Coming Home

by Alexa Land

Book Nine in the Firsts and Forever Series

Books by Alexa Land Include:

Feral (prequel to Tinder)

The Tinder Chronicles (Tinder, Hunted and Destined)

And the Firsts and Forever Series:

Way Off Plan

All In

In Pieces

Gathering Storm

Salvation

Skye Blue

Against the Wall

Belonging

Coming Home

Dedicated to Melisha
Thank you for your friendship
and all your amazing support!

Contents

Chapter One

When I was a kid, I wanted to run away to Saturn.

I was too dumb to understand the million impossibilities that went along with that. I only knew it was beautiful. That was enough for me.

It didn't take long before that fantasy was shot to hell by a teacher who probably thought she was being helpful by explaining all the reasons that would never happen. She didn't realize how much I needed that dream. I *needed* to believe there was a beautiful place out there somewhere that I could escape to, a million miles from Simone, Wyoming.

Even after I learned that going there would never be a reality, Saturn remained my safe place. When I was sixteen, I had a tiny line drawing of the planet tattooed on the inside of my right wrist, below my thumb. It was still my escape, even if I had to retreat inward to reach it.

As the cane came down on my ass for the fourteenth time, I concentrated hard on that little tattoo. I had to twist my wrist around a bit to see it under the rope that bound me to the bed. But it was there, my own private refuge, with me always.

The man beating me was becoming angry. He wanted me to scream or cry or beg him to stop. He was trying to break me. He didn't seem to realize I'd already been broken a long, long time ago and that absolutely nothing he did to me was going to give him the response he wanted.

He tried for another couple minutes. Every time the cane struck my body, a shockwave radiated through me. I couldn't help but flinch, it was involuntary. That in turn made me pull against the ropes, chafing my wrists. Damn it. The rope was cheap hardware store grade, too. It was definitely going to leave marks.

Finally he threw the cane down and put on a condom, then fucked me hard, slamming into my ass. It wouldn't be long now. Soon I could go home. He grabbed my hair and pulled my head up off the bed. I hated that so much. I still didn't respond, though.

After he came, the man, whose name ironically was John, rolled off me. He pushed his prematurely thinning red hair off his sweaty forehead and threw the condom on the floor as he griped, "Fucking you is like fucking a corpse. I'm through with you. You're a goddamn lousy whore." Was I supposed to find that insulting?

He got dressed and smoothed his douchey goatee in the mirror, then probably thought he was doing me a favor by cutting one of my wrists free before he left the cheap motel room. It took a while for me to pick at the knot holding my other wrist to the bedframe, then twist around and unbind my ankles. I was moving slowly as I got dressed. It hurt too much to wear my tight briefs, so I folded them up and put them in my jacket pocket. Fortunately I'd worn fairly loose jeans, but they still hurt like hell against the welts. I'd jammed the money he'd paid me in the pocket of my t-shirt. I took it out, folded it carefully, and hid it in my shoe. It was late and I was going home on public transit. I figured my chances of getting mugged were about fifty-fifty.

On the bus ride home, I kept my eyes on Saturn to distract myself from the pain, running the thumb of my left hand over the little drawing. I'd known the session would go exactly as it had, and I should have turned that trick down, but stubbornness made me agree to it. He'd fucked me four times before, and each time, his method for beating me had gotten more intense. He was always so pissed when I refused to cry. Didn't he realize there were boys that specialized in that kind of thing, turning on the waterworks like a switch and playing the victim?

But then, maybe that was exactly why he kept coming back to me. He wanted real misery, real tears. That was what he got off on. Breaking me probably would have felt like a victory to him. He just so totally didn't get the impossibility of his quest.

The bus stop was a block from my apartment and I walked slowly when I got off in the Lower Haight. I took my time on the stairs leading to my studio apartment, too. They were accessed by a metal security door to the left of the import store that occupied the ground floor of my building. The shop sold tchotchkes to tourists, so I didn't understand how it stayed in business. While plenty of them flocked to the famous intersection of Haight and Ashbury in the Upper Haight, few ventured this far down unless they were lost.

As I fumbled for my keys, my friend Zachary stuck his head out of his apartment and frowned at me. "What's wrong?" he asked.

"Nothing." I said that automatically as I glanced at him over my shoulder. Zachary was a chameleon, a lean guy of about twenty-three with skin like porcelain and big, dark eyes that gave the impression they'd seen way too much. He was a prostitute like I was, but worked for an escort service while I was more of an independent contractor. His appearance fluctuated on a whim, either his or one of his client's. Sometimes he looked Emo, sometimes Goth, sometimes clean-cut. I'd even seen him pull off high society. His hair was currently dyed black and a little on the long side. I had no idea what the real color was.

"Bullshit. I heard you on the stairs. You were moving like a senior citizen."

"I'm just tired."

Zachary narrowed his eyes at me. "You agreed to meet that asshole again, didn't you? John the john, the one who beat you with a riding crop last weekend." When I didn't reply, he exclaimed, "You totally did! What the fuck, Chance? Why don't you leave that asshole to the boys who specialize in that BDSM shit? At least they charge a premium. Did you charge him extra at least?"

"I did," I said as I swung open the door to my apartment.

"What did he use on you this time?"

"A thin bamboo cane."

His eyes went wide. "Shit. Nothing hurts worse than that. I let a trick do that to me once. *Once.* That was more than enough. Are you alright?"

"I'm fine."

"But you probably don't feel up to hanging out or anything," he said, breaking eye contact. Zachary would never actually admit to being lonely, but if he was asking to hang out it meant he needed a friend.

"Come on in," I said. "I'm going to get a shower, but you're welcome to wait for me."

He pulled the door to his apartment shut and made sure it was locked, then crossed the small hallway barefoot. Zachary was dressed in a baggy t-shirt and a pair of cotton shorts, which made me think he'd gotten out of bed when he heard me come home. He'd been doing that more and more lately.

"Fuck," he muttered as he slipped past me. "It's like the equator in here. I'm going to open a window." The whole floor had once been one big apartment, but had been carved up by the landlord into two little studios and a decent-sized one-bedroom. The thermostat for all three was in the one-bedroom unit and the couple that lived there liked to keep it set to a balmy eighty or so, year-round.

"Go ahead. Help yourself to a drink, too. I'll be out in a few minutes." I grabbed a couple things from my closet and took them with me into the bathroom.

After standing under the warm water for a while to ease some of my soreness, I dried off and got dressed in a pair of loose-fitting pajama pants and a long-sleeved t-shirt, which I pulled over the marks on my wrists. They were bruising up pretty good.

When I left the bathroom, I found Zachary sitting on the tiny counter of my pseudo-kitchen. There was a sink, a two-burner cooktop and a dorm-sized refrigerator in one corner of my apartment, along with an upper and lower cabinet. Even the term 'kitchenette' was overly ambitious.

He held his hand out to me palm-up, revealing two ibuprofen tablets. I took them from him and he offered me a glass of water. "Thanks," I mumbled before washing down the pills.

Zachary relocated to the floor on the other side of the tiny studio and leaned against my twin bed, which doubled as my couch. The reason he was sitting on the floor was pretty obvious, and I went ahead and stretched out on the mattress as he'd intended. "I wish you'd change your mind and be my plus-one at my friend Christian's wedding tomorrow," I told him as I tucked my arm under my head.

"We already talked about this," he said. "Spending the day with a bunch of rich people isn't my idea of a good time."

"Christian may have money, but he's totally not some spoiled rich kid. He's a great guy."

"If you say so. But still, no. You told me your wedding gift to him was being his photographer, so it's not like you'd be hanging out with me anyway."

He had a point, but it still would have been nice to have some company. I studied my friend's profile as he ran a short fingernail along the edge of my mattress and asked, "Are you okay, Zachary? You look like you have a lot on your mind."

"I'm fine. It's just, you know. Weekends." I didn't have to ask what he meant by that. The majority of his work at the escort service happened Friday through Sunday. He'd been turning tricks for a couple years, but I got the impression he'd never fully acclimated to the job. I, on the other hand, had been a prostitute for well over a decade. It was all I knew.

I began to lightly stroke his hair, because I knew he found it soothing. "You don't have to do that," he murmured, even as his eyes slid shut and he leaned into my touch.

"I know." I kept right on doing it.

"I should be the one comforting you after the night you had."

"You *are* comforting me, just by being here."

He was quiet for a while before saying softly, "I love you, Chance."

"I love you, too."

We both knew this would never be anything but a friendship. Neither of us was looking for more, and even if that had been the case, we were far too similar to even consider dating each other. Zachary was my best friend, and I was pretty sure I was his only one. We cared about each other and filled a void in each other's lives. I'd been really lonely before he moved in across the hall a couple years ago. Recently, I'd become friends with Christian, who in turn brought other people into my life. But that was just because Zachary's kindness had shown me it was okay to trust and let other people in. He was a very private person who never talked about himself and sometimes disappeared for days at a time without explanation, but I respected his limits and was grateful for what he was able to give me.

That night was typical of our friendship. He tended to gravitate to me in the hours past midnight, that part of the night when loneliness could just swallow you whole. We didn't always feel the need to talk. Just being together was enough.

I started to drift off after a while, my fingers stilling in his soft hair. I felt him lightly kiss my forehead. "Good night," he whispered.

"Night," I mumbled before sleep took me.

*****

I slept in way past noon. Zachary was gone when I got up, same as usual. He reminded me of a ghost sometimes, a pale, quiet boy who haunted my apartment in the middle of the night, rarely seen in daylight. I got up and used the bathroom, then paused to straighten a couple photos. The one solid wall in my apartment was covered floor-to-ceiling with pictures I'd taken, held up by thumbtacks. I assessed them with a critical eye, then went back to bed and stayed under the covers with a book until I absolutely had to get up and get ready for my friend's wedding.

After I showered, spending a long time under the hot water to ease the soreness that remained (which was considerably better than the night before), I got as close to dressed up as I could manage in black pants, a tie, and a long-sleeved shirt, pulling the cuffs down over the red and purple marks around my wrists. Then I took my time checking my equipment and my camera. It was my most prized possession. Christian had given it to me, back when he thought he was dying and wanted to make a grand gesture. The why behind it wasn't hard to guess. He'd wanted to give me a way out of prostitution, and the camera was meant to be an opportunity for a new life. It wasn't that simple, though. People weren't exactly lining up to hire me as a photographer. Still, the gift was by far the nicest thing anyone had ever done for me, and I looked forward to repaying his kindness by doing the best I could on his wedding photos.

When my camera bag was packed, I left my apartment and quickly weighed the pros and cons of driving to the wedding. I'd recently bought a used car, after Christian's friend Gianni hired me to be his assistant for a few weeks and paid me way too much for what turned out to be an incredibly easy job. Christian was getting married at the new house he and his fiancé Shea had bought, which was on a hill above the Castro, and parking was going to be pretty much nonexistent.

But then again, coming home late on the bus with all my expensive camera equipment was just asking to get mugged, so I walked the two blocks to my car and unlocked the little blue Civic. It was pretty nondescript, but it was the first car I'd ever owned and I was proud of it. I got behind the wheel and placed my camera bag on the passenger seat, then put the seatbelt around it to keep it safe. Only then did I pull away from the curb.

Chapter Two

I was early. I'd done that on purpose, since Christian and I had decided to take a few portraits before the wedding, but I overshot. The grooms were still up in their bedroom getting dressed when I arrived, and Christian's best friend Skye let me in.

I really liked Skye. He and Christian had met in art school, and he was very much what I assumed an art student would be like, right down to his shaggy blue hair. He greeted me with a hug and his ever-present smile, then led the way to the kitchen, where his brother River and River's boyfriend Cole were hard at work. The couple was catering the event as a wedding present to the grooms, and both paused to shake my hand when I came in. Skye's husband Dare was seated at the counter chopping vegetables, and he greeted me with a smile and a little wave.

Stepping into Christian's world always felt good. I didn't know his friends all that well, but they were consistently nice to me. I offered to help with the meal prep, and when I was told it was almost done I pulled out my camera instead and began snapping a few photos of the couples working in the kitchen. I liked the way Cole and River cooked together. They were totally in sync, one of them dropping some herbs into a pot on the stove, then moving on to something else while the other one swooped in and stirred it. It was a dance that came from comfort and familiarity, and I thought it was beautiful.

Christian's fiancé Shea was part of a large Irish-American family, many of whom were police officers. His cousins Kieran and Brian arrived about twenty minutes after I did, along with their husbands. Kieran was a former cop, and he was married to a sweet guy named Christopher Robin, who'd gone to art school with Christian and Skye.

Brian was a big, muscular brunet, an ex-Marine who'd lost both his legs in Afghanistan and was getting around on a pair of prostheses. He was married to Hunter, an absolutely gorgeous, slim, blond former porn star. I loved watching those two together. They were so different on the surface, but they clearly adored each other. When Brian settled onto a kitchen chair, he pulled Hunter onto his lap and put his arm around him, and Hunter rested his head against his husband's. I snapped a couple candid shots of the two of them and would have taken a lot more, but I was trying not to be completely intrusive.

Three of Shea's groomsmen, Leo, Cas and Ridley, were the next to arrive. His fairly nerdy former roommates all seemed more than a little awestruck by Hunter, who'd been a pretty big celebrity before retiring. They even embarrassedly admitted to having attended an autograph event of his back in the day.

Once they picked their jaws up off the floor, Ridley asked where the grooms were and Skye said, "They've been upstairs getting dressed for about an hour now."

"Uh huh, getting dressed," said Leo, a thin African American with close-cropped hair and a quick grin. "We all know they're up there having pre-matrimonial wild monkey sex. I, of course, condone this wholeheartedly. After that, it'll be nothing but married-people sex so they have to go all Wild Kingdom while they can."

"Oh believe me," Hunter said, "sex after marriage can still be plenty wild."

"I'm trying so hard not to picture that and completely invade your privacy, Hunter Storm," Cas said. His vivid blush made it clear he was failing in a big way.

"It's just Hunter Jacobs now," the blond said with a smile.

"Whatever your name is these days, you're still mighty fine," Leo said. "Your husband is one lucky man."

Brian smiled and said, "I tell myself that every single day." That earned him a sweet kiss from Hunter.

The kitchen contingent was soon joined by Nana, a little eighty-year-old firecracker who had decided at some point that both Christian and Shea were family. She and her driver, a cute blond named Jessie, were carrying an absolutely enormous box with Skye's help, and Dare jumped up to give them a hand as well. "We picked up the wedding cake from the bakery," Nana was saying, "but I still think I should have made one. I'm real good at that sort of thing."

Christian and Shea came into the kitchen just then, accompanied by applause and cat-calls. They both grinned shyly and made the rounds, greeting all their early arrivals. When Christian got to me, he gave me a hug and kissed my cheek, then said, "I'm so glad you're here, Chance."

"Me too."

Shea said hello too, then put his hands on his hips and eyed the huge box that had been deposited on the kitchen island. "I don't think the cake we ordered was that big," he said. "We're only expecting about forty or fifty guests, just close friends and immediate family. This looks like enough to feed an army."

Nana climbed up on a stool and began tugging at the tape that held the lid on. "Well, you know, this isn't all cake. They pack these things up real careful-like so they'll make it to their destination and there's going to be a lot of empty space in this box, though it did weigh a ton!"

"Here Nana, let me help you," Jessie said, climbing up on another stool.

Once they removed the tape, Jessie lifted the lid and all four sides of the box fell away. "Sweet baby Jesus, is that what you ordered?" Nana exclaimed. "I mean, I'm not judging."

I burst out laughing and began snapping photos of the cake. It had obviously been intended for a gay bachelor party and featured two cartoonish half-scale naked muscle men in a passionate embrace, rendered from the knees up. One was African American, the other white, and they were making out while sporting enormous erections. A little sash hung around the couple and said, "Good luck Ferdinand and Klaus."

Christian was laughing so hard that he'd doubled over. Jessie chuckled too and snapped a photo with his phone before saying, "I'll call the bakery and get it straightened out, even though this is the best cake I've ever seen in my entire life."

"We should have gone with the naked muscle men in the first place," Shea said with a smile. "That bakery actually specializes in racy bachelor party cakes, and clearly they're masters of their craft."

Nana had put on a pair of huge, round glasses and leaned in so her face was just a couple inches from the cake cocks, which were crossed like a pair of swords. "It's been a while since I saw a real life weenie dongle, but this is pretty much how I remember it. I don't think they're usually that straight though, I remember more of a curve to them. I'll fix it for Ferdinand and Klaus." With that, she grabbed the white figure's willie and tried to bend it, and the thing snapped off in her hand, balls and all. "Well, shit! That wasn't supposed to happen," she exclaimed. "All I was doing was trying to make it more realistic, like this." She tried to bend the dick on the African American figure and it snapped off, too. "Damn. It happened again! What do I do with these now?" She held up the pair of peckers.

Skye jumped up to assist and pulled open a drawer. "We can stick them back on," he said with a huge smile. "A couple skewers and they'll be good as new."

Jessie had been on the phone, and when he turned back to us his eyes went wide and he exclaimed, "Oh man, they've been neutered!" Then he asked, "Nana, what are you doing?"

She had a circle of chocolate frosting around her mouth, and one of the cocks was half gone. "Shit," she said, "I didn't think about it. I just got hungry and decided to have a snack!"

Jessie grinned and told her, "It's alright Nana, I'm sure the bakery can make some new willies. You just hold on to those." She seemed really pleased about that and gave the vanilla appendage a lick.

Skye and Dare went with Jessie and Nana to take the heavy cake back to the bakery. Meanwhile, the grooms and I moved to the living room and took some photos. The love and devotion between them was unlike anything I'd ever seen before. They'd been through so much in their time together, including Christian's battle with a brain tumor which he'd beaten through clinical drug trials, surgery and chemotherapy. It was obvious that throughout all of that, the two of them had become an inseparable team.

For some of the shots, I had them pose before a big mural that Christian had painted directly onto the wall of their high-ceilinged living room. It was a fanciful cityscape, the San Francisco of dreams and imagination, a million times removed from the reality of life outside these walls. I loved it, though. I'd been a fan of Christian's artwork long before I ever met him. He'd been a graffiti artist while in school, and I'd met him one night while he was evading the police. He mainly concentrated on running a nonprofit art center for kids now, and I wondered if he'd ever return to his roots in street art.

More guests kept filtering in, including Christian's mom and her husband. Zan, Christian's dad, arrived soon after with his boyfriend Gianni. Zan was a former pop star and a surprisingly nice guy. That wasn't what I'd expected from someone so famous. While the couple had been hiding from the paparazzi by Lake Tahoe a few weeks back, they'd hired me as their assistant, since Gianni and I knew each other a bit through Christian. They couldn't really go out in public for fear of being overrun by fans and photographers, which had been where I came in. I considered them both friends now, even though I would have felt way too intimidated to phone up either of them and ask to hang out. They were kind to me, but the gap between my world and theirs made the Grand Canyon seem insignificant.

We took a few posed family shots, first in the living room, then up on the rooftop garden where the ceremony was going to be held. Shea's parents were notably absent, since apparently they were really religious and had disowned their son when he came out. Several other members of his family were there though, including a couple uncles and aunts and quite a few cousins with their spouses and kids.

Shea's brother Finn arrived shortly before the ceremony was set to begin. He was a tall, muscular guy with dark brown hair and a little frown line etched between his eyebrows. Finn looked uncomfortable in his suit, or maybe he was uncomfortable with the whole situation. I wondered if he was only pretending to be okay with his kid brother marrying a guy. It was hard to tell. He was one of Shea's groomsmen, and took his place stiffly beside the couple, along with the three former roommates, who promptly shed their jackets and revealed red Star Trek uniforms. That made me grin.

Zan and Skye stood to the left of the couple, the brother and the Trekkies to the right. It was early evening, the sun just beginning to set as the ceremony got under way. I circled as unobtrusively as I could and snapped photos as the couple exchanged their vows, making sure to document everything to the best of my ability.

The reception that followed was casual and lighthearted. Music played, people visited the buffet, and cocktails flowed. I stayed behind my camera. I was glad I had a role to play, because it meant I didn't have to mingle and make small-talk. I was no good at that.

It gave me an excuse to study people too, which I enjoyed. Through my lens, I picked up on the subtle glances that Christian's mother kept directing at his dad and could tell she regarded him as the one who got away. I also watched Zan and Gianni together and got a couple nice candid shots of the two of them. It was so obvious that they were madly in love. The whole house probably could have fallen down around them and they would have gone right on dancing and staring into each other's eyes. Christian and Shea were the same, so much in love that it was evident in every touch, look and gesture. I couldn't even imagine what that was like.

I made a point of getting candids of all the guests. That was easier said than done in some cases. The Trekkie groomsmen were total hams, and would mug for the camera every time they noticed it was pointed at them. I did manage to get a few nice shots of the three of them and Shea doing a group hug, though.

Finn was a bit problematic as well. Every time I tried to get a shot, I found him looking directly at the camera. I did catch him off guard at one point as he leaned on the railing of the rooftop garden and looked out over the city lights, and got a couple pictures in profile. He looked really melancholy, so I didn't know if I'd end up using the photos. Finn ended up leaving early, making an excuse to his brother about getting called in to work. That struck me as odd, but it was really none of my business.

Later that night, I went into the living room and the group gathered there raised a toast to me and to the caterers. Being in the spotlight all of a sudden was pretty embarrassing. Gianni put his arm around my shoulders and said, "I didn't see you sit down once all evening. Come and relax."

I hesitated but finally agreed, perching on the loveseat beside him and Zan. My cuff rode up a bit and I pulled it down self-consciously. I'd forgotten about my bruised wrists and hoped they hadn't been too noticeable. I then took a look at the group that remained.

Christian and Shea were curled up together across from me in a big, upholstered chair, and Leo, Cas and Ridley were asleep on the couch. River and Cole snuggled to my left in another chair, and Skye and Dare manned the bar. They'd been trying to invent a drink for the newlyweds and seemed pretty tipsy.

Dare distributed some newly minted cocktails while I flailed around for something to say and finally told Gianni and Zan, "I've been meaning to say thanks again for hiring me as your assistant while you were in Tahoe. I bought a used car with the way too generous salary you paid me. I'm going to use it in the fall for a road trip and visit my brother and mom in southern Wyoming. After that, I'm going to drive to the opposite end of the state and see if I can track down the man who fathered me. It's a total long-shot, but I figure it won't hurt to go and ask a few questions."

"Wow Chance, that's huge," Gianni said. "Is anyone going with you?"

"I asked my friend Zachary, but he doesn't want to go. He doesn't see why I'd want to do any of this, both because he knows my mom and I have a lot of issues and because he doesn't think that man would be worth finding, even if I somehow managed it." I took a sip of the drink I'd been handed and added, "Actually, I'm glad my friend turned me down. This really is something I should do on my own."

"I hope that goes well for you. If you need anything while you're on the road, be sure to call us," Gianni said, and I thanked him as I broke eye contact. I was embarrassed that I'd just rambled on about myself like that. He and I had had a conversation once about the fact that I didn't know who my father was, so I'd wanted to tell him my plans. But I had no idea what had compelled me to blurt out all of that right then, in a room full of near-strangers.

I took another sip of my drink and declined the offer of a piece of cake. Jessie and company had returned before the ceremony with a sedate, two-tiered confection. It seemed like a downgrade from the naked body builders.

Since there wasn't much more to photograph, I made my excuses after a few minutes and started to go. Christian insisted on sending some cake with me before he walked me to the door. He gave me a big hug and said, "Thank you so much for coming and for taking all those photos. I feel bad, I don't think you really got to enjoy yourself."

"Sure I did. Taking pictures is fun for me." I kissed his cheek and said, "Have a great time on your honeymoon. I'll talk to you when you get back."

"Take care of yourself, Chance," he said. There was real concern in his green eyes. That was usually the case. I'd made the mistake of calling him soon after we met, when I'd gotten beat up pretty severely on the job. I'd regretted that call ever since. He'd been incredibly sweet and he'd really helped me out, but from that point on he looked at me with so much worry, all the time. I felt like enough of a disaster around him already, even before adding that layer of patheticness to the mix.

I walked to my car quickly with my head down, clutching my camera bag, and made it without incident. But then I had to repeat the process when I got back to the Lower Haight and the only parking space I could find was several blocks away. I felt like I'd never reach my apartment building. I was out at night all the time and it didn't really bother me, but this time I had something worth stealing. When I let myself into my building and pulled the security gate shut behind me, it was a relief.

The light was on under Zachary's door, so I knocked softly. He opened it right away. "Hey. How were the rich people?" he asked.

"They're all really nice."

"Did they treat you like a charity case? The poor little rent boy?"

"No."

"Why don't I believe you?"

"Because you're suspicious of anyone with money?"

"Possibly."

I changed the subject by holding up the little white box in my hand and saying, "They sent a piece of cake with me. Do you want some?" Zachary smiled at that, and picked up his keys from a little table just inside his door. He locked up behind himself and I let us into my apartment.

I got a couple forks and we sat side-by-side on my bed and ate the rich chocolate cake. "This is so good," he mumbled between forkfuls. "Thank you for sharing it with me." I claimed to be full and let him have the rest. He ate slowly, savoring every bite. It made me happy to see him enjoying himself.

I got up and changed into pajama bottoms and a t-shirt while he ate, and when Zachary finished he stretched out beside me on my little bed and picked up my hand. "Rich people have better cake than the rest of us," he said.

"They do."

"What was the wedding like?"

"It was beautiful. Let me show you the photos, I want to take a look at them too and see if I got some good shots. I really hope I did." I reached over him and pulled my camera out of the case. Then we shared my pillow, our heads touching as we watched the little view screen.

I flipped through the photos slowly and was happy to see many of them had come out like I'd wanted them to. I'd taken a photography class at City College a couple months back, and it had shaken my confidence a bit because the instructor had been really critical of my work. When Zachary said, "Wow Chance, you did an amazing job," I felt relieved.

"Thanks." I spun the dial with my thumb, bringing up the next photo, and said, "This is the couple who got married, Christian and Shea. Christian's on the left."

"So that's him," he said quietly. I knew he was threatened by my friendship with Christian, even though he had no reason to be.

"Yup. He had longer hair when I met him, but he had to shave his head when he had brain surgery. Then it fell out when he had chemo, and it's slowly growing back."

Zachary shot me a look. "You just told me that so I'd have sympathy for him, didn't you?"

"Maybe." I grinned a little and he did, too.

"Show me some more pictures." I went back to scrolling through the shots, and he kept asking who everyone was. He claimed to have nothing but disdain for Christian and his circle of friends, but his interest told another story. "He's cute," he said when Jessie appeared on the screen.

"Jessie's really nice, too. He's Nana's driver, that little old lady I showed you. Definitely not a spoiled rich kid. Want me to introduce you?"

Zachary shook his head and took over the job of flipping through the photos. "There's no point." I knew he'd say that, and knew he was right, too. Neither of us dated. I wondered if any prostitutes did, and if so, how they managed it. What kind of guy would somehow be okay with his boyfriend going out and sleeping with other men to earn a living?

"Oh wow." Zachary's fingertip stilled on the dial. "He's really handsome. There's a story behind those eyes."

He'd stopped on a picture of Finn, who was looking directly at the camera in a tight close-up taken from across the room. There was sadness and a lot of emotion in his blue eyes. "That's Shea's brother, he was one of the groomsmen. I couldn't quite tell what was going on with him. He seemed pretty unhappy and left early."

Zachary continued scrolling through the photos. Eventually he reached the end and said, "That looked like a wonderful wedding."

"Do you regret not going with me?"

"No." I grinned at that and set my camera on the little table at the head of my bed, then draped my arm over my friend's midsection. He felt small and fragile under his baggy t-shirt.

Zachary was quiet for a long time, and I thought he'd fallen asleep. But then he asked randomly, "Do you think you're really a bottom?"

"Where'd that come from?'

"I was just thinking. I worked this evening, nothing elaborate, just a couple hours in bed with this guy. It was important to him that I was enjoying myself, which was weird. I mean, normally they really don't give a shit, you know? But this one kept asking me, 'Is it good? Do you like it?' I guess he needed the reassurance or something. I told him I did, but that wasn't true at all. I hated everything he was doing to me. So, I don't know. I guess I just started to wonder. Maybe I'm not even a bottom, maybe that's why I hated it so much."

"What did you like to do before you started turning tricks?"

He shrugged and muttered, "I dunno."

I thought about it for a while before saying, "I guess I don't really know what I am, either. Sex has always been something that's done to me. I never, like, called the shots or anything."

My friend didn't look at me as he said, so quietly, "Do you want to try? With me, I mean? You can fuck me if you want. Maybe you could figure out what you like that way."

"You just told me you don't like to bottom."

"I know, but maybe it'd be different with someone I actually liked."

"You're not serious, are you?"

"I don't know. Never mind." I tried to take his hand, but he sat up and said, "I'm going back to my apartment."

Zachary swung out of bed and headed for the door, but I went after him and gently caught his arm. "Don't go."

"I have to. I'm being stupid tonight. I hate it when I get like this."

"What's going on with you, Zachary?" I asked as I let go of him.

He looked at the floor as he mumbled, "Nothing. I'll talk to you soon, okay?"

"Okay." After he left, I locked the door behind him and leaned against it. The apartment was so quiet. Too quiet. Two a.m. was really lonely without my best friend.

"Just you and me, kid," I said to the little brown teddy bear on the table beside me, my one possession from my childhood. Bobo stared at me with his button eyes. He wasn't much of a conversationalist, but I was still glad for his company.

Chapter Three

Zachary avoided me for the next few days. He was really good at that. I never heard him coming and going on the stairs, and when I knocked on his door, there were no sounds from inside the apartment.

Meanwhile, life went on. It was lonely with Zachary M.I.A. and Christian off on his honeymoon, but I was used to loneliness. I spent my days either lost in a book or hiding behind the lens of my camera, and my nights working.

I didn't have many regular customers and none were calling that week, so I worked the street. Friday night was the same as any other, but I felt a bit off for some reason. Around midnight I was in a back alley, getting used by some guy in an expensive suit that had been too cheap to get a room. He thrust into me hard as I braced myself against the rough masonry wall and kept my eyes on Saturn. He was one of those guys that got off on verbal abuse, and told me how worthless and pathetic I was as he fucked me. At least he came in just a couple minutes, and when he finished, he threw the condom on the ground and left without another word.

I zipped my jeans, wrapped my arms around myself, and leaned against the wall. I was definitely out of sorts, a little too tired and cold and hungry, all at the same time. But I was also behind on my monthly income and knew I needed to get back to work. First though, I was going to give myself the luxury of two quiet minutes by myself. I exhaled as I let my eyes slide shut.

"Hey. You okay?"

I jumped at the deep voice, my hands coming up automatically to protect myself and my heart thudding in my chest. A large police officer was backlit by a distant streetlight. I couldn't see his face, but I knew he was a cop by the outline of the radio on his shoulder and the gun on his hip. He shone his flashlight at me. Surprisingly, this one was nice enough not to shine it right in my face. Most of them did that. Instead, he shone the light along the ground, pausing on the used condom, then ran it partway up me and kept it on my midriff. Since my eyes had been used to the dark, it was still too bright and I squinted.

"Is your name Chance?"

That startled me. Why would a cop know my name? I'd been arrested twice, but the last time had been over four years ago. Not like they'd remember one hooker among hundreds.

I nodded quickly, looking at the ground. The big cop came up close to me, directing the beam of the flashlight off to the side. "Are you a prostitute?"

The question was surprising. Usually the cops didn't come right out and ask. I looked up at him. Man, was he big. I was about five-eleven on a good day, and this guy had to have at least six or seven inches on me, not to mention eighty pounds of sheer muscle mass. I still couldn't see him very well with the flashlight disrupting my night vision, but there was something familiar about him. I asked hesitantly, "Finn Nolan?"

Shea's brother nodded and said quietly, "You didn't answer my question."

"Why would I answer that? Getting thrown in jail isn't exactly on today's to-do list."

"I couldn't arrest you for that, not unless you solicited me."

"Like I'd be dumb enough to solicit a cop."

He paused for a moment, studying my face, and I looked down again. "I don't get it," he said. "You're a wedding photographer. Why would you be out here turning tricks? Is it for the thrill? Because frankly, there are much safer ways to get your kicks."

That made me lock eyes with him and knit my brows. "Yeah, it's for the thrill. It has nothing to do with paying rent or feeding myself or providing for my family. I totally get off on letting any asshole with a handful of twenties use my body any way he wants." I immediately regretted snapping at him. Getting on a cop's bad side was such a terrible idea.

"Providing for your family?"

"Never mind, forget I said that. Am I under arrest?"

"No."

"Good." I turned and walked down the alley, wasting no time in putting plenty of distance between myself and Officer Nolan.

*****

Next time I saw him, it was Monday night. I'd had a relatively slow weekend, so I was working once again. He approached me dressed in street clothes, and I glared at Finn and said, "If this is an attempted sting operation, it's such a total fail."

"No! Jeez, of course not. I just...um...can I talk to you?" He shifted uncomfortably, stuffing his hands in the pockets of his jeans. He also wore sneakers and a khaki-colored canvas jacket over a t-shirt, but the casual outfit didn't make him look any less like a cop.

"You *are* talking to me."

"I mean, you know, can we go somewhere and talk?"

I raised an eyebrow. "You get that I'm working here, right?"

"Yeah. But maybe, I don't know, take a walk with me?" He fidgeted again, clearly nervous about something.

"Do you swear this isn't some elaborate, jacked up attempt at arresting me?"

"It's not. I'm not even on duty tonight." I studied him for a moment, then sighed and started walking. He fell into step with me. After a minute he said, "I need you to promise not to repeat this conversation to my brother, his husband, or any of their friends. That's really important. You absolutely cannot talk about this with anyone who knows me. Will you do that?"

"If whatever you're going to say is a big secret, here's an idea: don't tell me in the first place." He sighed at that, and after a moment I said, "You don't have to worry, I'll keep quiet." The light changed and we crossed the street. We were heading out of the Tenderloin and the neighborhood was slowly improving, block by block. Since it was fairly late, all of the shops were closed and the street was nearly deserted.

Finn blurted, "I thought about this all weekend, and it has to be you. Having some common ground is reassuring, but it also makes this a hundred times more insane than just finding a stranger, because you could blackmail me, or even just tell my brother about this out of spite. I just...I don't think you're the type to do that. I'm pretty good at reading people, that's a big part of my job. God, I hope I'm right in this case." He was speaking quickly, his nerves still getting the better of him.

"What exactly are we talking about here?"

"I want to hire you." I stopped walking and stared at him. Finn seemed completely mortified, looking at anything but me.

"Not as a wedding photographer," I guessed.

He shook his head. "No. I, um...I want to hire you to do *this* job." He gestured at our surroundings awkwardly.

"You want to take me to bed?"

"Oh God." He turned away from me, but then he nodded.

"I'm going to go ahead and guess you don't have a lot of experience hiring prostitutes," I said.

"Absolutely none. I've thought about it before, but I could never go through with it. Between my job, my family...." He turned to look at me. "You could destroy me, Chance, and I'm not being dramatic. You could tear down my world if you chose to. But...somehow, I don't think you will."

"Why would you take that risk?"

"Because I want this so damn bad. It's all I can think about. Please, tell me I can trust you."

"You can."

"I know this has to be awkward for you, too," he said, "and keeping it confidential goes both ways. You probably don't want Christian or Shea to find out about our, um, arrangement, and I swear I'll be discreet, for your sake as well as mine."

I studied him for a long moment, then told him, "I don't get it. There are dozens of hookers out on the street right now. Why wouldn't you just pick someone who has no idea who you are and take them to the closest motel for an hour? It doesn't make sense that you'd turn to the one prostitute who knows your name, your family, and where you work. It's just asking for trouble."

"Like I said, it has to be you," he mumbled, studying the dirty sidewalk. "I don't want to do this with anyone else."

"Okay," I said softly.

Finn looked up at me. "Really?" When I nodded, he fumbled with an inside pocket of his jacket and pulled out a small, white envelope, which he thrust at me as he said, "Based on what I know from working vice, I think this is about right. I know you're probably worried about naming a dollar amount, since I'm a police officer and that would set you up for a potential arrest. So, you don't have to name a figure. If that's not enough, just say no and I'll add to it."

I took the envelope from him and untucked the flap, then counted the ten crisp hundred dollar bills inside it by running through them with my thumbnail. "This is way, *way* too much," I said as I tried to give the envelope back to him.

"Not for what I want."

Oh man, here it comes, I thought. *The guy's going to turn out to be a total freak. He's probably going to want to do some damage for that kind of money.*

It seemed like he had to force himself to blurt out, "I want you to sleep with me. I mean...well, both of the things that expression implies. After we...you know, I want you to spend the night with me. I want ten hours of your time, ten p.m. to eight a.m. I don't want to have to hurry or worry about how much time I have left or feel any pressure. I'd also like the option to maybe...you know. Do it again with you after I've rested up a bit." He actually blushed as he said that, shoving his hands back in the pockets of his jeans.

That was all fairly surprising, but again I said, "Okay."

He seemed slightly relieved. "Great. So, um, I guess we should talk about ground rules. I have a couple and I assume you do, too."

"Sure. Go first."

"Alright. So, I guess...I guess I need you not to initiate anything. Let me take the lead. But if I do anything you don't like or that hurts you, you have to tell me. Do you promise you will?" When I nodded, he said, "Okay, good. There's one more thing. I'm not a big talker. I don't want to make small-talk or answer questions or any of that."

"Not a problem."

"Great. Okay, so what are your rules?"

"I don't do bareback. No exceptions. Do you have a problem with that?"

Finn shook his head. "I'm glad you have that rule. What else?"

Now it was my turn to study the pavement. "If you decide you want to get rough with me, I need you to confine any marks or bruises to parts of my body that are normally covered by clothing. For the amount of money you're paying, you basically get an all-access pass, with the two exceptions of using a condom and where you can hit me. If you mark up my face, neck or wrists, that makes things difficult for me."

"Oh God," he said and started to reach for me, but then he stopped himself. "I'm not going to hurt you, Chance. You really...you let people do that to you?"

I looked up at him and pinned him with a sharp stare. "I have one more rule. You don't get to ask me questions, either. What I do and why I do it is my business and none of yours. Got it?"

"Yeah, okay."

After I put the envelope in my pocket, I started walking again, and he hurried to catch up to me. I glanced at the time on my phone and said, "It's a quarter to ten. Where do you want to go, since I assume you want to get started?"

"Oh." Finn looked around and said, "Um, let's turn right at the next intersection. There are a couple hotels outside the Financial District that are kind of off the beaten path." He thought about it as we walked up the street and added, "Maybe I should go first, then call you when I've gotten the room. Just, you know, so we can be discreet."

I stopped walking, took out my wallet, and handed him one of my business cards, which had only my first name and phone number on them. I'd thought they were classy when I first ordered them, but now the sheer white vellum with white ink just looked tacky. "Text me when you have a room and I'll be right there."

When I took the white envelope from my pocket and tried to hand it to him, he asked, "Why are you giving that back to me?"

"I figured you'd want to hold on to it. There's a thousand dollars here. Who's to say I won't just run off with it?"

He frowned a little. "I trust you, Chance. I have to, otherwise this whole thing's going to fall apart. I'm planning to go to sleep with you in the same room. I know you're not going to rip me off or, hell, I don't know, murder me in my sleep or something."

"Wow. Super grim example."

Finn shrugged. "Given some of the things I've seen in my line of work, it's pretty easy to go grim." I actually totally understood that. He turned and headed down the sidewalk as he said, "I'll call you in about fifteen minutes."

Chapter Four

He really did call too, as opposed to texting. "I'm in room two-fifteen at the Hotel Whitman. Do you know where that is?"

"Yeah. I'll be right there." I disconnected and got up from the cement stairs I'd been sitting on. I'd trailed Finn at a distance and settled in on the far corner, then watched him as he stood on the sidewalk outside a small hotel for a couple minutes, apparently psyching himself up. At one point, he ran up the stairs, turned around, and ran back down. But then he'd turned back, resolutely marched up to the door and disappeared into the lobby.

Once he'd gotten inside, it had taken him a while to call me, and I started to wonder if he was going to back out. I'd watched a light come on in a left-hand corner room on the second floor, and could see him pacing through the sheer curtains. He did that for a good ten minutes before he finally pulled out his phone.

It wasn't all that unusual for people to be nervous the first time they went to a prostitute. That was a little above and beyond, though. I wondered as I walked up to the hotel and pushed open the door if it was also his first time with a guy. That wasn't terribly uncommon, either. We were often a way for people to experiment or try out hidden desires.

Finn looked nothing short of terrified when he opened the hotel room door for me. He'd taken off his jacket, shoes and socks, which were all stacked neatly on a chair in the corner. A new box of condoms and a sealed plastic bottle of lube were lined up on the nightstand.

Since he'd said he didn't want small-talk, I didn't say anything as I closed the heavier set of drapes and began to undress. I turned my back to him automatically. It was an old habit, a weird urge to keep a little of myself private just for an extra minute or two before handing my body over to whoever had paid for me.

I studied my surroundings as I stripped myself. The hotel was a lot nicer than most of the places I usually ended up. It wasn't fancy and the room was really small, but it was clean and well-maintained. The walls were a sunny yellow and the white bedding looked crisp and fresh. I focused on a fairly generic painting of a bunch of white magnolias on the wall to my right. It was kind of an odd choice for a hotel that must cater to business travelers. So was the color scheme. I liked it, though.

When I was completely naked, Finn came up behind me, stopping a couple feet away. "Is it okay if I touch you?" he asked. His voice was a choked-off whisper.

"You can do whatever you want."

I flinched a little when his fingers grazed my back, and I took a deep breath. The reaction was involuntary. I didn't know if I could relax around him yet. Despite all his big talk about not wanting to hurt me, I'd heard that before from plenty of men who quickly turned abusive when they got me alone.

Finn pulled back when I flinched, but he tried again, resting his fingertips lightly on my right shoulder. His hand was trembling, and his breathing was fast and shallow. He traced the outline of my shoulder, then followed the length of my spine but stopped before he reached my butt and pulled his hand away.

I turned around and looked up at him. He was absolutely *huge* and seemed to fill that cramped hotel room. Our size difference was more apparent than ever as I stood naked before him. He could hurt me so badly if he wanted to.

Instead though, he gently brushed my hair back from my eyes, then traced the outline of my face with shaking fingertips. "You're so incredibly beautiful," he murmured before gathering me in his arms. Finn held me carefully, and I could feel his heart racing as I put my head on his chest. He took a couple deep breaths to try to calm himself, then guided us over to the edge of the bed and sat down with me on his lap.

He seemed to be in no hurry, even though I could feel his erection against my hip. Finn nuzzled my hair and breathed me in as his big arms enveloped me. It was so different than what I was used to. Zachary had told me about clients at the escort service who treated him like this, but street hustlers like me didn't usually experience that sort of thing. It threw me off my game a bit, but I just tried to go with it.

Finn caressed my skin for a few minutes, exploring my arms, back and shoulders before asking, "Is it okay if I kiss you?" When I nodded and looked up at him, his lips met mine. The kiss was so tender. God it felt good. I felt myself relaxing in his embrace.

Abruptly, I jumped off his lap and stepped back from him, mumbling, "I need to use the bathroom."

I hated the fact that he made me want to lower my guard. That sent up an entire battalion of red flags. When the bathroom door was locked behind me, I leaned against the sink and took a few deep breaths. Then I stared at my reflection, muttering, "Get it together, Chance."

This was a well-paying gig and I needed to get back out there and give the customer what he wanted. After a minute, I flushed the toilet to sell my lie and fixed a neutral expression on my face. Finn was leaning against the headboard with his knees bent, a little worry line between his eyebrows when I returned to bed. "You okay?" he asked.

I nodded. "Do you want me back on your lap?"

"Yes please." I straddled him and he put his arms around me. When he kissed me, it seemed more urgent, like it was getting him worked up instead of just kissing for its own sake, so it was easier to go with it. I rocked my hips slightly, rubbing myself against the bulge in his jeans and hoped that didn't cross the line in terms of initiating anything.

Finn seemed to like what I was doing and moaned against my mouth as his hands glided down my back. He held my hips and pushed up a little, rubbing his cock against mine. I started to get hard and wrapped my arms around his shoulders, letting my eyes close as his tongue slid between my lips.

After a while, he pulled off his t-shirt and fumbled with his belt as his nerves geared up again. Eventually he got his clothes off, then reached for the box of condoms and knocked them on the floor. Once he retrieved them, his hands were shaking so hard that he had trouble getting the box open.

I took it from his hands and said, "Some men enjoy it when I put the condom on for them. Would you like me to do that for you?" Okay, so I was once again violating the taking charge rule, but the poor guy obviously needed some assistance.

Finn nodded, his voice gravelly when he whispered, "Thanks."

I tore open a condom and rolled it down over his shaft, then grabbed the lube and peeled off the seal. I drizzled some over the condom and stroked him to slick him up. His cock pulsed in my hand. "How do you want me?" I asked.

"I...um...." He stared at me for a moment, then stammered, "What are my choices? I mean, it's not like I've never watched porn or anything. It's just really hard to think right now."

Oh yeah. Definite first-timer. I said, "Do you want me on my back facing you, or on my knees facing away?" No need to complicate things with the full menu.

"Facing me, please." I got on my back and spread my legs for him, rubbing the leftover lube onto my opening. "Do we…I mean, aren't we supposed to do something to prepare you?" he asked.

I shook my head and said quietly, "I already have lube in me. I don't need anything else."

A sheen of nervous perspiration dampened his forehead and his chest rose and fell rapidly as he knelt between my legs and took hold of his cock. He positioned it at my hole and pushed into me carefully. His nervousness was replaced by an expression of pure bliss as he bottomed out in me. "You feel amazing," he said, and then he started to move in me.

I liked watching him as he began to gain confidence in what he was doing. A little smile played around his full lips, and when he locked eyes with me, it got a lot bigger. Gradually his thrusts sped up, instinct replacing overthinking.

It didn't take him long to cum. He cried out and pushed into me as deep as he could. His arms went around me and he held me to him as he rode out his orgasm. When he finished and started to pull out of me, I reached down quickly and held the condom to the base of his cock. He took hold of it when he realized what I was doing and eased out slowly. "Be right back," he said, rolling out of bed and grabbing his boxer briefs from the floor as he headed to the bathroom.

I turned off the overhead light, leaving the room lit only by a small lamp on the nightstand, and curled up beneath the thick blanket. The bed was comfortable and the crisp, clean sheets smelled so good. I rubbed my cheek against the pillow and closed my eyes.

He was gone for a while, and I started to drift off. When the mattress creaked beneath Finn's weight, I gasped and started to sit up. He drew me into his arms and said softly, "Go back to sleep, Chance."

"Can't. You paid for the whole night," I mumbled.

"I paid to sleep with you, not just have sex. I've been looking forward to this part almost as much as what we just did," he said as he settled in.

After a couple minutes, he said quietly, "I always thought it'd be so nice to spend the night with a beautiful guy in my arms, and I was right. You feel incredibly good."

"You feel good, too," I said softly.

"Can we do this again on Thursday?" he asked. "That's my next night off."

"All night again?"

"Yeah, if you can."

"Sure."

"Great. Meet me here at ten. I'll come early and check in, then I'll call you with the room number."

"Okay."

Finn drifted off a few minutes later, and I tilted my head back and watched him as he slept. He had to be in the closet. It was the only explanation for his inexperience, or why he'd turn to a prostitute in the first place. Any man with that face and body would be able to find a sex partner within ninety seconds of setting foot in any gay bar in the city.

I was surprised he wanted to meet again so soon. That was a hell of a lot of money. Actually, he'd probably cancel after he came down off his sex high and realized the expense involved. Two thousand bucks in one week on a cop's salary was pretty steep. More than two thousand, actually, since he was also springing for a decent hotel room. But if he did go through with it, that was great news for me. It would actually put me ahead for once, and I'd be able to build up my savings a bit.

I reached across him and turned off the little lamp on the nightstand, and he snuggled against me. I'd assumed I wouldn't be able to sleep in the same room as a stranger, but instead, I found it surprisingly easy to relax. Finn seemed trustworthy, and the fact that we knew some of the same people was reassuring.

I closed my eyes and let myself enjoy how good this felt. I knew I shouldn't, but I did it anyway. I was going to have to get it together though, if this guy became a regular. It was so important for me to maintain a lot of detachment on the job. That was what made it possible to do the things I did. I reminded myself, *it's just my body, the job can't touch my soul.* I'd told myself that a million times in the early days.

I'd started turning tricks as a fourteen-year-old runaway. It was the only way I could survive. Besides, my innocence had already been taken from me by that point, so what difference did it make? At twenty-six, I was still selling my body, but I didn't feel any of the things I used to in the early days, the fear and hopelessness and heartbreak. I didn't feel much of anything at all.

Chapter Five

When I awoke the next morning, I was alone in the hotel room. Finn had left a note, written on the little notepad by the phone. It said simply, *thank you.* For such a big guy, his handwriting was surprisingly small and tidy.

I still had some time before checkout, so I took a long, hot shower and used the nice soap and shampoo that came with the room. They smelled like oranges. After that I got dressed in my clothes from the night before and used the plastic comb I kept in my jacket pocket.

By the time I rode home on the bus, it was almost noon. I barely recognized the slender guy exiting through the metal security door as I walked up to my apartment building, and I greeted my friend with, "Hey, Zachary."

He looked surprised to see me. His hair had been dyed golden blond, and he was dressed in a nice, dark blue suit, white dress shirt and a light blue tie. He managed to pull off the confidence and aloof detachment that rich people gave off effortlessly. "Hey. Are you just getting in?" he asked.

"Yeah. I had an overnighter. I don't get many of those."

"With one of your regular clients?"

"No, a new one."

Zachary frowned a little. "You spent the night with someone you just met? Sounds like an awesome way to get murdered in your sleep."

"It was fine. I obviously lived to tell about it." I said that lightly, but my friend's frown deepened.

Instead of berating me for my lackluster personal safety efforts, Zachary shifted his weight from one foot to the other and said, "I'm sorry about the other night. I hate it when I get needy like that. It sucks."

"There's no need to apologize."

He glanced at the cab that had pulled up at the curb. "I gotta go, but I'll talk to you soon, okay?"

"Okay."

Zachary slipped on a pair of sunglasses, which added to the rich kid vibe he had going on. He hesitated, then said, "Thanks for putting up with me. I know I act like an idiot sometimes."

"You don't, but even if you did, I'd still love you." He grinned embarrassedly and started to walk over to the cab, and I called, "Hey." When he glanced at me over his shoulder I said with a grin, "Be sure to report back about whether blonds really do have more fun." It was a dumb thing to say, but it made him smile, and that had been the whole point.

Once in my apartment, I took the little envelope from my pocket and looked around for a hiding place. I was always worried about break-ins and that was a lot of money. I ended up pouring the last of some instant oats into a bowl and stashing the envelope inside the empty cardboard canister, which I put back in the cupboard.

After I made my breakfast, I carried the oatmeal over to my bed and perched on the edge of the mattress. I'd added some brown sugar and a few raisins, using them both up since I'd just gotten a big payday and would be able to restock my cupboard. They made the oatmeal seem like a special treat. I ate slowly, just like every meal, savoring each bite. When breakfast was finished, I returned to my kitchenette and washed my dish, then looked around me.

The little studio was quiet and lonely, but I had a solution for that. I retrieved the paperback I'd been reading, then remembered something and pulled a slip of paper from my wallet, which I slid between the pages as a bookmark. It wasn't every day someone wrote me a thank you note, and something had made me want to hang on to it.

Soon I was lost in the pages of the book. I had an inexplicable love of detective novels from the 1920s to the 1950s, and had found a used bookstore that sometimes had them in their three-for-a-dollar bin. I stopped by often. Most days, I found nothing. But every once in a while, I went home with an armload of books. Those days felt like Christmas.

I'd been reading for about an hour when my phone jingled on the end table. Reluctantly, I tore myself away from Los Angeles, 1939, and looked at the caller ID. "Hey Jessie," I said after putting the call on speaker.

"Hi Chance. Got a minute?"

"Sure. What's up?"

"Nana's starting a project and needs a photographer. You were the first person she thought of. She wants to put together a cookbook as a tie-in to her cable TV cooking show and needs someone to take pictures of the finished dishes, plus step-by-step how-to photos. Does that sound like something you'd be interested in?"

"Yeah, that sounds—"

Before I could finish my sentence, Jessie swore and the phone hit the ground with a clatter. In the background, I could hear him yelling, "No, Tom Selleck! Down!" I had to grin at that. Nana had adopted a big mutt of some sort, and named him that because he was, according to her, 'such a handsome boy'. She never failed to put a smile on my face.

When Jessie picked up the phone again, he said, "You still there?"

"Yup."

"Sorry about that. All of a sudden, the puppy has discovered his sex drive. He's humping everything! Nana even had him fixed, and it didn't help at all. In the last couple days, the dog has decided I'm way more interesting than pillows or stuffed animals, which were what he was sexually molesting before he decided I was his type. I keep trying to explain to him that I just want to be friends, but there really is no reasoning with a horny puppy."

I chuckled at that and said, "Wow. You need hazard pay."

"I just need to remember to stay vigilant. I hadn't been paying attention and was leaning on the kitchen counter, and all of a sudden it was like dropping the bar of soap in a prison shower. Anyway, now I'm locked in the downstairs bathroom, so Tommy will just have to go off and do unspeakable things to the Tickle Me Elmo doll he found in one of the closets."

I smiled at that and tried to steer the conversation back on track by saying, "So, the project sounds great. When does Nana want to get started?"

"Immediately. You know how she is. She gets so excited about things! She had me call you because she's busy writing up a list of the recipes she wants to include. Last time I checked in, she had about a hundred and twenty dishes on the list. I'm gonna need to talk her down a bit, or else we'll never get the cookbook done." There was a rustling sound, as if Jessie switched the phone to his other ear, and then he continued, "I know it's super short notice, but do you want to come over this afternoon and then stay for dinner? It's okay if you're busy. I can convince Nana we need more prep time."

"It's fine, I can tear myself away from Raymond Chandler," I told him.

"Is that your boyfriend? Feel free to bring him!"

"No, he's an author. I was reading one of his books."

"Oh! My bad. Okay, well, head on over around four if you can. We'll need to run to the store, but we'll be back by then. I'll tell Nana you're coming, she'll be so happy."

"Sounds good." After we disconnected, I turned my attention back to The Big Sleep. I'd read the book at least a dozen times before, but I loved the comfort and familiarity of reading a great book over and over again.

*****

When I arrived at Nana's house that afternoon, it was total chaos. I suspected that was always the case. Two puppies were barking excitedly, a few little boys were running down the hall, and several people were setting up equipment around the big kitchen, which was brightly lit by stage lights mounted to the ceiling.

Jessie smiled and hurried over when he spotted me. "Hey, Chance. Thanks for coming."

"Hi. What exactly is happening here?"

"Well, Nana's a big believer in multitasking, so she's going to simultaneously film an episode of her cooking show, make dinner for the family, and have you take photos for the cookbook. She's also moving from one video camera to three, because the executives over at the cable TV channel were complaining about her show not being professional enough.

She figures taking more dynamic footage from multiple cameras will solve that problem."

"So, she hired a camera crew?"

"Not exactly, but she did bring in a couple people with video experience, including her hairstylist, Mr. Mario." He gestured at a man in his sixties who'd used so much self-tanner that he was the color of an Oompa Loompa. "He used to make adult films in the 1970s. I'm not sure what side of the camera he was on back then, but Nana says he's good at making videos."

"Ah."

"And that guy over there," Jessie said, indicating a man of about forty with a shaved head, camouflage utility vest, and camo Crocs, "is a Bigfoot researcher. I'm not sure where Nana found him. I think his name's Hoss, or Moss, or something. I didn't quite catch it. Anyway, he spends tons of time out in the Santa Cruz Mountains trying to film Bigfoots. Or Bigfeet. Or whatever. So he's really skilled with a camera. And of course you know Trevor."

The slender brunet was setting up a video camera on a tripod just a couple feet from us, and he grinned and said hello. He was married to Nana's grandson Vincent and was actually a chef's apprentice, but seemed to have been permanently roped into the job of chief cameraman for Nana's cooking show. His adopted son Josh, who was probably twelve or thirteen, sat in a corner with a paperback, trying to look aloof. But a little half-smile appeared on his face whenever he peered over the top of the book at all the activity in the kitchen.

I pulled my camera from its case and had just slung it around my neck when Nana burst into the kitchen. She was barely five feet tall, but the chef's hat she was wearing added a couple more feet. "I'm excited to get started," she said as she rubbed her hands together. "We're gonna make a nice cioppino. It's one of my favorites." Nana spotted me then and said, "Hi there, Chance! Thanks for coming. I'm gonna want you right up here with me so you can get close-ups of all the action." I went around the large kitchen island and stood by her side as I pocketed the lens cap.

"I think we're ready to get started, Nana," Jessie said, taking his place on her other side and smoothing down his short, blond hair, which tended to spike up on top. He'd originally been hired as her limo driver, but his job description had expanded to include assistant, companion, and cooking show co-conspirator.

I looked around as the three video cameras started to roll and said, "I'm going to be in the shot if I stand here. Maybe I should step aside."

"That's fine," Nana said. "You're cute, you'll probably boost ratings. Now get some shots of what we have here." She gestured at a big metal tub on the counter, which was full of ice.

Jessie pulled it a bit closer, and Nana got up on a stepstool as he said, "Don't forget to tell the viewers what we're making, Nana."

"Cioppino! Didn't I already say that?" She looked at the camera Trevor was manning and said, "It's basically a fish stew. You got some onion in there, some fennel, some tomato paste. It's good stuff. If you're thinking you don't like fish, get over it! Look at all the gorgeous seafood we got here." She started pulling plastic bags from the ice while I snapped a few pictures. "We got some halibut, some mussels, some shrimp. We went to this real nice fish market in North Beach. You know what they were out of though? Clams! How can a fish store run out of clams, I ask you? They said a customer came in right before us and cleaned 'em out. But here's a tip for you: no matter what you're cooking, always be ready to improvise! Cioppino's gotta have clams, or else it ain't cioppino. But really, it don't have to be them little Manila clams like I'm used to. Take a look at this."

Nana pushed back the sleeve of her pink Chanel suit and plunged her hand into the ice. "Where the hell'd it go? I know that fucker's in here somewhere," she muttered as she dug around. Finally she announced triumphantly, "Got it!"

What she pulled out of the ice looked exactly like a thick, ten inch cock with a shell where the balls would be. From the corner, Josh snort-laughed loudly. "Now, I know this ain't the type of clam you're used to. Me neither if I'm bein' honest.

But the fishmonger assured me these are real tasty," Nana said. "It's called a gooey duck clam. I got no idea what that name means. I sure as hell never seen a duck packin' anything that looks like this."

Jessie chuckled and snapped a picture with his phone, then asked, "So, what do we do with it, Nana?"

"Well, before we do anything, we gotta get it out of its shell." She tried prying the shell loose with her fingers, but it didn't budge.

"Should we just trim it off above the shell, Nana?"

"No. We got several inches of good meat there. It's a shame to waste all those inches."

Jessie grinned at that and said, "Truth."

"What we just gotta do," Nana said, handing Jessie the shell end of the clam, "is yank it. It'll release eventually."

"It usually does, when you yank it," he said with a smile.

Nana wrapped both hands around the fleshy appendage and started pulling on it with a series of quick, short tugs. "I know I can jerk it off," Nana said. "I just gotta keep tugging." I had to bite my lip to keep from laughing. Behind the camera, Trevor was shaking with silent laughter and turning red.

Jessie braced his feet on the floor as Nana hopped off the step stool and really started going at it. I snapped a couple pictures, because I didn't know what else to do, and Hoss or Moss circled with his camcorder. Mr. Mario, the orange hairdresser, took his video camera off its tripod and circled around behind the kitchen island as he exclaimed with a thick Spanish accent, "Show eet who is the boss, Nana!"

"Oh, I'm showing it," she said as her chef's hat listed to the side. She was really putting her back into it, digging in her low heels and tugging the meaty monster with both hands.

Jessie almost toppled over, so he bent at the waist to try to lower his center of gravity. Immediately Tom Selleck, Nana's great, big mutt, ran in and tried to mount the petite blond. "No! Stop! No means no!" Jessie yelled, trying to dodge the dog. He ended up stepping over his left arm to point his butt away from the animal, but kept hold of the clam, which now jutted out between his legs. The dog yipped and bounced up and down excitedly. While all of that was happening, Nana's grandson Nico, a straight-laced law student, came into the kitchen, took one look at the scene before him, turned and walked right back out again.

Nana wasn't deterred in the slightest by her lack of progress. She got up right behind Jessie and kept pulling with both hands, thrusting her skinny hips back and forth to really put her weight (all eighty pounds of it) behind each tug. "Holy crap," Josh muttered from the corner. "It just got all Skinemax up in here." His father shot him a look and the kid said, "Come on, I'm in junior high. I have questions."

"Then talk to me! Don't learn it from softcore porn with poor production values," Trevor exclaimed. "How'd you even manage to access those shows? I have all the parental controls set up."

Josh rolled his eyes. "You password is your wedding anniversary. Duh."

"I'm changing that as soon as we get home," Trevor said before turning his attention back to the video camera. His son just grinned.

I snapped a couple pictures, just because it was too funny not to, then jumped out of the way as Mr. Mario slid in from underneath and got the shot from between Jessie's legs, his adult entertainment background suddenly quite obvious. This seemed to inspire the Bigfoot researcher/videographer, who came in for a tight shot of Nana's death grip on the clam cock. Trevor stayed right where he was, calmly filming all that transpired, as if any of that was going to be useable for the cooking show.

Finally, after a few more firm yanks, some liquid leaked from the end of the clam and the whole thing drooped a bit as Nana let go of it. "I gave it my all," she said, mopping her brow with the back of her hand. "That shit was hard. I need a drink now, and I feel like smoking a cigarette, even though I stopped smoking forty years ago."

Jessie straightened, holding up the sagging sea creature, and said, "This victory goes to Long Duck Dong. Or whatever this thing was called."

"I'm spent," Nana said. "Let's take five." She grabbed a bottle of wine off the counter, which had probably been meant for the cioppino, and chugged about half of it while Jessie tossed the clam back on ice and washed his hands.

As she carried the bottle out of the room, Jessie said, "I don't suppose you got any useful shots out of that."

"Not so much."

He thought for a moment, then pulled a shallow, white bowl from one of the cabinets and put it on the counter. As he opened the bag of mussels and dumped them into the bowl, he said, "Maybe you can take a few pictures of the ingredients. I'll get 'em arranged for you. I always wanted to moonlight as a food stylist."

I grinned at that. "A food stylist? Really?"

"Not as like, my dream job or anything. But I saw a show once on people who make food look good for a living and thought it'd be fun. I'm a try anything once kind of guy."

"So, what is your dream job?"

"Don't laugh, but I've wanted to be a race car driver since I was six. Like that'll ever happen. The closest I've come is street racing. I wrecked my car though, so now I'm not even doing that, although I've been saving up and should be able to buy another car soon." As he was talking, he knit his brows in concentration and tried to get the mussels to form a pyramid. They kept slipping off.

"That takes a lot of balls. I could never race. Hell, I just bought my first car ever at the age of twenty-six, so I'm not exactly what you'd call a gearhead."

Jessie straightened up and looked at me, the mussels forgotten. "What did you buy?"

"Nothing fancy, just an old Honda Civic."

"Good call, they run forever with a little TLC. Some people even soup them up for street racing. There's a lot that can be done with that car. What type of Civic is it?"

I grinned and said, "A blue one. It's from, like, the mid-1980s. I honestly don't know shit about cars, aside from where the gas goes."

"Do you want me to teach you how to work on it? You can save a lot of money by doing your own oil changes and routine maintenance. Plus, if you want, I could get it running real nice for you, maybe even boost the performance a bit."

"Does 'boost the performance' mean make it go fast?"

He grinned and said, "That's one option. But I can also make it run really efficiently to save you money on gas."

He looked excited, but I said, "I'm sure you have better things to do than work on my car."

"Not really, and besides, that's totally fun for me. Please?"

That made me grin, too. "You're actually begging to work on my Honda?"

"I've done all I can do to Nana's limo, short of a sick paint job with some flames. Her grandson Dante doesn't want me to do that, even though it'd be tight. So yeah! I'm itching to get under the hood. Until I can afford my own car, I'm at the mercy of whoever will let me tinker with theirs."

"Well, hey, tinker away then."

Jessie beamed at me. "Awesome. We can work in Nana's driveway if you want, since all my tools are here. Can you come by Friday around ten a.m.? That's when Nana leads an exercise class for a group of her girlfriends and they usually have cocktails afterwards, so she won't want me to drive her anywhere for at least a couple hours."

"Sure, I'll be here."

I looked around as Jessie turned back to the mussel pyramid. Things were considerably calmer. Mr. Mario had grabbed a second bottle of wine and gone off with Nana, and the Bigfoot researcher had let the dog into the backyard and was filming him, probably just in case the brown, hairy beast turned out to be a baby sasquatch. Meanwhile, Trevor rounded up his three little nephews and gave them each a squeezable pouch of apple sauce, then tossed a dog treat to their multicolored puppy, who was aptly named Gismo. His son Josh tried to reject the offer of a pouch at first, claiming he was too old for that kind of thing. But finally, he accepted the apple sauce, sucked it down quickly and asked for another.

It felt good to be in that gorgeous home, watching the everyday interactions of such a loving family. Those little boys probably took it all for granted, but I couldn't. It was just too far removed from anything I'd ever experienced. Being in a clean, beautiful kitchen with enough to eat and a family who cared about them was an incredible gift. So was the fact that they let me be a part of it, at least for a little while.

Nico stuck his head in the kitchen, decided the coast was clear, and crossed the room to pour himself a cup of coffee. He then joined Jessie and me and said, "Hi guys. Do I even want to ask what was happening a few minutes ago?"

"Cooking show," Jessie said. That was explanation enough.

Nico nodded knowingly and took a drink from his mug as I studied him from beneath my lashes. He was a strikingly handsome guy, probably in his mid-twenties with jet black hair that grazed his collar, flawless olive skin and glasses that framed intelligent, dark eyes. He always looked tired though, every time I saw him. I knew he was in law school, and that he'd really thrown himself into it after a bad break-up. It always seemed like school was wearing away at him, and even though it was summer, that apparently hadn't lessened any. I asked him, "Are you on break now?"

He shook his head. "The regular semester ended, but I'm taking three classes this summer in the hope of lightening my load a bit next term."

"Which is so crazy!" Jessie exclaimed. "Dude, you need a break!"

"I'll have one during our four weeks in Italy." Nana's grandson Gianni and his boyfriend Zan had bought Nana a trip to Italy, and were sending Jessie and Nico with her for company. They'd probably included Nico because he was desperately in need of some downtime.

"But that's not until August and this is only June! You're gonna, like, implode or something!"

"I'll be fine, as long as we don't suddenly run into a worldwide coffee shortage." Nico took another drink from the white mug he was holding, then said, "I'm going to get back to the books. If all of this actually ends up turning into dinner, would you let me know?"

"Sure thing, Cousin," Jessie said with a big smile.

That made Nico grin. "Thanks. But you know we're not actually related, right?'

"We are now. Nana adopted me."

"You can't actually adopt twenty-three-year-olds," Nico told him.

"Not officially, but close enough."

Nico's expression softened and he gave Jessie's shoulder a squeeze. "You're a good addition to the family," he said before leaving the kitchen.

Jessie looked really pleased with that. I asked him, "Do you have an actual family somewhere?"

"Yes and no. I have a mom and dad and three brothers and sisters. But my dad's a Baptist minister, and let's just say having a queer kid doesn't sit too well with him." A shadow passed over his normally cheerful features, but he pushed it aside and smiled at me.

I got the impression he did that a lot, hiding pain behind a smile, and it made my heart go out to him. "If you ever feel like you want to talk about it, I'm a pretty decent listener," I told him.

"Thanks, I might take you up on that sometime. I do go to a weekly support group at the LGBT community center, but it's also nice to have friends to talk to." He turned his attention back to the seafood on the counter and once again tried to stack the mussels. "We should probably get to those photos while this is all still fresh. I want to make sure this turns out really good for Nana." He said that so sincerely. I picked up my camera and went to work.

*****

My time spent in Nana's big, beautiful home, full of family and life and activity, was such a huge contrast to the rest of my life. The one hundred and forty square feet that comprised my studio apartment felt really empty when I got back later that night. There wasn't anything I could do about that, though. I'd already knocked on Zachary's door, but he wasn't home.

I pushed my shoes off, hung up my jacket and cracked a window to offset the ever-present heat. That increased the noise from outside as cars and buses rattled by and voices drifted up from people out on the sidewalk. I was used to it.

After retrieving my paperback, I sat on my bed and tucked my feet under me. For some reason though, it was tough to concentrate on the pages. I really didn't know why I felt kind of sad, there was no reason to. I'd had a good day among people who were nice to me, and I was full from a wonderful Italian dinner. Once Nana gave up on the big clam, she and her family had made a terrific meal. Also, thanks to Finn Nolan, I could afford the luxury of staying in and reading, instead of spending the night hustling. I knew for a fact that being safe and warm with a full belly was nothing to take for granted.

*****

I'd been trying to focus on the book for about half an hour when I heard footsteps on the stairs. They were immediately followed by a knock on my door. When I opened it for Zachary, he launched himself into my arms.

I held him tightly as I asked in alarm, "Did someone hurt you?" He shook his head no. I led him over to the bed and sat down with him, then went right back to holding him. "What happened?"

When Zachary pulled back to look at me, his eyes were red and a bit swollen. He was still dressed in the suit and tie, and the shirt was now unbuttoned at the collar. "Can we please not talk about it? I just...I can't."

"Sure, as long as I know you don't need to go to the hospital or anything."

"I don't. I just need a friend."

"I'm right here," I said as I hugged him and he wrapped himself around me.

After a while he whispered, "I'm so glad you were home tonight."

"You can always call me if I'm not here."

"But what if you're working or something?"

"You're way more important."

He was quiet for a while before saying, "I've tried so hard not to become dependent on you. The last thing you need is some clingy, desperate loser making demands on your time. But you're all I have, Chance."

"You're not even sort of like that."

"I know I am. You're just being nice."

After a pause I said, "If you wanted to, I could help you meet some new people. You don't have to feel so alone, Zachary. I'm going over to Nana's house on Friday because her driver Jessie offered to work on my car. Why don't you come along? They'd love you."

"I wouldn't fit in."

"Like I do? They accept me anyway, and they'll accept you, too. Come with me. It'll be really low-key. We'll pretty much just hang out in the driveway with Jessie. Remember the blond from the wedding photos who you thought was cute? He's one of the friendliest people you'll ever meet."

Zachary sat up a bit and mulled that over while smoothing out the fabric of his suit jacket. Finally he asked, "Do they know what you do for a living?"

"Some do. Others just assume I'm a photographer."

"I don't want to tell them I work for an escort service. I'd feel like they were judging me."

"You don't have to tell them if you don't want to," I said.

"But then what am I supposed to say? It's always one of the first questions people ask, 'what do you do for a living?' My two choices are telling them I sell my body, or lying to them. Both options seem kind of shitty."

"Just tell them you're between jobs. It'll basically be the truth. You'll be between tricks while we're there."

He grinned a little for the first time that night. "Way to find the loophole."

"I'm good at that."

"I'll think about Friday." Zachary stood up and said, "I'm going to get out of this suit and take a long shower." He leaned over and kissed my forehead. "Thanks for everything, Chance."

"I didn't really do anything," I pointed out.

"You do way more than you realize," he said before leaving my apartment.

Chapter Six

It was cold and foggy, typical San Francisco summer weather. I tugged the collar of my denim jacket up a bit as I hurried down the sidewalk. The business district was deserted at nearly ten p.m. and the fog gave it a slightly eerie air.

That wasn't why I was hurrying, though. I rounded a corner and saw the light on in room two-fifteen of the Whitman. Finn was standing at the window, watching for me. He gave a little wave as soon as he saw me and I raised my hand in return. He closed the privacy curtains and I picked up my pace.

Finally I reached the hotel, and as I crossed the lobby, the middle-aged guy behind the reception desk watched me carefully. He'd also been working the first time I was here and was probably putting two and two together, figuring out what I was. I'd been kicked out of more hotels than I could count, and the confrontation always made me feel like trash. I was worried that was about to happen again, but he let me go without incident.

Finn was waiting in the open doorway when I got upstairs. His face lit up as soon as he saw me. The moment I was inside the room and the door was closed behind us, he scooped me up into an embrace. He actually lifted me off my feet, and I wrapped my arms and legs around him and held on tight.

"I'm glad you're here," Finn whispered, rubbing his cheek against my hair.

"Me too." I said, nuzzling his shoulder. He smelled good, like soap. His hair was still slightly damp, too. He'd gotten cleaned up for me.

"You don't have to say that."

"I know."

He pulled back a few inches to look at me, then kissed me tenderly before carrying me to the bed. Another little white envelope was lined up on the nightstand beside the lube and the box of condoms. After we kissed for a while, he looked in my eyes and asked, "Is it okay if I undress you?"

"Of course. You don't have to ask."

"It feels wrong not to."

He started with my shoes and socks, kissing each foot as he uncovered it. My jacket was next, and I raised my arms for him so he could pull my t-shirt over my head. He kissed my chest and stomach, then took off his short-sleeved button-down shirt before stripping off my jeans and briefs.

He ran his palm over my stomach, but then he hesitated. During our first session, he hadn't touched my cock. Not that that was unusual. The men who paid me were there to get themselves off, not me. He laid down on his side beside me and said quietly, his palm still on my stomach, "I want to make you feel good, but I'm worried about doing something wrong."

"You can't really mess this up. Just touch me the same way you'd touch yourself."

"I…um…I don't just want to use my hand," he said, clearly embarrassed by that admission.

"You can't really mess that up, either," I said, "unless teeth are involved."

"That's exactly what I'm worried about, not being careful enough and hurting you that way."

"Don't overthink it."

"I overthink everything. I also feel guilty about how one-sided everything was last time. You didn't even cum when we were having sex."

"If you want me to, I can jerk off while you're fucking me and cum for you."

"No, see," Finn said as he sat up, "that's the problem. I want you to cum because what's happening feels good, not because you're putting on a show for me. I know I'm paying you, but I hate feeling like you're just enduring it and not enjoying yourself at all."

I sat up too and said, "I do enjoy it. I like being with you."

"Really?" I nodded as he studied me closely. He asked, "What would make it even better for you?"

"Honestly, you and I would both enjoy it more if you let me initiate a bit. You can tell me what to avoid, and also just tell me to stop if I do something you don't like. As it stands right now, I'm pretty limited in the ways I can give you pleasure."

"I didn't want to feel out of control of the situation. It's probably pretty obvious that I don't know what I'm doing though, so forget what I said. Just don't...um...." A blush rose in his cheeks and he looked away.

"Don't what?"

"God this is embarrassing," he muttered, but finally he admitted, "I'm not used to having stuff inside me. I was worried you'd do something before I was ready."

"I'm glad you told me. I'll be sure not to finger you or—"

"No, see," he interrupted, "the thing is, I, um...I want you to do that." He put his hand over his face. "This is the most embarrassing conversation ever. I knew it'd be incredibly awkward to try to tell you what I wanted. It was part of the reason for my rule about not doing a lot of talking. I was trying to avoid this."

I knew I should give him some space, but for some reason I did the exact opposite, curling up against him and nuzzling his shoulder with my cheek. "You never have to be embarrassed with me, Finn. I'm here to make you feel good, and the more you can open up to me about what you want, the more fun you'll have."

"I'm not really an opening up kind of guy. In fact, I'm the exact opposite."

"Try to let this be your one exception. I mean, you're spending a ton of money and I feel guilty about last time. No way was what we did worth a thousand dollars. I really want you to get your money's worth this time around."

Finn dropped his hand and looked at me. "You're right, it wasn't worth a thousand dollars. It was worth a million. That was the best night of my life. On top of that, I took up ten hours of your time, which deserves compensation."

"Still though, I don't want to feel like I'm taking advantage of you. Let me earn my pay this time."

A little smile played around his lips. "You don't want to feel like *you're* taking advantage of *me?*"

I grinned, too. "That's right. Now how about laying back and letting me show you what I'm capable of?"

His lips parted and he drew in his breath. "One sentence and I'm instantly hard."

"Good." I rubbed him through his jeans as he kissed me. He hadn't been kidding.

Finn stripped himself quickly and settled back against the pillows. I slid between his legs, took his cock in my mouth, and slid my lips to its base before dragging them slowly back to the tip. "Holy shit," he exclaimed. Already? He had no idea what he was in for.

I concentrated on giving him the best blow job of his life over the next half hour, bringing him right to the edge before easing him down again. I did that again and again, and it was really gratifying to watch the way he responded. Finn started out trying to keep it together, but toward the end he was crying out and writhing beneath me, both hands gripping the bedding.

I could have just left it at that and finished him off, but based on what he'd said earlier, I eased my mouth off him, stroking his cock with my hand as I asked, "Do you want me to finger you?"

He could barely speak, but managed to rasp, "Yes. Fuck yes. Please." He parted his legs for me and I squirted some lube on my hand before letting a little run over his hole.

I took his cock in my mouth again before sliding my index finger inside him. He was incredibly tight, but I felt him trying to relax and let me in. Before long, he opened up enough to let me slide my finger in and out of him as I sucked him. When I grazed his prostate, he bucked his hips and moaned, low and deep.

I built him up again, then eased him down, sucking him as I worked his hole. Finn's entire body was shaking and his head was thrown back. I was surprised he hadn't asked me to finish him off, but I decided it was time to do just that. I began sucking him hard and fast as I massaged his prostate.

He cried out when he started to cum, arching off the bed. I slid my mouth from his cock and he erupted all over his belly, then onto his face and hair and the wooden headboard behind him. I wrapped my hand around his shaft and milked his orgasm, my finger still inside him as he bucked and thrashed around. His yells were almost sobs, his hips pushing his cock into my fist again and again, both hands white-knuckling the bedding beneath him as his muscular body glistened with sweat. He looked incredibly beautiful, totally lost to his pleasure like that.

I brought him down slowly, eventually easing my finger from him. When it was all over he laid on the bed shaking and gasping for breath, his chest rising and falling rapidly. One of his legs had been bent and he let it fall to the side, totally exposing himself to me and completely oblivious to it. "I'll be right back," I said, rolling off the bed and heading to the bathroom.

I washed up, then dampened a cloth with warm water and brought it and a hand towel back to bed with me. As I sat beside him on the mattress and wiped the cum from his face and hair, he whispered, "Thank you." I grinned at him and washed his chest and stomach, then quickly wiped down the headboard. I tossed the wet washcloth through the open bathroom door and dried him off with the hand towel. Once I'd tossed that too, he pulled me into his arms. "I mean it," he said, his voice a bit raspy. "Thank you. I just…." He shook his head. "I had no idea. Absolutely none. I thought an orgasm was an orgasm. That was…my God. How did you do that?"

I said softly, "I'm glad you liked it."

He rolled over so he was facing me, cocooned me with his big arms and draped his thigh over mine. I settled in comfortably as he lost the battle with his heavy eyelids. "Liked it," he murmured. "Huge understatement. Huge. That was life-changing. It was…my God." His voice trailed off. He was asleep in the next moment. I felt surprisingly content as I let my eyes shut.

*****

Sometime in the middle of the night, a tender kiss on my cheek pulled me out of a deep sleep. The room was dark, and Finn's arms were still around me. He kissed my cheek again, then ran a line of kisses along my jaw. When I stirred, he said, "Sorry to wake you."

"It's fine."

He nuzzled my ear and said, "Do you think it'd be okay if I did the same thing to you that you did to me? I mean, it won't be the same. Not even close. You're extraordinary and I'm, well, me. But is it okay if I suck you? I need to make you feel good, Chance. I need that so bad right now."

"Of course." I kissed him, cupping his face with my hand, and he returned the kiss before shifting around and kneeling between my legs. He kissed and licked the tip of my cock, then wrapped his hand around my shaft and began jerking me off. His movements were hesitant, but when I said, "That feels really good," he seemed to gain a little confidence.

Finn took a couple inches of my cock between his lips and tried sucking on it, his hand still wrapped around my hardening shaft. I pulled a couple pillows behind my head and stroked his short hair as he explored me with his lips and tongue. Gradually he got bolder, taking a little more of my cock in his mouth and sucking harder, encouraged when I moaned softly. What he was doing really did feel terrific, and I relaxed and let myself enjoy it.

He was trying hard, even to the point of accidentally gagging himself a couple times, and his efforts were paying off. I felt my orgasm building after a while and whispered, "I'm close, Finn. You might want to pull off."

He did, but only long enough to look up at me in the darkness and say, "I want to taste you, is there any reason not to?"

"No."

That one-word answer was all he needed. He wrapped his lips around my cock again and started sucking me hard. "Fuck," I muttered, letting my eyes close as I threaded my fingers into his hair. I needed just a push to take me over the top, and when he cupped my balls, that did it. I moaned as I came, shooting again and again, my cock twitching in his wet mouth.

Afterward, as I caught my breath, he gathered me gently in his arms again and asked, "Was that okay?"

"It was so good. I guess it'd been a while since my last orgasm, sorry. That was probably more than you bargained for."

"I loved it," he said, reaching up to stroke my hair as I put my head on his chest.

After a pause I said, "Here's a little public service announcement for next time you give someone a blow job, just because you seemed concerned. The rule to remember is 'spit or swallow, don't let it wallow.' I learned that from the San Francisco AIDS Foundation. In other words, if you hold cum in your mouth, it increases your risk of infection. Sorry to, you know, get all over-explanatory on you."

"That's fine. Thanks for caring."

"Just so you know, I get tested every six months and I haven't had unprotected sex in years, so you don't have to worry all that much with me. But it's just something to know in general, especially if you visit another prostitute." I felt kind of stupid for rambling on like that and added, "I didn't mean to get all after school special on you."

Finn chuckled a bit, his chest rumbling beneath me. "If only there had been an after school special about blow jobs. That would have been really beneficial. And thanks for looking out for me, but I actually already knew that. I'm a firm believer in doing my homework."

"That's good. Safety first," I said.

"Mmhmm," he murmured as he leaned in and kissed me.

His erection grazed my thigh and I reached down to stroke him as we kissed. After a while I asked, "Feel like fucking me?"

"I will if you do that for two more seconds," he said. Then he smiled, his teeth a flash of white in the darkness, and said, "Aaaand, we're there. What should we do? I'm open to suggestions. You could continue your educational programming."

I sat up and swung my leg over him, straddling his hips. "You might enjoy a program called Chance Rides Like a Cowboy."

That made him chuckle again. "Perfect." I fumbled for the lube and condoms, and he reached over and turned on the lamp on the nightstand. "I really should watch you do this, for purely educational purposes," he said with a smile, and I grinned at him.

I rolled a condom over his cock and slicked it with lube before lowering myself onto it. Finn moaned as I took all of him in me and started to ride him. He stared up at me with an awe-struck expression, and I rested my hands on his shoulders to steady myself.

He maintained eye contact as he reached between us and gently stroked my cock, asking, "Is it too soon after the last time, or do you think you could cum again?"

"I know I can." Between his thick cock massaging my prostate and the hand-job he was giving me, I was proven right a few minutes later. I shot onto his chest and he came soon after, thrusting up into me as he moaned and grasped my hips.

My legs were shaking when I slid off of him and removed the condom. "Back in a minute," I said, then hurried to the bathroom and repeated the wash cloth and hand towel routine, cleaning Finn up before snuggling into his arms.

"You're so incredibly sweet," he told me.

"So are you."

He chuckled at that. "If you said that to anyone who knew me, they'd call you crazy."

"Well, you're sweet to me."

"I feel better with you than I do with anyone else. You've even got me talking! I don't do that."

I grinned and said, "You don't talk?"

"Not much. I usually limit small-talk to reciting the Miranda rights."

Now it was my turn to chuckle. "You're funny, too."

"Again, no one would ever believe you if you tried to tell them that."

"Well, then I'm lucky that I get to see what no one else does," I said as he hugged me and rubbed his cheek against my hair.

*****

There was another note waiting for me the next morning. It said: *Thank you again for last night. It was perfect. I don't have my schedule yet for next week, but I'll call you when I know my days off. I'd love to see you again.*

I was both pleased and surprised that it seemed to be becoming an ongoing thing. I liked the overnighters with Finn, though I wondered how long he'd be able to afford them. I rolled out of bed and headed to the shower, looking forward to the luxurious orange-scented soap and shampoo.

Chapter Seven

"Oh my God," Zachary whispered as we stood on the sidewalk in front of Nana's house, pushing his once-again-black hair out of his eyes. Granted, it was a lot to take in. The three-story Queen Anne mansion was both regal and whimsical at the same time, the latter because it had been painted top to bottom in a sheer rainbow. Since the trim had all been left white, the effect was actually really pretty, and less 'the circus is coming to town' than it could have been.

"Explain Nana to me," he said as he stared up at the façade.

"Well, let's see. Some of her grandsons are gay, and I think that's what pushed her to be such a strong ally. That kind of explains the giant rainbow. Also, her family used to be in the mafia, that's how they made their money. I guess they're basically retired now, but that explains the mansion. Other than that...well, you just have to meet her and see for yourself. Nana as a whole kind of defies explanation."

Zachary looked concerned as he glanced at me, but I said, "You'll love her. Jessie, too. Come on." I led the way up to the front door and he trailed a couple steps behind me.

Nothing happened for a couple minutes after I rang the doorbell. When I rang it again, there was another pause before the big, white door swung open and muted, pulsating techno music spilled out. "Hi Chance," Nico said, stepping back and holding the door open for me. "I hope you weren't out here long. Everyone's upstairs and I was studying in my room. I wasn't quite sure I heard the bell at first."

"It wasn't long at all," I said, stepping into the huge foyer as Zachary took my hand. When I glanced at him, he looked dazed. I'd been like that too, the first time I came here.

"It's like something out of a movie," Zachary whispered, standing so close to me that our bodies touched. That about summed it up, between the marble floor, the huge crystal chandelier, and the sweeping staircase on the right curving up to a second floor gallery.

"Nico Dombruso, I'd like you to meet Zachary Paleki. We're supposed to be meeting Jessie, he wanted to work on my car."

"Yeah he mentioned that. Jessie's really excited about it," Nico said. He extended a hand to my companion and gave him a friendly smile. "It's nice to meet you, Zachary."

He looked up at Nico with wide eyes. "You too," he said softly as they shook hands.

"Nana's leading an exercise class upstairs in the grand ballroom and last I saw, Jessie was DJing for her. Come on, I'll take you to him." With that, Nico turned and led the way up the staircase. Zachary and I both checked him out automatically. He had a pretty incredible body, and the rear view was impressive.

We climbed to the third floor, and Nico stopped in front of a set of double doors. The music was louder there, and he raised his voice to be heard above it. "They're in here. I'm going to make my escape before you go inside. Nana keeps trying to get me involved in this exercise class. She likes to change it up for her girlfriends, and, well, you'll see." He smiled and said, "Good luck," before turning and heading back the way we'd come.

Zachary stared after him, and when Nico was out of earshot he said, "That's one of the most gorgeous men I've ever seen. He looks like a movie star. Is he?"

"No, he's a law student. All of Nana's grandsons are really attractive. Good genes." I smiled at Zachary as I grasped the door handle. "Here goes nothing."

When I opened the door, we both slipped inside and then just froze and stared. The huge room was absolutely beautiful. It had high ceilings and was bathed in sunlight thanks to a big row of windows, and someone had painted an absolutely perfect trompe l'oeil scene on the walls, a birch forest in winter. It was gorgeous and ethereal and such a weird contrast to the scene before us.

Four silver stripper poles were mounted on the right side of the room, three in a row, and one offset on a little stage. A tall, muscular guy with dark hair was demonstrating a move on that last pole. I recognized Skye's husband Dare when he stopped spinning. I knew he was a dance instructor with a background in ballet, but judging by his moves, apparently he also moonlighted as a pole dancer, because he clearly knew what he was doing.

"Alright ladies," Dare called over the music. "Take it slow now. Break it down just like we talked about."

The other poles were each manned by two tiny women over seventy in colorful leotards. "There's no way," Zachary whispered to me. "They can't possibly—" He stopped talking abruptly as three of the little old ladies stepped forward, grabbed the poles, and swung around in a rough approximation of what Dare had done. "I stand corrected," he said.

Jessie stood at a little table beside the stage with a laptop that must have been connected to hidden speakers, keeping the beat by swaying his narrow hips to the music. After a minute, he glanced over his shoulder and exclaimed when he spotted us, "Hey there, guys!" He turned down the music a bit, jogged over and startled me by grabbing me in a hug. "Is it ten already? I lost track of time." He then flashed a huge smile at my companion and stuck his hand out. "You must be Zachary. Chance texted me and told me he'd be bringing a friend. I'm Jessie, it's great to meet you!"

"You too." He stuck close to my side as he shook Jessie's hand, his other palm on my lower back. I was surprised at how shy he seemed all of a sudden, not that I'd ever watched Zachary interact with anyone before.

"I'll just be a few more minutes, the exercise class got off to a late start," Jessie said.

"Hot damn," Nana exclaimed, rushing over to us. She was dressed in a shiny, long-sleeved, hot pink leotard and matching legwarmers with purple tights. "Am I glad to see you boys! Come give us a hand."

"With what exactly?" I asked as she grabbed Zachary and me by the sleeves and started pulling us over to the poles.

"We need some spotters. Dare said we couldn't do the fancy stuff without 'em, and my grandson Nico is too much of a stick-in-the-mud to help. He was going on about us breaking hips and whatnot. As if all old people are made of glass!" She turned to Zachary and gave him a quick head-to-toe assessment, then said, "You're adorable. I don't think we've met. Are you a gay homosexual like Chance, and if so, are you two boyfriends?"

"Um, yes to being gay, if that's what you just asked me. And Chance is my best friend, so no to the boyfriend part," he said, coloring slightly. "My name's Zachary," he tacked on as an afterthought.

"Glad to know you, Zachary. Any friend of Chance's is a friend of mine," Nana said. We'd reached the pole in the center and Nana put her hands on her hips and turned to Dare. "Okay, Captain Cautious, we got our spotters! Time to bust out that slick upside down move."

"Wait, what are we supposed to be doing?" Zachary asked nervously.

"Don't worry, I'll team up with you, since you're little like me," Jessie told him. "Dare can take one pole and Chance can take the other. The ladies won't be satisfied until they get to try out one of the more advanced moves, and once they do, we can get to the fun of tearing Chance's car apart. You don't have to be too concerned about them either, they're actually pretty good at this stuff and probably won't fall, but we need to be there just in case. It's kind of like in cheerleading when they make a pyramid and some of the girls stay on the ground to catch the others, you know?" Zachary looked a bit panicked, but Jessie smiled at him and squeezed his shoulder. "It'll be fine. You'll see."

"Alright boys, let's do this thing!" Nana exclaimed, rubbing her bony hands together. She then grabbed a pole and tried to shimmy up it, but only got about a foot off the floor.

"Go get 'em, Stana!" The chubby little old lady standing beside us exclaimed. She was dressed in a turquoise leotard with lots of matching eye shadow, and pumped her fist in the air. "And be quick about it, I want my turn!"

"Keep your girdle on, Gladys," Nana huffed. She managed to gain maybe one more foot in elevation, and then she said, "Shit, I'm not getting anywhere," and hopped off the pole. "Show us again, Dare."

He grabbed the pole beside him with both hands and twisted around effortlessly, so his legs were over his head. He then wrapped a calf around the pole and extended his arms over his head as he said, "Keep your hands down like this to catch yourself if you fall, and don't go too high up." The ladies weren't listening at all. He was wearing a black cotton tank top and shorts, and the shirt fell around his shoulders, exposing his washboard abs. Immediately, Nana and her friends clustered around the stage, three of them putting on glasses to get a better look.

"The secret to this move is right here," Nana said, coming up on stage and grabbing Dare's ass with both hands. "That's how he can hold on to the pole with just one leg. See how his buns are clenched up nice and tight?" Nana gave them a squeeze and said, "I forget what we were talking about, but this is the best exercise class I ever dreamt up. I think we should start working out seven days a week with Dare as our instructor. Maybe we can even do some water aerobics after the pole dancing. Do you own a Speedo, Dare? I don't have a pool but I don't think that part's important."

Dare chuckled as he jumped off the pole, landing on his feet like a cat. "Come on ladies, your turn. Let's see what you can do."

"Yeah, okay," Nana said. "I'm gonna work that pole. Get ready, boys." She climbed off the stage, took a run at the metal apparatus, and grabbed it with both hands. Somehow, she managed to fling herself upside down, wrapping her skinny legs around the pole. Her wig fell off, revealing a beige hair net, and she exclaimed, "Shit, my hair! Somebody give me a hand." Gladys bustled over and grabbed the wig, jamming it onto Nana's head sideways, up to her eyebrows. "Thanks, you're a peach," Nana told her. "Now everyone stand back, I'm gonna bust a move! There's two more poles, girls, let's show 'em we still got it!" While she flung her legs out to the sides, Gladys ran at the pole to Nana's right, and another tiny lady with a bright yellow leotard jumped on the pole to the left. Both ladies flipped upside down at the same time, and both their wigs fell off.

"I feel like I'm on a super weird acid trip," Zachary whispered to me. When I glanced at him, he was smiling.

Nana wrapped her legs tightly around the pole and said, "Here comes my sexy move. Don't say I didn't warn you." She stuck her arms out to the sides and began vigorously shaking her chest and shoulders. Her wig fell off again, but she didn't seem to notice as she said, "It feels like my boobs are gonna flop out of the top of my leotard. If that happens, somebody stuff 'em back in." She then slid down until her back was on the ground, possibly accidentally, and jumped to her feet. "Big finish, girls, just like we practiced!"

Dare came over to us once all three ladies were on the ground and said, "For the record, I didn't teach them this next part. It's pretty well choreographed, though."

All three of them grabbed their wigs and jammed them onto their heads, then rushed to get into position. They grabbed the poles with one hand, straddled them, and started twerking wildly while making spanking motions with their other hand. A bubble of delighted laughter burst from Zachary, and when they stopped and took a bow, he started applauding, along with the rest of us.

All six little ladies got together then and did a round of high-fives, and Nana exclaimed, "We make eighty look good!"

"I'm only seventy-five," Gladys chimed in.

"Liar," the tiny lady in yellow said, fluffing her wig (which was on backwards). "I got a look at your driver's license when you got pulled over for speeding last week. It says you're—"

"Shut it, Miriam," Gladys interrupted. "You're not the only one with tales to tell. Two words: Tampa and margaritas!"

"What happens in Tampa stays in Tampa!" Miriam shrieked.

While Nana's cohorts bickered, we joined Jessie beside the stage, where he was packing up his laptop. "Sorry for the delay," he said. "It's really easy to get sidetracked around here. Is your car in the driveway?"

"No, there was a big, pink Lincoln Continental in the driveway beside Nana's limo, so we parked down the street," I told him.

"Oh, that's right. I forgot that Gladys fired her driver and drove herself here. No worries though, we can just hang out while the ladies have their Bloody Marys, unless you guys are in a hurry."

"I'm not. What about you, Zachary?" I asked, and he shook his head.

A phone on the tabletop started ringing, and Jessie glanced at the screen before shouting across the room, "Dare, it's your husband. Want me to get it?"

"Sure." He had a little old lady hanging off each arm, fondling his biceps.

Jessie poked at the screen and said, "Hey Skye, you're on speaker. Dare is currently in a Nanette sandwich."

"Hey, Jessie. So, um, this is my one phone call," Skye said, and everyone in the room stopped talking and turned toward the phone. "I got arrested for trespassing. I'm at the same police station where Nana and I got taken that one time. Dare, do you think you could come and bail me out?"

"Of course! I thought you were just going to the junkyard to buy some scrap metal, though. What happened?"

"I got distracted by the most awesome piece of metal ever. It was sticking out of a dumpster, so I figured it was fair game. Problem was, that dumpster was behind a great, big chain link fence, and going after it in broad daylight on a weekday? Not the best call ever."

"Skye's a sculptor," I explained to Zachary, then called, "Hi, Skye. It's Chance. Sorry you got arrested."

"My own fault," he said. "I rang the buzzer and no one answered, so I figured I'd just conduct some routine trash removal services for their company. Turned out the place wasn't deserted after all. I'm not sure what that company does exactly, but apparently it involves guzzling steroids and having your sense of humor surgically removed."

"I'll come with Dare to bail you out, Skye," Nana yelled from across the room. "Are you okay? Are you the victim of police brutality? Have they violated your rights as a Gay Homosexual American?"

"No Nana, I'm fine. The cop who processed me was kind of a douchebag, but it's no big deal."

Nana yelled, "I knew it, they're violating his rights! Jessie, fire up the limo. Dare, Chance, and cute friend of Chance's whose name I forgot, you're with me. Girls, half of you come with us, the other half go with Gladys in the Lincoln. We need to get down there pronto, all of us, and show The Man that we got our eyes on him. Sit tight, Skye, we're on the way! I just need to grab Nico, he's the closest thing we got to an in-house lawyer."

She ran from the room with all of her girlfriends right behind her, and Jessie picked up the phone and headed for the door as he said, "Looks like we're all coming. We'll be there in twenty."

"That's not necessary," Skye said. "I just needed Dare to bail me out."

"I'm on my way," his husband said as he fell into step with us. "You really okay, Skye?"

"I'm perfectly fine. Can you try to talk Nana out of storming the police station?"

"That's not gonna happen," Jessie chimed in. "You know how she is. It'd be like trying to force a cork back into an erupting champagne bottle. She won't stop until she sees you're okay with her own eyes."

"Yeah, you're right. I gotta go, they're telling me my time's up. See you soon," Skye said. A moment later, the line went dead.

As we all jogged down the stairs, Jessie asked, "You guys are coming along, right? We should all back Nana up."

I was going to decline, since a police station was hardly my favorite place to be. But then I glanced at Zachary and he said, "Can we? I want to see what Nana does next." There was a sparkle in his dark eyes that I hadn't seen before. I nodded and we all picked up the pace to catch up to the eighty-year-old.

*****

The limo and the big, pink Lincoln both parked illegally right in front of the police station, which was an interesting choice. Nana was the first one out of the vehicle, throwing the door open before Jessie brought the car to a complete stop. "Wow," Zachary said as we stepped out onto the sidewalk, "Nana's really concerned about this Skye person. Is he one of her relatives?"

"No, they're not related, but she sort of adopts stray gay guys, maybe because they remind her of her grandsons," I said.

"She has a really big heart," Jessie said. He came around the car from the driver's side just as Nico, frazzled and barefoot, stepped out of the back of the limo. Apparently Nana had plucked her grandson from his room with no time to get himself together. Jessie added, "She also has a really big .44 in the handbag she grabbed on her way out the door. I really hope she doesn't get the idea to brandish it in the police station. That would be bad." Nico's eyes went wide at that, and he took off at a sprint after his grandmother.

"Oh my God," Zachary said with a little, lopsided smile as we went after them. "Best granny ever."

All hell had broken loose inside the station, just in the forty seconds or so that it took us to get inside. Nana was standing on the front desk, and she and Nico were engaged in a tug-of-war with her purse while all of her girlfriends yelled at once. The big African American cop behind the desk was trying to talk her down, as if that would work, and Dare muttered, "Wow, that's…."

"Pretty typical," Jessie finished for him. He smiled and added, "It's so awesome when she goes full-on Norma Rae."

The lobby of the police station was filling with cops, many of whom were trying to herd the leotarded little old ladies to the seating area. While that was going on, Nico finally won the tug-of-war, staggering backwards when Nana let go of her purse abruptly and turned her attention to yelling at the cop behind the counter. Nico bumped into me, knocking me off my feet before awkwardly righting himself.

A big hand reached down to help me up. I ran my gaze up and over the police uniform until I met a pair of vividly blue eyes. Finn looked grave, a little frown line between his eyebrows.

I took his hand and let him pull me to my feet, and then we just stared at each other for a long moment. My gaze dropped to his full lips, and I remembered the way he'd looked while sucking me just a few hours before. My cock stirred at the memory, and I licked my lips without thinking about what I was doing. That, or maybe something else, made the frown line vanish, and he drew a deep breath.

I had no idea how much time passed as we stood there staring at each other. "What are you doing here?" he finally managed.

"We were at Nana's house and kind of got swept up in a field trip."

All of a sudden he realized he was still holding my hand, and let go as he stepped back from me. "I need to get back to work," he mumbled, then turned, cut straight through the mayhem in the reception area and disappeared into the back of the building.

"What the hell was that about?" Zachary asked. I turned to look at him, and he raised an eyebrow at me.

"Oh, um, I know him. That's Christian's brother-in-law. You saw his photo in the wedding pictures I took."

"The guy with the sad eyes, I remember," Zachary said. "Still doesn't explain that weird little moment."

"Just, you know, I wasn't expecting to see someone I knew, especially in uniform." I really couldn't offer more explanation right then.

Zachary nodded at that. "The uniform always makes me uncomfortable, too. I'm glad I came along, though. It would have been a shame to miss that." He grinned and tilted his head in Nana's direction. She was still up on the front counter, and was using her wig to swat at a cop who was trying to get her down. Meanwhile, I noticed Dare over to the left, calmly arranging his husband's bail with another officer.

"I'm surprised they haven't arrested her yet," I said.

"They have to catch her first," my friend pointed out.

Nana shimmied off the counter and took off at a run into the back of the police station, yelling, "I'm coming for you, Skye! Ain't nobody gonna violate your rights as a Gay Homosexual American on my watch!" She disappeared from view behind a sea of dark blue uniforms. We could still track her progress though, because she kept grabbing papers off the desks she passed and throwing them in the air, possibly to distract her pursuers.

It was miraculous that they didn't arrest her after all of that. Apparently cute little old ladies could pretty much get away with murder. They did detain her though, eventually herding her into a holding cell, and called her eldest grandson. Dante showed up half an hour later in an expensive, dark suit, a frown etched onto his handsome features. His husband Charlie accompanied him, trying to look serious even though his green eyes sparkled with amusement.

When Dante gave Nico a once-over, staring for an extra few seconds at his cousin's bare feet and the big handbag over his shoulder, Nico blurted, "You used to live with her, you know how it is! She's like a tiny hurricane, she just sweeps through and scoops you up into the mayhem!" Dante had to agree with that.

It took a good hour to get everything with Nana sorted out. While that was happening, Skye was released on bail. He sat in the waiting area with his husband and the ladies in their leotards, who were passing around silver flasks. Jessie struck up a conversation with Zachary, and I was glad that they seemed to be bonding.

I slipped outside for some fresh air at one point and went around to the side of the building. I closed my eyes and tilted my face toward the sunlight as I leaned against the police station. My stomach rumbled and I wondered how long it had been since I'd eaten, but I ignored it and wrapped my arms around myself.

After a while, I was startled out of my bubble by a deep voice close by that said, "Hey." I flinched and put up a hand automatically, but relaxed when I saw Finn standing there. He held out a candy bar and said, "Here."

"What's that for?" I asked, making no move to take it from him.

"I came out here to find you a couple minutes ago and heard your stomach rumbling, so I went back in and got you this out of the vending machine."

"You didn't have to do that."

"I know."

"It's really embarrassing that you could hear my stomach from a few feet away," I said.

"Would you please take this?" he said, and I slid it from his fingers, then looked at the ground.

"I'm sorry for coming here," I said. "I didn't mean to make things awkward or uncomfortable for you. I didn't know you worked out of this station. I didn't think you worked days, either."

"I'm working a double today because we're short-staffed."

"I see." I studied my worn-out formerly white sneakers, which were a huge contrast to his highly polished black boots.

"I didn't mean to make it weird for you, either. We know some of the same people, so we're going to see each other around occasionally. I just, you know, didn't expect you to turn up at my job, the day after...." He cleared his throat embarrassedly and shifted his weight, turning his head to focus on something in the distance.

I looked up at his profile and said softly, "I really am sorry, Finn."

"You didn't do anything wrong."

"I did. The last thing you need is someone like me showing up at your workplace."

"Someone like you? Chance...." He started to reach for me, but then he stopped himself. A few awkward moments passed, and then he asked, "What are you doing out here?"

"Just taking care of myself for a couple minutes."

"What do you mean?"

I struggled for a way to explain it, and finally mumbled, "It's just something I've always done. A teacher when I was in grade school said it was because I was an introvert and needed time alone to recharge my batteries. That's how she put it. I just need breaks sometimes, a few minutes to, I don't know. Check out from reality, I guess."

I'd really botched that explanation, but Finn nodded and said, "I get it. You just need to zone out occasionally."

"Yeah, basically."

"I do the same thing, but I usually put on headphones and listen to music when I need to check out for a while." I nodded at that, crossing my arms over my ribcage. After another pause, Finn said, "I need to get back to work. I just wanted to make sure you were okay."

He started to reach for me and hesitated, but then he touched my arm. It was a strange little gesture, just the lightest graze of his fingertips against the fabric of my jacket. Finn headed for the side door then, and I turned and went to the front of the building.

When I got back to the lobby, Zachary and Jessie both looked up and smiled at me. I sat down beside them, and Zachary asked, "Where were you?"

"Just getting some air."

"You going to eat that?"

I'd forgotten about the candy bar in my hand. He was eyeing it hungrily and I said, "You can have it." He thanked me and tore it open eagerly, then shared it with Jessie. When he tried to give me some, I turned it down to make sure he got enough to eat.

My mind wandered to Finn as we waited. I wondered how badly I'd blown it. He must have really hated having the whore he'd hired show up at his job like that. What man wouldn't? He probably wouldn't call me again after something like that.

A couple minutes later, Nana burst into the lobby and announced, "I'm free! The Man couldn't get any charges to stick. Let's get out of here before they dream up some reason to keep me in lock-up." She linked arms with Skye and led the procession out of the building. I glanced over my shoulder when I got to the door, but didn't see Finn. I didn't know what made me look for him in the first place.

Chapter Eight

I was lying in bed that night, staring at the ceiling in the darkness when my phone jingled on the table. I reached above my head and picked it up, and was surprised to see Finn's name on the screen. "Hey," I said when I answered.

"Hey. I'm sorry to call so late. I hope I didn't wake you."

"You didn't."

"Really?"

"Yeah."

There was a pause before he said, "Are you still going to want to see me after today?"

"Of course. Why wouldn't I?"

"Because I made things weird and awkward between us. I didn't mean to, but, well, I did it anyway."

"You didn't do anything wrong."

"I'm glad you think so." After a moment, he said, "I got my schedule tonight. My next day off isn't until Thursday."

"I can meet you then, if you want."

"It's so far away, though. Today's only Friday. Oh wait, shit, no it's not. It's after midnight. I'm sorry. I didn't realize it was that late."

I rolled onto my side, pulling the blanket up to my shoulder as I said, "It's fine. Really."

"Do you swear I didn't wake you?"

"I swear."

"What were you doing? Not that it's any of my business."

"I was just lying in bed. It's hard for me to get to sleep sometimes."

"Same here, except when I'm with you. I guess I just have a hard time sleeping alone. You'd think I'd be used to it." We were both quiet for a few moments, and then he told me, "I don't want to wait until Thursday."

"You don't have to."

"Can I see you tonight? I can't get a room at the Whitman, no one works the front desk this late, but maybe we could meet somewhere else for a couple hours. It's fine to say no, you're already in bed. I just…I thought I'd ask," Finn said.

I sat up and pushed my hair out of my eyes. "Sure."

"Really? Wow, that's great. Thank you."

I sat up and said, "Do you want me to come to your apartment?"

"No." He said that quickly. "Do you have a car?"

"Yeah."

"Could you meet me up on Twin Peaks? I know that's kind of random, but it's not going to be patrolled tonight, so there's no risk of my coworkers discovering us up there."

"Sure, that's no problem. I can be there in half an hour."

"Thank you again, Chance. See you soon." We disconnected and I hurried to the bathroom to get myself ready.

*****

I ended up being a few minutes early and sat on the half-wall of the scenic overlook, pulling up the zipper on my hoodie against the cool breeze. All of San Francisco sprawled out below me. The city looked better from a distance. You couldn't see the litter, graffiti, or the runaways and homeless people out there trying to survive one more night. That was San Francisco to me. I pivoted around, turning my back to the false promise of those glittering lights, and waited for Finn to arrive.

At two minutes before our designated meet time, an older, white SUV pulled into the empty parking lot. An immediate, involuntary fear reaction flooded me, since I didn't know if that was Finn and I was really isolated up here. If that was someone who wanted to do me harm, I was pretty much screwed. I chastised myself for not waiting in my car as I rose to my feet and squared my shoulders.

The SUV parked next to my Honda, and I let out the breath I was holding when Finn got out and started walking toward me. I closed the distance between us, and the moment he reached me, he grabbed me in an embrace, lifting me off my feet. I wrapped my arms and legs around him and breathed in his clean scent. He'd showered for me. The hair at the back of his neck was still slightly wet.

We held each other for a long time, and after a while he whispered, "I wanted to do this so bad today when I was talking to you outside the police station. I spent the rest of the day thinking about it. That's why I had to call you. I'm so grateful that you agreed to meet me." I kissed his cheek and buried my face in the space between his neck and shoulder.

Finn carried me to my car and sat me down on the hood, then kissed me with raw hunger. I slid my hand between us and caressed his thick cock through his sweats, which made him gasp against my lips, drawing the breath from my mouth. He was rock hard in no time, and took a step back as he fumbled with the lube and condom that he pulled from the pocket of his jacket.

As he prepped himself, I slid off the hood of the car, pulled my jeans and briefs down to mid-thigh and bent over for him, resting on my forearms. Once the condom was on and lubed, he pushed into me with one long thrust and whispered, "Oh fuck," when he bottomed out in me.

He grasped my hips and started fucking me hard and fast, the sound of his body slapping my ass filling the quiet night. My cock was hard, but I ignored it and concentrated on pushing back onto him to increase his pleasure. I rested my body on the warm hood of my car and reached behind me, spreading my ass for him so he could take me even deeper. He cried out and pounded me harder still. God it felt good. I moaned as he drove himself into me, his fingers grasping my hips.

Finn yelled when he came. He pushed into me so hard that it drove me onto the hood of the car, my feet coming up off the ground. Again and again he slammed into me. It was so wild and intense that I let myself stop thinking and just enjoyed how amazing it felt. I swung my arms around and braced myself against the car, my cock rubbing against the smooth metal.

It startled me when I came. It shouldn't have, since he'd been pounding my prostate, but I hadn't been focused on that at all. I made a weird little sound, almost a whimper, as my balls drew up and the orgasm detonated. He fucked me all the way through it and I writhed underneath him, riding out the wave of pleasure, letting it overwhelm me.

When it was all over, he collapsed onto my back for a few moments. Both of us were shaking as we tried to catch our breath. "Sorry," he managed, "I'll get off you in a second, soon as I can move."

"No hurry. I like it," I told him. It was true, too. His weight on top of me was a comfort somehow.

He got up a moment later. I just kept laying on the hood of my car, waiting for some strength to return. Finn took a sandwich bag from his pocket and deposited the condom inside, then zipped it shut and tossed it in a nearby trash can. I chuckled a little, and when he glanced at me I said, "You think of everything."

"I try to." After we both were dressed again, he scooped me into his arms and carried me to the spacious backseat of his SUV, then slid in after me.

I climbed onto his lap, straddling him, and put my head on his shoulder as he held me. "You feel so good," I told him.

"I'm glad you think so." He kissed the top of my head.

"Meeting in public like this was a pretty bold move," I said after a pause.

"It was a calculated risk. I used to work this beat, so I know only two types of people come up here: tourists, who aren't going to recognize us, and horny couples who are way too focused on getting off to care who we are or what we're doing." He thought about that and added, "Well, okay, I come up here too, sometimes. If other locals do too, then I guess it's not so private after all."

"Why do you come up here?"

"To gain perspective. I'm down there every day, dealing with people at their absolute worst on the job. It would be pretty easy to start to hate my hometown if all I saw were the criminals. But from up here, I just see San Francisco, and I'm reminded how incredibly beautiful she is."

"I don't buy that perspective, standing so far back that you don't see any of the ugliness."

"I don't come up here to fool myself, I come to literally see the bigger picture. It's not all ugly, not by a long shot. It can start to feel that way, after rolling up on my thousandth domestic violence call or drug overdose or homicide. But in reality, there's so much more to this city. I mean, just look at that."

He gestured behind me at the sparkling cityscape, and I glanced over my shoulder at it and muttered, "It's a lie," before turning away from the view again.

"What is?"

"The beautiful face that San Francisco shows the world. It's full of false promises. I fell for it and came here with the hope of a better life, back when I was young and stupid. Well, young anyway. I'm still stupid."

Finn shifted around and cradled me against him, lacing his fingers with mine. "If you hate it so much, why do you stay?"

"It's not like anyplace else is much better." After a moment I added softly, just to myself, "Moving to Saturn isn't an option."

"What?"

"Nothing." I was so startled when he stroked the little tattoo on the inside of my wrist with his thumb that I pulled my hand away.

As I sat up and stared at him, he said, "Shit, sorry. You said no questions, just like I did, and I must have crossed a line. I didn't mean to."

"It's fine," I lied, sliding across the seat, away from him. "Look, it's late. I need to go. No charge for tonight. You totally overpay me as it is, you were owed a freebie."

I got out of the SUV, and Finn tumbled out after me, calling, "Chance, wait. Please. I'm so sorry. I obviously fucked up, but I'm not sure what I did. If it was the questions, I'll stop, I promise."

"It wasn't that," I mumbled, dropping my keys as I tried to get the door to my Honda open.

"Then what was it? I don't understand. Why are you running from me?"

There was so much genuine grief in his voice that I turned to look at him. His face was partly lit by a distant streetlamp, the other half in darkness. But the bewilderment spelled out on his features was crystal clear. All of a sudden I felt like such an asshole. He had absolutely no idea why I was freaking out on him.

"It wasn't the questions. It was the way you touched me."

His eyes went wide. "Oh God, did I hurt you when we were having sex?"

"No, it wasn't anything like that." I took a step closer to Finn and looked up at him. Then I turned my right hand over and showed him the inside of my wrist. "This is mine," I said quietly, running the thumb of my left hand over my tattoo, exactly like he'd done. "I doubt I can explain this properly, but…this is my safe place. When things feel out of control, I retreat there. It's kind of like a little link to a place deep inside myself, a place where no one can hurt me. It just…it scared me when you touched it, especially because you did it without looking. I didn't like that you knew exactly where it was. It made me feel vulnerable all of a sudden, and I hate that feeling."

"You actually did an amazing job of explaining that," he said softly, "And I'm so sorry for making you feel that way. I didn't know."

I stared at the ground and said, "You didn't do anything wrong. You had no idea about any of this."

"I still feel like an asshole. The last thing I ever wanted was to make you feel unsafe."

"Don't. This is all me. All you did was touch my wrist. In what world is that reason enough for me to act like this?"

"I should have known it meant something to you, though."

I glanced up at him. The breeze was pushing my hair into my eyes, and I swept it out of the way as I asked, "How could you possibly know that?"

"Well, because I saw you at my brother's wedding. You seemed so shy and uncomfortable, except when you were taking pictures. Whenever you didn't have your camera to hide behind, you'd hold your right hand with your left and start rubbing that spot with your thumb. I don't think you even realized you were doing it. At first, I thought it was because the bruises around your wrists hurt, but when I got close enough to see the tattoo, I realized it must be something else, like a little personal talisman or something."

I looked away again and said quietly, "I was hoping no one saw the bruises."

"I doubt anyone else did. I'm a police officer, I'm trained to notice things."

I frowned at that. "Most of your family is in law enforcement, including your brother Shea. By that logic, half the people at the wedding would have noticed them."

"Not most. Some. There were only four or five police officers at the wedding. And anyway, so what if they noticed? They didn't know you were a prostitute. They'd probably just assume your sex life was a hell of a lot more interesting than theirs." He'd been trying to make a joke, but when my frown deepened, he said, "Well, who cares what my family thinks?" That was kind of ironic, since he obviously cared a great deal, but I didn't call him on it.

Instead, I stuffed my hands in the pockets of my jacket and shifted uncomfortably as I told him, "I'm sorry about this. You're not paying for drama and I acted like an idiot. I'm going to go ahead and go before I make things worse.

Like I said before, there's no charge for tonight." He didn't say anything as I retrieved my keys and drove off. But when I glanced in my rearview mirror, I saw him standing right where I'd left him, staring after me, his shoulders slumped.

I knew I'd messed up, but I had to get out of there. It wasn't just because of what had happened with my tattoo. It all felt really complicated, though there was no reason why it should. I was just his whore. I was nothing to him, and he was nothing to me.

"Bullshit," I muttered and then I sighed as I rolled up to a stop sign. The first part of that might be true, but the last part was a total lie, one I couldn't even sort of make myself believe.

But I didn't want him to mean anything to me! I didn't want to care about him and I didn't want to look forward to our time together. I hated the fact that I'd been happy when he'd asked me to meet him that evening, and that it didn't have a damn thing to do with getting paid. I knew better than to get attached to a trick. I knew better than to get attached to *anybody*.

I'd really lost sight of that over the last year or two. I'd let Zachary in because I felt like he needed me, and later I'd let Christian in because I was awestruck by him and his artwork and couldn't believe someone like him actually wanted to be my friend. Christian had proven to be a package deal, bringing all sorts of other people into my life. They were nice to me but I didn't fit in with them at all. I didn't fit in anywhere.

I pulled to the side of the road and took a few deep breaths as I thought about what had just happened with my tattoo. Like I'd told him, Finn hadn't done anything wrong. All he did was…well, pay attention. He'd noticed my bruised wrists at the wedding and my nervous habit of rubbing my tattoo. He'd *seen* me, when most people looked right past me. That wasn't a bad thing. If it made me feel exposed, that was my problem.

After a few minutes, I realized the SUV hadn't driven past me and started to wonder if Finn was alright. I shut off the engine and pocketed my keys, then walked back up to the parking lot. I'd barely driven two blocks before I'd pulled over.

My heart leapt when I saw him. He was standing on the retaining wall, arms outstretched to each side. My God, was he about to jump?

I yelled his name and took off at a sprint across the parking lot. At one point I tripped over a pothole and came down hard on my hands and knees, but I was right back up in an instant, running for him. Finn turned to look at me, then stepped off the wall into the parking lot.

He'd taken a couple steps toward me and when I reached him, I knocked him over in what basically turned into a flying tackle. He landed on his back with a surprised yelp, and I fell on top of him. I then sat up, straddling him, and grabbed the front of his jacket in my fists. "What the fuck were you thinking, Finn?"

"About what?" He looked genuinely bewildered.

"About fucking jumping off Twin Peaks! What a horrible way to kill yourself! You probably wouldn't even die you know, you'd just mangle yourself real good on the trees and bushes and shit down below. Not that I'm advocating finding a better way to kill yourself! Just, God, what the fuck?"

When my rant was over, Finn chuckled and said as he pulled me into a hug, "I wasn't trying to kill myself. I was just enjoying the view and the breeze. I didn't think I'd fucked up badly enough to warrant throwing myself off a cliff."

"Oh. Well, good," I said, putting my head on his chest.

He rubbed my back and said, "You were really worried."

"Well, yeah."

He kissed the top of my head and said, "Thank you for caring."

"You're welcome. I feel like a total idiot now, though."

"Don't. I love the fact that you tried to save me."

"Of course I did. What do you think I'd do in that situation, sit back with some popcorn and watch you end it?"

He smiled at that, then asked, "Why'd you come back? Besides obviously to save me from not killing myself?"

"I'd pulled over a couple blocks down the hill and realized after a while that you'd stayed up here. I wanted to make sure you were okay."

He sat up, taking me with him, and said, "I'm glad you came back."

"I shouldn't have left like that. All you did was notice me. That's what bothered me about the thing with my tattoo."

"Apparently you really hate that."

"Yeah, I guess I do. Must be that same part of me that desperately wanted to be invisible when I was a kid. I had to draw a picture once when I was in third grade showing me as a superhero with one special power. All the other kids drew themselves super strong or flying. I turned in a blank piece of paper. The teacher wasn't amused. I wasn't trying to be a brat, I just didn't know how else to draw myself as invisible." I was rambling and I knew it. I really needed to quit it.

"I think that's clever."

"Thanks." I rested my head on his shoulder and asked, "What would you have picked for your superpower?"

"Flight. I dreamed I was flying once when I was about ten. It was the best dream of my entire life. I always hoped I'd have that dream again, but it never happened."

"What did you like about it?"

"I felt so free, and that made me incredibly happy."

I thought about that for a while as I slowly stoked his short hair. Then I said, "Sorry, I just realized I asked you a bunch of questions."

"I don't mind questions like that."

After another minute, I climbed off him and extended my hand to help him up. He took it in both of his and turned the palm to face him, then said, "Shit, Chance, you're hurt."

"It's nothing."

He got to his feet and turned both my hands palms up. They were a bit bloody and scraped from the spill I'd taken on the asphalt. "It's not nothing. Come here." Finn led me to the back of the SUV, opened it and had me sit on the bumper. After rinsing both my hands with a bottle of water, he opened a big first-aid kit and said as he pulled out a brown bottle of hydrogen peroxide, "This is going to hurt like hell, but I want to make sure the cuts don't get infected." I stuck my hands out for him and he said, "Sorry," as he poured a bit of the disinfectant over the scrapes and I flinched slightly.

"It's fine," I said.

He then took out a roll of gauze and bandaged both my hands. I thought it was overkill, but I let him do it anyway. The way he knit his brows and concentrated on the task was cute. He was good at what he was doing, and when he finished, both my hands were lightly wrapped in an intricately woven pattern, my fingers and thumbs totally unimpeded. I thanked him and he kissed my forehead.

After he packed up the first-aid kit, he said softly, "Will you stay for a little while?" I nodded and followed him to the backseat of the SUV.

I curled up in his arms and he kissed me gently. Finn fell asleep a few minutes later and I sat up a bit and studied his handsome face. He looked so young and innocent when he was asleep, and a weird, misplaced urge to protect him flared in me. I sighed quietly.

I really was getting attached to him, and that wouldn't end well for me. It was easy to see why it had happened. The lines were so blurred with him. He didn't treat me like a prostitute, he treated me like I was something special. But come on! That was just because he was a nice guy. I needed to get a grip. I was nothing to him, just a warm body. It was so dumb to read anything into a kind word and a gentle touch.

Letting my emotions anywhere near the job was ridiculous, and I certainly knew better. This was a great gig, the best I'd ever had, and I was determined not to fuck it up. The job would run its course sooner rather than later anyway. No way could someone on a cop's salary keep spending that kind of money. For the next few days or maybe a week or two, I could keep it together. Then it'd all be over and I could return to life the way it had been before Finn Nolan came along.

I refused to let that thought depress me.

I awoke the next morning to light kisses on my cheek. When I opened my eyes, Finn smiled at me and said, "Good morning. Sorry to wake you, but we need to get going." I nodded and sat up, pushing my hair out of my face, then opened the car door and slid out a bit unsteadily. It was dawn and the sunrise colored the sky a vivid shade of pink. It was actually really pretty.

"Hop in and I'll drive you to your car," Finn said as he climbed out of the backseat and got behind the wheel. I slid in beside him as the big engine rumbled to life.

When we got to my little Honda, Finn leaned over and kissed my forehead. Then he smiled at me, his blue eyes crinkling at the corners, and said, "So, Thursday? Back at the Whitman, usual time?" I nodded again.

He waited until I was in my car with the engine running before he drove away. I watched the white Bronco disappear around a curve, then put on my seatbelt. A crinkling sound from the pocket of my hoodie caught my attention, and I reached inside and pulled out a small, white envelope. There was a note written on it in Finn's tight, controlled handwriting. It said: *Thank you for meeting me last night on short notice, and thank you for coming back after I fucked up. I bet you're going to argue about the amount in this envelope, but please just accept it. I wouldn't feel right about it being any less.*

I looked inside the envelope and sighed at the ten hundred dollar bills. He was right, I wanted to argue. I didn't even want to charge him for those few hours, especially after subjecting him to my drama. I sighed and slipped the envelope back into my pocket.

Instead of driving down the hill, I did a U-turn and went back up to the parking lot, then sat on the hood of my car and watched the sunrise. My right hand itched, and I turned it palm-up and scratched my scrapes through the meticulously wrapped bandage. Saturn caught my eye, and I ran my thumb over it before looking back at the panoramic view of the city.

It was pretty, I couldn't deny that. I'd believed it was Utopia once. I came here for the San Francisco in the postcards and for the promise of a place where people didn't judge you for being gay. God was I naïve.

But then, I'd been fourteen years old at the time. What did I know at that age? The reality of life in the city had been a harsh wake-up call, but it had toughened me, made me stronger. I'd survived, and was still surviving. Almost twelve years later, I had a roof over my head, enough to eat, and a warm bed to sleep in. All of that was a victory, considering where I'd started.

I slid off the hood of my car and flipped off the beautiful, seductive lie before me, and then I got in my car and went back to reality.

Chapter Nine

August

"I'm worried about you," Jessie said, easing out of the Civic's engine compartment and turning to look at me as he wiped his hands on a rag.

"Don't be. There's no way that car's going to break down on me, not after all you've done to it."

"That's not what I'm worried about. No way is Sharona breaking down, I guarantee it. But you're going to be on the road all by yourself. I wish I could come with you." He'd decided at one point that my car looked like a Sharona, so that was what he insisted on calling it.

"I know, but you're going to be in Italy, having the most amazing time," I said, "and there's no reason to be concerned. It's only a couple days' drive to Wyoming, no big deal."

"Chance is going to be fine," Nico said, coming into the garage with a pitcher of iced tea and three glasses. "He's perfectly capable of taking care of himself."

"Nico's right," I said as he filled a glass and handed it to me. He gave Jessie a drink too, then sat beside me on one of the patio chairs we'd set up in the garage. I'd spent a lot of time out there over the last few weeks as Jessie did things to the old Honda that made it run like a sports car, and once Nico's summer program ended, he'd started hanging out with us. I could tell he'd been making an effort to relax, but apparently it didn't come naturally to him.

After a few minutes, the door burst open and Nana's huge, rambunctious puppy launched himself out of the house, heading straight for Jessie. Apparently the dog was gay, and had quite a crush on my friend. "Oh shit," Jessie exclaimed, bobbing and weaving to stop the dog from humping him. "No, Tommy! We've been over this! I only like you as a friend!"

Nana rushed into the garage with Mr. Mario right on her heels. Her hair was set on rollers, and she wore a purple t-shirt that said: *Boys Will Do Boys*. "Tom Selleck got away from us," she said. "He's going to miss you, Jessie, I think he wanted to say goodbye."

Nico said, "I don't think that was quite the message the dog was going for," as Mr. Mario grabbed the dog's collar and took him back into the house.

Nana turned to us and said, "Are you boys packed? Nico and Jessie, are you sure you have your passports? And what about condoms? Oh wait, never mind. I forgot I bought a great big box of them at Costco. They're in my luggage already." Nico looked mortified and Jessie laughed and blushed at that, but Nana waved her hand and said, "Don't be embarrassed. I'm not some old prude, I know how it is. Cute young things like you on vacation in Italy, you're gonna want to have some fun. But no boom boom without a pecker protector!" With that, she spun around and headed back into the house.

"I wonder if anyone else's grandmother actually tries to get them laid," Nico said before taking a drink. Then he added, "I also wonder why I didn't spike this iced tea."

"She's just looking out for us. It's sweet," Jessie said. Then he let out a delighted little laugh and added, "I can't believe I'm going to be in Italy in just a few short days! But before that, can you even freaking believe where we're going to be tomorrow night?"

"It hasn't even sort of sunk in," I told him. Gianni had invited a big group of friends and family to southern California to watch his boyfriend Zan's return to the stage after years of retirement. He was headlining a concert for charity at the L.A. Coliseum and he'd given all of us tickets and backstage passes.

I'd been absolutely floored when he'd invited me along. I really didn't understand why he would, unless he thought he still owed me a thank you for those weeks last spring when I acted as their personal assistant. That was kind of nuts though, since they'd already totally overpaid me for that.

I was excited about the concert, but a little apprehensive, too. It was all so far out of my comfort zone that I'd actually wanted to make excuses and not go. But I just couldn't let myself chicken out. It was a once-in-a-lifetime experience, and I wasn't going to let shyness get in the way of that.

We were caravanning down the next morning in Nana's limo and a couple other cars. The day after the concert, Nana, Jessie and Nico were flying out of LAX for their month-long vacation. I'd be driving back to San Francisco with Gianni's brother Vincent and his husband Trevor, which was a little awkward since I didn't know them all that well. They were both quiet like me though, so hopefully the drive wouldn't be strained with awkward attempts at small-talk.

I planned to head out on my road trip the day after getting back to San Francisco. I'd put it off so I wouldn't miss the concert and was eager to get started. Well, really, I was eager to get it over with. But the sooner I started, the sooner I could be done with it.

Jessie let the hood fall shut on the Honda and announced, "Sharona is a thing of beauty, under the hood at least. I still think we should've given her a righteous paint job with sparkles and some flash, though."

"Sparkles and flash don't play well in Wyoming," I pointed out. "Dirt and bugs are more like it. I'm sure I'll be picking up plenty of both on the drive, so I'll be set by the time I roll into my home state."

"When was the last time you were there?" Nico asked.

"I haven't been back since I left at fourteen. I saw my mom and kid brother when they went to Reno for a wedding about five years ago, but that visit only lasted forty minutes. At that point, my mom and I had a huge fight and I got back on the bus and returned to San Francisco. We've always had a difficult relationship."

Jessie said, "This doesn't exactly sound like it's going to be a fun vacation."

"Nope. Trying to track down the guy who knocked up my mom twenty-six years ago also won't be a lot of laughs," I said. "It'll suck if I can't find him, but it'll probably also suck if I do, since I doubt he'll want anything to do with me. Failure or rejection, I can't decide which is worse."

"Okay, forget Italy," Nico said. "I'm coming with you to Wyoming. Nana doesn't really need me along, she has Jessie. No freaking way should you be facing that alone."

"That's sweet, but I actually want to do this by myself. The only thing worse than awkward family interactions are awkward family interactions with an audience. Plus, whatever the upshot of this ends up being, I'm going to want time by myself to process it."

"This is probably a stupid question," Jessie said, leaning against the car, "but do your family members know what you do for a living?"

"Hell no. My mother thinks I've been climbing the ladder at Taco Bell the last few years. I think the last thing I told her was that I was up to Assistant Manager."

I'd been reluctant to tell my new friends I was a prostitute, but had finally been honest with them a few weeks earlier. Between the cookbook photos and the work Jessie had been doing on my car, I'd spent a fair amount of time at Nana's house that summer. The more I got to know Jessie and Nico, the shittier I felt about lying to them. I still hadn't told Nana and really didn't intend to, but these two took the news more or less in stride. Jessie wanted to ask a million questions, but after I'd explained that I really didn't feel comfortable discussing it, he'd just moved on and that was that.

I glanced at the time on my phone and took a long drink of iced tea before getting up. It was a little after nine p.m., so I said, "I need to get going. I'll be back here tomorrow morning at ten sharp." That was when the caravan for L.A. was planning to roll out.

"You sure you don't want me to pick you up at your apartment?" Jessie asked. "It's really no trouble."

"No thanks. I have an errand I need to do in the morning, so I'll just come here afterwards."

After I said goodbye, I drove to the Whitman's neighborhood and was immediately reminded why I usually used public transit. It took nearly half an hour to find a parking space. It was so far away that it took another fifteen minutes to jog to the hotel once I parked.

As soon as I rounded the corner of the street the hotel was on, I spotted Finn in the window of room two-fifteen, watching for me like he always did. We'd met there twenty times before. He'd spent every night off with me from June to

August, as well as a few nights when he worked the day shift. I was approaching from a different direction this time, so he didn't see me. I could tell he was a bit worried from his body language, probably because I was never late. I waved to him, but he still didn't spot me.

I pushed open the door and nodded to the desk clerk as I called, "Hey, Robert."

"Hey Chance. You're late."

"I was dumb enough to drive down here and ended up parking in another area code."

"He brought you a present," the man told me with a grin. "Sorry, spoiler alert. It was cute, he was all excited." Robert's initial distrust of me had been replaced with friendliness as the weeks went on. I was pretty sure that was because Finn had been killing him with kindness, and that ended up spilling over to me.

I smiled at him as I crossed the lobby. "You're awful at keeping secrets. Do you tell your wife what all her birthday presents are beforehand?" It wasn't the first time Finn had brought me something, and it also wasn't the first time the desk clerk had told me ahead of time.

"She picks them out herself, otherwise I probably would. Birthdays are basically an excuse to go shopping as far as she's concerned."

The door to two-fifteen was closed when I got to the second floor. Usually Finn was in the doorway waiting for me. I knocked and he swung it open a moment later, then grabbed me in a hug and exclaimed, "You snuck up on me!"

"I did! I tried to get your attention when I was outside, but you didn't see me. I drove and parking was impossible. That's why I'm late, sorry about that."

He lifted me off my feet and carried me into the room, and as the door shut behind us, I wrapped my arms and legs around him. "I'm so happy you're here," he said. "I started to get worried. I thought maybe you'd left early for your trip."

"I wouldn't do that without telling you."

Finn kissed me before murmuring, "I'm going to miss you so fucking much, Chance. What am I supposed to do without you for a week or two?"

I felt a sharp pang of guilt at that. I'd decided to end it with him, using my road trip as the stopping point. He didn't know that, though, and I wasn't going to tell him yet. I didn't want a cloud hanging over us on our last night together.

It *had* to end. He was giving me his entire life savings. Tonight would bring the total to twenty-two thousand dollars, counting the grand from our night on Twin Peaks. That was insane. It wasn't like he was some trust fund kid, and I hated the thought of him damaging himself financially just to be with me.

There was another reason why it had to end, too. Over the past few weeks, I'd utterly failed in trying not to get attached to him. He was so sweet and kind and sexy, and just so damn beautiful inside and out. I was falling hard for Finn Nolan, and that could *not* happen. The fact that he was a cop and I was a prostitute was only the start of all that was wrong with that. I was in no way capable of being in a relationship, and it wasn't as if a closeted police officer would even want a relationship with me in the first place. Sure, he enjoyed our time together, but that was light years away from wanting to make it into something real. There was just no freaking way.

I pushed those thoughts aside as Finn laid me on the bed and stretched out beside me. He traced my face with his fingertips and whispered, "You make me so happy, Chance." Another wave of guilt accompanied that, but I pushed it aside and kissed him.

Things soon got hot and heavy, and after we undressed and he donned a condom, he fucked me slowly, watching my reactions. He'd learned a lot the last few weeks and knew just what to do to make me feel good. I came before he did, and he finished a minute later, throwing his head back and moaning.

He stayed in me for a while afterwards, kissing and caressing me, before finally going to clean up in the bathroom. When he came back, he jumped onto the bed playfully and grabbed me in an embrace, rolling us over so I was on top of him. He kissed my hand before saying, "I have something for you. It's in the nightstand."

I never told him that the desk clerk ruined his surprises because I didn't want him to be disappointed. I sat up and straddled him as I pulled open the drawer. It contained a cupcake in a white box and a small, flat package meticulously wrapped in blue-and-white-striped paper. "You didn't have to get me anything, Finn," I told him.

"I know, but I wanted to. I hope you like it." He pulled an extra pillow behind his head as I carefully unwrapped the package, preserving the paper.

Inside was a beautiful, indigo blue journal embossed with a compass rose. "I saw that in a bookstore and thought maybe you could use it on your road trip to record your memories," he told me. "I mean, you'll probably be doing that already with photos, but, I don't know. Maybe you'll want to write stuff down, too. Whenever I go on a long drive I end up lost in thought, to the point where I often have to double back to get to my exits because I roll right past them. Anyway, I don't know. Maybe that's a dumb gift, but I hope you like it."

"I absolutely love it. Thank you."

I leaned down and kissed him, and when I sat up again he said, "Really? You're not just saying that?"

"I promise I love it." I stood it up on the nightstand, and he shifted us around and cradled me against his side.

"I found a food truck today that sells insanely good cupcakes and had one of these with my lunch." He grinned at me and said, "Okay, I'm lying. I had three of these as my lunch. I know you like chocolate, so I wanted you to try this."

"Thank you, Finn." He'd been doing that a lot lately, bringing me little delicacies. I found it incredibly touching.

He broke off a bit of the dark, rich cake and fed it to me. "Oh my God, that's amazing," I exclaimed, licking the salted caramel frosting from my lips. I let him feed me two more bites before saying, "I'm full. Have the rest."

I broke off a bit of cupcake just like he'd done and held it to his lips, but Finn rolled his eyes. "You are not full! You just know I like it so you're trying to give it to me."

"No, really. I can't eat any more."

"I don't even sort of believe you."

I grinned at him and said, "Please have some."

Finn sighed and ate the bite I offered him, then licked my fingers clean. "You're so sweet. Sweeter than that cupcake," he said before kissing me.

He refused to eat more, and once he'd fed me the rest, he pulled the blanket over us and snuggled with me. After a while he said softly, "I need you to promise me something."

"What?"

"Promise you'll be so incredibly careful on your road trip. Drive really safe, okay? And watch yourself if you stay at any of those cheap motels right off the freeway, a lot of crime happens in those places. I need you to come back to me safe and sound, Chance."

My heart broke at that, and I wrapped my arms around him and held on tight. I was going to miss him so damn much. He'd been incredibly kind to me, kinder than anyone ever had been before and probably ever would be again. I buried my face in his shoulder and he hugged me to him and kissed my hair.

*****

I hadn't meant to doze off, but when I awoke it was morning and Finn was gone. I tried to push down the disappointment that welled up in me. I'd wanted more time with him, even just an extra hour or two, and was so mad at myself for falling asleep.

There was a white envelope on the nightstand, along with a note. It said: *I'll miss you so much. Please be safe, Chance. I'm looking forward to your return.* I felt like crying, but instead I sighed quietly and went to use the orange scented soap and shampoo for the last time.

After I showered and got dressed, checking and re-checking that the little journal was tucked in my jacket pocket, I said goodbye to the Whitman and retrieved my car. I drove to my apartment and picked up the backpack I was taking to L.A., along with a thick, nine-by-eleven envelope with Finn's name on it, which I'd hidden under the refrigerator. I slipped the little white envelope from that morning inside the bigger brown one, slung the backpack over my shoulder, and locked up behind me. I knocked on Zachary's door but he wasn't home, so I went downstairs and continued on to the police station. I knew Finn's schedule so knew he wouldn't be there, but that was the whole idea.

I went up to the huge, muscle-bound police officer with a crewcut who sat behind the front counter and put the brown envelope in front of him as I said, "Could you please make sure Finn Nolan gets that? It's important."

He frowned a little as he got to his feet and said in a deep voice, "I can't accept that for security reasons." God lord, the guy had to be about six-eight.

"Oh! Shit, I didn't think of that. Look, it's not, like, anything harmful. That's just something that belongs to him and I need to give it back." I pulled out my wallet and showed him my driver's license. "Here's my I.D. If I was a terrorist or something, I wouldn't show that to you. Please, just give the envelope to Finn. It's really important."

The guy glanced at my I.D. and looked surprised. "Your name's Chance."

"Yeah."

"Finn mentioned you."

Now it was my turn to look surprised. "He did?"

The cop nodded as I put away my wallet. "I don't think he meant to. I'm not always behind a desk, usually he and I patrol together. He was smiling about something and staring out the window of the squad car a couple weeks ago. Looked like he was a million miles away. When I asked what he was so happy about, he said, 'Chance.' I asked who that was and he got really flustered and changed the subject. What are you to him?"

"A friend."

The big officer knit his brows and studied me for a moment. Finally he asked, "What's in the envelope?"

"It's personal."

He picked it up and weighed it in his hands, then said, "There's a lot of cash in there."

I hadn't been expecting that, and no way was I going to tell him the envelope held twenty-two thousand dollars. There was just no explaining that much money. Instead I thought quickly and said, "You're right. That's nearly eight hundred dollars in small bills. Finn loaned me some money and I'm paying him back. You can see why I didn't want to put it in the mail."

The cop considered that, still studying me carefully, and asked, "What was the loan for?"

"A car repair. My Honda's older than I am. It needed a whole new transmission." I was completely bullshitting, but he seemed to buy it.

After another moment, he picked up the phone and hit a button, then spoke into it, saying, "Come up to the front desk for a minute." He hung up without waiting for a reply and told me, "Most people would have written a check. It's not a good idea to carry a bunch of cash around."

"You're right."

"Why aren't you giving this back to him in person?"

"Because I'm heading out of town and won't see him again before I go." I actually got to tell the truth that time.

Someone came up behind the cop, and a familiar voice said, "We talked about this, Duke. Don't just call people and then hang up without telling them why they're being summoned. I mean, I don't care, but it ticks off our coworkers."

"Sorry," the big cop said, turning and putting the envelope in Finn's hands. "Your friend's here. He wanted to give you that."

Finn looked shocked when the big cop moved aside and he spotted me, but he replaced it a moment later with a halfway decent poker face. "Thanks, Duke. I'm going to walk my friend out. I'll be right back."

He waited until we were on the sidewalk before asking, "What are you doing here?"

"You weren't supposed to be here. You told me you started at five."

"We've been short-staffed so I got called in for a double. Wait, you didn't come here to see me?" I shook my head, and he looked at the envelope in his hands. "What is this?"

"I have to go," I said, and turned and started to flee.

"Wait." I paused and glanced back at him. He unwound the string that held the brown envelope shut and peered inside.

"There's a note. I have to go, I'm expected at Nana's," I told him.

"What's going on?" He pulled a sheet of paper from the envelope, shook it to unfold it, and scanned the handwritten letter. Then he looked up at me. "I don't understand. Why are you ending it?"

I mumbled, staring at the pavement, "I just can't do this anymore."

He folded the note and stuck it in his pocket, then pulled a handful of white envelopes from the larger one. "Why are you giving me the money back?"

"Because it's fucking insane, Finn. That's twenty-two thousand dollars! What were you thinking? It must be your entire nest egg. No possible way can I take that from you!" I'd spent some of it at first, but as the money kept accumulating and I realized he had to be bankrupting himself, I'd replaced it with cash from my savings, so I was giving back every penny.

He put the envelopes back where he'd found them and tried to hand the brown envelope to me. "I wanted you to have this money."

"It's way too much. I really have to go." I turned and started to walk away, but Finn followed me.

"Just tell me what I did wrong."

"Nothing! Absolutely nothing."

"Chance, wait. Let's talk about this."

"There's nothing to talk about. I'm just not going to do this anymore."

"But I thought we had something good. I thought you liked being with me."

We'd reached the Honda and I went around to the driver's side, then looked at him over the roof of the car and said quietly, even though there was no one in close proximity, "Don't you get it, Finn? I like it too much. I like *you* too much. I can't keep being your whore, and I can't keep draining your bank account. Both of those things are breaking my heart, and I'm just not going to do either one anymore."

"You're not my whore, Chance."

I looked him in the eye and asked, "Then what am I to you?"

"You're…." He stopped talking and looked away.

That hurt so much that I actually felt it in my chest, a sharp stab of disappointment. But what did I expect, a declaration of love? Come on.

"Exactly," I said sharply. "I'm nothing, just some rent boy you took pity on. Was that money supposed to save me? Is that why you kept completely overpaying me? Were you going to keep going until I had enough to retire from the business? Well, I don't need or want to be saved. Put that money back in your retirement account or wherever you took it from, and let's forget any of this ever happened!"

I got in my car and drove away, muttering, "Shit," as I looked in the rearview mirror. He was standing right where I left him, a dazed expression on his face. I knew I'd fucked up. There had been no reason to get mad at Finn, he hadn't deserved that. I didn't even know what I'd been angry about.

A profound sense of loss settled on me, which just showed that I'd done the right thing by ending it. I'd lost all perspective where Finn was concerned and had gotten way too attached to him. He hadn't been my friend or lover or boyfriend, and the fact that it felt like I'd lost all of those things was fucking insane.

It was good that the trip to L.A. and my road trip were coming up. I desperately needed a change of scenery and some time alone to try to get a grip. Hopefully by the time I got back, I'd be able to manage the dull, empty ache that filled my chest.

Chapter Ten

"You okay?" Nico said that into my ear to be heard over the noise. We were at the L.A. Coliseum, and it felt totally surreal. Gianni's boyfriend Zan was performing songs I'd grown up with while ninety thousand people sang along. We were just offstage behind a big, black curtain and could see about half the audience from our position. The crowd was on their feet, swaying like the ocean. It was totally overwhelming, but Zan seemed to take it in stride.

I nodded and linked arms with Nico. I was still trying to process what had happened just that morning with Finn in front of the police station, and had spent most of the six-hour drive to Los Angeles staring out the window of the limo. Nico and I had sat up front with Jessie to keep him company, while Nana and her family had a party in the back.

This was a once-in-a-lifetime experience, and I tried to shake off the funk I was in and enjoy the concert. But I kept seeing Finn's face and his blue eyes. I kept remembering the way he'd touched me and held me the night before, and how good it had felt. *He wasn't your boyfriend*, I reminded myself. *He was just some guy who was paying you.*

But nobody had ever treated me like that. He'd been so kind to me. I touched my denim jacket and felt the little journal in my pocket. Regardless of what I'd been to him, he'd meant more to me than I wanted to admit and it was going to take time to get over him.

To try to stop thinking about Finn, I turned my attention to the crowd around me. Gianni looked awestruck and so totally in love as he watched his boyfriend performing. He was surrounded by his best friend Yoshi and two of his brothers, Dante and Mike, along with their families. Nearby, Nana was dancing like a teenager with Skye and Dare, while Gianni's other brother Vincent, his husband Trevor and their son Josh all held hands. Josh's look of total amazement was really sweet.

To my right, Shea stood behind Christian with his arms around him and the two of them swayed to the music. Christian looked a bit teary-eyed as he watched his father up on stage. The last time Zan performed had been in 2002, and that had ended mid-concert when Zan walked away from his career to head off a nervous breakdown. This was a huge moment for the singer and everyone who loved him.

I felt Nico stiffen all of a sudden and turned to look at him. His eyes behind his glasses were huge and full of heartbreak, his full lips slightly parted. He was staring past the stage into the crowd, and I leaned over and said into his ear, "What's wrong?"

"My ex," he muttered.

"Where?"

"Front row. Tall blond with a pink shirt," he said, raising his hand. I looked where he was pointing and easily spotted the guy in question. Holy hell. The blond was stunningly handsome, as was the shorter brunet that was hanging on his arm. They both looked like they could be models. "Oh God," Nico choked out before turning and darting backstage. I ran after him.

He ducked into a little alcove that was full of spare sound equipment and dropped to his knees, then he put his face in his hands and started sobbing, his entire body shaking. I knelt down beside him and wrapped my arms around him.

Nico let himself cry for several minutes before finally taking a few deep breaths and murmuring, "I'm so sorry. You're missing the concert. You should go back."

"This is more important."

He sat back on his heels and took my hand, using his other one to wipe the tears from his cheeks. "It caught me totally off guard," he said, his voice rough. "I was just enjoying the music, and all of a sudden, there he was. I should have known I'd see him here, I just didn't think about it. Erik's on the board of directors for the charity this concert's raising money for. He was wearing a VIP pass around his neck, I'm surprised I didn't run into him backstage."

"What happened between the two of you?"

"The oldest story in the book. He left me for my best friend, that brunet hanging on Erik's arm. We lived together for three years, and apparently those two had been having an affair at least half that time." Nico sniffed and took off his glasses, then wiped his eyes with the back of his hand.

"I'm so sorry that happened to you."

"I felt so betrayed. They were the two people I loved and trusted most in the world. It's been two years but it just won't stop hurting. I moved out of L.A. and tried to start a new life. I tried to leave both of them and what they did to me in the past. But it still hurts so fucking much, Chance." A fresh batch of tears spilled down his face.

I pulled him to me and he buried his face in my shoulder. His body trembled as he held on to me and let himself cry. It was several minutes before he finally managed to get it under control. He sat back, leaning against a big speaker, and I sat beside him with my arm around his shoulders as his ragged breathing gradually leveled out. "I hadn't seen either of them since the day I moved out," he said after a while. "I often wondered if they were still together."

"Nobody told you? You didn't keep in touch with any of your friends when you left L.A.?"

"I'd moved here from San Francisco to be with Erik. All my friends were his friends first, except for Gavin, who followed me to southern California. We'd been best friends since we were eight."

"God that sucks," I said.

"Tell me about it." Nico put his head on my shoulder and sighed. "They looked happy and in love, didn't they? I don't know why Erik stayed with me all that time and snuck around when Gavin was obviously what he wanted."

"They're both fucking assholes."

"You're not wrong." He pushed himself to his feet, brushed off his khakis, and smoothed out his light blue button-down shirt. I got up too as he said, "I really hope I don't run into them backstage tonight. I probably look disgusting now, don't I?"

"No. You just look like you've been crying."

"That's worse. I want them to think I've totally moved on."

"Come on," I said. "Let's get you cleaned up."

After we found a restroom and he washed his face and combed his hair, we rejoined our group and tried to concentrate on the concert. His eyes were still red, but other than that he didn't look much worse for wear. We positioned ourselves near the curtain, so his ex and former best friend were no longer in his line of sight. Jessie had seen us leave, and when he came over to ask if anything was wrong, I filled him in quickly. He and I spent the rest of the concert on either side of Nico with our arms around him.

When the concert ended, a hell of a lot of people wanted to get a piece of Zan, including countless photographers and reporters. He paused to take a picture with the head of the nonprofit, and then we all helped escort him and Gianni to the back of the building, where a car was waiting. I caught a glimpse of Nico's ex at one point in the backstage crowd. He was looking our way, but I didn't think Nico saw him.

After we thanked Gianni and Zan and said goodbye to them, the rest of our party headed to the VIP parking lot. "I want to party!" Nana exclaimed. Her dark eyes were bright, and she was dressed in a white leather ensemble and platform boots that made her look like an aging go-go dancer. "Let's find a nightclub, who's game?"

"We're going back to the hotel, it's past Josh's bedtime," Vincent said. His son rolled his eyes at that. To me, Vincent said, "We're in room twelve-twenty, come find us in the morning, Chance. We'll want to start heading back to San Francisco at about ten." I told them I would and they took off in the direction of their car, as did Mike and his girlfriend Marie, who carried his sleeping sons. Mike had one on each hip while Marie carried the third.

"I think we're going to head back to the hotel, too," Christian said. "It's been a hell of a long day. We'll see you guys at breakfast." He and his husband were staying in L.A. for the weekend, along with Skye and Dare, and the four of them said goodnight and left together. Yoshi took off too after admitting embarrassedly that he was hooking up with someone he'd met at the concert.

"I don't know if I'm up for this," Nico said as we headed to the limo with Jessie, Nana, Dante and Charlie.

"This is exactly what you need," I told him. "It's what we both need, some fun and distraction."

"Shit, there they are," Nico whispered. I followed his gaze across the parking lot and spotted his ex easily. The guy stood out, no doubt about it. He and his boyfriend noticed Nico at about the same time and looked shocked.

"Just ignore them," I said, and guided Nico into the back of the limo. Before I followed, I flipped off his ex with both hands.

Jessie saw what I was doing and asked, "Which ones are they?"

"The tall blond guy in the pink shirt that looks like a Viking," I said, "and the guy who's hanging all over him."

"Fuckers," Jessie said. When we got in the limo, Jessie called over the divider, "Want me to run them over, Nico? I won't, like, kill them or anything. I'll only bump them a little."

Nico grinned at that and said, "Nah, they're not worth the jail time. Thanks for the offer, though."

We ended up beside Erik's flashy red convertible as my friend eased the limo slowly out of the tight parking lot. Jessie grabbed a square, black mic from the dash, turned on the P.A. system with the flick of a switch and said, "Hey you! Yeah you, the asshats in the Dodge Viper!" Erik and Gavin turned to stare at the limo's tinted windows, their mouths falling open. "First of all, that's one of the douchiest cars ever made! Total fail! Do you realize how many completely righteous car choices you could have made for that money? Well no, obviously you don't, because you bought a total Douchemobile! You two totally suck ass, and not just because you don't know shit about cars."

Jessie turned up the volume on the P.A. system and said, "Hey, everybody! See those dumbshits in the lame, overpriced convertible? Oh sorry, we're in L.A., I need to be more specific. See the dudes in the red Viper next to the stylin' old-school limo?" Everyone in the crowded parking lot stopped to stare as Erik and Gavin slid down in their seats and probably totally regretted leaving the convertible's top open. "They're a pair of low-down dirty *cheaters!* Those assholes betrayed their best friend and their boyfriend! Erik and Gavin, you totally suck and you should be ashamed of yourselves! Karma's a bitch, baby, and I hope it comes back around and bites you on your ass!" Jessie turned off the mic and put it back it its cradle as he said, "Hang on kids, we're going off-roading."

We'd just cleared the gates of the parking lot, and Jessie slowly bore down on the Viper as all the other cars around us gave us a wide berth. He ended up squeezing Erik off the road in slow-motion, and the douchey sports car splashed into a muddy drainage ditch. I thought we were going to join them since we were driving on dirt at that point, but Jessie pulled out in time and we rolled back onto the pavement.

I turned and looked back at the Dodge as Erik stepped out of the car and sank into about a foot of mud, yelling and gesturing at the limo. Jessie pushed some buttons and started blasting I Will Survive through the exterior speakers as we left them behind, and Nana whooped and yelled, "That's my boy!"

"You just happened to have that song cued up?" I asked Jessie.

"No, but I did have Nana's Best of the 1970s CD in the player. Every now and then, she likes to bust some moves while we're driving around town."

I grinned and leaned back in my seat, and was glad to see that Nico was grinning, too.

*****

Jessie drove us back to West Hollywood, which was where we were staying, and Nana proceeded to take over a gay bar while her grandson Dante attempted to supervise her. Meanwhile, Jessie, Nico, Charlie and I found a relatively quiet table in the corner and proceeded to get drunk.

The more he drank, the quieter Nico became. It had the exact opposite effect on Jessie and Charlie, who ended up downright giddy. "Your husband is so damn hot," Jessie told

Charlie at one point. "I mean, my God, how do you even ever let him leave the bedroom? You're so freaking lucky!"

Charlie grinned at that, his green eyes sparkling as he watched his husband across the room. Dante was trying to talk his grandmother down from the bar, but Nana was totally ignoring him and dancing with a couple half-naked go-go boys. "I really am."

"He needs to give up on reeling Nana in, though," Jessie said. "I think his new approach should be, if you can't beat 'em, join 'em. Come on, let's see if we can get him to cut loose a little."

After the two of them went over to Dante, Nico said, "You want to hear something pathetic? Erik is the only guy I've ever slept with. It's been two years since it ended, but I just haven't been able to move past it. That's going to change, though. I'm going to loosen up a bit when I'm in Italy. That doesn't come naturally to me, as you can probably guess. Erik used to complain about how straight-laced I was, and I think it was probably sheer boredom that drove him to leave me for Gavin. But I don't want to be that guy, at least not while I'm on vacation. I don't think I can help being like that normally. But when I'm in Italy, I resolve to find somebody hot and sexy and totally unlike Erik, and do wild, impulsive things with him." He nodded his head at that and drained his martini glass.

"I support that idea, but you really don't have to wait until you're on vacation. This club is packed with hot guys. Someone as good-looking as you could hook up with any one of them."

He glanced around shyly and said, "I need to work myself up to it."

"Alright."

"What about you, why aren't you trying to hook up with someone? You've been getting plenty of looks since we got here."

I took a drink from the beer bottle in my hand and said, "Not interested."

Nico watched me for a moment before saying, "I'm sorry that I've made this evening all about me, when clearly something was bothering you earlier. You barely said two words on the drive down from San Francisco. What's going on with you, Chance?"

"I just have a lot on my mind with my upcoming road trip."

"That's not the only thing," he said. "I keep seeing this wistful look in your eyes. It has something to do with a guy, doesn't it?"

I sighed and admitted, "Yeah. I'm trying to get over someone who I never should have gotten attached to in the first place."

"Was he your boyfriend?"

"No. He was actually a client, and I started having real feelings for him. It's so stupid, too! I know better. It's not like I started turning tricks last week! You leave your emotions and your heart and soul at the door, only your body gets involved."

Nico thought about that for a while, spinning the stem of his martini glass between his fingers, and finally asked, "Why are you a prostitute, Chance?"

"Because it's all I'm qualified for." The fact that he asked that question and I actually answered told me we were both pretty drunk.

"That's not even sort of true. For one thing, you're an amazing photographer."

"Thanks, but nobody really cares if I'm any good at taking pictures. I was lucky that a few friends hired me to do some work, but aside from them, come on. San Francisco is full of photographers with more talent and far more education and training than I'll ever have. I can't compete with them."

"Who says you have to compete?" Nico said. "You can be amazing in your own right."

"Or unemployed and mediocre."

"You're better than your job, Chance."

"I'm really not. I dropped out of school in the ninth grade and I'm not qualified to do anything at all. This puts food on my table and keeps a roof over my head. I totally get that all of society thinks what I do is dirty and shameful, but to me, by now? It's just a job. It doesn't mean anything. I've become completely inured to it."

Nico raised an eyebrow at me. "The very fact that you just used the word 'inured' should show you how completely underemployed you are."

I grinned a little, looking at the half-empty bottle in my hand. "I read a lot, so I have a decent vocabulary. That's not enough to actually land me a legitimate job, though."

"I don't mean to come across as judgmental," he said. "If that job makes you happy, then more power to you. The thing is though, I don't think it does. I get that you've been doing it for a while now and kind of own it and make no apologies for it. But at the same time, I think it costs you more than you realize." I just shrugged at that. After another pause, Nico asked, "So, what are you going to do about that guy you mentioned?"

"I ended it with him this morning."

"Did you tell him how you felt before you ended it?"

"More or less," I said. "He doesn't feel the same way."

"He told you that?"

"Basically."

"I'm sorry, Chance. That must have hurt," he said.

"It's my own fault. I knew better than to get attached to him, and it was no surprise that he didn't want a whore."

"I wish you wouldn't call yourself that."

"It doesn't change anything if I dress it up and call myself a sex worker instead."

Nico asked, "Are you really willing to just let that guy go?"

"It's not like I have a choice. Besides, it wouldn't have worked out anyway. Relationships are impossible in this line of work."

"Really?"

"I mean, I assume so. I've never had a relationship, but I can't imagine that my job would sit well with a boyfriend."

"Literally never?" When I nodded, he said, "Isn't that reason enough to consider another line of work?"

Nico looked really sympathetic. I hated that. I pushed back from the table and said, "I'll be right back, I'm going to find the restroom."

As I made my way through the club, I assessed the crowd. It was a learned skill, something I'd honed in my line of work. It was easy to sort the men around me into categories at a glance: horny, cocky, aggressive, desperate. It was fairly easy to pick out the working boys, too, especially when they were assessing the crowd just like I was and sizing up potential tricks. They in turn probably easily figured out what I was too, even if I wasn't on the clock that night.

The restroom was crowded, and plenty of people were ignoring the sign on the door prohibiting sex on the premises. I ignored them and used the restroom for its intended purpose. As I was washing my hands, a big, blond guy in a tight t-shirt pushed up beside me and ran a hand down my back. "Hey, sexy," he purred.

I got a read on him immediately: drunk, over-privileged rich boy who was used to getting what he wanted. Men like that were trouble. "Not interested," I said as I turned from him.

He detained me with a hand on my shoulder. "You haven't heard what I'm offering yet," he said with a leering grin. "Are you a hooker? I can always tell. All I want is fifteen minutes of your time, but I'm gonna make you earn every penny." He pulled a fistful of hundreds out of his pocket and stuck them in my face.

I looked at the money, and then I looked up at the guy. Whatever he wanted wasn't vanilla, I could tell by the glint in his eye. He wasn't bad looking either, so if all he was looking for was something mundane like a blowjob, he could have gotten that easily in the club without having to pay for it. My gaze returned to the handful of bills.

I'd stopped hustling when Finn hired me, since he'd paid me so much. That morning (was it really only that morning?) I'd given back every cent I'd made all summer, including a good portion of my savings to make up for what I'd spent. I really could use that cash.

Somehow though, I just couldn't go through with it. Finn had been the only man to touch me since June and…oh God.

I suddenly realized that I'd feel like I was cheating on him if I let this guy fuck me. I really was messed up. "I said I'm not interested," I said, and tried to push past him.

He wasn't the type to handle rejection well, so he grabbed both my shoulders and hissed as he shoved me against the sink, "You think you're too good for me, bitch?"

"Let go of me," I growled. He had my arms pinned, so I couldn't take a swing at him, and my legs were trapped between him and the sink so I couldn't knee him in the nuts. He was also way too tall for me to head-butt him, so until he decided to let go of me, I was stuck.

"Or what? As if a skinny, good-for-nothing slut is going to do anything about it."

Someone tapped him on the shoulder, and he whirled around to confront whoever was interrupting him. A hard punch connected with his jaw, dropping him like a bag of rocks. As soon as he fell I saw Nico behind him, shaking out his left hand. "I forgot how much that hurts," my friend said. I must have looked as shocked as I felt, because he added, "My family was in the mafia for the better part of two centuries. You'd better believe I was taught to throw a punch."

I stepped over the prone douchebag, who was moaning and making no effort to get up. Pretty much everyone in the restroom had stopped what they were doing to stare at us.

"Come on Rocky Balboa, let's go before we find out he's here with a pack of giant, douchey friends," I said.

We left the club, waving to our friends on our way out, and walked the few blocks back to our hotel. "Thanks for coming to my aid," I said. "It wasn't really necessary, I would have kneed him in the family jewels as soon as he got off me. But still, it was nice of you to intervene. Is your hand okay?"

"I'll be fine," Nico said as he flexed his fingers. "I'm going to ice it when we get back to the room to keep it from swelling."

"I have to say, that seemed utterly unlike you."

"It is. I'm not even sort of a violent person, despite my family history. But I heard the way he was talking to you and it really pissed me off. I can't blame it on the alcohol, either. I'd have decked that jerk even if I was sober."

"You're a good friend, Nico."

"Thanks for saying that."

Despite the late hour, the Sunset Strip was crowded with young, beautiful people, scantily dressed on that warm summer night. Nico and I joined hands as we wound our way through the throng. A warm breeze rattled the long rows of palm trees overhead, and scores of lit, colorful billboards vied for attention. It was a lot to take in, and the quiet lobby of our hotel felt soothing after all of that.

When we got to our shared hotel room, I got him some ice and wrapped it in a washcloth. We then sat cross-legged on one of the two queen beds and I held his hand between both of mine as I kept the pack on his knuckles. They'd begun to discolor a bit and were probably going to bruise. After a while I said, "Did your family really teach you how to throw a punch?"

"My cousin Jerry did. He was always the tough guy, still is. He's running the west coast side of the family business now and my brother Andreas is running east coast operations."

"I've never known what to make of the fact that your family is or was in the mafia. Is, by the sound of things."

"It's not like it used to be. I'm pretty sure all of my family's sources of revenue are legal these days. There are still a lot of old rivalries though, some of which go back generations. That's why the Dombrusos will always make a big show of being strong, united and organized, regardless of how they're earning their income. Any sign of weakness and it's entirely possible some of the rival families might try to swoop in and settle old scores."

"Damn," I muttered.

Nico said, "I know how insane all of that sounds. It sounds insane to me too, even though I grew up with it. It has very little to do with me, I've never been even remotely involved in the family business, but there is this whole overarching reality that comes along with the Dombruso name."

"You don't judge me for being a prostitute, and I'm sure as hell not going to judge you for your family history."

"Thanks for that." He slid his hand out from under the ice pack and flexed his fingers again as he said, "That history has been on my mind a lot lately, since tomorrow I'm flying back to the place where it all began. Part of our vacation will be spent in the town in Sicily where Nana was born, Viladembursa. Our history goes back centuries in that place, and much of it was very violent and bloody. Nana still has a lot of family there, which is why we're going. It'll be strange to be in a place with that kind of legacy. I visited once when I was fourteen, but haven't been back since." He grinned suddenly.

"Apparently you have some good memories from that visit."

He said, "Oh. Um, yeah. One in particular. I had my first kiss in Viladembursa. I met this beautiful boy at the fountain in the town square. I never even knew his name, but I'll never forget him."

"That sounds amazing."

"It's my fondest memory, and it's still so incredibly vivid. I remember every little detail, the green of his eyes, the little chip in his front tooth, the three freckles in perfect alignment on his collarbone. I even remember the smell of the water in the fountain and how cold it was when he pulled me in with him." Nico smiled, looking more wistful than I'd ever have thought possible.

"It'd be wild if you ran into him again."

"That's impossible. Viladembursa has grown to almost thirty thousand people. I know I'm not going to run into one guy from over ten years ago." He returned the ice pack to his knuckles as his smiled faded.

"Yeah, probably not. I hope you have a great time on your vacation, though."

"I'm really going to try."

Chapter Eleven

The sun was low in the sky as my car bounced down a deeply rutted dirt road. It led to the ranch house that had been my home for the first fourteen years of my life. I'd returned to San Francisco from L.A. two days earlier, said goodbye to Zachary (who'd tried to get me to bail on the road trip) and started heading for Wyoming. I'd slept in my car the night before to save money on a motel room, and had gotten on the road before dawn and knocked out the rest of the thousand mile journey.

The house was in the middle of nowhere. My mother had inherited it and the twenty acres of nothing which it sat on from her father, who'd passed before I was born. The nearest town was called Simone, and it was centered around a natural gas plant that was the lifeblood of the community. The homestead was almost twenty miles from town, surrounded by brown scrubby weeds in the middle of a brown, treeless wasteland.

It looked even worse than I remembered it. The roof was sagging, and the whole thing was covered in a layer of dirt, as if the land was slowly claiming it. It was two stories with a wrap-around porch and had been white and probably nice once, but years of neglect had taken their toll. The house would have looked abandoned if it wasn't for the pickup parked beside it. The truck was filthy too, but the windshield showed a clean half-circle carved out by one wiper blade, suggesting recent use. The dust layer would have settled right back in a day or two.

I pulled up outside the house and waited for the dirt cloud to settle before I opened my car door and stepped out into a stifling August heatwave. As I stretched my stiff neck and shoulders, my brother came out of the house and fidgeted on the porch. Colt had been a child the last time I'd seen him. He was far more man than boy now, skinny and so long-legged that he lived up to his name. He wore a baggy formerly red t-shirt and ratty gym shorts, shifting his weight from one sneakered foot to another. Even though we had different fathers, we looked a lot alike. We both took after our mother with our blue eyes and hair so dark brown it was almost black. He'd probably end up taller than me, judging by the fact that he was already my height and most likely not done growing yet.

"Mom's not here," he called as I approached the house. "She's on vacation. Sorry that you came out here for nothing. I hadn't checked the P.O. box in a couple weeks, so I only got your letter this afternoon. Otherwise, I would have written back and told you to save a trip."

"Oh. Where'd she go?"

"Ohio."

"Why Ohio?"

"Because her boyfriend wanted to visit some friends there."

"When's she coming back?"

"I don't know. Like, a couple weeks?" He stared at the dusty porch, shifting uncomfortably.

"So, she just left you here by yourself?"

He looked up at me and knit his thick brows. "I'm sixteen. I'm not a kid. I can take care of myself."

I stepped up onto the porch and tried to look him in the eye, but Colt looked away. He seemed nervous for some reason. "I know. I didn't mean to insult you. I'm just surprised she didn't take you along."

"She went with her boyfriend. I would've been in the way."

"I didn't know she had a boyfriend."

"Why would you? It ain't like you been around," he muttered.

"I know," I said softly. "I barely recognized you, Colt. You got all grown up on me."

He glanced at me, then looked away quickly. "I barely recognized you either. You growin' a beard?"

"Nah. I just haven't bothered to shave in a few days."

"I wish I could grow a beard," he said. "It'd make me look a lot older, I bet."

"Why do you want to look older?"

"Because it totally sucks gettin' treated like a kid."

"True. I remember." He just kept staring at the porch, tracing an arc in the layer of dirt with the toe of his worn-out sneaker. After a moment I asked, "Is it okay if I come inside? I really need to use the bathroom."

He looked at me with wide, frightened eyes, and for a moment I thought he was going to say no. But finally he said, "I guess that'd be okay."

I followed him in, through the bent, duct-taped screen door. It was even hotter inside than outside. There was a swamp cooler in the living room window to the right of the front door, and even though it was making plenty of noise, it didn't appear to actually be cooling the place down any. The living room was a total mess, and the kitchen, which was straight ahead, was even worse. Every surface was cluttered with trash, including a huge number of Styrofoam ramen soup bowls. That was surprising, since my mother had always kept the inside of the house tidy, even if she'd given up on the outside long ago.

Movement to my left caught my eye. A thin, blond boy of maybe fifteen or sixteen with big, dark eyes hung back in the shadows outside Colt's bedroom door, dressed only in a pair of threadbare cotton shorts. His long hair was gathered into a messy ponytail, the escaped tendrils wet with sweat and sticking to his neck and forehead. "Hi, I'm Chance," I called. Instead of replying, the boy darted into the bedroom.

"That's Elijah. He's a friend. You remember where the bathroom is, right?" Colt said quickly.

I nodded and headed down the hall to the left of the living room. The bathroom was beyond filthy, as if it hadn't been cleaned in months. I wondered why my mom had let the place go like that. I used the toilet and washed my hands, drying them on my jeans since the towel looked like it could get up and crawl away.

As I reached for the door handle, I heard someone, presumably Elijah, say, "I thought you weren't gonna let him in." He had a thick southern accent.

"I had no choice," Colt said. "He had to use the bathroom. I really couldn't say no to that."

"You coulda said the toilet was broken or something," Elijah said.

"Both of them? There are two bathrooms. He used to live here, so he knows that."

"Okay, you're right."

"Everything's going to be fine, baby. I promise."

Baby. *Oh.* I came out of the bathroom and crossed the hall to my brother's room. When I stuck my head in the door, Elijah took a step back quickly, away from Colt. I said, "I'm sorry I barged in on you two. You must have been trying to have fun while Mom's away, and I showed up and interrupted."

"I…um," my brother stammered.

"I had no idea you're gay, Colt, but obviously I'm totally fine with that," I added.

Colt looked startled. "How did you know?"

"I overheard you just now. You called Elijah baby. I'm gay too, I'm not sure if you knew that." He just stared at me. After an awkward pause, I asked, "Is it okay if I spend the night here? I didn't just come to see mom, I wanted to see you, too. I get that it's weird because we barely know each other, and I'll leave in the morning. I just…I'd like it if we could talk a little."

There was that frightened look again, and it made my heart ache. Was I so much of a stranger that my own brother was actually scared of me? He muttered, "Um, yeah. I mean, this is as much your house as it is mine." He and I both glanced at Elijah, who looked terrified. Why? There really wasn't anything intimidating about me.

I asked, "Will you come for a walk with me, Colt? I just spent all day on the road and could use a little exercise."

"I guess so." He turned to Elijah and touched his arm gently, then told him, "I'll be back in a little bit. Okay?"

Elijah hugged his boyfriend quickly and said softly as he let go of him, "Okay. Be careful." Be careful? We were just going for a walk, it wasn't as though I was taking him skydiving.

Colt touched Elijah's face tenderly and said, "I will, baby."

My brother and I left the house by the back door. As we cut through the kitchen, he said, "I keep meaning to clean this up." It really was disastrous, with flies buzzing around the empty soup bowls and fast food wrappers. It smelled bad, too.

"How long ago did Mom leave on vacation?" I asked him.

"Like, um, two weeks ago," he mumbled.

We walked down a path overgrown with weeds, the only things that thrived in that part of Wyoming. Eventually, we came to a bench my grandfather had built decades ago. The fact that it wasn't dusty told me my brother came out here sometimes. Before us, the land dipped down into a shallow valley. In the distance, Simone was just barely visible. Only three thousand people lived there, so it wasn't exactly lit up like Vegas, but it did give us something to look at amid the brown nothingness.

"I always liked this spot," I said as I settled onto the bench.

"Me, too."

"How long have you and Elijah been together?" I asked after a pause.

"Five months."

"Where's his family from? My guess would be Georgia, but I'm no good at pinpointing accents."

"He's from Mississippi."

"I'm glad you have someone," I said.

"Really?" When I nodded, he said, "It's weird that you're okay with me likin' a boy. I'm not used to that. Usually, we just get a lot of funny looks and rude comments even if we ain't even holdin' hands or anything, because he kinda looks like a girl."

"People are assholes."

"You ain't wrong."

"Is Mom okay with it?" I asked.

"She doesn't know," he admitted, turning away from me.

"Oh." After another pause, I asked, "So, how's school? Is Simone High the same hell pit that I remember?"

Colt stood up and said, "Are you gonna, like, keep interviewin' me? I ain't exactly fond of that, so if you're gonna keep doin' it, maybe we should cut this short." I grinned at him, and he asked, "What?"

"You and Elijah must spend a lot of time together. You're developing his southern accent." He frowned at me, and I said, "It's cute. And I'm sorry about the interview. I don't know anything about your life, so I was just curious. I can see why that'd be annoying though, so I'll knock it off."

My brother hesitated, then sat back down on the edge of the bench, keeping as much distance between us as he could. After a moment, I said, "I'm sorry this is so awkward for you. I should have made an effort to see you when you were growing up. It's just...it's weird for me to be back here."

"I kinda remember when you ran away. Mama wouldn't talk about it afterwards, but I remember a lot of yelling and crying before you left. You were so mad at her."

"Yeah," I said quietly, "I was."

"But then you started sendin' the checks. You weren't even gone six months before the first one arrived. Why'd you send money home if you were so mad?"

"Mom lost her job because of me," I said. "I knew she'd never be able to find another one in Simone, not one that paid more than minimum wage at least, and I was worried about you, Colt. You were just a little kid. I wanted to make sure you had enough to eat and that the electricity stayed on."

He was quiet for a few moments before saying quietly, "Thank you."

That meant more to me than he could possibly realize. There was a lump in my throat as I murmured, "You're welcome."

"I know you're not plannin' to send those checks forever. When you gonna cut them off, when I turn eighteen?"

"No. As long as you need the money, I'll keep sending it."

He was quiet for another minute before saying, "Mom said you were workin' at Taco Bell. I found out what that pays, so I don't know how you can afford to send all that money."

"I don't work in fast food," I admitted. "I only told her that."

"Oh. Then what do you do?"

"I'd rather not talk about it."

Colt turned to look at me. "Is it something bad?"

"I said I don't want to talk about it."

"But you been sendin' a thousand bucks a month without fail for more than ten years. That's so much money."

"I know."

Colt looked down as he said. "I feel guilty 'bout taking your money, but at the same time, I'm so damn terrified about you cuttin' me off. I don't know what I'm gonna do when the checks stop."

"They're not going to stop. You have my word."

He smoothed out the frayed cuff of his shorts, still not looking at me as he said, "You don't even know me, but you're sendin' me half your income."

"It's not half. And you're my brother, Colt. I'll always take care of you."

He was quiet for a little while, and then he said softly, "You're a nice person. I wish you'd been around when I was growin' up."

My heart broke as I whispered, "So do I."

He looked up at me, his big blue eyes searching my face in the fading light. "Why'd you run away?"

"It's complicated."

"Did somebody hurt you?"

"Let's not talk about this."

"That's what happened though, isn't it? I just remember bits and pieces from back then. There was something about a man. He did something to you. But Mama, she didn't believe you. Is that right?"

"I said I don't want to talk about it." That came out a lot sharper than I'd intended. When Colt flinched a little I said, "Shit, I'm sorry. I don't mean to be an asshole. I just really can't talk about this."

"I'm sorry, too. I'm doin' the same thing I asked you not to do with all the questions. Mama always used to tell me, 'curiosity killed the cat.' I hate that expression. But I guess I've always had a bad habit of bein' way too nosy about stuff."

"Being curious isn't a bad thing," I said as I got up from the bench. "Come on, let's head back while there's still a little light. I don't feel like tripping over a coyote on the way back."

My brother grinned a little as he got up and fell into step with me. "I know you're kidding, but there is a coyote that comes around here. He's always by himself. I named him Colt, Junior. Sometimes I leave out scraps for him, like if I been to town and got KFC and have some chicken bones. I really want to get him to eat out of my hand, but he won't come close. Elijah says I'm nuts for trying."

"Elijah may have a point."

"Colt, Junior would never do it anyway," he said, "but it's still nice to have him around. I used to get real lonely out here before I met Elijah. That coyote was my only friend for a while."

"I remember how lonely it gets out here," I said quietly. "Do you think Mom would ever sell this place and get the hell out of Simone?"

"She tried. She had the house and the land on the market for six years after you left, but she got zero offers on it. Finally, she gave up."

"I never understood why she didn't just walk away from it."

"I dunno. I mean, partly it's 'cause this place is ours free and clear, anyplace else we'd have to pay rent. But aside from that, I think stubbornness kept her here. This house has been in our family a long time. I think walkin' away from it woulda felt like just one more failure, you know?"

"I guess." We were getting close to the house, and I stopped walking and turned to my brother. "I want to ask you something before we go inside. Don't take this the wrong way, okay? I only bring this up because I care about you."

"Why do I get the feeling that you're about to say something super embarrassing?"

I grinned a little. "Probably because I am. Are you and Elijah practicing safe sex?"

"Oh my God," Colt exclaimed. "I can't believe you just asked me that!" Even in the dim light, I could tell he was blushing ferociously.

"I wouldn't ask if it wasn't important."

"Okay, this is like, seriously none of your business, but I'm gonna tell you anyway just so you never, ever ask me again." Colt took a deep breath and blurted, "Elijah and I don't have sex. I mean, we mess around and stuff, but we've never…you know. He had some bad stuff done to him before he met me, so that's not somethin' he's comfortable with. And I love him so much that I don't care if we ever do it. All I need is for him to feel safe and be happy. Nothin' else matters."

"I see," I said gently.

He looked at the ground and said, "Normally, I wouldn't tell anyone that things happened to Elijah. But…I think maybe those same things happened to you, too. You probably feel like I'm still a kid and need to be protected from the truth, but I'm not. I grew up a long time ago. I think I've been able to help Elijah by being a good listener, and maybe I could help you too, if you felt like you wanted to talk to someone."

"I just…I can't," I whispered, my throat suddenly dry.

He looked disappointed, but said, "I get it. I'm a stranger to you, too, just like you're a stranger to me. I don't blame you for holdin' back."

Colt turned and went into the house, the screen door squeaking as it swung shut behind him. An overwhelming sense of loss settled on me as I stood out in the hot, still, August night, looking up at the dirty windows. I'd missed so much. My brother had grown up in the blink of an eye.

I felt compelled all of a sudden to do more for him than just those monthly checks. I didn't know what my mom had been doing, but it was clear that Colt needed a hand. I dragged an empty fifty-five gallon metal barrel away from the house, then went inside and started opening drawers. On my fourth try, I found a box of wooden matches and stuck them in the pocket of my t-shirt. I then propped the screen door open, carried a big armload of fast food wrappers outside, and set them ablaze in the barrel.

I'd made three trips back and forth with armloads of trash when my brother stuck his head in the kitchen and asked, "Why are you doing that?"

"Because it needs to be done."

"You must be tired, though. You drove all day."

"I'm fine." He watched me for a moment, then went into the living room and came back with a big armload of wrappers.

Elijah emerged from the bedroom after a while and joined in wordlessly. It didn't take long to burn all the garbage. After that, I went to work cleaning the kitchen.

"This really isn't your responsibility," Colt said.

"Doesn't matter. Just needs to get done."

"I'm sorry I let it get so bad. This heatwave has been draining the life out of me. Not that that's an excuse. I been lazy, too," he said.

"It's alright. Easy enough to make it better," I said as I pushed my sweaty bangs off my forehead and started scrubbing the sink. The boys took some cleaning supplies with them and went to work in the downstairs bathroom.

We all ran out of energy maybe an hour later, but by then we'd made real progress. "I'm going to grab my stuff from the car," I said. "Do you care which room I sleep in?"

"Yours is pretty much how you left it," Colt said. "Mama brought your desk downstairs for me a few years ago when I needed a place to do my homework, and she gave me your clothes as hand-me-downs, but other than that everything's the same."

He wasn't kidding. It felt so strange to be back in my childhood bedroom. The room was tiny and furnished with just a twin bed and a light blue dresser decorated with stickers. Some of my drawings and a few old posters were still stuck to the walls. It was also hot as hell, and got no better when I pried open the window. I went across the hall and opened the window in the bathroom, too, on the off chance that a breeze might come up out of nowhere, and left my door open.

After flopping down on top of the faded quilt, I pulled my backpack over to me. My phone had run out of charge and I wanted to plug it in before I passed out. As soon as I got it plugged in, the screen lit up, and a moment later the message icon appeared. I was surprised to hear Finn's voice when I played my voicemail. He'd been calling me several times a day, but he'd hang up when I didn't answer. This was the first time he'd left a message.

"Hey," he said. "I know you're on your trip, but I really need to talk to you. I hate the way we left things. There was a lot I needed to say, and I just…didn't. I'm no good at talking, you know that. But…shit, Chance. I shouldn't have let you walk away like that, and I sure as hell shouldn't have let you give that money back. I really wanted you to have it. That's not because I was trying to save you or whatever…. Okay, maybe that is why, but so what? I wanted that money to make a difference in your life. I wanted it to help. I'm sorry that I'm rambling right now. I have to confess, I've been drinking, so I don't really know what I'm saying right now, and I don't know if it makes any sense, but…call me, Chance. Please? So, okay. Bye for now." I sighed quietly as I turned my phone off again.

*****

It had been tough to sleep in the heat, and I awoke feeling stiff and groggy. At least the morning was considerably cooler and a breeze was stirring the light blue curtains. That was a relief. The heatwave had actually been pretty unusual, I didn't remember it getting that bad when I lived in Wyoming. I rolled out of bed and showered and changed in the bathroom across the hall (which was a lot cleaner than the other one), then slung my backpack over my shoulder and headed downstairs.

Colt and Elijah were sitting at the kitchen table, holding hands. Their heads were close together and they were deep in a whispered conversation. Elijah seemed to be worried about something, and my brother was reassuring him. He reached up and gently brushed Elijah's hair back. I was touched by the tenderness that seemed to come naturally to Colt.

As soon as they saw me, they broke apart guiltily. I really didn't understand that, since they knew I was fine with it. "I need to get going," I said. "Colt, will you walk me out?" He nodded and got up from the table as I said, "It was good to meet you, Elijah."

"You too," the blond murmured, avoiding eye contact.

When we got to my Honda, Colt said, "You didn't stay long."

"I know. I don't want to intrude on your time with your boyfriend. Mom will probably be home soon, right? So, I doubt you two want me hanging around." Colt looked at me with sadness in his eyes before looking away. I asked him, "Do you need me to take you into town for some groceries before I take off?"

"No, I can drive."

"Do you have a license?" He looked up again and frowned at me, and I let it drop. I pulled a folded bundle of bills from the pocket of my t-shirt and said, "Here, take this. I can tell money's tight by what you've been eating. Maybe get yourself some fruit, some milk, you know. Stuff like that. Both you and Elijah look half-starved. He's living here while Mom's on her trip, isn't he?" Colt fidgeted, wrapping his thin arms around himself, and I added, "It's totally fine with me if he is."

He didn't answer my question. Instead, he took the money hesitantly before crossing his arms over his stomach again. "Thank you," he said quietly.

"You're welcome. You have my number, right? In case you need anything?"

"Yeah, it's in Mama's address book."

"I noticed the phone had been disconnected when I tried to call yesterday and let you know I was close."

"It was just another monthly expense," he said. "We didn't really need it. If I need to call you I can go to the gas station up on the highway."

"That's almost twenty miles away."

"I know."

"Will you please do something for me, Colt?"

He looked at me and asked, "What?"

"Write me a letter now and then. Let me know how you're doing. You have my address in San Francisco, don't you?" He nodded and I said, "I'd love to hear from you."

"Alright. I can do that," he said, shifting his weight from one foot to the other.

"Great. So, I'm going to go. Please take care of yourself and Elijah."

"I'm really trying," he said.

I wanted to hug him goodbye, but thought it would make him uncomfortable so I didn't do it. Instead, I got in the car, pushing down the emotions that wanted to overwhelm me, and started the engine. I then straightened the little brown bear that was seatbelted to the passenger seat and said softly to the stuffed animal, "On the road again, Bobo. Step one is that horrible dirt road, prepare yourself."

I felt lost as I put the car in gear and drove away. When I looked in the rearview mirror, I saw Colt and Elijah on the porch, watching me go. Elijah clung to my brother, who was stroking the smaller boy's hair. Those two had a secret, no doubt about it. I didn't have a clue what it was, and wondered if I'd ever know.

I thought about Colt as I slowly made my way back down that rutted road. So much had been taken from me as a child, but I hadn't realized what the greatest loss of all had been until then. I'd missed out on my brother and all those years we would have had growing up together. He'd become a loving, remarkable person, one who didn't know me at all. I was just some guy who sent a monthly check. A stranger.

I swallowed hard, pushed the pain down and concentrated on the road ahead.

Chapter Twelve

I hadn't thought it was possible, but I'd managed to land in a town worse than Simone. The inappropriately named Gala, Wyoming was little more than a cluster of businesses along a not particularly busy highway. The biggest city nearby was Gillette, which had maybe thirty-five-hundred residents. It seemed like a boomtown compared to Gala.

My mother had passed through on an ill-conceived (ha!) road trip the summer after her twenty-first birthday. She and a girlfriend went to visit friends in southeastern Montana, and ended up spending the night in Gala on their way back. The friend had been tired and stayed in the motel while my mother went out for a drink. At a bar named Washington's, she'd hooked up with a guy whose name she remembered as 'Tony something Greek'. Forty weeks later I was born, a lifelong souvenir of her trip to Gala.

I'd asked my mother once why she never went back to look for Tony, and she'd said, "Why bother? He was nothing to me, just a horny guy in a bar. Plus, he was obviously dirt poor, not like he could have supported us." That was the sum total of what I knew about the man who made up half my DNA.

It was more than a little surreal to stand in front of Washington's twenty-six years later and know that this was where I began. I wasn't sure what I'd expected, but it turned out to be a totally unremarkable, squat, brown-shingled, windowless building in the parking lot of an abandoned Chinese restaurant. It probably hadn't looked any better two and a half decades ago.

I stood out on the cracked asphalt for a long time, psyching myself up and sweating a bit in the early afternoon sun. I'd tried calling the bar about a year ago and asking about Tony, but the person who answered had promptly hung up on me. If that was any indication, this probably wasn't going to go well.

There was no reason to be nervous, though. Nothing would come of this. Just because the bar was still there didn't mean anyone would remember a patron from a quarter-century ago. But what if they did? Washington's seemed like a place that would be frequented by locals and was several blocks from the highway, so it probably didn't draw a lot of people that were passing through.

If I actually managed to track Tony down, then what? What would we even talk about? I thought maybe I could ask him about my Greek heritage, but that was all I could really think of. I'd adopted a few Greek customs over the years, just as a way of, well, being a part of something, maybe. My mother had given me her last name and described herself as a mutt, so I'd gotten no traditions from her side of the family.

Other than that, I really didn't know what I'd say to this man, but maybe what we'd talk about wasn't all that important. What I really wanted was just to see what he looked like, find out what kind of man he was, maybe spend a little time with him. I had these stupid fantasies about him giving me a hug, inviting me to his house, chatting over dinner about anything at all. Just…having a dad.

"You're totally stalling, Chance." I said that out loud, but quietly. I really was, too. I took a deep breath and crossed the parking lot, then pulled open the heavy door.

It took a moment for my eyes to adjust to the relatively dim interior. The place smelled like paint, and I saw why as soon as I stepped from the little entryway into the main part of the building. A man in his early forties was touching up the red backsplash behind the bar with a plastic cup of paint and a small brush. His shoulder-length black hair was shot through with grey, as was his short beard, and he wore a Ramones t-shirt, making him look a bit like an aging rock star. "You open?" I called.

"Yup. Just taking advantage of the lull before the after-dinner crowd filters in." I'd be willing to bet that 'crowd' was pretty ambitiously stated. "What can I get you?"

I ordered a beer and looked around me as I sat at the bar. The place was nicer inside than I'd expected, neat and clean with a new-looking tile floor and comfortable seating. The bar itself was dark wood, polished to a high shine. "Is this your place?" I asked the bartender. When he nodded, I said, "It's nice. Shows real pride of ownership."

"Thanks. I'm going to get around to fixing up the outside. I bought it eighteen months ago, and so far all my effort's gone in here." I took a long drink from my beer, trying to figure out how to ask the question I'd come here for, and he asked, "Where you from?"

"California, but I grew up in Wyoming. I came back to visit family."

"Did you grow up in Gillette?"

"No, down south. A place called Simone."

"Never heard of it."

"You wouldn't, not unless you're from there. And if you were, I'd offer you my condolences."

He smiled at that, his dark eyes crinkling at the corners. "That good, huh?"

"Oh yeah. It's awesome."

"So what brings you to Gala?"

There was my opening. "I'm looking for somebody by the name of Tony. He used to come to this bar, back in the late eighties. Or, well, he did once."

The bartender's expression became grave. "He owe you money or something?"

"No, nothing like that. He, uh…he knocked up my mom." I took another drink of beer, feeling like a complete idiot.

"So, you're…."

"His son."

"What the fuck are you playing at?" The man's sharp tone startled me.

"Nothing!" I stammered. "I just want to find my dad."

"Get out of here," he growled. "Now!" He was furious, and I had no idea why.

The barstool almost fell over when I slid off it quickly, but I righted it and fished in my pocket with a shaking hand. I found a five dollar bill and put it on the bar for the beer, then took a step backwards as I asked, "Please just tell me, do you know him?"

"I said get out!"

My pulse was racing as I turned and fled, equal parts startled and baffled. When I got to my car, I pulled out of the parking lot and circled around Gala for a few minutes to try to calm down. I had absolutely no idea what had just happened or what I'd said to make that man so angry, and his reaction had really rattled me.

A heavy weariness settled on me as I drove around. The last few days had finally caught up to me, all that driving combined with barely sleeping or eating. I desperately needed to get some rest, then I could regroup and figure out what I needed to do.

The only place I could find in town was called the Gala Holiday Motel, right beside the I-90. It looked run-down and was adjacent to a truck stop, neither of which were good selling points. I was too tired to care, though.

When I checked in, my heart jumped as I was handed the key to room two-fifteen. As I climbed the stairs to the second floor, it was clear that the Gala Not-Holiday-Inn was worlds removed from the Whitman. In my room, its orange shag carpet was stained and the nylon bedspread smelled like it hadn't been washed since it was bought in the 1970s. I peeled it off the bed and rolled it into a ball, which I deposited in the far corner of the room. Then I pushed my sneakers off and climbed onto the bed. At least they'd washed the sheets between customers.

I started to worry as I laid there, and sat up, pulled out my wallet, and counted my cash. I had seventeen dollars on me and another hundred-twenty hidden beneath the seat in my Honda, just in case I got mugged. I hadn't planned on giving my brother that extra four hundred dollars, but then I hadn't expected to find him living in squalor and existing on ramen noodles either. I calculated how many times I'd had to fill my gas tank coming here, and what I'd need to get back. This was the only night I'd be able to afford staying in a motel, and my food budget would have to be somewhere around five bucks a day. I fell back onto the pillow and stared at the ceiling.

Zachary had been right to try to talk me out of going. This trip had been such a stupid idea. My mom hadn't even been home, my kid brother was a stranger, and the only lead I had for finding my dad had ended with some nut job screaming at me for absolutely no reason. I felt lonely, hungry, tired, and more than a little defeated. I curled up on my side and pulled a pillow over my head to drown out some of the noise from the truck stop. Fortunately, I was so exhausted that I fell asleep almost immediately.

*****

I slept for a couple hours and was awakened by a particularly loud shriek of air brakes from the truck stop. Ugh. I wanted to go back to sleep, but I was absolutely starving. No surprise, since my last meal had been fast food sometime around noon the day before. I rolled out of bed, slipped on my sneakers and used the bathroom, then pulled my phone out of my pocket to check the time. It was just past four p.m. There were two missed calls from Finn but no new messages. The charge indicator read seven percent. I'd used the phone to navigate to Gala and that had drained the battery. When I went to plug it in, I realized I'd left my backpack in the car.

I pulled my keys from my pocket, left my room and jogged down the exterior staircase to the parking lot. Then I stopped short and looked around. It took me a long moment to process the fact that the Civic wasn't where I'd left it. It wasn't anywhere. "Oh God," I rasped, panic rising up in me.

I ran to the front office and exclaimed, "I think my car was stolen!"

The young guy behind the counter blinked at me. "Did you lock it?"

"Of course!"

"Don't know what to tell you, dude." He was utterly indifferent.

"Fuck!" I left the office, ran to the street and looked in both directions, not that I expected to see the car. I just didn't know what else to do.

I felt crushed as the full reality of what had happened hit me. I dropped to my knees on the sidewalk and tears rolled down my face. It was gone. Oh God, I was so fucked.

My phone vibrated in my pocket. Finn's name was on the screen, and when I answered it, a sob slipped from me. "Chance, what's wrong?" he asked, sounding alarmed.

"Everything. Every fucking thing. They stole my car. Why the hell would someone steal a twenty-eight-year-old Honda? All my stuff was inside it. Oh God, my camera was in the trunk! And Bobo. Shit, Finn, Bobo was in the car!"

"Who's Bobo?"

"My teddy bear. He was the only thing I brought with me when I ran away from home. I loved that bear," I said, my voice breaking.

"Where are you?"

"Fucking Gala, Wyoming at the fucking Not-Holiday-Inn. They gave me room two-fifteen, Finn. It made my heart ache." I doubled over, absolutely sobbing. I barely knew what I was saying.

"Chance, take a deep breath, try to calm down." I just kept crying, curling up into a ball on the cracked, weedy sidewalk.

My phone beeped and I mumbled, "Shit, my phone's about to die. The fucking charger was in the car. Everything was in the car. Oh God, what am I going to do?"

"Baby, just hang on. Everything's going to be alright."

"It's not, Finn! Nothing's going to be alright! They stole my fucking car in broad daylight! How am I supposed to get home? I only have seventeen dollars on me, the rest was in the car. I shouldn't have given my brother all that money, but I thought he needed it more than I did."

"Chance—"

The phone beeped again, and another sob slipped from me. I muttered, mostly to myself, "Fuck, I'm going to have to turn tricks at that truck stop to make enough money to get home. That's gonna suck in a place like this. I think my odds are dead even on landing some jobs or getting the shit beat out of me."

"Chance, no! I—"

My phone went dead in my hand and I wrapped my arms around myself. My whole body shook as I cried. Several minutes passed before I calmed down enough to sit up and drag my palm over my wet cheeks. My head was absolutely pounding, and I realized I'd attracted an audience. Several people stood at a distance watching me, but no one made a move to ask if I needed help.

I pushed myself to my feet unsteadily and went back to my motel room, where I curled up in a ball on the bed and pulled the covers up to my ears. I knew I needed to report my car stolen, but there wasn't a phone in the room and I needed a few minutes to get it under control before I went outside again. I hadn't cried like that in years. I hadn't felt that helpless and scared in just as long.

It reminded me of how I'd felt when I'd first arrived in San Francisco, and the reality of what I would need to do to survive hit me like a ton of bricks. Sometimes I thought I'd left that frightened little boy far behind. Other times, I realized that was complete bullshit and I'd never actually stopped being him, not for a moment.

*****

I awoke with a start sometime later. It was nighttime, but the room wasn't dark because the light from the motel's garish neon sign filtered in through the thin curtains. I'd cried myself to sleep, which hadn't been my intention. The dead phone was still in my hand, and I slipped it in my pocket as I got up and went into the bathroom.

The person looking back at me in the mirror was a total mess. Washing my face helped, but only a little. My eyes were red and swollen, my pale skin mottled. I tried to fix my hair with my fingers, since my comb was in my backpack, and wished I'd taken the time to shave that morning. Some men looked good with a bit of razor stubble. I looked like I'd been living on the street, which I soon would be if I didn't raise enough money to get myself home.

I pocketed my room key, walked over to the truck stop and called the local police department from a payphone. The indifferent voice on the line took some information, told me the officer on duty was out on another call, and suggested I come down in person to file the report. "You just heard the part where my car was stolen, right? How am I supposed to get down there?" I asked.

"That's not my problem," the dispatcher said. I sighed and hung up the phone.

I sat down on a bench and took a few deep breaths. Behind me was a twenty-four-hour convenience store and gas station, and ahead of me was a parking lot full of huge trucks. I'd never worked someplace like that before. When I was street hustling, it was pretty clear why I was there, and the customers would come to me. I'd worked clubs and bars too and done some active soliciting, but they'd been gay businesses so my chances of getting punched in the face for propositioning someone were pretty slim. A redneck truck stop in Wyoming was another thing entirely.

My left knee bounced nervously, and I wiped my sweaty palms on my jeans. I seriously needed to get a grip, but the day had left me rattled. I was still so fucking hungry, too, which was probably why my head was pounding. But until I earned a few dollars, I couldn't worry about anything else.

I pushed off the bench and wandered among the trucks. I realized after a while that I was practically wearing a hole in my wrist by the way I was rubbing my tattoo and shoved my hands in my pockets. Whenever I caught someone's eye, I'd smile, but that just earned me funny looks. Clearly subtlety wasn't going to work out here. I spotted a younger truck driver that didn't look like a total douche and took a deep breath, then went up to him and said hi.

"Hey."

I tried my best to look flirtatious, which made me feel like an idiot. "Want a date?" Ugh, that was so cheesy.

He knit his brows and growled, "Hell no! Fucking faggot," before pushing past me roughly to head to the convenience store. Well, hey, at least I didn't get punched.

I wandered to a different part of the truck stop, trying the same line a couple more times with similar results. There were very few people around, since most of the truckers were bedded down for the night. I propositioned everyone I saw, even guys I'd normally avoid. I wondered how long it'd be before one of them reported me to the manager of the truck stop and the cops got called.

Finally, in the farthest corner of the lot, I tried the line on a big, tatted guy of about twenty-eight with a shaved head and a beer gut. He eyed me for a moment before asking, "How much?" I named a figure and told him that price was for a blow job. He considered it, then offered me a lower amount. Ugh, he was actually haggling!

I was too desperate to argue though, so I agreed to the price and climbed into the cab of his truck. As soon as the door was closed behind us, he started pawing at me and trying to unfasten my belt. "What are you doing? This was just supposed to be a blow job," I said as I tried to push his hands away.

"I don't want a blow job, I wanna fuck you." His breath smelled like cigarettes and alcohol.

"That's not what we agreed to."

"So what? I'm changin' it."

"We can't have sex. I don't have any condoms." I tried to slide away from him, but he grabbed my wrist and tried to climb on top of me.

"I don't like fuckin' with condoms," he slurred, his hands all over my body. Shit, he was really drunk.

He had size on his side, but I had agility. I managed to wriggle out from under him as my heart pounded and somehow got the door of the truck open, but he grabbed my t-shirt and tore it completely off me as I jumped out of the cab. He wasn't done, either. He followed me out of the truck and caught me before I'd made it five yards, grabbing me by my hair as he hissed, "Come back here you fuckin' whore! You're bought and paid for!"

"No I'm not. You didn't give me any money and I sure as hell didn't agree to getting barebacked!"

He slapped me so hard that my vision faltered and I fell to my knees. "You're getting' fucked, faggot," he told me, and started to drag me back to the truck by my hair.

I fought wildly. He almost had me back to the cab of the truck. If he got me in there again, I was in trouble. I grabbed a bit of crumbled asphalt and kicked his leg, and when he spun on me I threw it in his face.

All that did was enrage him. He dropped me with a hard stomach punch, all the air leaving my body at once as pain shot through me. I tried to struggle to my feet, but he pulled something from his pocket, grabbed my hair again and yanked my head back. I froze as a long, thin switchblade caught the light from a distant streetlamp. "No! Please," I rasped, fear overwhelming all my senses as my heart pounded in my ears.

"It's too late for please, you fuckin' whore," he growled, his eyes glinting.

"Police! Drop your weapon," a deep voice bellowed from somewhere behind me.

The man dropped me instead, then turned and hauled ass back to his truck. Not ten seconds later, the eighteen wheeler was barreling out of the parking lot. While the man retreated, I curled up on the ground, hugging my knees to my chest as I tried to come down from the sheer terror of what had almost happened.

I gasped and brought my hands up to defend myself when someone touched me. "Shhh, baby, it's okay," a familiar voice said.

"Finn!" I threw my arms around his neck and clung to him with all the strength I had left. As he carried me out of the parking lot I stammered, "But how? There's no way you can be here right now! It's absolutely impossible."

"I came as soon as I knew you needed me." We reached a white rental car and he unlocked the door with a key fob and sat me down on the passenger seat. Then he crouched down and brushed my hair out of my eyes as he asked, "Baby, are you hurt? Do I need to take you to a hospital?"

I shook my head no, then whispered, "It's more than a thousand mile drive from San Francisco. How can you be here?" My body started shaking as the adrenaline drained away, and I wrapped my arms around myself.

"Gillette has an airport, I flew out of SFO. I was lucky, because I was able to catch a flight that departed at six. It had a layover in Salt Lake City though, otherwise I would have been here sooner." I stared at him, completely dumbfounded, and he asked, "You sure you're okay? Should we have you checked out by a doctor just in case?"

"I'll be fine."

"Okay. Tell me what you need."

"A shirt," I said, touching my bare chest. "And something to eat. Something cheap, I only have seventeen dollars. Wait, no, sixteen-fifty. I had to use some change to call the police about my car. Fifty cents seems high for a local call, don't you think? Not like I had a choice, though." I knew I was rambling a bit, but I couldn't help it.

Finn got behind the wheel and started the engine, then asked, "Is there anything of yours back at the motel?"

"No, nothing. Everything was in the car."

I put my seatbelt on and watched his profile as he pulled onto the interstate. "How did you know where to find me?"

"You told me exactly where you'd be, the truck stop by the only motel in Gala, Wyoming."

"I...um...I didn't do anything tonight. I mean, I didn't turn any tricks. I tried to, but it didn't pan out," I mumbled embarrassedly. I didn't know why, but it was really important to me that he knew that.

"We're going to have a talk about this, later on when you're not so shaken up," he said calmly. "Actually, I'm going to yell at you for about half an hour for endangering yourself like that. But now's not the time."

"I know it was dangerous to try to hook in someplace like that, but I really didn't have a choice."

"Yes you did. You could have called me back from a payphone. Or, if you didn't feel comfortable asking me for help, you could have called my brother-in-law. Christian's a good friend of yours, he would have wired you some money with no questions asked."

"It didn't even occur to me to ask for help," I admitted.

"Seriously?"

I looked down at my hands, which were dirty from the asphalt. "I've always taken care of myself. When things go wrong, I just deal with them."

"I can understand that, actually," he said quietly.

We drove the rest of the way to Gillette in silence and I leaned back in my seat and closed my eyes. I hurt all over and couldn't stop shaking. Finn pulled into the parking lot of a twenty-four-hour diner, and I got out of the car and steadied myself with a hand on the roof. He was unbuttoning his shirt when he came around the car and helped me into it, then buttoned it up for me, leaving himself in the pristine white t-shirt he'd been wearing underneath. His shirt was huge on me, but it was also incredibly comforting, since it enveloped me in Finn's clean scent.

When we went inside the diner, I spotted a restroom and said I'd be right back, then washed up thoroughly. I took an extra couple minutes in there as I tried to calm down and stop shaking. Finally though, I felt bad about keeping Finn waiting and went to find him in the restaurant.

He was on the phone, and I realized after a moment that he was talking to the Gala police department about the theft of my car. Surprisingly, he was able to recite the Civic's license plate.

The waitress came by while he was doing that and put a bowl of clam chowder in front of me, along with a basket of crackers. She gave me a critical once-over, frowning slightly at the way my hand shook when I picked up the soup spoon, and asked flatly, "Anything else?" She probably thought I was a druggie.

"No thank you," I mumbled. As soon as she left, I started shoveling the soup into my mouth with one hand while stuffing the pocket of Finn's shirt with several packets of crackers. It was so good, warm and soothing on my empty stomach.

Finn disconnected and put his phone on the table. "I went ahead and ordered for you since I knew you were hungry. Soup always comes up fast."

"Thank you," I said before ladling more into my mouth. I knew my table manners left a lot to be desired, but I was too hungry to care. I polished off the soup, scraping up every last drop, then tore open a packet of crackers and ate them in a couple bites.

I was startled when the waitress came back and deposited two plates heaped with burgers and fries on the table, then went off to refill Finn's coke. "I can't afford that," I said quietly. "It'll take up too much of the money I have left."

"Dinner's on me." I started to protest, but he cut me off by saying, "No arguments." I still tried to protest, but he interrupted again and said, "I mean it."

"Thank you again. I'm paying you back when I get some money," I told him before diving into the food.

"You're welcome."

"So, what did the police say?" I asked before stuffing a French fry in my mouth.

"We need to go down in person tomorrow and finish the paperwork since the one officer on duty is tied up tonight, but they have the information and a description of your vehicle and will notify the neighboring jurisdictions."

"The car's probably long gone, but thanks for helping. Thank you for all of this. I still can't believe you're here!" But then a thought occurred to me and I said, "Wait, what about work? Aren't you going to get in trouble for taking time off with such short notice?"

"It doesn't matter."

"Sure it does. Your job's really important to you."

"It is, but you're far more important."

I absorbed that for a few moments, eating another fry as I stared at the tabletop. Finally I said quietly, "I don't know what I would have done if you hadn't come along right when you did. That wasn't the first time a john pulled a knife on me, but that time I really believed he was going to use it." Finn swore under his breath, and I glanced at him from beneath my lashes. "My job's not always that bad," I told him.

"I'm adding that to the list of things I'm going to yell about later," he said levelly.

I ate everything on my plate and washed it down with three cokes, after making sure refills were free. By the end of the meal, I was absolutely stuffed but feeling worlds better. Finn paid the bill, then drove us to a cluster of hotels near the airport.

He picked the nicest of the chain hotels. After he parked and grabbed a backpack from the trunk, I followed him into the plush lobby, hanging back a bit when he got us a room. We rode to the third floor in silence, and he let us into three-twelve. It was neat and clean, all done in earth tones with a little couch, table and two queen beds. "I'm paying you back for this, too," I told him, "as well as that last-minute plane ticket. That must have been insanely expensive."

"No you're not," he said as he tossed the backpack onto one of the beds.

"Of course I am. It'll take me a little while to get the money together, but I'm paying you back, every cent of it."

"I won't accept it, and when we get home, you're taking that envelope back, too. That money is yours."

I shook my head. "No chance. No fucking way am I going to let you financially damage yourself for me."

Finn's voice rose slightly. "Who says I'm 'financially damaging' myself? I can afford it, and you're taking that damn money."

"How can you possibly afford that?"

"I have a lot of savings."

"You'll have a lot more when you put that twenty-two thousand dollars back in the bank!" I exclaimed.

"Why are you being so stubborn?" Finn was almost yelling by that point and put his hands on his hips. "That money could be life-changing for you! There's absolutely no reason to turn it down!"

My voice rose, too. "Yes there is! If I take that money, it means all I was to you all summer was just your whore! And I don't want to be that, Finn. I know I'm being stupid and ridiculous and self-deluded, but don't you see? Our time together meant so fucking much to me, and I need it to not have been about money!" I turned away from him.

Finn was quiet for a long moment before saying softly, "It meant everything to me, too."

"You don't have to say that just because I did."

"I'm not! I just…shit, Chance, what do you think I'm doing here?"

I looked at him over my shoulder. "I really don't know."

"I'm here because I care about you *so much*! You asked what you were to me when we were in front of my station and I didn't have an answer ready, because like I keep telling you, I'm no good with words. But that doesn't even sort of mean the answer is *nothing*, it just means it was too complicated for me to explain it right then." He pulled a white piece of paper from the back pocket of his jeans and held it out to me. "I tried to write it down when I was on the plane. I wanted to be ready in case you asked me again. I think maybe you should read this."

I took the paper and unfolded it, then realized it was a barf bag. That made me grin a little. The front of the bag was covered in a big logo for the airline (because of course you'd want to brand something people threw up in). On the back of the bag, above some utterly unnecessary printed instructions, Finn had written something in blue ballpoint pen.

I took a deep breath and read out loud, "You're the boy I can't stop thinking about. My first thought every single morning is about you, and you're my last thought before I fall asleep at night. In between, I think about you a million times each day. You're the person who makes me happy, more than anyone else on this planet. You're the reason I've smiled more this summer than I have in all twenty-eight years of my life, combined. You're everything, Chance." I folded the bag and held it to my chest with both hands. "For someone who thinks he has trouble with words, that's actually so great," I told him, fighting to keep my voice steady.

"That says some of what you are to me, but not nearly all of it," he said shyly. "I only had the one barf bag. Even if I'd filled up every single bag on that plane, it still wouldn't have been enough to explain what you are to me." His eyes went wide and he added hastily, "With words! If I'd filled them up with words. Oh God. That sounded disgusting."

I chuckled and said, "I knew what you meant."

Finn grinned a little. "I'm glad I could make you laugh, after the day you had."

"It was such an epically shitty day," I said as I went over to the small nightstand between the two beds and stood up the barf bag by leaning it against the base of the lamp. I then took the five packets of crackers from my pocket and lined them up beside the bag before sitting on the edge of the mattress. "What are the chances that a stolen car will be recovered?"

"Not bad," Finn said, crossing the room to sit on the mattress across from me. "My concern though, since it was right beside a highway, is that the thief headed out of state with it. That'll make it harder to find. Was it insured?"

"Yeah, but liability only since it was so old. Why would anyone even steal a twenty-eight-year-old car? That makes no sense."

"It happens all the time, actually," he said. "Older cars are easier to break into and often don't have alarm systems. Plus, those little Hondas are really popular with street racers and get stolen pretty frequently."

"Awesome," I muttered. Then I asked idly, "How'd you know my license plate number?"

"I'd noticed it when we were on Twin Peaks."

"You weren't kidding when you said cops were observant."

"Well yes, we are, but I couldn't help but notice that license plate."

"Why?"

"Because it happened to be my initials, F-O-N. The numbers I just remembered incidentally."

"What's the 'O' stand for?"

He grinned a little. "Never you mind."

I grinned too, then asked, "What about the stuff inside stolen cars, is that ever recovered?"

"Sometimes. We can check the local flea markets, see if anything turns up. What did you lose?"

"There were three things in that car that meant everything to me. My camera was in the trunk. It was worth a hell of a lot more than the car." I sighed and added, "I loved that camera. It was a gift from Christian and the nicest, most expensive thing I owned by far. I should have left it home, but I was worried about my apartment getting broken into while I was gone. Plus, I thought maybe I'd want to use it if I found my dad, but that was just stupid."

"If you found your dad? Is he a missing person?"

"No, I didn't mean it like that. I was in Gala trying to find the man who knocked up my mom over twenty-six years ago. I've never met him and don't even know his last name. I went to the bar where they met, and the owner of the place yelled at me and kicked me out. Just part of the tremendous shit fest that made up this day."

"Oh wow, I had no idea. You just said you were going to visit your family."

"I did that too, or tried to. I spent last night in southern Wyoming, in the house where I lived as a child, but my mom wasn't home. I did get to see Colt, my kid brother, and I met his boyfriend. It was super awkward. Colt and I barely know each other, and I didn't stay long because I just felt like I was in the way."

"I'm sorry this trip has been so awful."

"You know, I expected it to be bad, but not quite *this* bad."

"Why didn't you ask me for help in tracking your father down? I certainly have the resources," Finn said. When I shrugged, he sighed. "It's that whole not asking for help thing again, isn't it?"

"Maybe. Is it Oliver?"

"Is what Oliver?"

"Your middle name."

He grinned a little. "I'll tell you mine if you tell me yours."

"I don't have one."

He looked surprised. "Really?" When I nodded, he said, "Fine, I'll tell you. It's O-D-H-R-A-N."

"What the hell did you just spell?"

"My middle name. It's pronounced Orin, but my parents went with a more traditional spelling."

"Could you be more Irish?" I said with a grin.

"The funny thing is, my family's been in the U.S. for five generations. But it's like, the further we're removed from Ireland, the harder my parents try to cling to tradition."

"Is Finn short for something? Finnegan, maybe?"

"Nope. It's a traditional Irish name in its own right, taken from the hero of legend, Finn MacCool, who became all-knowing after he ate a magic salmon. I always thought that was special," he said with a smile.

I burst out laughing. "Finn MacCool and a magic salmon? Really?"

He raised his hands palms-up and said, "That's where the name comes from."

"That's awesome."

"It's so good to see you smile," he said with a sweet grin.

"It's because of you, one hundred percent. I'm so glad you're here, Finn."

"I am, too." That made me feel kind of shy for some reason. I looked down at the beige carpet, which I was carving a little trough into with the toe of my sneaker. "I always wanted to ask this," Finn said. "But you don't have to answer if you don't want to. Is Chance your real name?"

"It is. People ask me that a lot, because it sounds so much like a made-up hooker name. But I was born Chance Matthews."

"I assume that's your mom's last name."

"Yeah. Even if she'd known my dad's last name, she still would have given me hers."

"Where'd she get the name Chance?" Finn asked.

"Well, when my mom found out she was pregnant, she went straight to an abortion clinic. I'd obviously been a total accident, and she didn't even sort of want me. But at the last minute, she couldn't go through with it. She decided, as she put it, to give me a chance. Hence the name." Finn looked shocked. I said as I pushed my shoes off and curled up on my side, "Sorry. I realize that the majority of my personal anecdotes should be accompanied by a tiny violin. But, well, you asked."

Finn took his shoes off too and did the same thing I'd done, curling up on his side on the other bed, facing me. We watched each other across the small divide for a while, and then Finn asked, "What were the other two things?"

"What?"

"You said there were three things in the car that were irreplaceable. One was your expensive camera. What were the other two?"

"A stuffed animal from my childhood, and the journal you gave me."

Finn rolled over and grabbed his backpack, then turned so he was facing me again. He unzipped the pack and handed me a blank journal that looked exactly like the one he'd given me before, and a little brown bag that said *The Imagination Station at Salt Lake City Airport*. "What's this?" I asked as I sat up.

"I was trying to replace what was stolen. I would have bought you a camera too, but I didn't have time to shop for one. I know for a fact you would have complained about the expense, but I would have done it anyway," he said with a little half-smile.

"This is the exact same journal," I said, putting it in my lap and running a fingertip over the embossed compass rose on its dark blue cover.

He sat up, facing me, and said, "I'd bought myself one too, because I thought it was really pretty. I never go anywhere though, so you should have mine. Fortunately, it happened to already be in my backpack."

I stood the journal up next to the barf bag and said thank you. Then I reached into the paper bag and pulled out a soft little brown teddy bear. "How did you know?" I whispered.

"You told me when I called, before your phone went dead. I know he's no substitute for Bobo, and maybe we'll still get him back, but in the meantime, I wanted you to have this little guy. We can call him B.B., or I don't know. Whatever you want."

I stared at the adorable little bear for a long moment, and then I startled the hell out of myself and Finn by bursting into tears. "Shit, Chance, I'm sorry," he exclaimed, quickly moving to my bed and putting an arm around me. "I didn't mean to make you cry. Does he remind you too much of Bobo? Should I get rid of him?"

I clutched the little bear to me and shook my head no. It was a full minute before I managed to choke out, "I don't know why I'm crying. I think…I think I'm just not used to people being nice to me or something."

"You've had such a long day, baby," he said gently. "Here, stand up for a minute." I did as he said, and he pulled the blanket out from under me.

I climbed into bed, curling myself around the little bear, and Finn tucked me in as I said, "I never cry. Never. Except for today. God I'm sorry. I'm such a mess."

"You have to be mentally and physically exhausted," he said. "I'd cry, too."

I took a couple jagged breaths to calm myself, then said, "You would not. You're a big, tough cop. And you probably think I'm being such a wienie right now."

He grinned at me as he sat down on the edge of the bed and brushed my hair back from my forehead. "I think you're a strong, capable person who hit his breaking point. Don't beat yourself up over it. Life already beat you up enough for one day."

I nodded at that as I took a few more deep breaths. Finn stroked my hair for a while, and once I'd calmed down, he kissed my forehead and moved back to the other bed. He got under the covers and offered me a sweet smile.

I stuck my hand out from under the thick, white comforter, and he reached out and took it. After a while, he said, "I don't know how I'm supposed to act around you. I don't know what's okay and what isn't. It kind of feels like I'm meeting you for the first time, even though we just had that intense, intimate summer together. I always thought I was ruining any real chance with you by approaching it as a business arrangement, but…damn it, Chance, I really wanted you to have that money."

"Where'd you get it? I know you told me you had it in savings, but what guy in his twenties has that much money saved up?"

He grinned a little and said, "So, the no questions thing is totally out the window now, right?" I grinned too and nodded, sniffing a bit since my nose had started running with the tears. He admitted quietly, "That was my house."

"What do you mean?"

"I'd been saving for a house since I was twenty. It had always been my dream to own my own place, but I didn't want to move out of San Francisco. It's my hometown and I love it, despite its flaws. Obviously the San Francisco housing market is insanely expensive, which is why, eight years later, I was still working on putting together a down-payment big enough to make the monthly payments affordable on a cop's salary." He shifted a bit under his blanket and said, "So, anyway, that's where the money came from."

"You gave me your dream," I whispered.

"Well, but not unselfishly. In return, I got the best summer of my life."

"Would you have done that with any other prostitute?"

"Absolutely not."

"So, why me?"

"Because I wanted you, Chance. I wanted you so fucking much. I thought you were so incredibly beautiful the first time I saw you, over a year ago when we both went to say goodbye to Christian before he went in for those clinical drug trials. Then I saw you again at the wedding, and I realized there was so much more to you, too. You were sweet and shy and such a good friend to my brother and his husband. You didn't take a single break all through the wedding and reception. You didn't eat anything, either, you were too busy trying to capture every moment of their big day. I really wanted to take you by the hand and make you sit down for a couple minutes and bring you a plate of food. But how weird would that have been, coming from a total stranger?" he grinned self-consciously.

"You saw me," I said quietly. Tears started to prickle at the back of my eyes, but no way was I going to cry yet again.

"Yeah. I saw you, Chance. And I saw myself too. I saw everything wrong in my life that made it impossible for me to just walk up to you and ask you out. Nobody knows I'm gay. I think a couple people have their suspicions, but that's it. I still live at home, pathetic as that sounds, because it's rent-free and I was saving my money for a house. My parents are completely homophobic. I watched the way they turned their backs on Shea when he came out, and I was too much of a coward to follow my kid brother's example. Instead, I just stayed in the closet. I haven't even told Shea the truth! Isn't that ridiculous? I'm so fucking deep in there that I can't even be honest with my own gay brother! What the fuck is wrong with me?"

I squeezed his hand and said, "Nothing."

"Bullshit."

"I'm serious. There's nothing wrong with you, Finn. Not every choice you make is the right one, but, God, who among us is perfect on that count?"

"I don't expect to be perfect, but I could be a hell of a lot better than this. Sometimes I think I secretly wanted you to slip up and tell Christian that I was seeing you, because then my brother would find out I was gay without me having to tell him."

"Why don't you just talk to him? You know he wouldn't judge you."

"It's not that I think he'd judge me, he'd know how much I failed him. I let him go through all of that alone. If I'd manned up and come out first, maybe it would have been easier on him. And if he knew I was gay too, he would have had someone to talk to, not just when he was coming out. I had so many questions when I was younger, and I bet he did, too. But I was too busy being afraid to be there for him."

"You should really cut yourself some slack," I said.

Finn grinned, just a little. "Yeah, I don't really do that."

"You know what? Shea turned out fine. Better than fine! He's madly in love and married to a great guy, and the two of them couldn't be happier. Maybe it's time to forgive yourself for all these alleged shortcomings."

"Definitely in the easier said than done category."

We watched each other for a little while, and then I asked, "If I hadn't ended it, how much more of your savings were you planning to give me?"

"All of it, all eighty-three thousand, every last cent until the account was empty."

I sat up and exclaimed, "That's totally nuts!" He just shrugged. I stared at him for a long moment before saying,

"You know you could have gotten laid for free at any gay bar in the city."

He sat up too. "It wasn't just for sex. You know that. It was for you. I wanted to be with you more than anything."

"It would've been a hell of a lot cheaper to ask me out."

"Would you have said yes? If I'd walked up to you at my brother's wedding, introduced myself properly, and said, 'Chance, will you go on a date with me?' is there any possible way you would have agreed?"

"Honestly? No. I thought you were really attractive, but I still would have said no to you. I don't date, never have. How can I with this job?"

"You know what I think? You use your job as an excuse. I think you're as afraid of getting close to someone as I am, if not more so. I think we both needed the excuse of me hiring you to let ourselves have what we really wanted," he said. "Or maybe I'm just completely self-deluded and telling myself all of that to keep from feeling like such a total creep for paying you to have sex with me."

"Oh no. Don't even try to feel guilty about that. I loved being with you! I loved every single minute of it. And you're probably right about that being the only way we'd ever manage to get together."

"I'm afraid to ask this question," Finn said after a pause, "but I need to ask it anyway. Where do we go from here?"

"I have absolutely no idea. I'm still a hooker, you're still not out, and it really doesn't seem like either of us would have the first clue how to be in a relationship, even if those two huge barriers didn't exist."

Finn sighed quietly. He did that almost as much as I did. Then he got under the covers and laid back down on his bed facing me, and I laid down on mine. "I wish things were different," he whispered.

"So do I."

We watched each other for several long moments across that small divide. Then I scrambled out of my bed and into his, taking B.B. with me. Finn wrapped me up in his arms, and I snuggled against his chest as he kissed my forehead. Finally, I was able to let myself relax, exhaling slowly as my eyes slid shut. I felt better and safer than I had in days.

Chapter Thirteen

Finn was gone when I woke up the next morning, and there was a note on the nightstand. I felt like I was back at the Whitman. When I read the note though, it said he'd gone out to get some breakfast and would return soon.

I used the toilet and took a quick shower, then got dressed again in the only clothes I had. By the time I came out of the bathroom, Finn was back and setting up breakfast for two on the little round table by the window. "I got a couple things I thought you might need," he said, "but the only place I could find that was open early was a gas station convenience store, so it's all a bit random."

"Thank you," I said as I peered into the plastic shopping bag on my bed. The items near the top were a toothbrush, a dark green t-shirt with 'Wyoming' written across the front of it in big letters, and several candy bars. "I'll pay you back. I probably already owe you about "

He cut me off. "Please stop keeping a running total. I'm here to help, so just let me." I quit talking about it, but added the purchases and breakfast to the list in my head. As I sat down at the table, Finn said, "I got the room for another night, and we can add more as needed. We should hang around and see if your car turns up, and it'll also give us a chance to work on tracking down your father."

"Don't you need to get back to work?"

"There's no hurry."

"Really?" When he nodded, I said, "Well, alright. What do you suggest?"

"Tell me exactly what happened when you went into the bar where your parents met." I told him the whole story, in between sips of hot coffee and bites of a fast food breakfast sandwich.

Finn fidgeted with his coffee cup as he said, "We could go back and question the bar owner, but if he was that defensive I doubt we'd get very far. Instead, maybe we can find a diner or someplace in Gala that's frequented by locals and see what we can find out there."

"I'm sure that'll go over big. People in small towns just love outsiders, especially ones that ask questions," I said.

"I know. I'd approach it another way and do a records search, but that's pretty tough without a last name." Finn drained his coffee cup, then said, "I really want to find out a bit about that bar owner. He has to know Tony, or at least know of him. Otherwise, his response makes absolutely no sense. You said he seemed friendly until you started asking about your dad."

"Yup. It was like flipping a switch."

Finn polished off his breakfast sandwich and pushed back from the table. "I'm going to get a shower and then we can take off." He retrieved his backpack and looked inside, then started to chuckle as he dumped its contents on the bed.

"I did an awesome job packing." All he'd brought was a toothbrush and about twenty pairs of underwear. "In my defense, I packed in about fifteen seconds, because I was trying to catch that flight out of SFO."

"You were obviously taught never to leave the house without clean underwear," I said with a grin. "Nailed it!" He flashed me a smile, then went into the bathroom with the toothbrush and took a shower while I finished my coffee.

I was changing from his shirt to the dark green t-shirt he'd bought me when Finn came back into the room sometime later, wearing only a towel and looking so damn sexy that my breath caught and my cock instantly stirred. His gaze locked with mine when he noticed me staring.

In the next instant, we were all over each other. I tore the towel off him as his mouth devoured mine and he pulled me onto one of the beds. I was absolutely desperate for him, clutching his big body as we ground our hips together. He fumbled with my belt and zipper, then yanked my jeans and briefs off me. As soon as I was naked, Finn dove onto my cock and sucked me to the root. I threw my head back and cried out, thrusting into his warm, wet mouth for a few moments before I told him, "I need you in me so fucking bad, Finn."

He released my cock, grabbed his wallet from the nightstand and pulled out a little individual packet of lube and a condom. As he prepped himself, I got on my knees and elbows, arching my back. Both of us moaned when he pushed into me. He wrapped an arm around my chest and pulled me against him as he began to pump in and out of me. His other hand snaked down my body and grasped my cock. With each thrust into me, he slid his hand down my shaft, which was slick from his mouth, establishing an intense, steady rhythm. I completely gave myself over to the pleasure, crying out beneath him, driving myself onto him as everything else, all thoughts, all worries, fell away.

I came first, yelling as I shot onto the bedding, my ass tightening around Finn's thick shaft. "Oh fuck," he rasped, clutching me to him as he slammed into my body. He pushed in deep when he came, rocking both me and the bed with several hard thrusts.

He kissed my shoulder when he finished, holding me as he caught his breath. He then slid from me carefully, discarded the condom, and pushed the soiled top sheet off the bed. We settled onto the mattress and Finn wrapped himself around me, his chest against my back. I grinned happily.

After a few minutes he said, "I wish we could spend the whole day in bed. I know there are some important things we have to do today though, so I guess we should get up and get going."

I nodded as I sat up and pushed my hair from my face. When I turned to look at him, Finn flashed a beautiful smile and pulled me back into his arms. "But five more minutes won't hurt anything." I smiled too and kissed him.

*****

Five minutes turned into a few hours. That was fine, though. I really wasn't eager to get to the day's tasks.

Once we finally got up and dressed, we went to Gala's one-room police station and finished the paperwork on my stolen car. Finn had a good rapport with the forty-something female officer who assisted us. She was full-figured with a friendly smile, and apparently in the process of growing out her blonde hair in favor of her natural salt-and-pepper, leaving her with a two-tone effect. She was the only person in the station and seemed glad to have someone to talk to. It also didn't hurt that Finn was nice to look at, and more than once I caught her checking him out. He didn't seem to notice.

When the report was completed, they engaged in a bit of cop talk, comparing notes about their jobs. "I've thought about transferring to a bigger city," the police officer said, whose name badge read C. Hanson. "Nothing ever happens in Gala, except for theft or vandalism. It's always either kids bored out of their minds or someone passing through on the highway. Then again, a big city might be entirely too much excitement."

"Did you grow up in this town?" Finn asked.

"No, in Gillette."

"I suppose you've gotten to know the citizens of Gala pretty well, though."

"Not all, but a lot of them. There are only four hundred and fifty-two residents," she said.

"What can you tell me about the owner of Washington's bar?"

Officer Hanson raised an eyebrow at that. "Why do you ask?"

Finn told her, "My friend went in there yesterday because he's looking for a family member, and the bar owner flipped out on him. I was wondering if he's always like that."

"Cap used to be the nicest guy in the world. I always heard money changes people, and apparently there's truth to that. He got a huge inheritance a couple years ago, and ever since then he just hasn't been the same."

"Really?" I asked.

"Yup. He got close to a million dollars, bought Washington's and has been putting all kinds of money into fixing it up. I don't know why. It's the only bar in town. His regulars would drink there even if the roof fell in and chickens roamed the dance floor."

"You said his name's Cap?" Finn asked.

"He's been captain of the volunteer fire department for the last decade, ever since he got sober, so that's his nickname," she said. "His real name's Antonio Asturias, but no one ever calls him anything but Cap."

That made me sit up as my breath caught. "Antonio," I repeated, and she nodded. "Is Asturias Greek?"

"No, Spanish. His father was a Guatemalan immigrant. You sure are interested in this guy," Officer Hanson said. "What's your story?"

"I came to Gala looking for my dad," I admitted. "I've never met him, but he and my mom hooked up at Washington's Bar more than a quarter century ago. It seems like a place that would mostly draw locals, so I asked Cap if he knew this guy and that was when he threw me out."

"Really? Just for asking a question?" When I nodded, she said, "That's peculiar. Cap's had a short fuse lately, but not *that* short."

"It struck us as odd, too," Finn said. "The man we're looking for is named Tony. Do you know of any men by that name in town? He'd have to be in his forties or fifties, and we think his last name is Greek."

"Not offhand. I can think of three…no wait, four men named Tony in Gala, but none of them are Greek or the right age. The person you're looking for could have been passing through though," she told him.

"That's a definite possibility," Finn said. "He could have also been a resident back then and moved away."

"True, but that's less likely," the police officer said. "Gala's the type of place where the families go back generations. Not a lot of turn-over."

Finn pushed his chair back and got up. "I think we should try talking to Cap again. Thanks for your time, Officer Hanson."

"Christine," she corrected as they shook hands. "If that doesn't pan out, come on back and I'll see if I can give you a hand tracking this fellow down. Everyone should have a chance to know their father."

I thanked her and we went out into the parking lot, where I turned to Finn and said, "Asturias could easily be mistaken for Greek, and Tony could be a nickname for Antonio. Did I meet my dad yesterday?"

"I was wondering the same thing. Maybe he bought the bar he used to hang out in."

"Oh man, what if that's him? He's such an asshole," I said.

"It might not be the right guy. Maybe his name's just a coincidence, and if so, we can come back and see if Officer Hanson can help us access the town records. But as soon as I heard his name, I wanted to ask him some questions."

"Me, too. Let's go see him," I said. "The bar was totally empty this time yesterday. It's probably best not to confront him with an audience of drunk locals."

I told Finn how to find the bar, and when he parked in front of it he asked, "You do want me to come in with you, don't you?"

"Yes, please. I'm guessing this guy won't be thrilled to see me, and you're probably good at defusing hostile situations." He gave me a half-smile and got out of the car.

I went into the bar first, and as soon as Cap saw me, he growled, "Was I unclear yesterday? Get the fuck out." When Finn filled the doorway behind me, the man said, "Oh great, you brought muscle. Look, if you start anything, I can have the Gala Police Department over here in ninety seconds."

"I didn't bring 'muscle', I brought my boyfriend," I said as I walked up to the bar. "And if you feel like calling the police, go right ahead. Christine seemed pretty bored when we were talking to her a couple minutes ago and she'd probably welcome a little excitement."

"What the fuck do you want?" Cap said, glaring at me and bracing both hands on the bar.

I took my wallet from my pocket and fished out a worn photo, which I held in front of his face. "That's my mom. Her name's Janet Matthews. She would have looked a bit younger when she was passing through Gala in August of 1988. That's my kid brother in the photo. He doesn't know who his dad is either, but that's a different story. Anyway, that summer Janet was on her way back from visiting friends in Montana, but she and her girlfriend left late and decided to spend the night in Gala. My mom came to this bar and hooked up with a guy whose name she remembers as 'Tony-something-Greek'. It was just one night, and she never saw him again. Nine months later, I was born. My name is Chance Matthews. Coming here was a total long-shot, but I had to try."

Cap had been staring at the picture with his brows knit. He looked at me as I tucked it away and returned the wallet to my pocket, and said in a low voice, "That's a really compelling story. There's only one thing wrong with it, the fact that I'm infertile. Other than that little hitch in your well-spun tale, bravo. You sounded really convincing. I think I even vaguely remember Janet. She must have put you up to this, right? Well, go back and tell her nice try, but I'm not falling for it."

"Did you sleep with her?"

He knit his dark brows at me. "Get the fuck out of here."

"But—"

"But nothing!" he yelled. "Didn't you hear the part where I can't have kids? My ex-wife and I tried for six years! That's why she left me, because I couldn't—" Cap stopped talking abruptly, gritting his teeth and looking away.

I said quietly, "Look, all I know is this: in August of 1988, a guy named Tony in Gala, Wyoming conceived a child with my mother. Maybe it was you, maybe it wasn't, although I have to say, it sure sounds like it might have been you. I know you say it's impossible, but hell, maybe that was your one and only viable sperm or something. Who knows?"

He looked at me again with raw anger in his eyes. "I'm so fucking sick of people like you coming to me with their hands out. I wish I'd never gotten that damn inheritance. Since then, it's been this ongoing procession of fake long-lost aunts and cousins and uncles, all wanting a piece of the pie, not to mention half the residents of Gala with their sob stories, expecting me to cut 'em a check just because they said please. Claiming to be my son is a new all-time low, though. I wanted a kid more than I wanted anything in my entire life, you asshole. But it's *not fucking possible!*"

"Look, if you need a paternity test, I'll do that gladly because I'd love to know the truth."

"Just get the fuck out!" He yelled that at the top of his lungs and came at me from behind the bar.

Finn cut him off, stepping in front of me and putting his hands up palms out. He said in a voice that resonated authority, "I need you to step back and calm down, sir."

"I'll calm down when you and that fucking lying gold-digger get the fuck out of my bar!"

Finn pulled two business cards from the pocket of his t-shirt and placed them on a table beside him as he said, "One of those cards tells you who I am, my cellphone's on the back. The other is where we're staying, room three-twelve. We're going to be in town a couple more days. Once you've had a chance to calm down and realize not everyone's interested in your fucking money, you should come see us."

Finn's voice dropped a couple octaves as he added, "But when you do, I expect you to treat Chance with respect. He drove all the way here from California, not for your goddamn money but because he wanted the opportunity to meet the asshole who knocked up his mom. I don't know if that's you, but it's easy enough to do a paternity test and find out. I'll even pay for it. If you decide that's too much trouble, you're going to miss out on getting to know the sweetest, kindest, most genuine person you'll ever meet, and believe me when I say, that is your fucking loss."

Finn put his arm around my shoulders and we left the bar. When we got in the car, I said, "Thank you for stepping in."

"I just wish I could have done more."

He started the engine and pulled out of the parking lot, and then I exclaimed, "Shit, I'm sorry. I just realized I outed you back there. I called you my boyfriend. It won't happen again, I promise. I'll be so careful when we get back home."

"It's okay. I actually loved hearing you say that," he said quietly.

"Still, though. I'll watch myself."

We drove in silence for a few minutes. Eventually, he said, "I really respect the fact that you're so upfront about your sexuality. That man could potentially be your father, and you told him you had a boyfriend with no hesitation."

"If he's going to reject me, he might as well reject all of me. I wasn't going to hide who I am. If he has a problem with the fact that I'm gay, it's just that, his problem, not mine," I said as I watched the landscape roll by. This part of the state was a lot greener than where I'd grown up. It was kind of nice, actually.

Finn fell silent again for a while. When he took the exit for our hotel, he said, "You should eat something. What do you want for lunch?"

"I can't eat right now, my stomach's in knots. Let's get you something, though. You have to be hungry."

He drove us to a sandwich shop and ordered way too much food, then told me when I glanced at him, "There's a mini-fridge in our room. It'll keep."

Once we were back in our motel room, Finn drew me into his arms. I clutched him tightly and asked, "Do you think that guy might actually be my dad? He didn't come out and say he slept with my mom, but that seemed to be the implication."

"No real way of knowing unless he agrees to a test."

I played over what had happened at the bar and my stomach twisted itself up even tighter. I hated confrontation, always had. "What do we do now?"

"Now we give it a couple days," he said. "See what develops." I nodded and he kissed my forehead before sitting down to eat.

While Finn polished off a foot-long sub, I borrowed his phone, pushed my shoes off and sat cross-legged on one of the beds. A search under the name Antonio Asturias produced some interesting results. "Find anything?" Finn asked.

"Yeah. There's an almost two-year-old article from the local paper about Tony. Cap. Whatever. When he first got his inheritance, he bought a firetruck and donated it to the Gala volunteer fire department." I expanded the grainy black and white photo, which showed Tony standing in front of a small truck with three other men.

"A fire truck? That must have cost a fortune."

"It wasn't a huge ladder truck, but yeah. The article says it cost three hundred thousand dollars. It kind of looks like a big ambulance." I scanned the article and said, "Listen to this: Asturias, a lifelong resident of Gala, received an inheritance of nearly one million dollars from an uncle he'd never met. When asked what he planned to do with the rest of his money, Asturias said he was in the process of buying Washington's Bar, as well as making a donation to the Gala Elementary School library so they could purchase new books." I looked up at Finn and said, "This Tony sounds a hell of a lot nicer than the one we met."

"Yeah, no kidding."

I read the rest of the article and said, "That's interesting. The reporter got a few quotes from local residents, and some strayed pretty far from the topic of the firetruck. A couple of them had opinions about Tony buying the bar, since he's a recovering alcoholic. Gotta love small town reporting. Simone's paper was always like that too, as much opinion and gossip as actual news."

There was one more, slightly older article, written when Tony first found out about his inheritance. It said he'd been working off and on as a handyman and included an interview, which basically consisted of Tony saying he was shocked a dozen different ways. That article also mentioned he'd been a star pitcher on his high school's team before a shoulder injury dashed his chances for a scholarship. It concluded with reactions from a few town residents, the majority of which again mentioned the fact that he was a recovering alcoholic. I read the article to Finn and then said, "From town drunk to its wealthiest resident. This guy's certainly colorful, I'll give him that."

Finn had finished his lunch by that point and put the rest of the food away when I told him I still didn't want to eat. He propped himself up behind me on the bed and I rested my head on his thigh as I flipped through the online paper. As I did that, he gently stroked my hair. After a while, I forgot about the news and said softly, "I love this. It feels so good just to be with you."

"Same here."

When I closed the internet browser, I glanced at his screen and told him, "You have several texts from Shea."

"I know."

I turned my head to look at Finn, who was frowning slightly. "What's going on?"

"Nothing."

"Yes there is. Did you two have an argument?"

"No, nothing like that," he told me.

"Something's up, though. I can tell by your tone of voice," I said.

"Shea's just worried about me. Obviously for no reason, since I'm fine."

I sat up and turned to face him. "Why is he worried about you?"

Finn hesitated for a long moment, chewing on his lower lip. Finally he said, "Promise not to make a big deal of this."

"I can't really promise that, since I have no idea what 'this' is."

He sighed and told me, "I kind of…quit my job."

"What? Why?"

"My captain wouldn't give me the time off on short notice."

"So you *quit*?"

"Well, technically, I got fired. I explained to him that I had to go, because a friend of mine was in trouble and needed my help. I also pointed out that I worked a ton of overtime and hadn't taken a vacation day in over three years, so I was due for some time off. He was mad about the short notice, but I couldn't keep arguing with him because I had a plane to catch. I told him this was something I needed to do, and then I hung up on him," Finn said. "According to my coworkers, most of whom called or texted me after that, the captain was furious. He's really not the type of person you hang up on. Someone called my brother and he's worried about me, but I don't know what to tell him. I already texted him and said I was fine, but he wants to know what I'm doing, and I don't know how to explain us to him without coming out of the closet."

"Finn, you love your job. How could you do that?"

"This was so much more important."

"What are you going to do?"

"Well, the good news is, I have a shitload of savings. I'll be fine until I figure something out."

"You mean your house money?" He nodded and I said, "Oh God. I ended up costing you your dream after all." Finn grinned a little and I asked, "What?"

"If I was a different kind of man, I'd point out that all I did was swap one dream for another, being with you instead of buying a house. That's a huge upgrade as far as dreams go." His grin widened and he said, "But I can't say something that sappy. I'd feel like a total dork."

I climbed onto his lap, straddling his hips as I put my arms around his shoulders. "You're an amazingly sweet man, Finn, but you can't keep sacrificing so much for me."

He rested his forehead against mine. "It's no sacrifice."

I played with the soft, short hair at the back of his neck and said, "You need to call your brother."

"I will, tomorrow. I just need to figure out what to tell him first." He tilted his head a bit and rubbed my nose with his.

"Okay, tomorrow. Promise?" I kissed him lightly.

"I promise," he said and kissed me again. "Right after we go through the town records and see if we can find any more candidates, in case Asturias is a dead-end."

"What do you think we should do between now and then?"

He gave me a lopsided smile and said, "This," before he brushed his lips to mine.

Chapter Fourteen

Christine Hanson was a big help, both with searching the town records, as well as accompanying us to a few local businesses and asking questions. We spent all day pursuing every idea we could come up with, but that didn't produce any new candidates. It was entirely possible that the man my mother had met had been passing through just like she was, but Asturias' admission that he remembered her made me think I'd found who I was looking for, especially once we exhausted all other possibilities.

Hanson also accompanied us to the town doctor's office. She told him my story and convinced him to do a paternity test, even after he insisted that Asturias couldn't father children. He finally relented and took a quick sample from me. "I'll go by Washington's and see if I can convince Cap to come in and give a sample," Christine told us. "He's stubborn as hook, but maybe he's a little curious, too."

When we were back out on the sidewalk in front of the doctor's office, we both shook hands with Christine and thanked her for her help. "It was my pleasure," she said. "I don't get to do much investigating on the job, but this came close. I hope you find your dad, Chance."

"Thanks. I kind of think I already did, but unless Asturias agrees to get tested, we'll never know."

We got back in the car and Finn pointed it east, toward Gillette. I stared out the window for a while before murmuring, "How weird would that be if Asturias turned out to be my dad? That would mean I found him on my first try. It'd also mean he went absolutely nowhere in all that time, he was still right where my mother met him. That's kind of sad."

"I really hope he goes in for the paternity test."

"I bet he won't, though. He was sure it was impossible, since the doctors told him he couldn't have kids. But I can't shake the feeling that it's him."

"Doctors can be wrong about all kinds of things. And with something like infertility, maybe it's not so black and white, a clear yes or no. Maybe his chances of conceiving were one in a million, but that's still a chance."

"I'm pretty aptly named in that case." Finn drove past our exit and I asked, "Where are we going?"

"I'm taking you on a field trip," he said with a little grin.

"What kind of field trip?"

"You'll see." I grinned too and laced my fingers with his on the center console.

A few minutes past Gillette, I read a road sign and said, "Devils Tower. Is that where we're going?"

"Yup. I was reading up on Wyoming on my phone when I was killing time in Salt Lake City and found out it's only an hour from Gillette. I've always wanted to see it, ever since the movie Close Encounters. Have you ever been there?"

"No. I've actually seen very little of my home state."

Finn pulled over a few minutes later at a gas station with a general store. I used the restroom while he filled the tank, and then we both went into the market, because he wanted to put together a picnic for dinner. He got a selection of items from the small deli counter, then embarrassedly put some lube and condoms in his basket. As we walked through the store, he threw a few miscellaneous items in the basket and asked me if I wanted anything in particular, but I shook my head.

There was a souvenir section near the door, and he selected a wool blanket with "Wyoming' woven into the design. He then picked up a little brown teddy bear wearing a Wyoming t-shirt and said, "Want to get B.B. a friend? We can relieve him of his t-shirt if you're sick of all the reminders of your ill-fated road trip."

"Actually, ever since you showed up, this trip has been great," I said. He smiled shyly and put the bear in the basket.

When we went to check out, the young guy working the cash register smirked at Finn when he got to the lube and condoms. Finn looked away embarrassedly. But when the cashier tried to smirk at me, I stared him down unflinchingly until he squirmed uncomfortably and went back to ringing up our purchases. Then it was my turn to smirk.

*****

Since we'd spent all day in Gala, it was late afternoon when we reached the National Monument. "Holy crap, look at that," Finn exclaimed when we got out of the car near the visitor center, which had closed for the day. He looked so cute with his sparkling blue eyes and his lips parted in awe.

"Beautiful," I mumbled.

Finn glanced at me and said, "You're not even looking at it."

"I found something better to look at," I said, and he grinned at me, took hold of my shoulders, and turned me to face Devils Tower.

It was pretty impossible not to be awed by the twelve hundred foot monolith that jutted out of the surrounding countryside. "That's just surreal," I said. "I've seen a million pictures, but to see the real thing is kind of mind-boggling."

Finn retrieved our picnic and the blanket from the backseat and we headed off on a hiking trail. A few people were heading back to the parking lot, but we seemed to be the only ones heading in. We walked for quite a while, until Finn said, "Hang on a minute, I'm going to scout a dinner location," and then disappeared into the bushes. He was back a few moments later, and said, "Follow me."

I pushed some branches out of the way and said, "I think we're going to get in trouble for straying off the marked path. Can rangers arrest people?"

"It'll be fine," he said as we emerged in a little clearing. He spread the wool blanket on the ground and we both settled down on it.

When I looked up, I exclaimed, "Oh wow." We had a great view of Devils Tower, and the sun was beginning to set. It was so stunningly beautiful that I murmured, "All of a sudden, I feel like I'm in a movie."

"Me too. I keep expecting Richard Dreyfus to run past and a big alien spaceship to rise up over the tower."

"Not Close Encounters," I said softly. "A romance. I've never been on a real date before, but here I am having a picnic at sunset with a gorgeous guy in this incredible setting, and it just doesn't feel real. My life is never like this."

"Shit," Finn whispered. When I looked at him he said, "I'm so damn sorry it took me this long to take you on a date. I totally blew it, all summer long. You deserved so much more, and I want you to know I'm going to try my damnedest to make it up to you."

"You don't have to make anything up to me. I loved this summer and our time together. Those nights at the Whitman were the best of my life."

Finn slid close and brushed his lips to mine, and arousal flared in me like a struck match. We stretched out on the blanket, kissing as we caressed each other, and after a while he pulled back to look at me and asked hesitantly, "Do you, um, have any interest in topping me?"

"If that's what you want, sure."

"But is that what *you* want?"

"I…never really thought about it," I admitted. My cock seemed fully on board with that idea, though, judging by the way it was swelling and throbbing. I grinned shyly and placed his hand on the bulge in my jeans.

Finn let out a low, "Mmmm," and rubbed me through the denim before slipping his hand under my belt and tracing a circle on the head of my cock. "I've been thinking about this a lot," he said, his voice low. "The idea used to really freak me out, but I feel so good with you. You're the only person I could possibly do this with."

"Are you sure you want to do it out here? We're kind of exposed."

"Nobody'll find us here, and I don't want to wait any longer. I've been thinking about it for such a long time, including all day today. I even, um, prepared myself this morning." He couldn't look at me as he said that.

I distracted him from his embarrassment by kissing him, long and hard. A warm breeze stirred the brush around us and felt good on my bare skin when I stripped myself. I undressed him next, then found the lube and used it to work him open, taking my time. His opening was tight and warm around my fingers, and he looked so sexy as he laid back on the blanket and spread his legs for me. I tasted his mouth as I fingered him, and when I stroked his prostate he moaned against my lips.

When I thought he was ready, I eased my fingers from him and wiped my hand on a wet-wipe from a plastic canister that he'd thought to bring along, then prepped myself with a condom and lube. I instructed him to push back as I sank into him slowly. He winced a couple times, but begged me to keep going when I asked if he wanted to stop.

Eventually, I was able to start moving in him, thrusting carefully. "Oh fuck," he rasped as I grazed his prostate, relaxing under me as pleasure edged out discomfort. I felt him open up a bit as he relaxed, and I picked up my pace, sliding in and out of him with shallow movements.

It took a while for me to relax too and just enjoy myself. I could only do that once I knew he was okay. We held each other's gaze as I began taking him harder and faster. I watched his every reaction, looking for signs of distress, but saw only bliss. His cock was rock-hard between us, and I reached down and stroked him as I sank deep into him, my other arm sliding under his head to act as a pillow. "Oh God yes," he whispered as I bottomed out in him.

We were both being quiet, which was a good thing since we suddenly heard voices. Finn and I froze as a large party walked down the path we'd been on, heading in the direction of the parking lot. I glanced over my shoulder and could see the beams from their flashlights through the foliage. They were only about twenty feet away when they passed us, but we were well-concealed by the bushes.

I looked at Finn, expecting him to be a bit freaked out, but he just smiled at me, his eyes crinkling in the corners. I thrust slowly, sliding all the way into him, then pulling out almost to the tip. I did a couple more slow-motion thrusts before the group was out of earshot, our eyes locked on each other. We then both held still for a moment and listened as Finn ran his hands down my back and cupped my ass.

Once I was sure we wouldn't be discovered, I kissed him deeply and smiled at him, then picked up my pace, fucking him hard and fast. In just a couple minutes, he bit his lip to keep from moaning and arched his back, then shot all over his stomach and chest, his cock twitching in my grasp. After a few more quick thrusts I came too, fighting to keep from crying out. I pushed into him as deep as I could, his ass squeezing my cock as I unloaded in him.

It was so incredibly intense that I was shaking by the time it was over. I laid down on top of him, trying to bear my weight on my knees and elbows, and Finn hugged me as we both caught our breath. "You okay?" I whispered when I could speak again.

"Oh yeah." I reached down and held the condom in place as I eased myself from his body, then looked at him closely in the fading light and chuckled softly. "What?" he asked.

"You just look so happy. It's cute."

"I *am* happy," he said. "Happier than I've ever been, and not because I just lost the last vestige of my virginity. I can't believe this is my life right now, it's so utterly unlike me!"

"What is?"

"All of it. I was always the guy who worked constantly, saved my money, played by the rules, and did what everyone expected of me. I never, ever rocked the boat. And it was fucking *exhausting*. But look where I am right now! I'm buck naked next to freaking Devils Tower with a sexy, naked guy in my arms! Me! Finn Nolan! Good old, reliable, predictable, uptight, totally boring Finn. I never even knew it was possible to be this happy."

I smiled and kissed him. "It looks good on you."

We cleaned up with the wet-wipes and remained naked while we had our picnic. Finn set the little bear beside us on the blanket, and we sat cross-legged with our heads almost touching, enjoying our little feast. He'd bought way too much food as usual, but we ended up eating almost all of it.

I was startled when Finn's phone rang. "Good thing that didn't happen when those people were walking by," he said with a smile before answering it. The call was from Christine Hanson, who told me, "We found your car, Chance. Someone took it for a joyride out on a fairly deserted country road, crashed it into a ditch, and abandoned it. Sounds like it got pretty banged up. I haven't seen it yet, but it's going to be towed to the police station first thing in the morning. I can meet you there at nine if you want."

"We'll be there. Thanks for calling, Christine." After we hung up, I looked at Finn and said, "I never thought I'd see that car again. I wonder how bad the damage is. I also wonder what the hell we're going to do with a broken-down car."

"I can exchange the rental car for a bigger vehicle, and we can tow the Civic home. I know a couple mechanics in San Francisco, maybe it'll prove to be salvageable."

"I know one, too." I reached for my t-shirt and pulled it over my head, then asked, "What do you suppose the chances are that my stuff is still in the car?"

"Hard to say."

We both got dressed and packed up the remains of our picnic. Then I said, "Wow, look at that."

I'd glanced up at Devils Tower, which was just a big, black silhouette at night. But all around it, the stars had begun to come out. "I haven't seen that many stars since I was a kid," I said as Finn and I leaned against each other and took in the view.

"It's beautiful."

After a minute I asked, "Can we head home by way of southern Wyoming? I want to check on my brother again. I saw him on the way here, like I told you, and there are all these pieces that just won't fall into place. He's keeping a secret from me, and I have a bad feeling about it."

"What kind of secret?"

"I really don't know. When I got there, the house looked like it hadn't been cleaned in months, and he'd been eating nothing but fast food and ramen noodles. He said our mom had been on vacation for a couple weeks, but that just doesn't make sense. She was always a bit of a neat freak, and I can't imagine that she'd let it get that bad."

"Do you think she abandoned him?"

"It's hard to believe, since she always adored Colt. Something's up though, and I want to know what it is. It seems like my brother's barely holding it all together. He's trying to take care of himself and his boyfriend, and…I don't know. I just have to do something."

"His boyfriend?" I told him about Elijah, and Finn said, "Oh yeah, we're definitely heading back there tomorrow. I hate the thought of a couple kids fending for themselves like that."

I grinned and said, "Just don't call them kids to their faces. My brother thinks he's all grown up at sixteen."

Finn laid back on the blanket, picked up the little bear, and held him in the crook of his arm. I curled up beside him, sliding my hand under his t-shirt to rest on his belly. "I'm really glad we came here," he said. "I feel like I'm on vacation."

"Me too, to both."

"Can we stop off and see Yellowstone after we check on your brother?"

"Sure, but it's not on the way. We'll have to make a big 'V' down to Simone and then back up to the northwestern part of the state."

"Fine with me."

"I've always wanted to see Yellowstone," I told him.

"You never did when you were growing up here?"

"Nah. My mom was always working, since she was a single parent. She never took vacations."

"It's surprising that she didn't try to track your father down for child support."

"Well, if that man's Asturias, look at what we know about him. He was an alcoholic who worked 'off and on' as a handyman, which basically means he was unemployed a lot. She must have known there was no point."

"Are you going to try to talk to Asturias one more time before we head out?"

"No point in that either."

We watched the stars for a couple minutes before Finn muttered, "Shit, I was supposed to call my brother today. I almost forgot." He put the bear on my stomach, sat up and pulled his phone from his pocket. "It's earlier in California, I'm going to go ahead and call him now."

He hit a number on speed dial, then put it on speaker. Shea sounded agitated when he answered with, "What the hell's going on, Finn? Where are you? I've left you about a million messages!"

"I know," he said. "I'm sorry. I'm in Wyoming. Chance was in trouble and I needed to get to him ASAP. He's right here, by the way, and you're on speaker." I sat up and raised an eyebrow at Finn.

"Oh! I didn't know you and Chance were friends," his brother said.

Finn took a deep breath before blurting, "We're a lot more than that. Chance and I have been seeing each other since just after your wedding. I told him to keep it quiet, but that's bullshit and I need to be honest with you, Shea. I've been in the closet my whole life. I should have told you years ago, and I'm sorry to be doing this over the phone, but I don't want to keep any more secrets from you." My mouth fell open.

"I kind of always suspected," Shea said.

"You did?"

"Yeah. There were signs."

"Like what?"

"You serial-dated all those girls in high school and college, but it was so obvious to me that you were just going through the motions."

"You're really observant," Finn told him.

"Do Mom and Dad know?"

"Not yet. When I come out to them, I'm going to need a place to stay because you and I both know how it'll go over. Is it okay if I crash with you and Christian for a little while, just until I find my own apartment? I promise not to stay long. You two are newlyweds, so I really don't want to be in the way."

"You can stay as long as you like. Want me to be there when you tell our parents?"

"I think I need to do this on my own. Thanks, though."

Shea asked, "Is everything okay with you, Chance? Hi, by the way."

"Hi Shea. It is now," I said, "thanks to Finn."

"We'll tell you all about it when we get back to the city," Finn said. "Should just be a few days."

"What are you going to do about your job? The captain is livid."

"I don't think there's anything to do. I hung up on him and took leave without permission. I'm sure that cost me my job."

"You were always an exemplary officer, though. If you go see him and apologize when you get back, maybe he'll just issue a formal reprimand and let you return to work," Shea said.

"It's worth a shot. Listen, I'd better go. I'll talk to you soon, Shea. And I'm really sorry I worried you."

"I'm just glad you're okay, and I'm so damn glad you finally came out."

"Me too. It was ridiculously overdue."

The brothers chatted for a minute more before we all said goodbye and Finn disconnected. When he stretched out on the blanket again, I curled up against his side and said, "I can't believe you came out to your brother, just like that!"

"I was so nervous that I thought my heart was going to explode. It really wasn't just like that, though. I'd rehearsed that moment a million times. I kept trying to figure out the perfect time and place to tell him, but ultimately that really didn't matter. I just had to say it, and it felt right in that moment."

"I'm proud of you," I said as I picked up his hand.

"Well, that was the easy part. I always knew Shea would understand. Telling everyone else, that's going to pretty much suck. Still needs to be done, though."

"Why now, after all this time?"

"In part, I'm doing it for us. No more sneaking around, you deserve so much better than that. But I'm doing it for me, too. I'm just so sick of all the lies and pretending. Twenty-eight years in the closet is just way too fucking long."

"I want you to know I'll be there to support you, every step of the way."

He grinned and kissed me before looking back up at the heavens. We were quiet for a while before Finn pointed at the sky and said, "I'm pretty sure that's Saturn. My cousin Kieran is a bit of an astronomy nerd, and he taught me some stuff. I wish I remembered more of it now."

I stared at the little speck of light he'd indicated and whispered as I squeezed his hand, "I like it so much better here."

Chapter Fifteen

The Civic rattled behind Finn's rented SUV as we slowly wound our way down the dirt road leading to my mother's house. The front end of the little car had been smashed in when it hit the ditch, but at least it could be towed along on its four wheels. Maybe Jessie could work a miracle when he got home from Italy, once I saved up enough money for replacement parts. I figured it was worth asking, at least.

The thief had missed the money I'd tucked under the driver's seat, and he'd dumped the backpack out in the backseat and rummaged through its contents, which he left behind. But he'd taken my teddy bear and the bag in the trunk containing my expensive camera. I was still cursing myself for having brought them along in the first place.

My phone rang and I picked it up and looked at Zachary's name on the screen. I'd plugged it in when I'd retrieved the cable from my backpack and found I had a couple texts from him, so I'd left him a voicemail with a quick overview of my trip. "Hey," I said when I answered.

"Hi. Are you really okay?"

"I'm fine. We're almost to my mom's house. Once we get things sorted out here, we're going to spend a day or two in Yellowstone and then head home. I'll be seeing you soon," I told him.

"Who's this guy that you said flew out to help you?"

"His name's Finn. I'll tell you about him when I get back."

"Can you trust him?" my friend asked.

"With my life."

"I miss you. I'll be glad when you're home."

"I miss you too, Zachary. How've you been?"

"You know, same as ever. I'd better let you go. Be safe."

"I will."

When we disconnected, I sighed and Finn asked, "Everything okay?"

"I guess. I always worry about Zachary. He never says much, but I think he gets really lonely. I'll be glad when I'm back and can check on him." Finn gave my hand a quick squeeze, then grabbed the wheel with both hands and tried to dodge a particularly deep pothole. The big SUV and its beat-up cargo both rattled loudly.

When we pulled up in front of the house, we waited for the dust to settle. Two faces peered at us through the dirty front window to the left of the door. After a minute we got out of the SUV and Colt came out onto the porch. He was dressed in the same ratty gym shorts as the last time I'd seen him, and nothing else.

"Why'd you come back?" he asked, then looked Finn over from head to toe. "And who's this guy?"

"This is my boyfriend, Finn Nolan. Finn, Colt Matthews. I came back because I needed to make sure you're okay."

"I'm fine." Colt glanced over my shoulder. "What happened to your car?"

"Somebody stole it and took it for a joyride. The police found it in a ditch."

"That sucks. I really am fine though, so you didn't need to come all the way back here."

I stepped onto the porch, stopping about four feet from my brother. "I have to ask you something, and I need an honest answer. What's going on? I don't buy your story that mom's only been gone a couple weeks. Did she take off and leave you to fend for yourself?" I tried to look him in the eye, but he avoided my gaze. "Just talk to me, Colt. Please? If Mom abandoned you, I can help."

"She didn't abandon me," he exclaimed. "She wouldn't do that! Mama loved me!"

"Oh God," I said, catching the past tense. "Did something happen to her?"

"Shit!" He tried to run past me, but I caught him by the shoulders.

"Colt, did something happen to Mom?"

"Please go away! I'm fine! I've got it all under control."

"You really don't," I said, still holding him gently by his bony shoulders. "And you don't have to. You're sixteen years old, Colt. Whatever's going on, you don't have to deal with it alone."

He started crying and said again, "Please go away."

I drew him into a hug which he didn't return, his body rigid in my arms as I asked, "What happened to her?"

He was sobbing now, and choked out, "I'm sorry I didn't tell you. I know it was wrong not to. Please don't put me in foster care, Chance! I couldn't stand it if you did that. I'd run away! Please?"

Dread settled in my stomach like a lead weight. "Colt, is mom dead?" He nodded against my shoulder. I felt sick. "How?"

He took a couple deep breaths and said, his voice choppy, "She went on vacation with her boyfriend. He rides a motorcycle. They went to Ohio to visit some friends, like I told you before, but they had an accident. Mama was killed instantly." He started sobbing again and put his arms around me.

I drew in my breath and rubbed his back. I couldn't begin to process what he'd just told me. It was just too overwhelming, too unexpected. It was a full minute before I had the wherewithal to ask, "When did this happen?"

"Right before Thanksgiving."

"You've been on your own for nine months?" He nodded again and I hugged him tighter. "You should have called me right away."

"I'm sorry." Colt stepped back from me, wiping his eyes with the back of his hand.

He took several ragged breaths and I said, "Come on. Let's get you a glass of water." Colt led the way into the house.

Elijah backed away from us as we came inside. "You told him," Elijah said to Colt. "You swore you wouldn't. How could you tell him, Colt?"

"I had to," my brother said. "She was his mom too. He had a right to know."

"You ruined everything," the little blond yelled. "They're not going to let us keep living here, and I'm not going into the system! No fucking way!"

"You're not, I promise," I said. Elijah was still backing away from us, into the kitchen.

"Why the hell should I believe you?"

"Because I love my brother, and he loves you. I'm going to help you."

Elijah shook his head. "You're lying. Grown-ups always lie!" He spun around and bolted through the back door, and Colt took off after him.

"Elijah, wait!" Colt yelled. His boyfriend was wearing sneakers and sprinted across the rough terrain easily, heading out into the barren landscape. When my brother tried to follow, he stepped on something sharp and fell to his knees with a little wail.

He scrambled back to his feet and tried to keep moving, but I caught up to him and said, "You can't run after him, Colt. You're hurt."

"Come back!" he yelled, still trying to limp after his boyfriend. Elijah was some distance away by that point and just kept running.

Finn had followed us out the back door and said, "I'll go after him." He took off at a dead sprint. I was surprised by how fast he could move.

I told Colt, "Come on. We need to go inside and get you cleaned up."

"I'm fine," he said, still trying to follow even though his right foot was dripping blood onto the dirt and he could barely put his toes on the ground.

"No you're not." I got in front of him and took hold of his shoulders again. "If that cut gets infected, you're really screwed. Just let Finn handle it. He's a police officer and really good in a crisis. He'll get Elijah back here."

"Shit. He's a cop? Elijah hates cops, he'll never come back with him."

"Finn will handle it, you'll see. If your foot gets infected, you'll end up in the hospital. Then how will you take care of your boyfriend, or yourself for that matter?" He swore under his breath but didn't fight me as I put an arm around him and helped him back to the house.

Once in the kitchen, he sat on the counter beside the sink and we rinsed his foot. He'd managed to grind a lot of dirt into the cut on his instep and I kept the water running over it as I went in search of some first aid supplies. I was surprised that I remembered their location.

When his foot was patched up, I helped him to the couch and said, "I'll bring you a sock to put on, it'll keep the bandages clean and dry."

I started to head to his bedroom but he said, "I, uh, don't have any clean socks. I've been meaning to do laundry."

"I'll wash some, then. Don't get up."

I grabbed an armload of smelly clothes from the floor of his bedroom and carried them to the laundry room off the kitchen while Colt watched me sheepishly. "You don't have to do that," he called.

"I know."

The avocado-green appliances were the same ones I remembered from my childhood. It was kind of a miracle that they were still running, and no less miraculous that my brother had actually thought to buy detergent at some point. I got a load going and returned to the living room. Colt was standing on one foot by the window, staring out in the direction that Elijah had gone.

I dropped onto the sagging couch and said, "Tell me what happened to Mom. How did she die?"

My brother turned to look at me and leaned against the windowsill. "She was on the back of her boyfriend Pete's motorcycle when a big RV cut into their lane. Pete wrecked the bike trying to dodge it. He said mom died instantly, and he ended up with two broken legs. They were somewhere outside Cincinnati when it happened."

"Didn't Pete try to help you?"

"I didn't want him to. I lied to him and told him I could move in with a friend's family. He was relieved. It's not like he wanted to deal with me. He wasn't a bad guy or anything, but he and Mama had only been going out about four months and I knew he didn't want the responsibility of figuring out what to do with me after she died."

"What happened to her body?"

"Pete paid to have her cremated and he sent her remains to me. That's what that box is over on the mantel." I felt a little nauseous as I glanced at the taped-up cardboard box with a hand-addressed mailing label. I wondered if the postal service had any idea what they'd delivered. "I didn't really know what to do with it." I didn't either. Colt pivoted a wooden chair to face the window, glancing at me as he sat down on it. "You're taking the news really well. I had no idea how you'd react."

"I'm completely numb," I admitted. I looked around the dusty living room. The empty ramen bowl collection had started to build back up again. "Do you eat those noodles three meals a day?" I asked idly.

"No."

"Because you don't eat three meals a day?"

He nodded, craning his neck to look out the window. "It's hard to make a thousand dollars last all month, so we skip breakfast. Those noodles are really good, though. They're always on sale at the Gas-n-Go by the highway, two-for-a-dollar, and they fill you up. We go and buy all they have twice a month. It really stretches our budget." He turned to look at me and said, "Do you think that SUV could go off-roading? Maybe we can drive after them. I'd take the truck, but the engine wouldn't turn over when I tried to drive it yesterday."

"The ground's way too rocky, we'd break the SUV is a matter of minutes. Just trust that Finn will handle it. There's no way he'd let anything happen to Elijah."

Colt glanced at me again and asked, "How long has he been your boyfriend?"

"Not long. We'd been seeing each other all summer, but things got serious between us this past week. I kind of fell apart after my car got stolen with all my stuff in it, and he dropped everything and came to help me."

My brother considered that for a minute, then turned back to the window. "He sounds like a good guy."

"He really is."

We were quiet for a while, before Colt said, "What are you going to do now that you know Mama's gone? I meant what I said about not going into the system. I'll run away before I let that happen, and I'll take Elijah with me."

"Why would you think that's even an option? You're my family, Colt, and I'm going to take care of you."

"You're not going to let me stay here and keep doing what I've been doing though, are you?"

"Definitely not. All of this would be too much responsibility for an adult, let alone a teenager."

"I really hate it when people treat me like a kid," he grumbled.

"That's not what I'm doing."

I got up and went out the back door, then just stood outside for a while, staring into the distance. Tears spilled down my cheeks, but I quickly brushed them away. There would be time to mourn later. For now I needed to hold it together. There was so much to figure out.

A gentle touch on my shoulder startled me, and I turned to look at my brother. He had tears in his eyes, too. "I'm so sorry I didn't tell you right when it happened," he said. I pulled him into a hug and his thin body shook as the crying started up again. "I miss her so much," he whispered. "I was so scared when Mama died. I didn't know what to do."

"I wish you'd called me right away. But at least I know now, and I'm going to help you, Colt. Do you want to come to San Francisco with me, you and Elijah?"

He let go and took a step back so he could look at me. "Are you actually giving me a choice?"

I nodded. "I'm not going to try to tell you what to do. It's your life. But the only other option I can see is me moving back here, and I really don't want to do that. I have no idea how I'd support us in Simone. I'd move back anyway and we'd figure things out, but it would be a lot harder, so I really hope you'll consider coming to California with me."

Colt wiped his eyes with both hands and said, "I hate Simone. I hate it so fucking much. Sorry about the bad language. I'll have to talk to Elijah and see what he thinks, but I'd love to get out of here. Isn't it going to be weird for you, though? You and I barely know each other. Do you really want me living in your apartment?"

I had no idea how we'd all fit in my tiny studio until I could afford something bigger, but that didn't matter. I nodded and said, "I'm glad I'll finally have a chance to get to know you, Colt. I've missed out on so much of your life."

He wiped his nose with the back of his hand and said, "I can help pay rent and stuff. I'll get a job at McDonald's or something. I bet if I do that I'll even get a discount on the food, so that'll help, too."

"I just want you to concentrate on school. You just finished your sophomore year, right?" Colt looked away, and I said, "Shit. Please tell me you didn't drop out."

"I had to. It was just too much after Mama died. I was all alone at first, before I met Elijah, and I kinda fell apart for a while there."

"So, the first thing we'll do when we get to San Francisco is enroll you in school for this fall, both you and Elijah. What grade is he in?"

"He'd be going into his junior year, too," Colt said. "We're the same age. We both missed most of our sophomore year though. Do you think they'll make us do it over?"

"I think they'll probably give you some tests to see which grade you belong in, since you're moving to a new state and a whole new school system."

Colt considered that and said, "Elijah needs to go back to school. He's really smart. I'm just gonna try to find a job though, so I can help us make ends meet."

"No way. You're getting your high school diploma, Colt. That's not negotiable."

He frowned at me. "It's just a piece of paper. No one cares. I know it's gonna be hard for you to afford a bigger place, but if I'm workin' full time, I can help out financially."

"Let me worry about the money, Colt. That's my job. Yours is getting an education."

His frown deepened. "You're treatin' me like a kid again."

"No I'm not. I'm just saying you need to go to school."

"But you dropped out your freshman year and it didn't affect you any. You still got a job that pays enough for you to send a thousand bucks home every month! Why can't I do the same thing?"

"No way, Colt," I exclaimed. "That is not happening! You're going to finish high school, and then I'm going to figure out how to pay for college. I'm going to do everything in my power to make sure you have a good life and that you don't end up like me!"

"What does that mean? How did you end up? It looks like you're doin' pretty good from where I'm sitting."

"I'm not. I had to do some awful things to survive, things I'm not proud of. Almost twelve years later, I'm still doing them because I have almost no options. Getting your diploma will open doors, and getting a college education will open even more. You're going to do better than me, Colt. You just are. And there's no point in arguing with me, because I'm never, ever going to change my mind about you going to school."

My brother watched me for a long moment, and then he asked, "How'd you survive, Chance? You left home at fourteen. You already told me the Taco Bell job was bullshit. Tell me the truth." I looked away, and he said softly, "Are you a prostitute? I can see why you wouldn't want to tell me that, but it's the only thing I can think of. I know what happens to runaways, I'm not totally ignorant. Is that what happened to you?"

I couldn't look at my brother, but I gave him a single nod. As much as I'd always wanted to shelter him from the truth, I also needed him to understand the reality. "Now do you see why you need to go back to school? It's so damn hard to get by in this world, and an education can be your ticket to a better life. I need that for you, Colt."

He flung his skinny arms around me and hugged me tightly. "I'm so damn sorry, Chance," he choked out.

"What are you apologizing for?"

"For taking your money all these years. Now that I know what you had to do for it, I feel terrible."

"No. Don't go there," I said. "The things I did were my choice, and I would have done them even without sending money home. I needed to survive and that was the only way I could do it."

He pulled back to look at me. "I'll make you a deal. I'll go back to school with no arguments if you do, too. I don't know how people get those high school equivalency diplomas, but I want you to find out."

I grinned a little. "You're negotiating with me? Really?"

Colt grinned too and nodded. "You just got done telling me how important it is to get an education. You don't want to be a hypocrite, do ya?"

"I'm already going to have a hell of a lot on my plate when we get back to San Francisco. I don't know if I can handle any more."

"You're making excuses."

"How about if I promise to look into it? That's the best I can do right now."

"Fine. I'm gonna make sure you follow through, though," Colt said.

"All of a sudden, I feel like I'm taking in a parent, not a sibling," I told him with a smile.

"I keep tellin' ya I'm not a kid. I'm gonna be seventeen in a few months! I didn't think I needed you to take care of me, but really, maybe we both need to take care of each other. I think that could work out real good."

"You're right." I glanced over his shoulder and said, "We also need to take care of those two."

Colt turned his head and yelled, "Elijah!" when he spotted his boyfriend, then took off running with a limping gait. He'd put on sneakers before he came outside, and since they were absolutely filthy, I made a mental note to check his cut later.

I followed my brother at a brisk walk, picking my way around the rough terrain, and he reached Elijah a minute before I reached Finn and grabbed him in an embrace. I too took my boyfriend in my arms, and Finn said, "I'm really gross and sweaty."

"I don't care." I kissed him and said, "Thank you for doing that."

"Of course."

As we walked back to the house, the boys fell in step beside us and Colt told Finn, "Dude, you can really haul ass for a big guy."

I looked up at my boyfriend and said, "He's not wrong."

"I stay in shape by training and competing in triathlons," Finn told me.

"Explains a lot," I said with a smile.

"I'm sorry I ran off like that," Elijah softly said as we neared the house. He was hugging Colt's arm with both of his and told him, "I really didn't mean to leave you behind. I just kinda panicked."

"Did everything get straightened out?" I asked.

Elijah shrugged, looking at the ground, and Finn said, "We had a good talk once he ran out of steam. I promised him that no one's getting put in the system. I think we reached an understanding."

When we got inside, Finn and I went upstairs so he could get cleaned up. He pulled me into another embrace once we were in my room, kissed my forehead and said, "I'm so incredibly sorry about your mom, Chance."

"Thanks. It still doesn't feel real." I buried my face in his chest and whispered, "What the hell am I going to do, Finn? How am I going to take care of those two boys? I'm barely keeping my head above water."

"You're not going to take care of them, *we* are. You aren't in this alone."

I looked up at him and said, "You and I just started going out. There's no way you should have to take on that kind of responsibility."

"You've meant everything to me for months, so it's a technicality to say we've just begun going out. Besides, I love kids and want to help those boys. I know we can really turn things around for them." I wished I shared his optimism.

Chapter Sixteen

Colt looked at me uncertainly. "Do you think we'll ever come back here?"

"Sure," I told him, "if you want to."

We'd spent a day and a half going through the house and packing up what we wanted to take with us. The Honda was full of boxes, and so was the trunk of the SUV. Mostly, we'd packed Colt's belongings, but I brought along some keepsakes from my room, the photo albums, and a few things that had sentimental value for my brother and me. On a more practical note, Colt also loaded the trunk of the Civic with his stash of ramen noodles and canned goods. He really was a survivor.

We'd also packed two big file boxes stuffed with papers that had been in our mom's closet, so I could somehow begin the process of closing out her estate. I had no idea what needed to be done when someone died, but I could learn. We didn't know what to do with our mom's clothes and the rest of her things, so we'd just left them in place.

The four of us finished off by cleaning the house. We got rid of all the trash to try to avoid a rodent invasion while the house stood empty. I really didn't know when or if we'd ever come back here, but I wanted to leave it in good condition.

The last thing I did was pick up the cardboard box with my mother's remains. I carried it to the Civic and set it in the driver's seat, then put on the seatbelt to keep it safe. A lump formed in my throat, and I swallowed hard as I closed and locked the door of my beat-up little car.

Colt had followed me out of the house, locking up behind me, and we stood out front looking at the only home he'd ever known. He put the keys in his pocket, then turned to me and asked, "What about Colt, Junior?"

"The coyote?"

My brother nodded, his eyes full of grief. "We're leaving him all alone. Do you think he's going to be alright?"

"He'll be fine. He's a survivor, just like the guy he's named for. You really don't need to worry about him."

My brother chewed his lower lip for a moment, then mumbled, "Okay," and crossed the grassless front yard. He went to take Elijah's hand, but his boyfriend put his arms around him instead, holding my brother tight and looking up at him for reassurance. Colt put on a show of confidence and said, "This is going to be such a good thing, Eli, just you wait and see. Remember how you told me you always wanted to see California and the Pacific Ocean? You're finally going to get that chance." Elijah nodded and hugged him tighter.

Finn came around from the back of the house and said, "I shut off the water and power at the main breaker and made sure the fire was out in the trash barrel. The back door and all the windows are locked, is everything secure in the front?"

"Yeah. I think we're set."

The four of us climbed into the SUV with Finn behind the wheel and the boys huddled against each other in the backseat. As we pulled away, Colt pivoted around and watched the house through the cloud of dust we kicked up. When he turned back around, he swallowed hard, his Adam's apple bobbing up and down. Fear and uncertainty showed in his eyes for a moment, but when Elijah looked at him, he smiled and put his arm around his boyfriend's shoulders.

*****

Despite all the stress we'd been under, or maybe because of it, we decided to proceed with our plan of visiting Yellowstone before we left Wyoming. It took about seven hours to get there, and it was totally out of the way, but I didn't mind. I wasn't in a hurry to return to the rest of my life.

The drive gave me a lot of time to think, not that I wound up with any answers. I had no clue how I was going to support myself and two teenagers, or how we were all going to live in my tiny studio apartment. I really didn't know what to do about my line of work, either. It didn't exactly make me a good role model, and it was going to get in the way of whatever was happening between Finn and me, I knew that for a fact. But I was going to be desperate for cash very soon, and I didn't know any other way to make that kind of money.

I had to stop thinking about it after a while because I was getting so discouraged, and stared out at the open road to distract myself. Having Finn beside me was a comfort. He wove his fingers with mine as he drove, and I leaned over and rested my head on his shoulder. I'd been worried about giving the boys stability and a sense of security, and I realized that Finn just radiated those things.

He said he'd help me, but why would he want to take on that kind of responsibility? He was going to have enough to deal with when we got home. He was currently unemployed and living at home with his bigoted parents, and if he came out to them, which seemed to be the plan, he'd also be looking for a new place to live. Finn had enough on his plate. I'd have to do what I always did and figure out a way to get by on my own.

*****

I was surprised when we pulled up to the Old Faithful Inn a little before sunset. Finn parked the car and its makeshift trailer in a space made for an RV, and got out and stretched. I got out too and looked at the beautiful, sprawling lodge with its steeply pitched roof. It looked like something out of a movie. I asked, "We're not staying here, are we?"

"We are. I got lucky, they'd had a last minute cancellation when I called last night. Normally they'd be all booked up this time of year."

"But wasn't it expensive?"

"It's not so bad. We have a standard unit in the old part of the lodge, nothing fancy. I figured, since we're just going to spend one day here, why not stay right in the park and really soak it in?" Finn looked happy, and that made me smile.

We all grabbed our backpacks before the boys and I followed Finn into the breathtaking lobby. It was a rustic composition of dark wood and high ceilings, with four tiers of balconies opening around a huge common area dominated by an absolutely enormous rock fireplace.

"Holy shit," Elijah whispered. His eyes were huge as he looked around, and he held on to Colt's arm with both hands.

"This is amazing," my brother said. He turned to Finn and asked, "Are you rich?"

Finn shook his head, a look of amazement on his face as he took in our surroundings. "Not by a long shot," he said, his eyes traveling up the absolutely gigantic fireplace.

After Finn checked in, we dropped our backpacks in our room and headed out to explore. I took my phone out and snapped a few candids of the boys. Elijah was really shy and never let go of Colt, practically hiding behind him as we negotiated the clusters of people outside. They seemed even more childlike in this setting as they reacted to everything with wonder. "Let me get a picture of the three of you," I told my companions, framing up a shot with the lodge in the background.

"Why don't you get in the picture, too?" A voice beside me said.

I turned to look at the older woman with short silver hair and an engaging smile, and said, "Yeah, okay," before handing over my phone.

I stood between Colt and Finn with Elijah on Colt's opposite side, and we all smiled for the camera. The woman took several shots, and when she gave the phone back, she told me, "You have a beautiful family."

"Thank you," I said softly. When she'd gone, I scrolled through the pictures she'd taken. We really did look like a family. A non-traditional one, sure, but no less a family. I stared at the screen for a long moment and smiled before turning to Finn. He took my hand, which surprised me a little since we were in public, but he just grinned at me.

"What's going on over there?" Colt asked, indicating a crowd that was gathering a short distance away.

"Let's go see," I said, and we all went over and joined the crowd. I knew what we were looking at, but the boys didn't so I decided to let them be surprised.

"It's about to happen," someone nearby exclaimed as we found a spot at the edge of the wide walkway.

"Wait for it," I murmured, and winked at Colt when he glanced at me. He turned back around just in time to watch Old Faithful erupt, shooting steam and water a hundred and forty feet into the air.

"Oh my God!" my brother exclaimed as the crowd cheered. Elijah clapped and let out a burst of surprised laughter before grabbing Colt's hand.

Finn looked no less enchanted. He had a huge, delighted smile on his face, his eyes bright and sparkling. I took a few pictures so I could always remember him in that moment of perfect happiness. I snapped a few of the geyser, too, but Finn was more captivating.

The eruption lasted about two minutes, and when it was over, the crowd applauded before beginning to disperse. "I can't believe I just saw Old Faithful!" Colt exclaimed. "I heard about it and saw pictures, like, a billion times, but seeing it for real was epic!" He turned to Finn and said, "Thanks for bringing us here."

"You're welcome. Come on, let's explore a bit before it gets dark," Finn said.

A few people stared at us as we strolled on the walkways through the steaming, bubbling geyser field, since Finn and I were once again holding hands. Fuck 'em. Whenever someone tried to give us a disapproving look, I stared them down, and Finn ignored them. The boys followed our example and held hands, too, and Colt did the same thing I was doing, glaring at anyone that dared look at him judgmentally. He caught me grinning at him at one point, and said, "Finn's really big. If anyone hassles us, he can punch 'em in the face."

Finn chuckled at that. "I could, but I'm not going to."

When it started to get dark, we went to dinner in the lodge's big dining room, which was decorated in the same woodsy style as the rest of the place. I probably looked a little shell-shocked when I saw the prices on the menu, and Finn must have noticed because he said, "Dinner's on me. Order anything you want. That goes for all of you." Colt and Elijah thanked him excitedly, while I mentally added the boys' and my meals to the ever-increasing running total of all I owed Finn.

I just ordered a bowl of soup, but the boys went nuts and ordered a ton of food. After their diet of fast food and ramen I could see why they'd be excited, and I didn't try to discourage them. They were both so skinny, and it was their first real meal in ages.

Somehow, they both polished off dessert after their huge dinners, and then my brother moaned and said, "Oh man, I'm so full that I could pop like a tick! Is it okay if we go lay down in the room?"

"Sure," I said, and handed Colt my key.

Elijah pushed back from the table. He'd said next to nothing throughout the meal, but now he glanced at Finn from under his lashes and said quietly, "Thank you, sir. That was the best meal I ever ate."

"Yeah, thanks," Colt seconded. "That was delicious."

"You don't have to call me sir. I'm just Finn. And you're welcome." Once the boys took off, he said, "They're good kids. Polite."

"Except for the part where my brother said he was going to pop like a tick at the dinner table," I said with a grin.

Finn grinned too. "That's typical." He watched them as they exited the dining room and said, "I feel like I'm being an irresponsible adult for letting them go to the room by themselves, like maybe I should chaperone them or something."

"I know what you mean, but they already lived together for months, totally unsupervised, and already did whatever they're going to do." I took a sip of water, then said, "Colt told me they've messed around but haven't had sex."

"And you believed that?"

"Yeah, because he also told me Elijah was sexually molested when he was younger, so now he has some hard limits."

"Poor kid. It seems really unfair that they've both had so much to deal with in their young lives."

The waiter came by, and Finn ordered some coffee and dessert. To me he said, "I wasn't going to do it, but that cake the boys polished off looked good."

"Well, you might as well enjoy your pseudo-vacation."

"I'm glad we took this detour. I think we all needed it, especially the boys."

The waiter came back with the coffee and a slice of chocolate cake with two forks, and Finn insisted on sharing it with me. We savored it slowly.

After a while Finn said, "I'm kind of surprised Colt told you about Elijah. He's so protective of him, and that was some pretty private information."

"He told me because he suspected something similar had happened to me before I ran away, and was trying to get me to open up to him. He, um...he wasn't wrong," I admitted quietly.

Finn reached across the table and took my hand, and I stared at the white table cloth. "Chance, I'm so sorry," he said softly.

"I've never talked about this. Colt wanted me to, but I just couldn't. I want him to know why I left, but how do I tell my kid brother about something like this? I was sexually abused for over a year, and when I finally told my mom, she didn't believe me. No one did. The man that did those things to me was her boss, a leader in the community, and I was just this punk kid. I got in trouble all the time. I lied, cut school, acted out. So, when I tried to tell the truth, everyone believed him and not me. Even my own mother." I stopped talking and swallowed hard.

"Oh God," Finn whispered, squeezing my hand.

"He ended up firing her shortly after I tried to tell everyone what he did to me. She was his assistant at the biggest employer in town, the natural gas company. He told people he'd caught her stealing, so she couldn't find another job after that. And here's the really pathetic thing: she knew he'd fired her on false pretenses, but she still took his word over mine about the molestation. She told me he must have fired her for the lies I told. Somehow, instead of making her see that he was a liar and a terrible person, it all just came back to me instead." I kept staring at the spot on the tablecloth where my thumbnail was wearing a little groove in the fabric.

"What kind of parent would take a child molester's word over that of their own son?" Finn's voice was choked with anger.

"The whole town believed him. Once I finally decided not to keep the secret anymore, I raised a huge stink about it. I wanted everyone to know, so no other kids would get hurt by him. I even tried to go to the police, but he was a pillar of the community, and like I said, I was just this little delinquent. I wondered in later years if that was why he picked me, because he knew no one would believe me if I decided to speak up. All these people came forward, boys he'd coached in Little League and kids he'd mentored as a youth minister, his grown sons and their friends, and they all vouched for him. They swore he'd never laid a finger on them. I had no evidence, it was my word against his. I became a pariah, the little shit who tried to tarnish the name of the town's most prominent citizen with my lies. The whole town turned on me. I was only fourteen years old. I had to get out of there. That's why I ran away." I let go of Finn's hand and quickly wiped the tear off my cheek before anyone saw, though the only other patrons in the restaurant were clear across the huge room.

"I want to kill him." Finn's voice was low and oozing venom.

"Cancer beat you to it. Henry Aimsley died three years after I left town. He took the truth to the grave with him."

Finn banged his fist on the table, making the silverware rattle. The few people in the dining room glanced our way. His eyes were bright with unshed tears, a muscle in his jaw working as he ground his teeth together. He pushed his chair back abruptly and pulled me to my feet, then crushed me in an embrace. "I can't stand it," he whispered. "I can't stand that this was done to you, and that he got away with it. I can't stand the fact that he wasn't punished to the full extent of the law, and that all the assholes in your town couldn't pull their fucking heads out long enough to see the truth. It's a good thing he's dead, because if he wasn't, I'd go to jail for killing him."

I rubbed his back and whispered, "Come on, baby, let's go outside." He nodded and let go of me, then flipped open the leather folder that held the bill and tossed a pile of twenties on it, including a very generous tip.

We went out the back of the lodge, to the patio overlooking the geyser field. Only a little steam was visible in the moonlight. Finn pushed his hair back from his face and took several deep breaths to calm down. "I'm sorry," I said quietly. "I shouldn't have told you here. I didn't want to spoil your vacation."

He turned to me and cupped my face with both hands, resting his forehead against mine, and said softly, "Please don't apologize."

I chewed my lower lip, not looking at him, then said softly, "My timing sucked, though. I wanted to tell you, but that wasn't the right time."

"Thank you for trusting me enough to tell me."

"I trust you with my life, Finn. It's so hard for me to trust people, and now you know why. But I've always known I could trust you. I've been absolutely sure of it."

He drew a deep breath, then took my hand and started walking. It was late, so we almost had the place to ourselves. Eventually he asked, "You said you kept the secret for almost a year back then. What made you finally come forward?"

"My brother. When he was about five, I took him to Mom's workplace on her birthday because he wanted to bring her some flowers. Aimsley came out of his office while we were there. He basically ignored me, probably because it was uncomfortable to have his dirty little secret in his place of business. But he was paying a lot of attention to Colt, acting really charming and joking around with him. Then he put his hand on Colt's shoulder, and I snapped. I was so afraid he'd try to do the same thing to my little brother, and I created a huge scene. Some big guy that worked maintenance ended up carrying me out of the building. That was the day it all started. I tried to tell anyone who would listen, and, well, you know how that turned out."

"Do you think he hurt your brother, too?"

I said, "God I hope not. Before I left, I sat Colt down and explained that Aimsley was a monster, and that he needed to be sure he was never alone with him. I didn't handle it right, the poor kid probably thought the man was a werewolf or something. But I was a kid, too, I did the best I could. Even though he was little, I think Colt understood."

We were quiet for a while as we wandered along the walkway and out into the geyser field. Finally I said, "I want to explain all of this to my brother, so he understands why I left. He begged me not to go, it broke my heart. He was just this tiny little kid, all skin and bones and big, blue eyes. I wanted to take him with me, but of course I couldn't do that." After another pause I told Finn, "When I saw Colt again on the first leg of this trip, I realized how much Aimsley took from me. He didn't just take my innocence and my childhood. He took my family."

"I can't even imagine how furious you must be."

"I'm sad more than anything, especially now because my mother and I were never able to move past it. I always held out hope that someday, somehow, I'd finally get her to believe me. But now she's dead, so that's never going to happen. I waited too long to try to talk to her."

"Chance, I'm so incredibly sorry."

I rubbed my cheek against his shoulder, then looked out over the open terrain for a while before saying, "Can we go back to our room?"

"Absolutely. You getting tired?"

"No, I want to talk to Colt. I can't keep putting off telling him why I left. He's already figured out a lot of it, and I kind of feel like I'm on a roll now. I told one person, so hey, why not tell two more?"

Finn nodded. "If you want to, then sure."

"I do, because I just realized something. I put off talking to my mom way too long, and I don't want to do the same with Colt. I want him to understand what happened. I feel like I've always owed him an explanation."

When we went back to the room, we found the boys lying on top of the covers on one of the queen beds. They had a big park map unfolded above them, each holding one side. Colt peeked around the edge of the map and said, "Do we have time to do some stuff here tomorrow, before we head back?"

"Sure," Finn said. "What do you want to do?"

My brother sat up and swung the map around to show us. "There are buffalo here. Look at the picture! Can we see a buffalo?"

"We can try," I said. I sat down on the other bed facing my brother, and Finn sat beside me as I said, "Can I talk to you a minute?"

Colt's face fell. "Shit. What did I do?"

"It's nothing like that. You'd asked me some questions when I first came to see you, and I didn't answer. I, um, I want you to know why I left Wyoming when I was fourteen."

My brother looked surprised, and Elijah sat up and peeked at me from behind Colt. "Do you want me to leave?"

I said, "No, please stay. If we're all going to figure out how to be a family, I don't want secrets between us."

I told the boys a pared down version of what I'd told Finn. When I finished talking, Colt whispered, "I knew it," and got up and gave me a hug.

Elijah had been studying the bedspread as I'd been talking, and after a pause he said softly, "I'm sorry that happened to you. I know what it's like and how scared you must've been." He swallowed hard and told us, "My uncle hurt me the way that man hurt you. He said if I told anyone, he'd just say I was lying, and then he'd tell everyone he caught me messing around with some boys from school. He said everyone would believe him because they all knew I was a faggot, and that my father would beat me to death if he found out what I was."

"Elijah, I'm so sorry."

"You can see why I ran, and why I'm never, ever going back there," he said, his voice a whisper.

"I'm glad you opened up to us about that," I told him.

"I knew you'd understand, after what happened to you."

"I really do."

After a pause, he asked as his slender hands smoothed out the bedspread, "Is it really gonna be okay if I live with you when we get to California? I know you don't know me or anything."

"You'll always have a home with us, for as long as you want it, Elijah. I promise."

"Thank you," he said, a little color rising in his pale cheeks, probably because everyone's attention was on him.

Finn seemed to sense his discomfort and changed the subject by telling the boys, "So, let's see that map. I bet we can cram the best of Yellowstone into one day. We just need a plan of attack." Colt swung the big fold-out onto Finn's lap, sat down beside him and started pointing out highlights.

Elijah sat on Colt's other side and took his hand, watching the discussion silently. When he and I happened to catch each other's eye, he gave me a shy little smile. It felt like an incredible gift.

Chapter Seventeen

It took us almost three days to get back to California. We could have pushed and done it quicker, but Finn thought the boys would enjoy Circus Circus since we'd be passing through Reno. We spent a night and part of a day there on the way home.

He was right. Colt and Elijah were absolutely enthralled. He gave them some money for the arcade while he and I relaxed with a couple cocktails, and when they came to find us two hours later, they both had an armload of stuffed animals that they'd won and were grinning happily.

"Which was better," Finn had asked them jokingly on the drive home the next day, "Yellowstone or the arcade at Circus Circus?"

"Yellowstone, because it had buffaloes," Colt had said, and Elijah nodded in agreement. We'd spent a whirlwind day in the national park and managed to see everything on the boys' to-do list. They left with t-shirts, a few souvenirs and good memories, all thanks to Finn and his incredible generosity. Best of all, those experiences had given all four of us an opportunity to bond and to get to know each other a bit, and I was really grateful for that.

I thought about the last couple days as we crossed the bridge into San Francisco. I was behind the wheel and glanced in the rearview mirror. Colt and Elijah were sound asleep in the backseat, curled up against each other while my brother snored softly. "So, I had an idea," Finn said, looking up from his phone. He'd been texting for the last few minutes. "You were saying your apartment is tiny, and I've been looking for a solution. I texted my cousin Jamie, and he suggested we stay with him until we can find you a bigger place. You know Jamie, right?"

"A little. We've met a couple times. He and his husband have a baby though, so I'm sure he wouldn't want us intruding."

"Lily is a toddler now and sleeping through the night, and Jamie and Dmitri love kids. They both come from huge families. They have a big apartment, too, right above the bar and grill they own. I know that sounds dicey, an apartment over a bar, but Nolan's is a really nice establishment."

"It is, I've been there. I'd feel like I was imposing by staying in their apartment though, since I'm basically a stranger."

"Yeah, but I'm not. Jamie and I are close, and I'd be staying there with you, if you're alright with that," Finn said.

"Really?"

"I don't want to go back to my parents' house, aside from picking up my things. As soon as I come out, I won't be welcome there."

"It wouldn't be nearly as weird if you were staying with us," I said.

"So should I tell Jamie we're coming?"

"I guess so. I just can't see all of us cramming into my tiny studio, and I really don't want the boys to feel like they're in the way. Hopefully we won't have to stay too long, even though it'll take me some time to put enough money together for a deposit on a bigger apartment. It's going to take a while to pay you back, too."

Finn knit his brows as he sent a text and said, "You really have to quit it with the paying me back thing."

"I owe you a shitload after this week. I've been trying to estimate, because you won't give me receipts. I bet my estimate was low on the cost of renting this SUV and dropping it off in a different state. That had to cost a bundle. Maybe nearly as much as that last-minute plane ticket."

"Let's talk about this later, when I can raise my voice without waking a couple sleeping kids." I grinned at that. He never made good on his threats of getting mad at me.

We parked in the alley behind Nolan's, Jamie and Dmitri's Irish pub in the Richmond District, and Jamie came downstairs to open the security gate for us. He looked very much like a surfer and very little like an ex-cop, both of which applied to him. He was tan, blue-eyed like most of the Nolan clan, and about six feet tall with sun-streaked hair, a loud Hawaiian shirt, and camo cargo shorts. Jamie greeted both Finn and me with a hug, and I said, "I'm so sorry to put you out like this."

"You're not putting us out at all, we love having company," Jamie said with a smile. "What do you want to bring upstairs? I'll help you carry some stuff."

I frowned at the loaded-down SUV and stuffed-full Civic and said, "I guess we'll just bring up our backpacks with our clothes, and…well, one other thing." I got my keys and retrieved my mother's ashes from the front seat of my car. It really wouldn't be okay if that got stolen.

Elijah and Colt each grabbed a couple of the stuffed animals they'd won in Reno and tumbled out of the backseat half-asleep. When we got upstairs, Jamie showed the boys to the attractively decorated guestroom, and Colt murmured, "Thanks," before he and Elijah collapsed on top of the comforter. They were asleep again in seconds.

Jamie had set up a thick air mattress in his home office for Finn and me, made up with fresh, cream-colored bedding, and said, "I hope this'll be okay."

"It's great. Thanks so much," Finn said.

"I, um, don't know where to put this," I said, looking at Finn as I indicated the box in my hands.

"Let me take it, I'll find a safe spot for it," Finn said, then took the box with him into the living room.

While he did that, Jamie asked, "What's in the box?"

"Oh. Um, it's my mother's ashes. Sorry, that must sound incredibly morbid. I recently found out she died, and I haven't figured out what to do with them yet."

"I'm so sorry for your loss, Chance," Jamie said, reaching out to give my arm a friendly squeeze.

"Thanks. And thank you so much for this. It's incredibly nice of you to open your home to us."

Jamie said, "You're more than welcome. I was surprised when Finn texted, since he's the type of guy who never asks for anything. It's obvious that he cares about you and those boys."

"I do," Finn said as he came back into the room. "Chance is my boyfriend, and I'd do anything for him." I was once again surprised that he outed himself without any lead-up.

Jamie took it in stride, smiling as he said, "I knew you were gay. Kieran owes me five bucks, we bet each other."

"You did? When?"

"A few years ago."

Finn shook his head. "And here I really thought I'd kept it under wraps."

"Have you told your parents yet?"

"No, only Shea and now you. Apparently my approach is to tell each of my gay relatives first, one by one, so I get a lot of practice before the main event. Maybe after that I'll go through a couple dozen of my straight cousins. Most of them took it in stride when you came out, so that'll be good practice too before outing myself to my parents."

Jamie said, "I see why you said you were going to be moving out when you texted me."

"I have to. You know how they've shunned my brother. No reason to believe it'll go any differently for me."

"I'll help in any way I can." Jamie added, "You both look exhausted, so let's continue this conversation in the morning. If you get up before we do, help yourself to anything you want in the kitchen. I really want you to make yourself at home."

"Thanks again," Finn said.

Jamie left the room, pulling the door shut behind him, and I asked Finn, "Where'd you put the box?"

"In a high cabinet in the living room, out of toddler range."

"I have no idea what I'm going to do with her ashes," I said as I sank down onto the mattress and pulled my shoes off. "It feels so weird to be carrying my dead mother's remains around with me."

"Maybe we can find someplace nice and distribute them there."

"Yeah, maybe."

Finn took off his shoes and jeans, then laid down with a little, "Ahh." He got comfortable and said, "This bed feels amazing after all those hours in the car."

I turned off the lights and stretched out beside him. He rolled onto his side and put his arm over me, and after a pause I said quietly, "What the hell am I going to do?"

He knew I wasn't just talking about the ashes. "You're going to let me help you, and we're going to figure all of this out together."

"I'm worried about Elijah. What if he bolts? I know all too well what'd become of a teen on his own in this city if he did that."

"I don't think he'll run. He obviously loves your brother, and that's reason enough to stick around."

"But he ran from Colt back in Wyoming, when you had to chase after him."

Finn said, "I know, but it took very little convincing to get him to come back. I think he mostly just ran off so he could cry without anyone seeing him. When he finally stopped running and let me catch up to him, he was sobbing and made me promise we wouldn't hurt him. It broke my heart."

"I'm really grateful that you took them to Yellowstone and Circus Circus. I loved seeing them enjoying themselves and getting to act like kids for once."

"I had as much fun as they did." Finn took my chin in his hand and gently turned my head to face him. I studied his features in the semi-darkness as he said, "I know it was hard for you to relax and enjoy yourself, given how much you have on your mind right now, so I hope when we get everything sorted out you'll let me take you on a real vacation. I want to take you somewhere beautiful for a few days, so you can finally relax."

I rolled over, into his arms, and said softly, "You're such a good guy, Finn. I'm really lucky to know you."

"I'm the lucky one."

"Hardly. I have no idea why you'd want anything to do with an unemployed ex-hooker with a couple teenagers to look after and absolutely no plan for the future." Finn looked surprised, and I said, "I can't go back to prostitution. I already knew I had to give it up because it would drive you and me apart. But now on top of that I have the responsibility of those two boys, and I need to be a good role model for them. I need to be better for you, too. If I expect to have a shot at holding on to you, I know I have to get my shit together."

He ran his fingertips over my cheek and said quietly, "That job needed to go because it was dangerous and because it damaged your self-esteem. But you really don't have to worry about holding on to me, Chance. You've got me, for as long as you want me."

I wanted to believe him. God I did. But I'd meant what I said, I had no idea why he'd want a train wreck like me.

*****

I woke up fairly early the next morning, but Finn was already up and gone. He was a habitually early riser. When I left the office, I noticed the door to the guestroom was still closed, and could make out the faint sound of my brother snoring.

After using the bathroom in the hall, I wandered into the living room. I hadn't gotten a good look at it the night before, but it was really something. It had high ceilings and big windows that let in lots of light. Sleek, modern furniture played off some quirky details, like a river of surfboards suspended from the ceiling. It was beautiful, but more than that, it really felt like a home. Dozens of pictures of family and friends crowded the big mantel, and toys and stuffed animals dotted the room.

Jamie and Dmitri were seated at their kitchen table across the apartment, flanking a cute little girl in a high chair. She had blue eyes and dark brown hair, and was feeding herself with a spoon, so a lot of porridge was landing on the Wonder Woman bib she wore.

I totally felt like I was intruding and started to turn to head back into the office, but Jamie spotted me and called, "Good morning, Chance. There's coffee if you want some."

I murmured a greeting and went into the kitchen, where I filled a mug. "Come sit down," Jamie said. "You remember my husband Dmitri, don't you?"

"Yeah. Good to see you again," I said. I took a seat and glanced at Dmitri as I took a sip of coffee. He was very much Jamie's opposite in terms of physical appearance, a pulled together and sophisticated Russian-American with a perfect smile, perfect black hair, and perfect clothes.

"Good to see you, too," Dmitri said. When he smiled at me, a set of dimples appeared. "We'd been meaning to call you, actually. Christian and Shea sent us copies of some of the photos you took at their wedding. We loved the candid shots of the three of us. In fact, we framed a couple and put them on the mantel."

"I'm glad you liked them," I said, looking at the wooden tabletop.

"We've actually been wanting to call to make an appointment for a photography session. We have a lot of pictures of Lily, but very few of the three of us together. Would that be something you're interested in? We'd pay your usual fee, of course," Jamie said.

I glanced at him and asked, "Did Finn put you up to this?"

"No. Why would he?"

"Because he knows I'm kind of desperate for money right now," I said quietly.

"He didn't say anything about it."

"Do you know where he went this morning?"

"He said he had to run an errand and that he'd be back soon."

I took another sip from my mug, then said, "I'll be happy to take some pictures for you, but there's no charge. You let us totally impose on you, so it's the least I could do."

"It's no imposition," Jamie said. "You're my cousin's boyfriend. That makes you family, and family is always welcome in our home."

"Well, if you insist on paying, please just give whatever amount you think seems right directly to Finn," I told him. "I owe him a bundle after this last week."

"Not a problem. Do you want to do it this afternoon? Maybe we could go to Golden Gate Park," Jamie said.

"Sure. I'll bring the boys, I think they'll like it there. Oh, and Elijah really wants to see the Pacific Ocean. Maybe we could go to that end of the park, so he and Colt can cross over to Ocean Beach."

Dmitri grinned at me. "Being a parent comes naturally to you."

"I don't know about that. I'm just trying my best to do what's right for those kids."

"That's exactly what makes you a good parent," Dmitri said as he picked up a napkin and wiped his daughter's messy chin.

"I'm totally clueless though. There's so much I have to do, and I don't know how to do any of it. For one thing, I have to figure out how to get them registered for school," I said. "It's probably starting in just a couple weeks. But maybe

I have to be appointed as their legal guardian before I can register them. It's probably no problem with my brother since I'm a blood relative, but I don't know what to do for Elijah. He ran away from a bad home situation and I don't know how to get custody of him. I just have absolutely no idea what I'm doing."

"It's a good thing that Finn brought you here," Dmitri said as he pulled his phone from his pocket. "A good friend of ours is one of the best lawyers in the country for family law. We had Lily with a surrogate, and wanted to make sure we'd both have full legal rights where she was concerned. He took care of everything, and I know he can help you, too." Dmitri fired off a text and said, "I just asked him if he and his wife can come over for dinner. It sounds like you need to get this handled immediately with that school deadline."

"I can't afford a lawyer," I said.

"Hayes does a lot of pro bono work. I'm sure as soon as he hears about your circumstances, he'll be more than happy to help." I hoped he was right.

The door to the guestroom opened, and a couple disheveled, uncertain-looking teenagers stepped into the living room, holding hands. When I waved to them, they came into the kitchen and looked at our hosts shyly. "Colt and Elijah, I'd like you to meet Jamie, Dmitri, and their daughter Lily. Jamie is Finn's cousin."

"Are we in San Francisco?" Colt asked.

"Yup. We got in last night, a little before midnight. You two were pretty out of it," I said.

The teens stood there uncomfortably, and Jamie got to his feet and flashed them a friendly smile as he said, "Come sit down. Do you guys like pancakes? I've got the batter all ready to go."

"I love pancakes," Colt said as he and his boyfriend sat at the table. Elijah slid his chair over so it was right beside Colt's and took in his surroundings from beneath his lashes.

"I was just talking about getting you two registered for school," I said. "I was saying that to do that, I think I'd have to be your legal guardian. We'd need to do that for a lot of other reasons, too. We're going to talk to a lawyer, but first I wanted to talk to both of you. Colt, since I'm your brother this is pretty much a given. But Elijah, I want to know how you'd feel about this."

He fidgeted under the attention, pushing his shoulder-length golden blond hair behind his ear. After a moment, Elijah said, so softly it was hard to hear him, "I guess that'd be alright. I don't reckon my folks would fight you on it. They probably figured good riddance once I took off."

Jamie took a pen and a pad of paper from a drawer and put it where Elijah could reach it. "The lawyer's going to want some information to start with, so could you write down your full name and your parents' names and address?"

The boy did as he was asked before handing the pad to me. He'd written Elijah Ezekiel Everett, above his parents' names and an address in a town in Mississippi that I'd never heard of. When I asked him where it was, he said, "It's just a fly speck on the map in northern Mississippi, 'bout fifty miles outside Holly Springs. Reminded me of Simone in some ways."

"How'd you get to Wyoming, anyway?" I asked as I tore off the piece of paper and put it in my wallet.

"I was tryin' to head west. I was hitchhikin' and a trucker picked me up, said he was going to California. Turned out that was bullshit, though. Pardon my language. He was actually headed to Idaho. He started getting' some ideas 'bout how I was gonna repay him for the ride, so when he stopped for gas outside Simone, I bolted."

"I met Eli at the gas station convenience store," Colt said. "The one I always went to for the Ramen bowls." The boys exchanged shy smiles and Elijah wrapped his arms around Colt and put his head on his shoulder.

Finn returned a few minutes later and joined us for breakfast. He'd unloaded the SUV and the Civic, stashing our things in a storage room at the back of the building, and then returned the SUV to the rental company. He sat at the table and smiled at me, but a little crease of concern appeared between his eyebrows when he looked at me.

Later on, when the boys were stuffed full of a staggering number of pancakes and taking turns in the shower, and our hosts were in the nursery getting Lily cleaned up, I said quietly, "They probably do a background check when someone applies to be the legal guardian of a minor, right?"

"I assume so," Finn said. "Why do you ask?"

I looked at my hands, which were splayed out on my thighs, and admitted, "I have a criminal record. I was arrested twice for prostitution, once at eighteen and again at twenty-two. Also, I have no employment history, since I've only ever worked as a prostitute. Who in their right mind would give me custody of a couple teenagers?"

"We'll discuss it with the lawyer, he'll know what to do. If your past ends up being a sticking point, I can apply for guardianship," Finn said gently, taking my hand.

I glanced up at him. "You'd do that?"

"Of course. I care about those kids. We'll do whatever it takes to keep them out of the system." I was so overcome with emotion that all I could do was hug him.

*****

Later that morning, Jamie and Dmitri took Lily and the boys downstairs to the restaurant, Finn went to beg for his job back, and I went to my apartment for my camera and some of my things. I climbed the stairs and knocked on Zachary's door, and he flung it open and launched himself into my arms. "You're back! Thank God! Are you okay? Please tell me you're okay!" The words tumbled out of him.

"I'm fine. How are you?"

"Better now. I missed you so much."

I kissed the top of his head and said, "I missed you, too. I have so much to tell you, I don't even know where to begin."

We went into my apartment, and I told him everything as we sat cross-legged on my bed, from the stolen car, to possibly meeting my dad, to finding out my mom had died, to taking in my brother and his boyfriend. Finally, I told him about Finn, and then I said, "I want this so much, Zachary, but I'm worried, too. I've never had a relationship before. I never even dated! But he's amazing, so kind and gentle and caring, and even though I don't know what the hell I'm doing, I'm determined to figure out how to make this work. He means so much to me, and I must matter to him, too. Why else would he drop everything and rush to Wyoming?" Zachary just stared at the cuff of his indigo jeans. After a moment I said, "Say something."

"I'm going to miss you," he said softly.

"What do you mean? I just got back."

"But you're about to start this whole new life. It's kind of funny when you think about it. You went off to find your family, you wanted to meet your dad and patch things up with your mom. But instead, you came home with a whole new family, you and your boyfriend and those two kids. That's kind of amazing, Chance, and I'm happy for you. I get it, though. You're starting this whole new life, and there's no room for me in any of that."

"Who says?"

Zachary looked up at me. "You're turning over a new leaf. I'm not. I'm still a prostitute, and that's not going to change any time soon. You're not going to want someone like me hanging around, being a third wheel with you and your man or being a bad role model around those teenagers. And that's fine. I totally get it."

"Zachary, you're my best friend. No matter how much changes in my life, that never will."

He got up from the mattress and said, "I'm sorry to make this about me. I really am happy for you. This is everything I could have wanted for you and then some."

He turned and started to leave the apartment, and I jumped up and grabbed his hand. "Come on, Zachary. Don't go. None of this has to come between us. Instead of walking away, join in! Come with me to the park and meet Finn and my brother and Elijah. Be a part of our family."

"But I'm *not* a part of any of that, Chance. And you're already worried about getting custody of those kids as an ex-hooker. You think a social worker is going to like the fact that you have a prostitute hanging around those kids?"

"It's none of their damn business who I'm friends with!"

"Good sentiment, but let's face it, I'll just be one more strike against you."

He turned and tried to go again, but I held on tight. "I'm not just going to let you walk away, Zachary. You mean way too much to me. I'm not bullshitting when I say you're my best friend."

"I'm not like you, Chance. You've always been better than that job. I'm not. You have friends, and a boyfriend, and people that care about you, and you're so fucking talented that it just blows me away." He waved his free hand toward my wall of photos as he said that. "The only thing stopping you from working as a photographer is the fact that you don't believe in yourself. There's so much more to you, Chance. You're right on the verge of a really great life, it's finally starting to happen. Don't let someone like me hold you back."

"You're not holding me back, Zachary. I love you and I want you to be a part of it."

He startled me when he pulled his hand away and yelled, "Damn it Chance, don't you fucking get it? I can't! I need to step the hell away from you!

"Why?"

"Because I'm in love with you, and you love me as a friend, nothing more! You've always made that clear. I fucking get it. And I'm sorry, but I really can't stand by and watch the guy I love swooning over someone else. That'd fucking kill me, Chance!"

"But…you never said anything. All that time. You never said a word," I stammered.

"Of course not, because I always knew it wasn't mutual."

"You should have said something."

"If I had, would you have returned my feelings? Is there any part of you that ever thought of me as anything more than a friend?"

I whispered, "No," as tears prickled at the back of my eyes. "I'm sorry, Zachary."

"Don't apologize. There's no reason to. This is my problem, not yours. I fucked up, I fell for someone who'd never feel the same way. I really hope you have a wonderful life, Chance. I always wanted that for you."

He turned and fled the apartment. I could hear his footsteps on the stairs. A moment later the security gate clanged behind him, and a moment after that, my front door finished swinging shut. I sank onto the edge of the mattress and took a deep breath, then whispered, "Oh God."

I'd been so stupid. I'd had no idea. I always thought Zachary and I were firmly on the same page, best friends, nothing more. I felt like such an asshole when I thought about how I'd been going on and on about Finn and what a great guy he was. That must have felt like salt in a wound.

I sat there for a long time, replaying the conversation over and over. There was no way I was going to let that be the end of our friendship, no chance in hell. He was going to need some time though, which was why I hadn't run after him.

Eventually, I got up and retrieved my old camera from the closet. Before Christian gave me my pride and joy, it had done the job decently enough, even if it was kind of beat-up and held together with duct tape. I slung the camera case over my shoulder, then started to leave the apartment. At the front door, I paused and looked back at the little space that had been my home and refuge. It already felt like part of the past.

Chapter Eighteen

September

I pushed my bangs off my forehead with the back of my hand and looked around the restaurant. The lunch rush at Nolan's was over, thank God, and the dining room was almost empty. The fact that it was so busy was a good thing, because it meant I made a lot in tips, but I was always exhausted at the end of each shift.

I forgot all about how tired I was when the front door swung open and Finn came in. He was dressed in his police uniform and looked so handsome. "Hey," he said, crossing the dining room to me with a big smile. He kissed my cheek and said, "Is the kiddo ready to go?"

A voice in the corner called out, "I'm way too old for you to call me a kiddo. I'm going to be seventeen in three months." Elijah slid from the booth and carried his empty plate to the bussing station, then went back and stuffed a bunch of books and papers in his backpack, which he slung over his shoulder. As he came up to us, he said, "We need to go, I don't want to be late."

"We're going, keep your shirt on!" Finn grinned at him and then kissed me again, this time a light peck on the lips, and said, "See you tonight. I'm working a double, so I'll be home late."

"I am, too. Be safe."

"Always am." My boyfriend winked at me and the two of them exited through the front door.

Finn had been granted temporary custody of Elijah while our lawyer worked on making the arrangement permanent, and the same had been done for Colt and me. As my brother's only blood relative, our lawyer felt confident that I'd be given custody, especially after Jamie hired me as a waiter at Nolan's and agreed to be one of my references. Things looked good for Finn and Elijah too, which was great because they'd really bonded over the last few weeks.

When the boys did their placement testing for high school, we'd been in for a big surprise. Elijah's math scores were off the charts. We learned that the shy, quiet little teen was a prodigy, a fact that seemed to embarrass Elijah.

His scores were so remarkable that several school administrators held a meeting to discuss what was best for him. They decided high school would be a waste of his talents, so instead he'd been enrolled at San Francisco State while plans were being made to transfer him to UC Berkeley. He'd missed both universities' enrollment deadlines, but for a boy as gifted as Elijah, that apparently didn't matter much. Classes at S.F. State had begun that week, and Finn picked up Elijah on his lunch breaks and drove him to the campus, since the kid was pretty overwhelmed with big city life and afraid to take public transit on his own. When classes were over,

Finn would take another break and drive him home. That was just one of the many ways Finn had stepped into a parental role, and he seemed to take it perfectly in stride.

After wiping down the booth Elijah had been using, I took one last look around to make sure my station was spotless and fully stocked. Then I picked up the plastic bussing tray and carried it to the kitchen. I put it down next to the dishwashing station, and when Jamie finished chatting with a couple of the cooks, I told him, "I'm going upstairs to rest before the dinner shift. If it gets busy early, give me a call and I'll come down sooner."

"You look exhausted, Chance. Are you sure you're up for working a double today? It'll be your third one in a row. Maybe I should find someone to cover."

"I'm fine, and I'll be even better after I nap for an hour," I said. "Thanks for your concern, though." Jamie gave me a sympathetic smile and squeezed my shoulder. We'd bonded a lot over the last month, and he felt much more like a friend than an employer.

The apartment was quiet when I let myself in with my key. We were still living with Jamie and Dmitri, since finding an affordable place big enough to accommodate all of us had proven to be a challenge. I'd given up the studio to save money, and felt kind of adrift without my own place.

I untied the black apron that was around my hips and put it on the coffee table, then dropped onto the white leather couch, took my shoes off, and sighed with relief. I pulled my phone out of my pocket and turned the ringer back on, then checked my texts. I had two messages, both from Jessie.

The first was the Honda's daily health report. He and Nana had gotten back from Italy a little over a week ago, looking tanned and happy, and Jessie immediately and enthusiastically jumped into the project of fixing up my smashed-in Civic. Nico had decided to stay on an extra week or two, and still hadn't returned. The second message was: *Nana wanted me to remind you about Sunday dinner. She said you and your family should come over at five, because she's going to be filming an episode of her cooking show before dinner and she likes to have a big audience.*

I wrote back, assuring him we'd be there, and then I sent my daily text to Zachary. I hadn't seen or spoken to him since the day he'd confessed his feelings to me. I'd knocked on his apartment door day after day, until a new tenant answered and told me he'd moved out. I'd called his cellphone and left dozens of messages, but he never called me back. No way was I going to give up on him, though. I sent a text every day, letting him know I was thinking about him and begging him to get in touch with me. I knew he needed some time, but weeks had passed and we really needed to talk.

I put the phone on the coffee table and had just leaned back and closed my eyes when Colt burst in, asking, "Did Elijah leave for school already?"

"Yeah, you just missed him."

"Shit." He sank onto the couch beside me and wiped his sweaty forehead with his arm. He'd obviously run home from the bus stop. "No matter what I do, I just can't get back here in time." He'd started classes at one of the local high schools and took the light rail back and forth (riding public transit didn't concern him in the slightest). What did upset him was the fact that he'd been enrolled as a sophomore as a result of his test scores. He'd hoped he'd go in as a junior, and was self-conscious about the fact that he was one of the oldest kids in his class.

He was upset, so I told him, "It's okay. He'll be home in three hours."

"I know. I just...." He stopped talking and looked away. When he turned toward me again, there was so much sadness in his eyes. "He's not gonna want me anymore, Chance."

"What are you talking about?"

"Elijah. Why would a genius want to be with a dummy like me?"

"You're not dumb. Not at all!"

"Yeah, right. Eli's this total math whiz and I'm completely lost in pre-Algebra."

"You just have different strengths than he does. And if you're struggling with pre-Algebra, why not ask Elijah to tutor you? I'd volunteer to help, but I'm actually having a hard time with that one, too." Both to better myself and to show the court I was making an effort so they'd grant me custody of my brother, I was taking online courses and preparing for the high school equivalency test. I'd been away from school a long time, and was kind of horrified by how much I'd forgotten.

"If I ask him to tutor me, he'll just see first-hand how stupid I really am, and it'll just speed up the process of him realizing he's way too good for me." I noticed idly that the southern accent he'd picked up from his boyfriend had almost totally faded out, now that my brother was spending time around a lot of people.

"Elijah loves you, Colt. He won't hold the fact that you're struggling in math against you."

"It's not just math. I don't know if it's because I took a year off, or if this school is just way harder than the one in Simone, or what, but I feel like I'm barely keeping my head above water."

"I can relate," I said, mostly to myself. I wasn't just talking about my classes, either. "Let's see your homework, maybe we can work on it together and both learn something."

Colt slid onto the area rug and pulled a pile of schoolwork from his backpack. I reviewed his textbook while he started on a worksheet. After a while, I noticed that he was staring at the coffee table, and asked, "You alright, Colt?"

"I was just thinking. What happens if you and Finn break up?"

That took me by surprise. "Why do you ask?"

He turned to look at me. "I know you haven't been having sex, because the walls of this apartment are pretty thin and if you messed around, I'd hear you."

"Which is exactly why we haven't been messing around."

"You're both working all the time, too. You never see each other, and that can't be good. I get why you have to, you're trying to afford our own place, and Finn's working a ton because he has to kiss his boss's butt after almost getting fired. But it can't be good for you two."

When Finn had gone to his captain to ask for his job back, he'd gotten yelled at for an hour, but had been reinstated. He'd been told if he stepped out of line again, he'd be fired immediately, and his punishment was a demotion on the roster. That meant he got all the crappy shifts and was expected to step up and cover any gaps in the schedule, so he almost always worked double shifts. It was all my fault, too. None of it would have happened if I hadn't fallen apart and he'd had to come help me.

I told my brother, "Just because we haven't been able to spend time together doesn't mean we don't care about each other."

He watched me for a moment, then said, "If you did break up, he'd take Elijah with him, wouldn't he, since he's gonna end up as his legal guardian."

"Okay, first of all, you're the only one that's talking about us breaking up. And even if, God forbid, Finn and I actually split up, we'd never try to keep you and Elijah apart."

He chewed his lower lip for a moment, then asked, "What if Elijah breaks up with me? What happens then? Are we supposed to just, like, pretend to be brothers and keep living together? Because that'd be super weird."

"I really don't know what we'd do in that situation, but you know what? There are enough real things in life to worry about without also worrying about the what-ifs. If that did happen, and I'm not saying it's going to, then we'd deal with it. But until then, there's really no point in dwelling on things that haven't happened and probably never will."

Colt mulled that over for a while, then gave me a little half-smile. "That's good advice. You're really smart."

I pushed myself to my feet and said, "Tell that to my high school equivalency classes. They're making me feel like an idiot."

His smile widened. "Sometimes it's super obvious that we're brothers. We're both totally in the same boat, aren't we?"

"Pretty much. Are you hungry? I'll make you a grilled cheese sandwich while you do your homework."

"Thanks. I'm starving." That didn't surprise me. He was always hungry and ate like a grizzly bear, but had barely put on a pound. I crossed the apartment to make him a sandwich, my nap long-forgotten.

When I brought it to him with a glass of milk a few minutes later, he glanced at it and said, "Don't we have any coke?"

"Oh, come on! Don't make me go all parental on you and lecture you about nutrition," I said as I sat back on the couch.

He thought about that for a moment, then said, "I know you're only ten years older than me and my brother and all, but you're the closest thing I'm ever gonna have to a dad. So, I guess I don't mind so much when you act like a parent. It shows you care about me."

I grinned at that as he tucked into the sandwich, devouring the first triangle in three bites. After a while I asked, "You don't have to tell me if you don't want to, but did Mom ever mention anything to you about who your biological father is?"

"No. Whenever I asked about it, she'd always get real defensive and angry. I could never figure out why. I took a look at my birth certificate, but all it says under father is 'unknown'. I always wondered if she really didn't know, or if she just wouldn't tell me. Seems like if she didn't know, she wouldn't have acted like it was some big secret." He chugged down half the milk, then went to work on the rest of the sandwich.

The phone rang and I glanced at Finn's name on the screen as I picked it up. I answered with, "Hey. Everything okay?"

"Yeah. Fine. Um, could you come down to the station, Chance?"

"Sure. Why?"

"There's someone here to see you."

"Who is it?"

"I kind of think you need to see for yourself."

"Is it Zachary? Was he arrested? Is he okay?"

"It's not Zachary. Please, just come down here."

I raised an eyebrow at that, but said, "Alright, I'll be there in about twenty or thirty minutes, depending on the busses, unless you think I need to hurry and take a cab."

"You don't need to hurry. I don't think he's going anywhere."

"Alright, I'm on my way. Will you still be there? I know you're supposed to be out on patrol today," I said as I stuffed my feet back into my sneakers.

"I'm definitely going to stick around for this."

After we said goodbye and disconnected, I looked down at myself. I was still wearing my work shirt, which was green and said 'Nolan's' across the front in big, white letters (I always liked that, since it was Finn's last name, too). I'd managed not to spill anything on myself during the lunch shift, which I took as a sign that I was getting better at waiting tables. I decided I was good to go and told Colt, "I need to go down to Finn's police station. I won't be long, especially since I start work again in ninety minutes."

"Why're you going down there?"

"Someone wants to see me. Finn didn't say who."

Colt got to his feet and said, "I want to go along."

"Why?"

"We can hang out and visit on the bus. You'll be working all night, so I'll barely see you."

"Except for the fact that you and Eli will be setting up shop in one of my booths for three or four hours and ordering everything off the menu, just like every night," I said with a smile. I actually loved the fact that they did that.

"Except for that. Let's go."

"Alright."

As we headed down the back stairs, he said, "You don't think it's something bad, do you? What if the lawyer went to see Finn at work with some bad news about the custody cases?"

"Our lawyer would call us and ask us to come down to his office, no matter what kind of news he had. He really wouldn't go to the police station."

"But then who could it be?" Colt asked.

"No clue."

As we rode the bus across town, I mulled over the same question and kept coming up blank. Why wouldn't Finn just tell me who it was? I wondered briefly if it was Finn's dad, if maybe he'd heard his son was gay from another relative and had come to confront him. Even though he'd moved out of their house, Finn had yet to come out to his parents. He kept saying he was going to, but kept finding reasons to put it off. That theory didn't make a lot of sense, though. Why would his father pick such a public venue?

Duke was at the desk when we got to the station, and greeted my brother and me with, "Hey Chance. Hey Mini Chance. They're back in the conference room, the one to the left that always smells like nacho cheese. Finn said to send you on back as soon as you got here."

"Thanks, Duke. Who's with him?"

The big cop grinned a little and said, "I'm not supposed to tell you anything. I think Finn doesn't want you to bolt before you hear what that guy has to say."

I frowned and said, "You're as bad as he is." Duke just went on grinning.

Colt and I cut through the police station, past the rows of desks to the long hallway that led to lockup, the break room, and the conference rooms (which all smelled like nacho cheese). When I swung open the door to the conference room on the left, I blurted, "What the fuck?"

Tony Asturias stood there looking nervous as hell. He was sweating through a plaid button-down shirt, which he wore open over a t-shirt, and clutching Bobo, my teddy bear, in both hands. I snatched the bear from his grasp and handed it to Colt, then stared Asturias down and said, "What are you doing here?" I noticed my camera bag on the table, the one that had been stolen from my car and said, "What the fuck are you doing with my stuff?"

Finn was standing over to my left, and he said, "Maybe you want to take a minute and hear what he has to say, Chance."

"He already said plenty. He called me an asshole and a gold-digger and told me he wanted nothing to do with me." I glanced at my boyfriend and asked, "How the fuck did he know where you work, Finn?"

"I gave him a business card when we were in Gala. Just sit down for a minute, Chance, and listen to him. This is important."

I crossed my arms over my chest and made no move to sit. "What is it?"

Tony cleared his throat and said, "I, uh, I went in and did the paternity test. Actually, I went in the day after you left town. I just…I mean, I was curious. Even though the chances of finding out I had a kid were a million to one, I just needed to know."

"And?"

He picked up some crumpled papers from the conference table and handed them to me. On top was a letter from the doctor's office where I'd gone to give a sample. The bottom two sheets were tables with numbers, which made no sense to me. I looked at the letter and one sentence jumped out at me: *I can confirm a 99.9 percent probability of paternity based on genetic test results.* "Holy shit," I mumbled.

"What?" Colt asked, and I handed him the papers.

"There's no way," I said, staring at Tony as my thoughts and emotions reeled. "We look nothing alike."

"No, we don't. You look exactly like your mother," Asturias said.

"Like you'd remember what she looked like."

"I do, just a little. Mostly, I remember the photo you showed me. Is this the little boy in the photo, your brother? It must be. You two look so much alike," Tony said, indicating Colt.

As I walked around Asturias in a wide arc and went to sit down, Colt said, "Yeah, I'm his brother. And shit, according to this, you're his dad. I think maybe I need to sit down, too." My brother took the seat beside me and held on to the bear while he looked over all the papers.

"Why did the results take a month to come back from the lab?" I asked, watching Asturias as he went around to the other side of the table and took a seat. Finn stood behind me and put his hands on my shoulders.

"They didn't," Tony said. "I had the results in a week. I then made them go back and recheck, because I couldn't believe it was possible. After the recheck came back with the same results, I had my doctor do a fertility screening, like I'd done when my ex-wife and I were trying to have a baby. It showed the same results as before. The doctor estimated my chances of being able to father a child at somewhere around one percent. I guess…well, I guess you were that one in a hundred, or maybe my stats were a bit better back when I was twenty-two, who knows. But…well, basically, this is kind of a miracle."

I just sat there, staring at the tabletop, trying to take it all in. Finn said, "Hey Colt, there's ice cream in the break room. Why don't you come with me and we'll get some? I think Chance and Tony might want to talk in private for a few minutes."

Colt looked at me and I nodded, so he got up and said, "I'm right down the hall if you need me, bro." He took the bear and the papers with him as he left the room with Finn.

Tony and I sat there for a solid minute, the silence between us thick and uncomfortable. Finally he blurted, "I'm so fucking sorry, Chance. I didn't know. I had so damn many people coming to me looking for a handout after I got that inheritance, and I was sure you were lying because I believed I couldn't have kids. My ex-wife and I tried for six years. We went to all kinds of specialists, in Cheyenne, Billings, Denver. She wanted a baby more than anything. We both did. All the tests told us the same thing: I was the problem. But like I said, I was twenty-two when your mom and I hooked up, maybe things were better back then, before a couple decades of drinking and smoking and God knows what else took their toll on me. I don't know." He ran out of steam and just sat there for a while before he said, "Say something, Chance."

I looked up from the fake wood grain of the conference table and asked, "Why did you come here?"

"Well, to tell you the news. I tried to write you a letter when I found out. I'm no good with writing, though. I tried over and over again but kept having to throw them out. I tried fifty times, actually. I know that because I started with a new legal pad and used it up. I never got farther than half a paragraph."

"Why? It only would have taken one sentence: 'Results came back, I'm your dad.' What's so hard about that?"

"There was a hell of a lot more to say."

"Why didn't the doctor call me and give me this news? My boyfriend's the one who paid for the test, we should have been notified."

"I asked Lem not to call you. I wanted the news to come from me."

"Lem. Of course you and the doctor are on a first-name basis."

Asturias shrugged and said, "Small town. Lem and I have known each other since kindergarten, aside from the years he went off to college and medical school."

I sighed at that, then said, "Is there some reason you didn't just call? Finn's cell number was on that business card."

"I started to dial your boyfriend's number a million times, I have it memorized by now. But it didn't seem right to tell you over the phone. And then three days ago, I ran into Christine Hanson at the market and she asked me about the results of the paternity test. You and your boyfriend made quite an impression on her. She really seemed concerned, so I told her the truth. And she told me just that morning, she'd recovered your stolen property. It was in the back of this kid's closet in Gala, his foster mother discovered it when they were packing him up to send him back to juvie."

I glanced at him. "A kid stole my car?"

"Yeah, Cory Previn, he's fifteen. He's no stranger to the police, but that was his first grand theft auto so they hadn't questioned him when your car went missing. Anyway, she told me she had your stuff, including a really expensive camera, and was concerned about sending it through the mail. I guess, I don't know. Maybe that was the extra push I needed to come here. I promised I'd return it to you, made arrangements for someone to watch my bar, and drove to California."

I frowned at that. "The camera costs a fortune. Why would Christine release my property to just anyone?"

Asturias frowned, too. "She didn't release it to just anyone. She released it to your father."

For some reason, it didn't really hit me until he said that. All of a sudden, it felt like all the air had been sucked from the room, and I struggled to draw a breath. I stared at the man sitting across from me, really looked at him. He looked tired. His shoulder-length hair was a mess, his shirt was wrinkled and sweat-stained, and he hadn't shaved in days. There were lines around his dark eyes, and those eyes were watching me intently. "Fuck," I said after a minute. "I actually found my dad. You were right where my mom left you. How did you never go anywhere in over twenty-six years?"

"That bar was always a second home to me. Before I was anywhere near old enough to drink, Ernie Washington would let me hang out there when it wasn't busy and sweep up in exchange for a hot meal and a bit of pocket money. He knew I needed a place to go because my home life sucked. All of Gala knew. There are so few secrets in a small town. Anyway, I'm totally rambling, but you're right. I never went anywhere. I drank at Washington's every single night back when I was an alcoholic, and when I dried out, I still drank there, I just switched from Jack Daniels to Pepsi. When Ernie said he planned to retire, I bought the place. Shit, I'm still rambling, but it's because you're not saying anything, Chance."

"I don't know what to say."

"Why'd you come looking for me after all that time?"

I thought about his question as I went back to studying the fake wood grain of the tabletop. After a minute I said, "I thought about finding you for years, starting when I was little. I guess it made more sense back then. I mean, when I was a kid, I wanted a dad to, you know, do all that dad stuff: take me to baseball games and show me how to shave and ride a bike and take me for ice cream and, shit, I don't know. What do dads do with their sons? I never had one, so I have no fucking idea. I'm pretty sure I got all of those ideas from an old TV sitcom. I guess…I guess I finally decided to go in search of my dad for that little kid inside me, the one who always felt he missed out."

He said softly. "I would have tried so hard to be a good dad to you. Why didn't Janet tell me I had a son? She didn't even give me a chance to do the right thing."

"I don't know."

"You must have asked her about me since you knew where to find me. What did she say?"

"Not much. I guess I got the impression that she didn't think you were up to the job."

He thought about that, then said, "If I was looking at myself through her eyes, I'd probably have thought the same thing. I was well on my way to becoming an alcoholic at twenty-two, couldn't hold down a job, and spent all my time in a bar. She probably figured no dad at all was better than some unemployed drunk. Still though, shit. I wish I'd known about you."

"Me, too." I pushed back from the table and slung the camera bag over my shoulder. "Thanks for bringing my stuff to me. Drive safe going back to Wyoming."

He stood up too and said as I headed for the door, "Wait, that's it? You're leaving?"

"I have to work a second shift at the restaurant tonight, and before that, I have to get my kid brother going on his homework."

"Hang on. Please?" When I turned to look at him, he said, "I get that this is awkward. I also get that I was a complete dick to you back in Wyoming and you probably can't stand me now. But, shit Chance. We already missed out on twenty-six years. Are we really going to miss the rest, too?"

"I don't know what to tell you."

"I know this was a lot to hit you with, and I know it came totally out of the blue, but I'm going to be in town for a couple days. Can we find some time tomorrow to get a coffee or something?"

I pushed my hair back from my face, and after a moment I said, "I guess."

"Good. Great! I'll text your boyfriend's number in the morning. Like I said, I have it memorized."

"Alright. Well, see ya." I left him in the conference room and found Finn and my brother eating Fudgesicles in the break room. "We have to go. I don't want to be late for the dinner rush," I told Colt.

Finn crossed the room to me and rubbed my upper arm. "You okay?"

"Yeah. I'll see you tonight." He nodded and kissed my forehead.

On the bus ride back to Nolan's, Colt said, "So that was probably the last thing you expected to happen today, huh?"

"Pretty much."

"Are you mad at that guy? What's his name, anyway?"

"Tony Asturias. And...yeah. I guess I am, but I'm not sure why."

"Because he wasn't there for you when you were a kid?"

"That's not his fault. He had no idea I existed."

Colt thought about it for a minute, then said, "Maybe it's really Mama you're mad at, but you don't want to be because she's dead. She's the one who didn't tell that guy he had a son."

"I don't know. Maybe."

"Or maybe you're just mad in general. That's okay, too. You can just be mad because life's not fair and stuff sucks."

I said, "I'm going to go with that."

When we got back to the apartment, we found Jamie and Dmitri curled up on their couch, kissing each other tenderly.

Lily was sound asleep in Dmitri's arms, her chubby little legs sprawled out on Jamie's lap. The two men stopped kissing and smiled at us, and Jamie raised a hand in greeting.

I returned the smile and wave as Colt snuck in and retrieved his schoolwork from the coffee table, and then he and I went into the office and closed the door. "We really gotta find our own place," he said. "Those two are the nicest guys in the world and they'd probably let us stay forever, but I totally feel like we're intruding."

"I feel the same way."

"Can we go stay with Finn's brother? Shea and Christian have that nice, big house." We'd all been there for dinner the week before.

"Finn thought about that, but then he decided against it. His brother is a newlywed, and before they got married, Christian had a ton of health issues. Everything's okay now, but they really need to just be able to enjoy being newlyweds without a bunch of chaos and interruptions."

"I'd be quiet. I promise," Colt said.

"I know. I don't mean you. It's just a lot to add four people to any household."

"I guess you're right." My brother chewed his lower lip as he sat down at the desk and spread out his homework. After a while he looked at me over his shoulder and said, "I wish you'd change your mind and let me get a job. I could be helping out financially. I could bus tables downstairs, I'm sure Jamie would hire me."

"We talked about this. You need to concentrate on school." I sat down cross-legged on the air mattress and carefully unpacked the contents of my camera case. It all appeared to be in perfect condition.

"I know, but I could do both. I hate seeing you and Finn bust your asses while I sit back and do nothing."

"You're not doing nothing. You're studying hard so you can get into a good college."

"Like that's gonna happen," he muttered before turning back to his schoolwork.

In an outside pocket of the camera bag, I found a green, zippered canvas pouch that I didn't recognize. I turned the worn fabric over in my hand. A Teenage Mutant Ninja Turtles emblem was so faded out that it was almost illegible. Inside the pouch were a child's treasures, a couple Hot Wheels, pretty rocks, baseball cards, a cheap adjustable ring with a blue stone, and several more trinkets. I picked up a tiny, unlined notebook, no bigger than two by three inches, and turned the pages. It was full of drawings of the same boy, and they were quite good. I wondered if they were self-portraits, but doubted it because the subject was always looking away, as if they'd been drawn while observing someone who didn't know the artist was there.

The fact that the boy in the drawings wasn't Cory Previn was confirmed when I took a look at the photos on my camera. He'd taken a series of selfies, which showed a kid with a ton of freckles, clunky glasses, and auburn hair that looked like he'd cut it himself. Not exactly the thug I'd been expecting.

In addition to the self-portraits, he'd also taken hundreds of pictures of anything he could find, like trees, old bottles, rusty barbed wire, often in close-up. They were exactly the kind of pictures I would have taken, and they showed he had a good eye. He'd take dozens of shots of the same thing, each time adjusting the camera settings, the focus, the angle. He was trying to learn, teaching himself. He was trying to get better.

"Shit," I whispered as I looked at his pictures. As if I didn't have enough on my plate. Now I actually found myself worried about a fifteen-year-old car thief in Gala, Wyoming.

*****

I didn't get off work until one a.m., but I still beat Finn home. He came in sometime around three and climbed onto the air mattress gingerly, trying not to wake me. I immediately crawled into his arms, and he pulled me close. "Sorry," he whispered. "I was trying to let you sleep."

"I was waiting for you to get home."

"Are you okay?"

"Yeah." I burrowed deeper into his embrace.

"I'm sorry I didn't tell you Asturias was at the station. I kind of thought you wouldn't come if you knew it was him, but I also thought you really should hear what he had to say."

"You were right, I might not have. Why am I so angry at him? He didn't really do anything wrong. Well, aside from being an asshole back in Gala, and waiting almost a month to tell me about the test results. And why the hell would he need the excuse of my camera to come and see me? Was 'I'm your father' not important enough on its own?"

"I don't know. Maybe he was scared to come see you, and the camera was enough to tip the scales."

I looked up at Finn in the darkness. "Why would he be afraid to come see me?"

"Well, because nobody likes rejection. I'm sure he knew he'd blown it back in Wyoming when he refused to listen to you and acted like a jerk. Maybe he thought you'd written him off after that."

"Life was already so damn complicated, Finn, and then he shows up out of the blue! I don't even know what to say to this guy! I don't know the first thing about him."

"So, maybe that's where you start. Just talk to him, get to know him. Isn't that what you wanted?"

I mulled it over for a while and finally said, "Yeah. You're right. I'm going to call him tomorrow. He came all this way, it won't kill me to have a cup of coffee with him."

"I'm glad you're giving him a chance."

We talked for a while, and then I leaned in and kissed him. He cupped the back of my neck as he deepened the kiss, and things soon got hot and heavy. We hadn't been able to do much since we'd been staying in his cousin's apartment, aside from a few stolen moments here and there, and Finn needed release. I knew that even before I ran my hand down his body and felt the growing erection in his boxer briefs. I climbed between his legs, freed his cock from his underwear and took it between my lips.

He let out a soft, "Ahhh," and wove his fingers in my hair as I began to suck him. I worked his shaft with my lips and hand and tongue while caressing his balls, and in just a few minutes he came, struggling to remain silent as his body shook and I swallowed his load. When he'd finished and was catching his breath, I pulled up his underwear and the blanket that had slid onto the floor and returned to his arms.

"Thank you," he said, and kissed my forehead.

"My pleasure."

"What about you, do you want a turn?"

"Next time."

He fell asleep a couple minutes later, and I rubbed my cheek against his chest and breathed in his scent, which was both familiar and comforting. I wanted to fall asleep too. My body was so tired, but my mind kept racing. After about half an hour, I gave up and slid out of bed. Finn stirred, but didn't wake up.

I decided I might as well do something productive as long as I was awake, so I picked up the cardboard file box I'd taken from my mother's closet. I'd already gone through the first box, which had been full of old bills, statements and receipts, and closed every account I came across. She'd had all of two hundred and thirty dollars in the bank. Since Hayes, the lawyer who was helping me on a pro bono basis, had filed the paperwork and I was named executor of her estate, I'd been able to close her account and move that money into a savings account for Colt. I thought 'estate' was a pretty ambitious word for a ramshackle old house and two hundred and thirty dollars.

I pulled the door to the office shut quietly, and when I stepped into the living room, I was surprised to find Dmitri on the couch. He was holding an e-reader in a black leather case, dressed in a black V-neck t-shirt and black cotton sleep pants. Somehow, he still looked pulled together and sophisticated, even at three a.m.

"I'm surprised you're awake," I said as I came into the living room.

"Lily woke up and wanted something to drink. I couldn't get back to sleep after that." Both of us spoke in a whisper, so we didn't disturb the rest of the household.

"I'm sorry to interrupt you."

"You're not at all. This book wasn't holding my attention. How are you doing, Chance?"

I sat on one of the white leather chairs on the other side of the big coffee table and put the file box on the floor at my feet. "Pissed off that I'm not asleep right now, but otherwise fine. How about you?"

He grinned and said, "The same. How much more paperwork do you have to go through?" He gestured at the file box when he said that.

"This is the second of two boxes I brought from my mom's house. The first was pretty straightforward and most of it went in the recycle bin when I was done with it, but so far this one has been less cut and dried." I pulled the lid off and set it aside, then took out one of the green paperboard folders and looked inside. "This, for example. It's full of Colt's report cards." I flipped through the papers and said, "All Bs and Cs. I see why she kept his and not mine, my grades were far worse. I guess I'll hang on to them, too."

I put that folder back in the box and pulled out the next one. It contained three birth certificates, mine, Colt's and my mom's. The folder after that contained only a sealed, blank envelope. I tore it open and read the one-page letter, written in my mother's girlish handwriting, then murmured, "Oh God."

Dmitri tossed his e-reader aside, came around the coffee table and sat on the edge of it, right in front of me. "Chance, what's wrong?"

My mouth was so dry when I said, "It…um…it's a letter from my mom."

"Oh wow."

"That's not the stunning part. It's what the letter says."

I handed it to Dmitri, and he read it quickly, then asked, "Who's Henry Aimsley?"

"He was my mother's boss. He was also the man who sexually molested me when I was thirteen and fourteen." I swallowed hard and said, "According to this, he's Colt's father."

"Oh dear God," Dmitri whispered.

I read the letter again. It explained how she'd gotten pregnant while she was having an affair with Aimsley and had been paid ten thousand dollars to keep it quiet, since he'd been married. It said she wanted to tell Colt who his father was, but because my "…lies had turned Colt against Henry," she was afraid to say anything. It also said that, if anything ever happened to her, Colt should go to Aimsley's family and ask for money.

"Fuck that," I muttered as I refolded the letter and put it back in the envelope.

"What are you going to do? Will you tell Colt?"

"I don't know. I do know this, though. I sure as hell won't let him go beg those rich, arrogant bastards for a handout. I don't care how many jobs I have to work, I'm going to take care of Colt without their help and make sure he never wants for anything. The Aimsleys can go fuck themselves." I handed Dmitri the letter and said, "Will you please hide this for me? If Colt does find out I want it to be from me, not from accidentally stumbling across that."

"Sure."

Dmitri took the envelope from me and I slumped in the chair and muttered, "Life just had to get even more complicated."

Chapter Nineteen

"I'm glad we had a chance to talk," Tony said as he leaned against the bar at Nolan's two days later. He'd planned to stay one more night, but the guy watching his bar was having some kind of meltdown, so Tony had come to say goodbye.

"Me too."

We'd met with each other twice during his visit to San Francisco. Our conversations had been more than a little awkward. We'd talked about random stuff, Gala and Simone, books, movies, the weather, nothing terribly personal. Neither of us was the type to open up quickly. "I wish we didn't live so far apart," he said, studying the wood floor. "Be nice if we could, you know, meet for coffee or have a meal together once in a while."

"I know." I shifted from foot to foot and adjusted the apron that was tied around my hips. "Oh shit, hang on. I almost forgot something." I went behind the bar, pulled out my old camera case, and handed it to him. "I need you to take this to Cory Previn."

"The punk who stole your car?"

"I don't think he's really a punk. He's just a kid with some problems."

"Why would you give him the benefit of the doubt like that?"

I unzipped the case, pulled out a paperboard envelope containing some prints I'd had made, and handed it to Tony. "Because of this. Anyone who can see beauty in the world like that has to have more going for him than meets the eye."

Tony flipped through the photos and said, "Previn took these?" I nodded, and he said, "They're good, I'll give him that, though I assume he took them with the camera he got out of the trunk of your stolen car."

"He did." I took the envelope when Tony handed it back to me and packed it carefully, beside Cory's Ninja Turtles pouch of treasures.

He glanced into the bag and said, "Hang on. Are you giving that delinquent your camera?"

"My old one. I don't need it anymore. Tell him this one might look beat up, but despite the duct tape, it has a lot of life left in it."

"You're out of your mind. You're rewarding him for stealing your car!"

I said, "What I hope I'm doing is letting him know at least one person in the world believes in him. Maybe that'll help in some small way."

"But you don't even know him."

"Tony, I *was* him, an artistic, troubled, gay kid growing up in a small town in Wyoming. I didn't go so far as grand theft auto, but I was constantly getting in trouble. I acted out all the time, in the hopes that my mom or someone else would notice me. When an adult did finally pay attention to me, it was entirely the wrong kind, and maybe I was singled out because I was so vulnerable."

"What does that mean?" Tony asked.

I told him quietly, even though the lunch rush was long over and the bar was empty, "I was sexually molested in my early teens. I'm not saying the same thing will happen to this kid, but he is vulnerable, not just to predators but to drug and alcohol abuse and dropping out of school and a million other things. Maybe it's not too late for him though, and maybe this one little gesture will make a difference."

I was startled when Tony grabbed me in an embrace. "God I'm sorry that happened to you."

"I'm okay now."

He let go of me and said, "I feel so fucking guilty for not being around when you were a kid, and I don't really know why, because I didn't even know you existed."

"You would've been a great dad, Tony."

"That's the nicest thing anyone's ever said to me."

"I mean it." We stood there awkwardly for a few moments, and finally I said, "I'm glad we had the chance to talk a bit. Thanks for coming all the way out here."

"Me too." He pushed his hair back and said, "Shit, I need to get on the road. But I'm going to come back for a visit next month, okay? I really want to get to keep getting to know you, Chance."

"I'd like that." He slung the camera bag's strap over his shoulder and I walked him to the door. When we got there, I said, "You know, you always wanted to be a dad, and it really sounds like Cory Previn needs a father. Maybe you two should talk a bit when you give him the camera." He raised a skeptical eyebrow at me and I added, "Just a thought."

We shook hands and he said, "I'll talk to you soon. Take care of yourself, Chance."

I nodded. "Drive safe going home."

Surprisingly, I felt a sense of loss when the door swung shut behind him. I didn't really understand that, since I'd gotten what I'd wanted, I'd found my dad. And at my age, it wasn't like I expected him to stick around and act like a parent. He had a life to get back to.

"You okay?"

I turned to look at Elijah, who stood a few feet away, fidgeting with a pencil. "I'm fine. I forgot you were back in that booth, you're always so quiet."

He said, "You don't have to automatically say you're fine. You do that a lot. It's okay if you're not."

"You're absolutely right."

"Your dad seemed like a pretty good guy. You gonna miss him?"

"Yeah, I am." I leaned against the wall beside the door and said, "Do you ever miss your family?"

"Is it really bad if I say no?"

"I don't think so."

He started dissecting the eraser on his pencil with a fingernail as he said, "I have four older brothers. They always knew I was different, from the time I was little, and they picked on me so bad. They called me a fag before I even knew there was such a thing as being gay. My parents didn't help at all. In fact, my dad would take my brothers' side and tell me I needed to 'man up'. That's a really fuckin' stupid thing to say to a five-year-old."

"It really is."

"Then there was the other thing that made me different, where I was super good at math and really liked it. I'd try to hide it, because it was just another way I didn't blend in."

"I'm sorry you felt you had to hide."

"That was how I survived, by trying to be invisible," Elijah said in his soft whisper of a voice. "I tried so hard. It didn't work, though. It just made me an easy mark for my uncle when he decided to molest me. Finally it all got to be too much, and I ran away. I had this idea that things would be better if I made it to California, that people would be more tolerant there. I really didn't think it through."

"I can relate to so much of that," I told him.

"I know. That's why I'm talkin' about it with you. I don't think most people will ever really understand what I went through, but I think you get it."

"Will you please promise me something?"

He glanced at me from under his dark eyelashes. "What?"

"If it ever gets bad here, if you and Colt have a fight, or if school starts to become overwhelming, or if things just go wrong in general, please promise me you'll come talk to me. I'm so scared you're going to run again, and that I won't be able to find you."

"You really want me around? I know Colt didn't give you a choice, he said you had to bring me or he wouldn't go with you."

"I absolutely want you around, Elijah. You're a part of this family and I care about you."

He closed the distance between us and hugged me, which surprised me because he usually avoided physical contact with everyone but Colt. He felt so tiny and fragile in my arms that it made me want to protect him more than ever. "I won't run, I promise. Y'all have been nicer to me than anyone's ever been in my life. I'm not gonna throw that away." He stepped back from me quickly, looking embarrassed, and said, "Alright enough mushy stuff. You gotta go get a shower."

I laughed at that and said, "Thanks! Do I stink?"

"No, nothin' like that. But I know somethin' you don't know." He gave me a little smile. "You might want to put on some nice clothes after you get cleaned up. Just sayin'."

"Alright, Captain Cryptic, I'm going. Are you going to stay down here for a while?"

"No, I'll come upstairs with you." He gathered up his books and papers and followed me as we cut through the kitchen, where I waved to a couple of my coworkers.

When we got upstairs, we discovered that Jamie had company. Two of his sisters, Maureen and Erin, were visiting, and so was his best friend Jessica. They relaxed in the living room and joked with Jamie and Dmitri as a couple giggling little blond boys ran around, pursued by Colt. My brother carried Lily on his shoulders and high-stepped like a horse, and the toddler howled with laughter.

It was such a perfect little moment that I had to pause and take it in. I'd had a hard time accepting so much help from Jamie and Dmitri, between the place to stay and the job, but they'd always made me feel so welcome, like I was part of the family. I was glad to see my brother obviously felt the same way.

Elijah went into the living room and perched on the arm of the couch. He was too embarrassed to join in when Colt took his hand and tried to pull him to his feet, but he was smiling. I took one last look at all that joy and smiled wistfully as I went to get my shower.

*****

Everyone was in on the secret but me. Their big, goofy grins were a dead giveaway. After I showered and got dressed in a dark blue button-down shirt and the one pair of pants I owned which weren't jeans, I went out into the living room and found Jamie and Dmitri, the sisters and Jessica, Colt and Elijah, and even the two little boys and Lily lined up in front of the kitchen. Even the toddler was grinning.

"Okay, when do I get to know what's up?" I asked.

"Any minute now," Dmitri said.

"Do you own a tie?" Colt asked.

"Yeah, one. Do I need it?"

"Couldn't hurt," my brother said. I grinned too and went to find it in the suitcase I'd been using as a dresser.

Someone knocked on the door just as I finished knotting my tie, and I returned to the living room. Everyone was still lined up shoulder-to-shoulder, blocking the kitchen from my line of sight. "I guess I'm getting that?" I asked. Nine grinning heads nodded and Lily giggled.

I opened the door to Finn, looking devastatingly handsome in a suit and tie. He held out a big bouquet of flowers in every shade of red and said, "Chance Matthews, will you go out on a real date with me?"

I smiled at him as I took the flowers and said, "With pleasure."

He stepped inside and kissed me on the cheek, and my brother yelled, "Oh come on! You can do better than that!"

Everyone laughed, and Finn took hold of me, dipped me and kissed me with everything he had. My heart raced and embarrassingly, my cock tried to get in on the action. When he swung me upright again, I had to hide behind him and adjust the front of my black dress pants. That resulted in another round of laughter, this time accompanied by some whistling. "What?" asked Jamie's nephew Brennan, the older of the two blond kids.

"He liked it," Colt said, and Jamie started laughing again.

"Yeah, that about sums it up. Come on guys, let's get out of here so Phase One can commence," Jamie said. He grabbed a nearby diaper bag and slung it over his shoulder while Dmitri scooped up Lily, and the entire group began to filter out of the apartment.

"Have fun, you two," Maureen said, tossing her strawberry blonde hair over her shoulder and winking at us roguishly.

"I helped make the tap-it-tizers!" Brody, the younger of Erin's sons, proudly exclaimed, stopping in front of us and beaming delightedly.

His brother took his arm and started to drag him out of the apartment as he said, "There apple-tizers, doofus. Now let's go. Uncle Finn needs to get all romantic with his boyfriend and stuff." Technically he was second cousin Finn, but he'd earned the honorary title somewhere along the line.

The boys started to bicker as they left the apartment, and Erin their mom sighed dramatically as she followed them.

"I'm guessing the tap-it-tizing will come later," Colt said with a huge grin. "Just a hunch. You two have the best time ever, for real. We won't wait up!"

Eventually, the rambunctious procession made it out the door, and Finn called a thank you and closed it behind them. I turned to look at the kitchen and a smile spread across my face. The big table had a white tablecloth over it and was dotted with candles, all of them battery-operated since the house was pretty thoroughly child-proofed. Lots of little glass vessels held white daisies, and two places were set, side by side, with the "good" china (in other words, not paper plates) and cloth napkins.

Finn took my flowers from me, peeled off the wrapping and put them in a water-filled vase that was waiting on the counter. He put them on the table as a centerpiece, then pulled my chair out for me. After I sat down, he kissed the top of my head and said as he headed to the refrigerator, "It's a bit early for dinner, so this is just appetizers and cocktails. We'll be eating later. I just didn't want you to be hungry." When he opened the fridge, he said, "Oh wow, they really went to town. I didn't think they'd make this much." He pulled out two big trays of appetizers and set them on the table, followed by a pitcher of martinis. Once he filled my glass and his, he sat down beside me and said, "Cheers."

We clinked our glasses together, and I said, "Thank you so much for this. You didn't have to go through so much trouble, though. We already went on a real date."

"What, you think you only get one? It'd be pretty tough to top our picnic at Devils Tower, granted, but still, I really want you to have a special evening. We've been so damn busy with work and the kids and everything else that there's been no time for us. I thought we needed to remedy that."

"You're so sweet," I said, and leaned in and kissed him before turning to the bite-sized treats. I had to chuckle. One silver tray began with a tidy row of round finger sandwiches, obviously done by an adult as an example. The kids had then obviously gotten into the cookie cutters, because that one neat row gave way to finger sandwich mayhem. Rocket ships, cats, and Christmas trees shared the stage with flowers, Easter bunnies and jack-o-lanterns. It was awesome. I put a rocket on Finn's plate and a tree on mine, then passed him the second tray of assorted delicacies, again ranging from sophisticated to kid-creative. He loaded up both our plates.

We ate our fill, and since we also polished off the entire pitcher of martinis, I wondered how he was planning to get us to our next destination. That question was answered when we went downstairs. Nana's white stretch limo was double parked in front of the restaurant. Jessie was leaning against the fender, and jumped up to open the door for us. He was more or less dressed like a chauffeur, which technically had been his job description when Nana hired him, although he'd evolved into much more since then. He wore a black cap, a short-sleeved black shirt, and a pink bowtie. But he was also wearing tight black shorts and combat boots, hence the less. It looked good on him, though.

"Hey guys!" he exclaimed. He gave me a hug and slapped Finn on the back when we came up to him.

"Hi Jessie. You look great," I told him.

"Thanks! You do, too, both of you. Hop in, we don't want to be late."

A bottle of champagne in an ice bucket and a box of chocolates were waiting for us in the back of the limo. "Well damn, you went all out," I told Finn as we settled in.

He picked up the bottle and popped the cork as he said, "I can only take credit for calling Jessie to see about borrowing the limo. The champagne and chocolates must be Nana's doing." He grinned and picked up something from the scat. "Along with this giant box of condoms."

Jessie called through the divider, "Nana was so excited when she heard Finn wanted to take you on a special date, Chance. She's a true romantic. She also told me I should give you some privacy so you can make out." He flashed us a big smile in the rearview mirror and put up the tinted divider.

"Well, if Nana insists," I said as I climbed onto Finn's lap. I straddled his hips and rested my forehead against his as

I said, "Thank you again. This is so over the top. I feel like we're going to prom."

"Oh man, my prom would have been ten thousand times better if I'd taken you!"

"I never got to go to any school dances. Sadly, I don't think my high school equivalency studies include one either. And they call themselves equivalent," I joked.

"I wish I had a do-over. I'd take you in a heartbeat." I grinned at that and kissed Finn as I stroked his soft, short hair.

A few minutes later, the limo pulled up in front of the Castro Theater. When I looked up at the marquee, I said, "Oh wow." It was a Raymond Chandler double feature. "I can't believe you remembered I liked Chandler. I mentioned that once in passing when we were at the Whitman."

We got a few looks when Jessie came around and opened the door and we stepped out of the limo. A guy in the crowd said, "Shit, I was hoping for Beyoncé!"

"Have fun! See you afterwards, guys!" Jessie said as he hurried to move the limo and unblock traffic.

We thanked him and turned toward the theater. I was worried we'd be overdressed, but some of the crowd had made it a 1940s theme night and there were a lot of suits and fedoras in the crowd. Finn handed over our tickets and we entered the lobby. When we stepped into the regal theater, I felt the same sense of wonder I did every time I came here. It was lush and opulent, built in the 1920s and later declared a

Historic Landmark. Since it was located in San Francisco's gay neighborhood, it also brought in one of the most fun, interactive crowds anywhere. They cheered, hissed at the villains (or applauded them, depending on the film), and took movie-going to a whole new level.

The theater was showing a double feature of The Big Sleep and Double Indemnity. We took our seats and I pulled Finn to me and kissed him. "Thank you so much for this," I said as I linked my arm with his.

He grinned and said, "You don't have to keep thanking me."

"Oh yes I do."

*****

Jessie timed our pick-up perfectly. He pulled up just as the movies let out, we hopped in the back, and he rolled on out of the Castro. "So how was it?" he asked.

"Terrific, but please tell me you haven't been circling for four hours," I said.

"Nope, I went to a club. Parking the Nanamobile was a bitch, but I actually managed it! It was like a Christmas miracle!" Jessie said.

"In September."

He grinned at me in the rearview mirror. "Christmas miracles can happen any time. That's part of the reason they're miracles."

As we rolled down Market Street I asked, "What are we doing now?"

"Beginning phase three," Finn said. He looked a little nervous for some reason, but he was smiling. Jessie drove us out past Hunter's Point, to the southeastern corner of San Francisco. As we wound through a sparsely populated industrial area, I asked where we were going, and Finn said, "You'll see. We're almost there."

Eventually, we reached a blocky two-story warehouse with rusty, corrugated metal walls, which backed up to the bay. It sat by itself on a patch of dirt and weeds, looking pretty forgotten. I was surprised when the limo stopped and Finn got out of the car. He helped me out by offering me his hand, then leaned back in and called, "Thank you so much, Jessie. I owe you one! We'll see you soon!"

"Good luck," Jessie called back. Finn closed the door and the limo pulled away, leaving us in the middle of nowhere.

I grinned at Finn and said, "I admire your unpredictability. Never in a million years would I have guessed our date would end up in the most remote corner of the city."

"It's good to keep you on your toes." Finn still held my hand, and led me to the nine-foot-high rusty door. He grasped the door's edge and said, "I need you to do something for me."

"Sure. What is it?"

"I need you to use your imagination."

"Um, okay." He slid the door open with a bit of effort, and my breath caught. The interior of the warehouse was lit with dozens of strands of white light bulbs suspended from the two-story ceiling, casting a warm, golden glow. The light reflected off the polished, honey-colored wood floor and the wall of glass at the back of the building. "It's so beautiful," I said as we stepped inside.

The warehouse was mostly empty, but someone had set up a picnic with flowers and candles right in the middle of the room. I looked to my right, where an industrial kitchen was tucked in the space beneath a second-story balcony. A row of offices lined the balcony, each with a glass door and a big front window. "What is this place?" I asked, looking up at the exposed ductwork on the high ceiling.

"In 1925, it was the Hofstedler Bottling Company. They made some kind of medicinal soda, which never quite caught on," Finn told me. "They went out of business in the 1950s, and the warehouse sat abandoned until 1988, when my cousin Shaun bought it. You remember him, right, the one whose wife's expecting their third child?"

"I remember."

"Shaun had this crazy idea to turn this into a trendy restaurant. The fact that it was totally out of the way didn't dissuade him. He felt that, if he built something special enough, people would seek it out, so he poured all kinds of money into this place, upgrading the electrical, the plumbing, adding the kitchen, reinforcing it against earthquakes. Unfortunately, he was dead wrong, and his restaurant went under just a year after it opened. He tried to sell the building after that, but no one wanted such a small warehouse, or the tiny lot it sits on. Not even developers were interested."

"So, what are we doing here?"

"Well, I ran into Shaun at the grocery store last week, and we got to talking about real estate. He knows I've been saving for a house for years, but the market keeps outpacing my savings. I asked him if he'd ever managed to sell the warehouse, and then I had a crazy idea. I asked him what he'd take for this place."

"Why?"

Finn said, "Well, it occurred to me that maybe I should broaden my definition of what a home could be. Shaun's willing to make me an amazing deal on this building, because he wants to be rid of it once and for all. I think he's being overly generous because I'm family, but he wouldn't listen when I tried to tell him that. Anyway, I'd love to buy this place, but it's not just up to me. I need to know what you think about it, Chance. Should I do it?"

"It's not really my call."

"Sure it is, because I wouldn't just be buying it for me. I'd be buying it for *us*, all of us, you and me and Colt and Elijah. I want this to be our home, but only if you think you'd be happy here." I must have looked startled, because Finn added, "I know we started living together out of necessity, but I want to make it official. If you think this could be the right place for us, then let's buy it together and make it ours."

"But you're the one with all the money," I said. "I couldn't really contribute."

"This isn't about money, Chance. Not even a little. It's about you and me, and it's about building a future together."

"But I can't just mooch off of you."

"If it's that important to you, contribute what you can toward the down-payment. It doesn't have to be fifty-fifty. I know you've been saving for an apartment, so maybe if you put that money into this place it'll help you feel like it's yours, too."

"As if a couple thousand bucks would buy a share of this place," I said.

Finn pressed his eyes shut for a moment. He then turned and walked across the warehouse to the glass wall at the back. It was made up of a couple hundred square panes in a metal grid with a large glass door in the center of it, and he unlocked the door and stepped outside.

I trailed after him and said, "I'm sorry. Please don't be mad."

He turned to look at me. A breeze off the bay ruffled his hair and his eyes reflected the ring of lights around the patio. "I'm not mad at you, I'm mad at myself. I always said I was no good with words, and I'm totally proving that right now. I don't know what to say or do to make you see this the way I do." He pushed his hair back from his forehead and told me, "I want us to be not only a couple, but a family, Chance. I want that so much. How can I convince you that it doesn't come down to my money and your money? Everything I have is yours. *I'm* yours. Don't you see?"

I whispered, "I'll never understand why you think you're bad with words. You actually say such wonderful things to me."

"There's so much more I want to tell you. In fact, there's something I've been wanting to say for a while now. I kept trying to think of the perfect way to say it, and the perfect time and place. But maybe that stuff doesn't matter. Maybe all that matters is saying it, so here goes." Finn drew a breath and blurted, "I'm totally in love with you, Chance."

I smiled at him as happiness bloomed in my chest. "I love you, too, Finn. I love you so much."

"I was hoping you'd say that."

Finn took me in his arms as I said, "You had to know I felt the same way."

He smiled as I looked up at him. "I thought so. But still, it's scary to say those words out loud. That was a first for me." Finn kissed me, and desire ignited in both of us at the same time. I sucked his tongue when he pushed it into my mouth, and his hands slid down my back and cupped my ass. He picked me up and I wrapped my arms and legs around him, rocking my hips to rub my cock against his through our clothes.

He spun us around and pushed my back against the glass wall as he gently nipped my lower lip. His warm breath on my ear gave me goosebumps, and he nibbled my earlobe and whispered, "I need to be inside you."

"I need that, too," I said before his mouth claimed mine in a demanding kiss. A shiver of pleasure went through me, my cock swelling as Finn carried me inside, kissing me the whole way, and laid me on my back on the wood floor. He stripped me quickly, licking and kissing each body part he exposed, starting with my shoulder, then working his way down. He lightly bit my nipple, then ran his tongue down my belly, licked my cock, and dotted a line of kisses along my inner thigh.

When I was completely naked he sat back on his heels and ran his gaze down the length of me with such raw hunger that I shivered again, thrusting my hips slightly, my cock throbbing. It was such a turn-on to be on display like this for him while he remained completely dressed in his suit and tie. "I belong to you, Finn," I said in a jagged whisper.

He looked me right in the eye as he ran both hands down my torso and said, his voice low, "Yes. You do. And I'm going to make sure you never forget it."

This was a different Finn, worlds removed from the man whose virginity I took all those months ago. He was confident, totally in control, and he knew what he wanted. It was clear in those focused blue eyes. Another tremor went through me, every nerve ending tingling with electricity. I made myself lay still, letting him call the shots, and that made my already hard cock swell even more and twitch as precum dripped steadily onto my naked body.

He climbed between my legs, pushing them apart with his knees, and pressed his tongue flat against the base of my cock, then dragged it slowly to the tip and licked the precum off me. "You taste so fucking good," he murmured before licking my stomach. I was shaking with need by that point and the one lick up my shaft was almost enough to push me over the edge. He was in no hurry to finish me off, though.

Finn cupped my balls, squeezing them lightly as he dipped his tongue into my navel. When he licked his way up my body and bit my nipple again, I drew in my breath and arched up off the floor. He caught me around the waist and held me there. When he stuck his face between my legs and lapped at the sensitive spot beneath my balls, I cried out and writhed in his grasp.

He laid me on the floor again and spread my legs with a hand on the back of each thigh, exposing me as he pressed my knees to my chest. I moaned when he drove his tongue into me, opening me up before he slid it out again and licked my opening. He kept that up for a while as I reached down and stroked my cock, and then he sat up a bit and pulled a bottle of lube from his jacket pocket.

I kept my legs right where he'd put them as he drizzled the lube over my hole and onto his hand. He pushed two fingers inside me and rotated his wrist, grazing my prostate and making me yell as a shockwave of pleasure pulsed through me. Then he slid his hand out and said, "I'm going to fuck you raw, baby." I stopped stroking myself and raised my head to look at him. "We both got tested last week, just like you've been doing every six months. We know it's safe."

"But still...knowing what I was?" I whispered.

"We're ready for this step, Chance."

I stared at him for a moment, and he held my gaze steadily. Finally I told him, "I'm willing if you are."

He gave me a sexy smile as his fingers slid into me again and slowly fucked my hole. "Oh, I'm willing." Finn rested his other hand beside my head and leaned down to kiss me.

He pulled back a few inches and looked in my eyes again as he said in a low voice, "Just so you know, I'm not going to hold back. We can make love some other time. Tonight, we're going to fuck. I want you to feel so damn good and cum so hard that you forget everything but my name. I'm going to make you mine with every thrust into you, and then I'm going to cum inside you. I want you to know for an absolute fact that you belong to me. Only me. Do you have a problem with that?"

I almost came just from hearing that and shook with desire as I ground my ass onto his fingers. "No problem at all," I told him, my voice husky, and added, "I like this side of you."

He grinned and kept fingering me as he unfastened the top button of his shirt, then draped his tie over his shoulder. When he leaned down to kiss me again, it was forceful and demanding. I fumbled with his belt and the button on his pants, and when I got them open I plunged both hands into his boxer briefs and grabbed his firm ass, pulling him to me and rubbing my cock against his.

He slid his fingers out of me, then pulled out his swollen cock and rubbed lube over the flared pink head and down the thick shaft. He licked his full lips, his eyes half-lidded as he ran his gaze from my face to my groin. I let my bent legs fall open, offering him all of me.

Finn bit my nipple at the same moment he plunged his cock into me, and I yelled from the sheer intensity of it, pleasure firing through me. He grabbed my body and pushed into me forcefully, again and again as I yelled, "Oh fuck yes," and drove myself onto him, trying to take him as deep into me as I possibly could.

At one point I grabbed his dress shirt and pulled it apart, buttons flying everywhere, then tugged off his tie and threw it out of my way. I ran my arms under his clothes, holding on to his strong body tightly as I rocked beneath him from the force of his thrusts. Finn pounded into me, both of us moaning and yelling incoherently. It was wild and primal and absolutely intense, and I completely got lost in it. Nothing existed in all the world but Finn and me and that moment.

He slammed into my prostate again and again, his big, thick cock filling me, stretching me, and I threw my head back and yelled as I arched up off the floor. I needed him closer. Deeper. I needed him to be a part of me. I clawed at his back, wildly, desperately, and when he yelled and came in me, I shoved his jacket out of my way and bit his shoulder, hard. All rational thought had completely fallen away. I was distilled down to sex and need and hunger, and he was, too. He fucked me like it might be our last time ever, urgently, almost frantically, pushing his seed into me with each thrust, yelling as he came in me. He dropped onto his elbows, his face inches from mine, his pupils so dilated that his eyes looked black, and told me, "You're mine." It was an absolute statement of fact.

"Yes. Fuck yes. Yours." The words tumbled from me. I was surprised I could talk.

When he pulled out of me, his cock was barely deflated. "Fuck me, Chance." His voice was pure gravel.

I sat up and pulled his jacket and shirt from his body, the buttons of both cuffs sailing off into the warehouse, then slid his pants and underwear to mid-thigh. He got on his hands and knees as I fumbled for the lube and slicked my throbbing cock. I pushed a wet finger into his warm opening, fingering him roughly as I told him, "It's going to hurt." I was way too worked up to think clearly, let alone prep him properly.

"Good."

I pulled my finger from him after just a minute and pushed my cock into his incredibly tight butt, grabbing his hips. We both moaned, and he mumbled, "Fuck yes, don't stop." I took him like he'd taken me, hard, fast, and rough. Our jagged yells shattered the stillness, along with the sound of my body slapping into his. My fingers dug into his flesh as I pulled him onto my cock, impaling him as he drove himself back in a steady rhythm.

We both knew I wouldn't last long, not after all of that. I bellowed when I came, not even recognizing my own voice as I emptied myself into him, thrust after thrust, driving my cum deep into him, claiming him in a way he'd never been claimed before. "Oh fuck, yes," Finn exclaimed as he grabbed his cock and started jerking off. I was astounded when he came again, shooting across the wood floor, his already tight ass clenching my cock, milking every drop of cum from my balls. I shot into him again and again until I had absolutely nothing left, and then I collapsed onto my side, taking him with me.

"Holy shit," I said as I gasped for breath. I was trembling and Finn was too, both of our bodies utterly depleted and covered in sweat. "Where did that come from?"

"Don't know." Finn rolled over to face me, then rolled me over too and spooned against my back, wrapping his arms around me and draping a leg over mine. "But my God was it good."

"Good. Such an understatement. That was epic," I said, smiling contentedly. "I didn't know either of us could be that uninhibited."

"You're amazing when you let yourself go."

"So are you." Something occurred to me and I asked, "Oh God, did I bite you? I did, didn't I?" I tried to look at him over my shoulder and Finn gave me a big smile.

"You did. It was awesome."

"I don't know what came over me. I didn't mean to hurt you."

"You didn't hurt me, and even if you had I wouldn't care. It was such a turn-on to watch you like that, so wild and totally caught up in the moment." He kissed my bare shoulder and snuggled against me.

I ran my fingertips down his forearm, which was draped across my chest, and after a while I said, "I used to wonder if I was really a bottom before I met you. I know the answer now."

"Which is?"

"I'm mostly a bottom, but I also love fucking you. Can I call myself truly versatile if it's eighty-twenty and not fifty-fifty?"

Finn said, "I think you can call yourself whatever you want. I used to wonder the same thing about myself, by the way. What I've realized is that I'm about eighty percent a top, twenty percent a bottom. Is that perfect or what? It's like we were made for each other."

I laced my fingers with his, raised his hand to my lips, and kissed it before asking, "How soon can we move in here?"

Finn sat up and said, "Really?"

I rolled onto my back and looked up at him. "I want to live with you more than anything. That's so much bigger than my money worries. And I love this warehouse. It's beautiful, and it'll be even better when we move in and fill it with life. I can just see it. We can get a couple couches and put them over there," I pointed to the corner diagonally across from the kitchen, beside the glass wall, "and make a cozy seating area with a coffee table and maybe a big tree in a giant pot. Wouldn't that be pretty? We can also get an enormous dining room table since we'll have so much space, and then we can have Jamie and Dmitri and Shea and Christian and all our friends and family over. Plus, there's already that great breakfast bar in front of the kitchen. Colt and Eli can sit there and study while you and I cook. Doesn't that sound great?"

He smiled at me and brushed my hair back from my face. "It really does. I'll have to learn to cook to make your little domestic fantasy a reality, but I have no problem with that."

"We can both learn to cook. It'll be fun."

"I think so, too." Finn stretched out on his stomach right beside me, arms folded under his head, and said, "To answer your question, we can probably move in any time we like. Shaun really doesn't care if we complete escrow first. The only problem is that there's no shower. There are his and hers restrooms down here with two stalls each, and one more small restroom upstairs. They all work, but this space wasn't designed with the idea of anyone living here."

"So, we'll improvise until we can have a shower built. Is it legal for us to live here though? It must be zoned commercial."

"It's zoned mixed use residential. A developer back in the eighties wanted to turn this entire area into condos and got it all rezoned before he went bankrupt."

"It's like it was meant to be."

"It was."

Finn leaned in and kissed me, then gave me the sweetest smile. It lit up his whole face, and I told him, "You look so happy. I love seeing you like this."

"Right back at you." He kissed me again before asking, "Are you hungry? It looks like Jamie and Dmitri totally went overboard when I asked them to set up the picnic I made us. I see a silver ice bucket with champagne and a whole cheesecake over there, which are their additions."

"I'm starving, actually," I said as I sat up, too. We washed up in the men's room (that was going to be an interesting feature once we moved in) then made ourselves comfortable on the white cotton blanket that had been spread out beneath the picnic. We were both still naked, but so comfortable with each other that it didn't matter.

As Finn loaded up my plate and his with all kinds of delicacies, he glanced at me and asked, "So, what you were saying before about your financial concerns…is that going to be an issue if we proceed with buying this place?"

"It definitely bothers me that I can't be an equal partner and pay my own way. I especially hate feeling like I'm taking from you and not giving enough back. But I don't want to let money get in the way of what we have. What I want more than anything is to build a future with you, and I love the idea of doing that here. I'll contribute as much as I can, but I guess I'm going to have to come to terms with the fact that it'll never be a fifty-fifty split."

"But there's so much more to a partnership than financial parity."

"You're right, but I still hate the fact that you have to bear so much of the financial burden."

"But I don't mind that at all. Plus, I make more than you for now, but just wait," Finn said. "Eventually you're going to get your big break because you're an incredibly gifted photographer, it's inevitable. When all the money starts rolling in from selling your work at the finest galleries, I fully intend to let you spoil me." He smiled at me, then popped an olive in his mouth.

"Because that's going to happen any minute."

"It could. Actually, you know what? My cousin Kieran's husband owns a successful art gallery. I bet Christopher would be glad to sell your work."

I shook my head. "No way. I'm not going to put Christopher in a position where he feels he has to put my stuff in his gallery because I'm dating a relative."

Finn raised an eyebrow at me. "It wouldn't have anything to do with nepotism. Your work is amazing."

"Thank you for saying that. But still, no."

"We're going to work on that," he said as he placed a couple glasses in front of us and popped the cork on the champagne.

"Work on what?"

"Your unwillingness to let people help you."

"I do let people help me. I let Jamie and Dmitri give me a job and a place to stay, and you completely saved my ass when I was in Wyoming."

"Okay, so maybe it's that you refuse to ask for help." Finn filled one of the glasses and handed it to me.

"You're right. But learning to accept help when it's offered is something. There was a time in my life when I wouldn't have done that, no matter how much I needed it."

He considered that as he filled his champagne flute, then lifted it in a toast. "To progress." I grinned at him and tapped my glass to his.

Chapter Twenty

The next morning, I awoke to a beautiful golden light filling the warehouse. I stretched my arms over my head and looked around me, then pushed myself to my feet and crossed the room to join Finn in the kitchen. He'd gotten cleaned up and was dressed in a white t-shirt and faded jeans that hugged his ass perfectly. Coffee brewed in a machine I recognized from Jamie and Dmitri's kitchen, and he was arranging a selection of pastries on a plate. I kissed him and he smiled at me and said, "Good morning. I brought you some clothes, they're in the men's room with a towel. Washing up is a little awkward in the sink, but doable."

"I'm once again astonished by your ability to think of everything."

He grinned at me. "I don't always. As you'll recall, I packed nothing but twenty pairs of underwear to go to Wyoming."

"Just shows how much of a rush you were in when you were trying to come help me." I kissed him again and said, "I'll be right back."

I used the toilet, then cleaned myself up as much as I could and brushed my teeth (he thought of that, too). Once I was dressed, I rejoined Finn and sat beside him on the kitchen counter. "How do you feel this morning?" he asked as I sipped my coffee.

"A little stiff from sleeping on the floor, but great otherwise. This place is beautiful in the morning light. Makes me wish I had my camera with me."

"I texted Shaun this morning and he's totally fine with us moving in any time we want to. Do you still feel the same way you did last night?"

I nodded and said, "I want this, Finn, I want to make this a home for both of us and for the boys. I think we could all be so happy here."

"I know we can."

"You sure we're not taking advantage of your cousin, though? The right buyer would pay him a fortune for this, even if it was just for the land."

"Like I said, he tried to sell it for years with no serious offers, and now he just wants to be done with it. Shaun isn't stupid. He was a lousy restauranteur, but he's made a lot of smart real estate investments and fully understands the value of this place. Yes, he's making me a great deal, but he's not giving it away. I wouldn't worry too much about taking advantage of him," Finn said.

There was a knock on the metal door, and Finn crossed the warehouse and let Jessie in. "Good morning, guys!" My friend came inside and looked around. "This warehouse is totally awesome! Please tell me Finn convinced you to buy it," he said to me.

I told him, "He did. I want us to move in right away."

Jessie clapped his hands. "That's so great! Finn was worried that you wouldn't like it. I think he fell in love with the place the moment he saw it, even though from what I hear, it was a huge mess when he came to look at it."

I glanced at my boyfriend and asked, "Really?"

Finn nodded. "I've been coming here and cleaning every day for a week, after each shift at work. I didn't want you to see it all dusty and full of cobwebs. It was already a stretch to think of this place as a home, and that wouldn't have helped its case any."

I grinned at him and said, "I think I still would have seen the potential in this place, but thanks for going to all that trouble. And hey, now it's move-in ready."

Jessie sat on the stainless steel kitchen counter with us and enjoyed some coffee and pastries before we got going. The limo was parked out front, though my friend had gone with a t-shirt, jeans and a baseball cap instead of the chauffeur uniform. Finn locked up behind us, and once we were in the limo he asked Jessie, "Would you mind if we made one stop before you take us home?"

"Not a problem. Nana's getting her hair done. It always takes a couple hours, so she won't need me for a while.

Where do you want to go?" Jessie said, and Finn recited an address.

"Where are we going?" I asked as I settled in beside him and Finn put his arm around my shoulders.

"My parents' house. There's something I've been putting off way too long."

I took his hand. "Are you coming out to them?"

He nodded. "I've been dreading this confrontation, but I can't keep living with it hanging over me."

"You don't have to face it alone, Finn. I'll be right by your side, if that's what you want."

"It's going to get really ugly, I guarantee it," he said, looking out the window. "You shouldn't have to be subjected to something like that."

"But would you feel better if I was there?" He hesitated, but then he nodded and I said, "Okay, that's settled."

The house he'd grown up in was a narrow two-story structure in the Sunset District. It was white stucco, fairly plain, and neat and tidy to a fault. It looked like the grass in the tiny front yard had been dyed green and trimmed with a pair of scissors, so that every blade of grass was exactly the same height.

We climbed the front stairs and Finn took a deep breath, then wiped his hands on his jeans and rang the doorbell. A shiny brass plaque above the bell said 'The Nolans'. The casing that contained the doorbell was shiny brass, too. Were there really people in the world that polished doorbells?

A tall woman with short, brown hair opened the door and exclaimed, "Finn! Why did you ring the bell, did you lose your key? Come in. Who's your friend?"

"Actually Mom, could you get Dad and ask him to come to the door? I need to tell both of you something."

She knit her brows at that and said, "Don't be ridiculous, Finn. Come inside."

"There's no point," he said. "You're just going to kick me out as soon as you hear what I have to tell you, so this saves you the trouble."

Her frown deepened, and she called over her shoulder, "Father, will you come to the door, please? Your son's here to see you but he won't come inside."

A huge man appeared behind her. He was as tall as Finn and fairly muscular, but he also sported a prominent beer belly. "What are you talking about, Mother? Why won't Finn come in?" He filled the doorway and looked me up and down. "Who's your friend, Finn?"

"This is Chance, my boyfriend." He reached over and took my hand. His palm was sweating and his hand was shaking slightly. Both his parents looked absolutely stricken, as if they'd just been told someone died. "I should have told you a long time ago, but, well, I'm telling you now. I'm gay."

For a long moment, his parents just stood there, completely immobile. But then his mother burst into tears and turned to bury her face is her husband's shoulder as she wailed, "Why is God punishing me like this? Why? What have I done to deserve two gay sons?"

Mr. Nolan patted his wife's back as he glared at Finn and bellowed, "Is this what you wanted, to upset your mother? Are you happy now?"

"No, Dad. I just needed to tell you the truth."

The man was turning red, a vein bulging on his forehead. "Get out! Do you hear me? Get out of here! You're no longer welcome in this home, you and Shea both!"

While he was yelling, his wife kept up a steady chant of, "Why? Why? Why?"

Finn sighed quietly and said, "I know. Bye, Dad."

"You should be ashamed of yourself," the man yelled as Finn and I turned and started down the stairs, hand-in-hand. "How could you choose a life of sin over your family? You're going to burn in hell for what you're doing, you and Shea and that faggot boyfriend of yours! All of you are going to burn, and that's just what you deserve!"

Finn let go of my hand and ran back up the stairs. "Oh hell no!" he yelled. "I don't really give a shit if you condemn me. Nothing I did was ever good enough for you anyway! But for you to condemn Shea and Chance is bullshit! They're the two kindest, sweetest, most decent men on this planet, and they deserve so much better!"

"Don't you raise your voice to me!" his father yelled.

"I have to raise my voice, or else you won't fucking hear me! If you two want to drive away your own flesh and blood, guess what? It's your loss, not ours! And you know what else? You don't speak for God! You don't get to decide who's going to heaven and who's going to hell! Only God decides that, and I don't believe for one moment that he would punish me for being what he made me!"

Mr. Nolan's face was completely red. "How dare you curse at me, you piece of shit!"

"Ironic much?" I said to myself, but then I drew in my breath as his father pulled his fist back and lunged at Finn, looking like he planned to deck him.

He didn't get the chance. Finn twisted his father's arm behind his back, spun him around, and mashed him against the stucco wall. Then my boyfriend said calmly, "You seem to have forgotten that your piece of shit son is a member of the SFPD, and if you come at me, you damn well better believe I'm pressing charges."

A lot of wind had been taken out of his father's sails, given how effortlessly his son had overpowered him. Finn turned and walked down the stairs, leaving the man seething on the landing. He picked up my hand again when he reached me, and when we got to the limo, Jessie held the door open for us. Once we'd climbed inside, Jessie spun around and flipped Mr. Nolan off with both hands, which made me smile. He then got back behind the wheel and said, "You okay, Finn?"

"Yeah. That actually went exactly how I thought it would," my boyfriend said as he shook out both hands and let some of his tension drain away.

"You did awesome. That took major balls, since you knew how they'd react," Jessie said.

Finn leaned against me and I put my arms around him. "At least I got it over with. I feel kind of nauseous right now, but I'm sure that'll be replaced with relief later on."

"What made you want to do that today?" I asked him.

"You and I are about to begin a new chapter in our lives and that was a loose end that needed to be tied up. It had been on my mind a lot and I didn't want it hanging over me, especially when I have so many more important things to focus on."

After a pause I said, "It's super creepy that your parents call each other Mother and Father."

He grinned a little and said, "I know, I always thought that was weird. Who knows what they're going to call each other now that they've disowned both their children."

Finn turned his head and stared out the window. I could tell he was just beginning to process what had happened. All I could do was hold him a little tighter.

When we got back to the apartment, we both hugged Jessie and thanked him. "It was my pleasure," he said with a smile that made his blue eyes crinkle at the corners. "I'm super stoked that you and Finn found each other. It's a great reminder to never stop believing in the power of love, no matter how dismal my own love life might be."

He gave us a little salute before getting behind the wheel. As the limo slowly made its way down the back alley, Finn drew me into his arms and buried his face in my hair. We just stayed like that for a while, wrapped up in each other. Eventually, he said, "It's kind of weird, choosing a day at random and knowing that would be the day I lost both my parents."

"I wish it didn't have to be that way."

"When I was younger, I used to think there had to be some way around what just happened, that if I could just think of the right words when I came out to them they'd understand and it'd be okay. I tried to figure out what those words were for such a long time. But the older I got, the more I realized it would never be okay. It just wouldn't. There were no magic words to make them keep loving me."

"Like you said, it's their loss. If they're stupid enough to put hate and prejudice ahead of family, then they don't deserve you and Shea." He nodded and I told him, "You don't need them anyway. You have me and Colt and Elijah, and your brother and brother-in-law, and about a thousand cousins and nieces and nephews and aunts and uncles, and we all love you so damn much. I'm going to make sure you know how much you're loved, every single day."

"God I'm lucky I have you," Finn said softly.

A voice close beside us asked, "What's wrong?" Finn and I broke apart, startled, and Elijah said, "Sorry. I didn't mean to sneak up on you. I saw the limo pull away a while ago, and then you didn't come upstairs."

"Finn just came out to his parents," I told him.

Elijah's brown eyes went wide and he asked, "Was it bad?"

Finn nodded and said, "I knew it would be." He looked surprised when the teen launched himself into his arms and gave him a big hug.

"It's gonna be okay, Finn. We'll take care of you," Elijah said.

Finn smiled at that and told him, "You're an amazing person, Eli."

The boy stepped back, coloring a little as he asked, "Why would you say that?"

"Because you've had some really horrible crap to deal with in your life, but you haven't let it shut you down. You're kind and loving and I'm so happy that you're a part of my family," Finn said.

Elijah's blush deepened, but he grinned a little as he tried to deflect the compliment. "We're havin' a love fest in an alley next to a dumpster. This family is weird."

"Damn right we are," Finn told him with a smile. "Wear it with pride, kiddo."

They both started for the back staircase at the same time, and Finn shouted, "Race you!"

He took the stairs two at a time, and Elijah burst out laughing and chased him as he yelled, "No fair! You had a head start!" I was smiling as I went after them.

*****

Later that afternoon, after the lunch shift was over, I returned to the apartment. Dmitri gave me a wave from the kitchen table, where he was giving Lily a snack, and Colt looked up at me and said, "Hi, bro."

He was sitting on the living room floor with a lot of his belongings spread out around him, and told me, "Finn says he's going to take Eli and me to see our new house after work! He told us it's a warehouse, right on the bay, and showed us some pictures on his phone. I'm trying to get my stuff organized because he says we can move in soon. It sounds amazing!"

"It really is." I sat on the couch and took my shoes off, then pulled out my phone and sent Zachary his daily text. I was relieved just like always when it went through. If he ever changed his number, I was going to have to get creative about tracking him down.

Just as I was about to return the phone to my pocket, a text popped up from my dad. All it said was: *Hey. Hope all is well. Was just thinking about you and wanted to see how you were.* As I wrote a reply and told him about the warehouse, Colt asked, "Who's the message from?"

"My dad, just checking in," I said as I hit send.

"You know, I've been thinking," Colt said. "You were able to track your dad down, and I was wondering if maybe I could do the same thing and find my dad. I was thinking I could talk to Mama's friends as a starting point, one of them might know something."

A sick feeling washed over me and I put my phone down and took a deep breath. Colt had been busy pairing up his socks, so he didn't notice my reaction. I'd been trying to figure out what to do ever since I found the letter, and right then I knew. I swallowed around the sudden dryness in my throat and said, "Can I talk to you for a minute, Colt?"

"We are talking."

"I mean...you know."

Colt glanced at me and said. "Oh, a 'serious talk'. I always think I'm in trouble when we have one of those."

"It's nothing like that. I just have something I need to tell you."

"Something super sucky, by the look on your face," he said as he got up from the floor and sat on a chair facing me. A thought occurred to him and he said, "Wait, you and Finn aren't breaking up, are you? Please don't! It'll tear our family apart!"

"No, Colt, it's not that. Finn and I are doing incredibly well. You really don't have to worry about us."

He relaxed a bit and said, "Okay, good. What is it then?"

"Well, you know how I've been going through Mom's old files?" I asked.

"Yeah."

"I found information in there about your dad, but...well, it's not good news. I wasn't even sure I should tell you, because you're going to be upset. But I've been thinking about it a lot, and you have a right to know."

Colt stared at me wide-eyed and repeated, his voice low, "Not good news?"

I said, "You don't have to hear this if you don't want to. It's up to you. We can wait until you're older, or we don't have to go there at all if you don't want to."

"I need to know," he said.

Dmitri had been watching the conversation with a solemn expression, and he got up, picked up his daughter and went into his bedroom. He emerged a moment later and handed me the envelope I'd asked him to put away for me, then said, "You two need some privacy. I'll be downstairs with Jamie. Please call us if you need anything." I nodded and he squeezed my shoulder before leaving the apartment.

I told Colt, "This is what was in the files. It was meant to be found if something happened to Mom, so you'd be taken care of. Want me to read it to you?"

My brother shook his head and stuck his slender hand out for the letter. When I gave it to him, he held his breath, pulled it from the envelope and unfolded the single sheet of paper. It took him just a few moments to read it, and when he got to the end, he exhaled and whispered, "Oh God."

"I'm so sorry, Colt. I wish it was better news."

"Half my DNA came from a monster," he said softly. He looked up at me and asked, "What does that make me?"

"The same sweet, wonderful, kind, loving person you always were. Who he was and who you are don't have a thing to do with each other."

"Are you sure?"

"I'm absolutely positive."

He sat there for a long moment, looking shell-shocked. Then he began to tear the letter into tiny pieces, and got up and carried them to the kitchen. I trailed after him and asked, "What are you doing?"

"This." He turned on the faucet and the garbage disposal, and began feeding bits of the letter down the drain. "I don't want to have anything to do with that family of stuck-up assholes. I'd rather die than hit them up for money."

"You'll never have to. I promise I'll always take care of you."

When the letter was gone, he shut off the water and the disposal and turned to face me. "Let's never talk about this again, okay?"

"Okay. I'm sorry. Maybe I shouldn't have told you."

"No, you had to. I would have been mad if you kept something that big from me. I had this fantasy about going on a quest when I was a little older like you did and finding my dad, someone like Tony who actually wanted a son. Now I don't have to waste my time or energy on any of that." He spoke quietly, staring at the floor.

"I wish it had been better news."

"Yeah, me too." He stepped around me and headed for the door as he said, "I'm gonna go for a walk. I just need to...I don't know. Think about stuff, I guess."

"Okay. Be careful." My heart broke at seeing him so disappointed. When he was gone, I pulled out my phone and called Finn, who answered on the second ring. "Hi. I'm sorry to bother you at work," I told him.

"It's fine, nothing's happening right now. We're on patrol, Duke's driving. What's up?"

"I just needed to hear your voice," I told him as I sat down on the kitchen floor and leaned against the cabinet, hugging my knees to my chest.

"What's wrong? Are you okay?"

"I'm fine."

"Are the boys okay?"

"Colt and I just had a talk. I told him about the letter."

"How'd he take it?"

"It seems like he's in shock. He just went for a walk to clear his head." I switched the phone to my other ear and said, "Did I do the right thing, Finn? Maybe I should have shielded him from the truth."

Finn said something to his partner, and then he told me, "You had to be honest with him and now that he knows, we can both help him deal with it. You went all those years wondering who your dad was and wanting to find him. There was no way you'd make Colt go through the same thing, not when you already knew the answer."

"But when I found my dad, he turned out to be a decent guy, not a sick fuck like Aimsley. Colt actually asked me what it meant that half his DNA came from a monster."

"Shit," Finn muttered. "That poor kid."

"I hated hurting him like that. I knew the news would hit him like a ton of bricks, given everything Colt knows about Aimsley. But he started talking about finding his dad, and I just couldn't lie to him."

"Colt is a strong kid, and he'll deal with this. It'll probably just take a little time to come to terms with this information."

"You're right," I said. "I can't stand seeing him hurting, though."

"I know, baby. Me too."

"Thanks for listening," I said quietly.

"Always. I just wish I could make you feel better."

"You are. Just hearing your voice is such a comfort."

"You know, when you told me about the letter, we only thought about your brother and what this information would do to him. But what about you, Chance? It couldn't have been easy to find out who Colt's father was."

"I can't even really process it." I heard a key in the lock and was surprised when Finn pushed open the door a moment later with the phone to his ear. I put my phone down and looked up at him as I said, "Hey. What are you doing here?"

"You sounded like you needed a hug, and we weren't all that far away."

I got to my feet and he took me in his arms. "Thank you," I whispered as he rubbed my back.

"It's going to be okay, Chance. Colt will be fine. The truth was the right choice." I nodded as I buried my face in his chest, and he said, so softly, "Thank you, too."

I looked up at him and asked, "For what?"

"You reached out to me when you were upset. That's the closest you've ever come to asking for help."

"You're thanking me for that?"

He grinned a little and said, "I like feeling needed. That's kind of a big thing with me. It's part of the reason I became a cop, not just because that's the default occupation for the Nolan family."

"You're incredibly needed," I said. "Our family would fall apart without you. I would, too."

"No you wouldn't. You're a survivor, just like your brother."

"You're right, I am. But that was all I was doing before you came along, just surviving. That was no kind of life. I'm worlds better now, thanks to you."

He tilted my chin up and gave me a kiss, then said, "I'll be back around six, I told the boys I'd take them to the warehouse. Are you working a double today?"

"No, I actually have the night off so I can join you."

"That's awesome." Finn kissed me again, then led me to the door by the hand as he said, "I have to get back to work, Duke's probably getting annoyed." He kissed me one more time. "I need to work this into my route, a daily stop-off for a hug and kiss."

"Your captain would love that," I said as we stepped out onto the little landing above the alley.

He said, "I know. See you in a few hours, baby. I'm so happy that we get two nights off in a row together!" He tipped me back and kissed me passionately, like something out of a movie, then put me back on my feet and smiled at me before jogging down the stairs.

I peered over the railing at the black and white police cruiser parked below. Duke was leaning out his rolled down window with his arm resting on the doorframe, and he grinned at me and gave me a little wave. I smiled at him and raised my hand in greeting.

"I miss you already," Finn called. He winked at me before he got in the car and they rolled down the alley. He'd come so incredibly far in the months I'd known him. The old Finn never would have yelled something corny like that in front of his partner. It was incredibly sweet, actually.

My phone vibrated as I went back inside, and I pulled it out and read a text from Jamie. It said: *Someone's here to see you. Do you need more time with Colt? We can keep your friend busy until you can come down.* I sent a message back, slipped on my shoes and headed downstairs.

When I poked my head into the office opposite the kitchen, Jamie's best friend Jessica was making funny faces at Lily and dressing her in a little black velvet coat while Dmitri chuckled. Jamie told me, "Your friend wanted to wait out there," and tilted his head toward the dining room. I thanked him and went to see who it was.

Zachary stood uncertainly among the empty tables, fidgeting with the zipper of a black jacket, which he wore over a baggy t-shirt and jeans. I broke into a run when I saw him and almost tackled him in a hug as I exclaimed, "I missed you so fucking much! Please don't ever disappear again!"

"I'm sorry. I'm a total asshole," he muttered as he wrapped his arms around me. One of my coworkers, who'd been wiping down her tables, went back to the kitchen to give us some privacy.

"No you're not."

"It was shitty of me to vanish on you like that, but I needed some time to get things in perspective."

I pulled back to look at him, holding him by his bony shoulders. He looked paler and thinner than usual, and his dark eyes were underscored with bluish shadows. He'd been growing out his hair, and it was currently black with a bright red stripe down the right side of his face. "Where have you been staying? Are you alright?"

"I'd been staying with a john. He was fucking me instead of charging rent, but then he started to get really possessive, so I had to bail. Now I'm just staying at a residence hotel."

"Why'd you leave your apartment?"

"I needed a change. I thought I could find a new place, but I hadn't realized what a good deal I'd been getting. When I started looking at other apartments, I almost died of sticker shock."

I took his hand and led him to a nearby table. When he sat down, I pulled another chair around so we were knee-to-knee and asked, "Are you still at the escort service?"

"No. I decided to go freelance. I was tired of them taking such a big cut of my earnings."

"How's that going?"

He shrugged and turned his head. "I dunno. Not great." After a moment, he glanced at me and said, "So, you really quit the business, just like that? Thanks for all those texts, by the way. I liked knowing what was going on with you."

"Yeah, now I wait tables," I said, gesturing at our surroundings. "I kind of had to quit, not only because I needed to set a good example for my kid brother and his boyfriend, but because I couldn't do that to Finn."

"It sounds like you're really getting yourself together." He pushed his chair back and stood up. "I should go."

I got up too and said, "No, not yet! I've been so worried about you, Zachary. Please just stay a little longer."

"You don't need someone like me hanging around. You've got this new job and a new man and a new family, and I'm the same as ever. I'm sure you don't want to associate with some low-class rent boy now that you got your shit figured out."

"Oh come on! You're my best friend, and I'm the same person I always was, too. I might have walked away from the job, but do you think I immediately forgot all about my past? I was right where you are for over a decade."

"You got out, though. I don't think I'll ever be able to." He sounded defeated when he said that.

"Come and live with Finn and me and the boys. We're about to move into a warehouse and we'll have plenty of room. It'll take off the pressure of making rent every month and give you more options."

Zachary frowned a little. "And just mooch off you? Yeah, right. As if I could do that."

"You're my best friend, Zachary. I'll gladly share all I have with you."

"And what's your boyfriend going to say about that?"

"He'll say welcome to the family. He has the kindest heart and the most generous nature of anyone you'll ever meet."

"Even after you tell him I used to have a crush on you? Wouldn't that make things super awkward?"

"It'll only be awkward if we let it. You've moved past the crush, right?" He nodded and I said, "So let's not let something from the past get in the way of our future. Just move in so you can stop worrying about rent and figure out a new plan."

"You make it sound so easy."

"It is! Just say yes."

But he was shaking his head as he took a step back from me. "I can't. No matter what you say, your boyfriend would resent me intruding on your new life together."

"He won't. Why don't you stick around and meet Finn? He'll be home in a couple hours and you'll see for yourself the type of man he is."

"There's no point, it'd never work out. Look, I gotta go. I'm expected across town in twenty minutes."

"Please at least think about it," I said.

"I can't. I need the money, and I won't make nearly as much doing anything else. I doubt I'd even be able to land a regular job."

"Sure you would. You're a smart guy, Zachary, and you're better than that job."

"Nah. I'm exactly right for it. I've got nothing else in me, but you do. I wish you'd stop ignoring that amazing gift you have. You should be taking pictures, every single day, and you should be carrying them into every gallery in town and making them look at what you can do. If the people in the first gallery are too stupid to want to sell your work, go to another one, and another one after that. Eventually, I know you'll find someone who doesn't have their head up their ass and then you can finally do what you're meant to. Do whatever it takes to make it as a photographer, Chance. For both of us, okay?"

"It's not even sort of true that you have nothing else to offer. You just haven't found your thing yet."

He frowned at me and said, "Did you hear any of the rest of that?"

"Yeah, I did. Thank you for thinking that."

His frown deepened. "I don't just think it, I know it. Do that for yourself, Chance, just give believing in yourself a shot. You go on and on in your texts about all you want for your brother and this Elijah kid, how you want to be able to pay for their college education and help them succeed, but you never say anything about what you want for yourself. I know how much you love photography, and I remember how passionate you used to be. Every time I saw you, you'd have your camera in your hand. But in the last year, bit by bit, you've been letting it go, and I fucking hate that. It all started when you took that stupid photography class at the community college and the teacher gave you a B instead of the A plus you deserved. Don't you get that that asshole was jealous of you? He only wished he had your talent! But somehow, you let some dipshit's opinion matter that much to you! What do you think, that because he got someone to let him teach a class that he's the fucking god of photography and only his petty, jealous opinion counts?"

I knit my brows and said, "How did we get on this subject? We were talking about you making changes, not me. I've already made plenty." I gestured at the restaurant again.

"Yeah, but this new job is bullshit. No offense. You're busting your ass and working a million fucking hours and are so tired at the end of the day that you can barely raise your arms."

"I never said any of that."

"You didn't have to. I worked the same job in high school, and during the summers I was always pulling double shifts just like you do," Zachary said.

"I didn't know you waited tables."

"That's not the point. Someone who can do what you can with a camera has no business waiting tables. You have no business doing any job other than photography, not with that insane amount of God-given talent. And here you are, worried about everybody else, me included, when you don't even give yourself a moment's consideration!"

"You're doing the same thing!" I exclaimed. "We were talking about you, and you completely made it about me!"

"This is different. I'm not the one with all that talent," he said, raising his voice.

"So, does that mean you can just make excuses and give up on yourself? I'm right here, Zachary, offering you a way out of prostitution and into a better life, and I'm doing that because I love you and care about you so fucking much! Just let me help you. Please?"

"You know it's not that easy. When have you ever accepted help?"

"I'm trying to learn to do that. I was exactly like you, unwilling to rely on anyone but myself. I was so used to other people letting me down that I stopped giving anyone the chance to do it again. My own mother didn't believe me when I told her I was sexually molested. You think I didn't end up with trust issues after something like that?"

Zachary's eyes went wide, and he said, "Shit, Chance. I'm so sorry."

"Thanks, but the point of that wasn't to dredge up my shitty childhood, it was to let you know I understand. You don't want to have to rely on anyone other than yourself. But I promise you, Zachary, I won't let you down. You know me, we've been friends for a long time. Please have some faith in me."

"I do. That's not the issue," he said. "You need to forget about me and focus on your photography career and your boyfriend and those two boys you're trying to look after. You already have a hell of a lot on your plate, and the last thing you need is me and my problems adding to it all."

"Do you really think I'm enough of an asshole to forget about my best friend and just go on merrily with my life?"

"I didn't mean it like that! I just mean you need to quit worrying about me. I'll get my shit together on my own."

"At least think about my offer."

"What if I keep turning tricks?" he asked. "Would you want a hooker living with your kid brother? I wouldn't exactly be a good role model. And you said you've been trying to get custody of those boys, you and Finn both. I can't imagine child welfare would be too thrilled that you took in a prostitute."

"You wouldn't have to keep hooking. You probably feel trapped, like I used to. But I'm opening a door for you, Zachary. All you have to do is walk through it."

"But your offer is contingent on me no longer being a sex worker."

"No, it isn't, actually," I said. "I can't force you to quit. All I can do is make it so you don't need that job. Without the financial pressure of keeping a roof over your head, you could look at alternatives."

He was quiet for a long moment before saying, "I'll think about it, that's all I can promise right now. I have to go, but I'll talk to you soon, okay?"

"Don't disappear again, Zachary. Please?"

"I won't." He started to leave, but he turned back before reaching the door and said, "Do something for me, Chance."

"Anything."

"Don't ever let anyone tell you you're not good enough. Not even you."

I gave him a half-smile and said, "I'm working on that."

"Good."

"I'll text you tomorrow."

Zachary grinned just a little and said, "I know," before he walked out the door.

*****

When Colt got back from his walk, he went straight to his room and closed the door. I was worried about him, but gave him some space. As soon as Elijah walked in the door a few hours later with Finn right behind him, Colt flung the bedroom door open and ran to his boyfriend. Elijah grabbed him in a hug and the teens held each other tightly.

Apparently my brother had already texted him with the news, because Elijah said, "Who and what he was doesn't have a thing to do with you, Colt. Just look at me and my old man. He's a mean drunk and a racist and a homophobe, but none of that changed who I am, and I actually grew up with him."

Colt nodded in agreement and said softly, "Okay. You're right." The young couple went to their room, Elijah's arm around Colt's shoulders as he continued to reassure him.

I told Finn, "I said the exact same thing to Colt, almost word for word. I can tell it meant a lot more coming from his boyfriend, though."

Finn grinned as he dropped onto the couch and pulled me onto his lap. "Of course it did. That's Teenager 101 right there. Boyfriends and peers always take precedence over parents."

"Parents?"

"Let's face it, you're his father figure and the closest thing Colt will ever have to a Dad."

"No pressure," I said as I settled in and put my head on Finn's shoulder.

"You're doing great with him. It's so obvious that he loves you and looks up to you."

"Thank you for saying that." I picked up his hand and kissed it before hugging it to my chest.

"So, I called the bank today and got the ball rolling on the escrow process. It looks like it'll go smoothly. I also added your name to my checking and savings accounts, and before you protest, just hear me out. If anything ever happened to me, you'd need access to that money. You have our family to look after."

"I can't even argue with you now that you put it like that," I told him with a little frown.

"Good."

"But just so you know, you're not allowed to let anything happen to you, ever."

"I always try my best to be safe," he said as he nuzzled my hair. "I didn't just add you for emergencies, either. We're building a household and we're going to have shared expenses."

"This is really happening," I said softly as he wrapped his arms around me. "It's just starting to sink in that we're buying a home and building a life together."

"Are you sure I'm what you want?"

I sat up and looked at him, and was surprised at the worry in those beautiful blue eyes. "I want you more than anything," I told him as I cupped his face between my palms. "I love you and I can't even imagine my life without you."

We kissed each other for a while, softly and tenderly, as Finn ran his fingers into my hair. Finally, we were interrupted by, "Do you think you two could quit makin' out long enough to drive us to our new home? We really want to see it." That had come from Colt.

Elijah added, "We want to spend the night there. Can we, please?"

"There's no reason not to. My cousin told me to keep the key and move in whenever we want," Finn said as I slid off his lap. "I'd already turned on the water and electricity, so that's good to go, but there are no beds or furniture."

"So we can move in tonight!" Elijah said, his eyes lighting up.

"You heard the part about no furniture, right?" Finn said.

"We can stop off at the Walmart and buy some sleeping bags," Elijah said. "We don't need anythin' else."

"No reason not to," Finn said as he got up, too. "We can buy some stuff for dinner while we're at it and make a night of it."

"Awesome. I'm going to go pack some of our stuff, Eli," Colt said as he jogged to the guestroom.

Elijah turned to us and said, "Thanks for agreein' to this. Colt really needed a distraction tonight and this is gonna make him happy."

"How's he holding up?" I asked.

The teenager shrugged. "Okay, I guess. I think he's just gonna need some time to work through this stuff, you know?" I nodded and he said, "I'm gonna help him pack. We'll meet you back out here in just a little bit."

Ten minutes later, as we headed to Finn's SUV with some of our belongings, we crossed paths with Jamie, who held a sleeping Lily in his arms. Dmitri caught up a moment later, loaded down with toys and a big diaper bag. Finn told them we'd be moving into the warehouse that night, and Jamie said, "Aw, we're going to miss you guys."

"I can't thank you enough for letting us stay with you," I said. "I know we totally crowded and inconvenienced you, but you were both so incredibly nice about it."

"It was great having you here. I hope you all know you're family," Jamie said, "and family is always welcome in our home."

Colt and Elijah smiled at that, and I said, "See you at work tomorrow," before we got in the SUV. Finn ended up stopping at a Target, and he let the boys pick out a few things for their rooms. They got a couple posters, a retro clock shaped like a rocket, and two big armloads of colorful throw pillows, and were so excited you'd have thought it was Christmas. We grabbed four sleeping bags and cushioned pads to go underneath, along with some groceries, and headed to our new home.

The boys were beyond excited when they saw the warehouse. They ran all around it, and bolted up the stairs to pick out their bedrooms. The two offices they selected had a connecting door and were at the far end of the landing, closest to the bay. Finn and I claimed the main office at the opposite end of the building to give us a little privacy, then went downstairs to start some dinner.

"This place is so awesome," Colt exclaimed when they joined us a few minutes later. "Beyond awesome! We're going to love it here." I felt exactly the same way.

After we ate, we went out to the patio and sat on plastic crates as we took in the view of the bay. It was after dark so the inky black water reflected the moonlight. A boat passed in the distance, and beyond it, the lights along the distant shore looked like faint stars in the night. Colt said softly, "This feels like it's a million miles from Wyoming."

"It feels like two million miles from Mississippi," Elijah said. "This has to be the best place in the whole entire world."

"You know, I didn't like San Francisco much, for about the first dozen years I lived here," I said. "But now there's no place else I'd rather be."

Finn glanced at me. "You mean it?"

"Absolutely. I just needed to look at it from a different angle," I said as I tilted my head and rested it on his shoulder.

"So, this place is for sure, right?" my brother asked. "I mean, I know you still have to do the paperwork and pay for it and stuff, but no one can take this away from us, can they?"

"Nobody's going to take it away, Colt," Finn said gently. "I promise you. This is your new home."

My brother thought about that for a while, then said, "I'll be right back." He went inside and returned a minute later with his duffle bag. I was surprised when he unzipped it and took out our mother's ashes.

"It doesn't seem right that she's in a box on the shelf," he said. "Do you think maybe we can let her out into the world?"

I said softly, "Sure, Colt, if that's what you want to do."

"It feels right. I was just looking out at the bay, and I remembered Mama talking about how much she liked the ocean. That's where this water goes, right? Out to sea?"

"Eventually," Finn said. "It circles around the bay first, but then it flows out under the Golden Gate and reaches the Pacific."

Colt peeled back the packing tape and said, "That's perfect. Should we, like, say a few words or something?"

Elijah got up and put his arm around my brother's shoulders. "I think that's a real nice idea. I'll go first if you want." The four of us walked to the eight-foot drop off at the edge of the bay, and Elijah looked out at the water and said, "I never got to meet you, Ms. Matthews, but I want you to know I'm in love with your son and I'll take good care of him for you. I hope you're at peace now."

A tear tumbled down Colt's cheek, and he whispered, "Thank you," to his boyfriend. Then he said, "I guess I'll go next." He took a deep breath and looked out over the water, too. "I miss you, Mama. I think about you every single day. You went away too soon, but I hope you're someplace beautiful now, someplace that's nothing at all like Simone, Wyoming. You made some mistakes, but I want you to know I love you. You took care of me the best you could. I wish you'd listened to Chance and taken better care of him, too. But we're together and we're a family now, me and Chance and Elijah and Finn. I know you used to worry about me, so I want you to know you don't have to worry anymore. I'm gonna be just fine."

When my brother fell silent, Finn said, "I'll go next." He cleared his throat and fidgeted a bit before saying, "I didn't know you either, Ms. Matthews, and Colt's right, you made some huge mistakes with how you treated Chance. But you also brought two absolutely wonderful human beings into this world, and I want to thank you for that. I hope you rest in peace."

I swallowed hard, trying to hold back tears as I said, "I came to see you this summer, Mom. I really hoped that we'd be able to talk without arguing, for the first time in our lives, and that maybe we'd find a way to put the past behind us. I was so mad at you for such a long time, but I never stopped loving you. I want you to know that. I always held onto the hope that we'd patch things up between us. That might never have happened…but I'm going to go ahead and believe that maybe it would have. I hope you're in a better place now."

Colt took a plastic bag out of the box and held it with both hands as I carefully opened it for him. There was a strong breeze blowing toward the bay, and when he shook the contents of the bag into the air, they dispersed immediately, out into the water and the air and the universe. "Ashes to ashes. Dust to dust. I get that now," Colt said softly as he stared out into the night. "Goodbye, Mama."

"Bye, Mom," I whispered, and my brother reached for my hand. He started to sob then, and I grabbed him in a hug.

Elijah hugged him too, pressing himself to Colt's back, and Finn put his arms around all three of us.

When he got his tears under control, Colt sniffed and said, "Thanks for doing that with me. I was going to do it by myself when I first got her ashes, but I didn't think anyone should have to spend all of eternity in Simone. I'm glad I got to take her someplace way better, and that I had you guys to help me out."

The four of us ended up putting our sleeping bags in the main part of the warehouse that night. Finn plugged in a couple strands of lights, and we lay there two-by-two staring up at their soft glow, Colt and Elijah a few feet to my left, Finn snuggling in close on my right.

"This is gonna be a really awesome place to live," Elijah said, his voice soft as ever.

"It really is," Colt agreed.

"You doin' okay after that?" Elijah asked him.

"I will be."

After a pause, Elijah changed the subject by asking, "Do you suppose there's any place around here to play miniature golf?"

Colt chuckled and said, "That's so random."

"I know. I was just thinkin' that it'd be fun if all four of us went on a double date," his boyfriend said. "I saw a movie once where these straight couples did that, and I always wanted to do it, too. I never been mini golfing."

"There was a really shitty course in Simone," Colt said. "Some guy just, like, built it in a vacant lot out of plywood and stuff, but we didn't have anything better to do so we'd go sometimes. On the eighth hole, you'd have to hit your ball up a ramp and into the mouth of this huge, horrifying clown face. I swear, to this day I still have flashbacks about that clown." My brother shuddered and Elijah grinned.

"Okay, there aren't going to be a ton of rules in this house," Finn said, "but there will be one: no talking about freaky clowns right before bedtime. I don't want to have nightmares."

Both boys burst out laughing and Colt said, "You're afraid of clowns? There's no way! Big, tough cop like you?"

"I didn't say I was afraid of them," Finn said with a smile, propping himself up with a hand under his head and looking across at the boys. "I'm just not a fan. At all."

"Dude, you're totally afraid of them!" Colt said as he and Elijah sat up, his eyes bright with laughter. "Oh man, the pranks are gonna be epic!"

"No! No clown pranks! Oh my God, don't do it!" Finn exclaimed, as both boys doubled over with laughter. He started laughing too, and I smiled as I closed my eyes and let the sound wash over me. It was unexpected in the wake of all the sadness we'd shared that night, and I was so grateful for it.

Chapter Twenty-One

October

"Enough pictures already!"

Colt raised his hands like a shield and started to walk away, and I straightened up from behind the tripod and implored, "Just a couple more. Please? The light's really good right now."

He frowned at me, but then relented. "Fine, two more, but can we do funny ones this time?"

"Two more serious ones, then all the funny ones you want," I bargained.

My brother said, "Okay, but hurry up. Everyone's gonna be here soon and I don't think we put enough food out."

We were about to host our first get-together in our new home. It had begun as a housewarming party because escrow had closed on the warehouse, but now we had even more reasons to celebrate. I'd been granted custody of Colt and Finn had gotten custody of Elijah. We'd all been so incredibly happy and relieved.

"There's enough food over there to feed half of San Francisco," I told him as I looked through my viewfinder and framed up my shot, which was a bit challenging given the height difference between Finn and Eli. I zoomed in fairly close, but made sure some of the amazing mural Christian was painting on the two-story wall of our living room still showed in the background. Then I jogged over to my family, took my spot, and said, "Smile!"

"My face hurts from all this smiling," Elijah said.

"Almost done!" I smiled too and clicked off a few shots with the remote shutter release I concealed in my hand. "Okay, crazy ones! Go nuts!" I announced, and all four of us mugged for the camera while I clicked away.

Shea had been raiding the chips over on the long counter separating our kitchen from the living area, and he chuckled and said, "Nice one. You all just made the same silly face. That needs to be your Christmas card." He noticed that Christian was trying to carry about two dozen spray cans at once, and jogged over to help him.

The big doors at the front and back of the warehouse were both open, and a crisp breeze wafted through the building, clearing the faint, lingering smell of spray paint. Christian's best friend Skye jogged up to the open back door holding a rusty, twisted piece of metal, and exclaimed, "Do you guys seriously not care if I help myself to that awesome treasure pile at the edge of your property?"

"You mean the Grand Tetanus Tetons?" Finn replied as I took my camera off the tripod and hung it around my neck. "We were saving it for you, so help yourself to as much rusty junk as you want. I'm going to haul whatever's left to the dump."

"Thanks, man," Skye exclaimed with a big smile, pushing his blue bangs out of his eyes. "I'm going to make you guys a sculpture out of it as a housewarming present!"

As he disappeared the way he'd come, I glanced at Finn and he smiled at me and said, "We can put a big baby gate around it when Lily comes over."

"Speaking of Lily," I said as the little girl wobbled unsteadily through the door with a dad on each hand. Jamie's best friend Jessica and her husband brought up the rear with armloads of toys, blankets, and a bulging diaper bag. Apparently going anywhere with a toddler was an extremely elaborate procedure. We exchanged hugs all around and Dmitri handed us a nice bottle of champagne before he and Jamie began a graceful dance of toddler redirection, away from the wet mural, the open back door, and the stairs. I turned to Finn and said, "I never realized how totally un-childproofed this place is."

"I know, but Jamie and his husband have the whole vigilance thing down to a science."

More and more people kept filtering in over the next hour. Finn had an astonishing number of cousins, and many came to the party along with their spouses and kids. Several of his coworkers also showed up, including Duke. We were chatting with Finn's cousin Brian and his husband Hunter when I spotted a thin figure hesitating outside the front door. I excused myself and made my way through the growing crowd.

When I reached him, Zachary dropped the big duffle bag that had been slung over his shoulder, and I grabbed him in a hug as he said, "You know a lot of people."

"Finn comes from a huge family. How are you?" I pulled back to look at him. We hadn't seen each other since the day he'd come by the restaurant, but he'd been texting me fairly regularly since then.

He paused for a long moment before he finally admitted, "I need help, Chance."

"Just tell me what you need."

He glanced at me from beneath his lashes and asked, "Can I crash here, just for a little while? Things feel really out of control right now and I need a safe place to stay until I figure some stuff out."

"Of course." I pointed to the second floor landing and said, "Those first three offices are open, we've been converting them into bedrooms."

"Aren't you going to ask your boyfriend if it's okay first?"

"I told him weeks ago that I'd extended an open invitation to you, and he was totally fine with it, just like I knew he would be. Come meet Finn and the boys."

I introduced my brother and Elijah first, who sat on the kitchen counter inhaling potato chips with Josh, Nana's great-grandson. "Welcome, bro," Colt said with a smile, wiping his greasy fingers on his jeans before shaking Zachary's hand. "We just got done painting the bedrooms in a reverse rainbow. The red, orange and yellow rooms on the right are available, take whichever one you want. The green room's a game room, Eli and I are in blue and purple at the end, and my brother and Finn have the big office toward the back. They haven't let us paint it yet, but we have big plans for those white walls." My friend grinned shyly and thanked him.

We deposited Zachary's bag in the walk-in pantry, and I led the way through the crowd as we went to find Finn. My boyfriend put his arm around my shoulders when he saw me and said, "Jessie just texted. Your dad's flight was slightly delayed, but they're on their way now." We'd planned our housewarming party to coincide with Tony's second visit to San Francisco, and when I'd mentioned it to Jessie and Nana, they'd volunteered to pick him up in the limo to, as Nana put it, 'make him feel like a big-shot'.

"Great. Hey, there's someone I want you to meet," I said, and spun us around a bit so he was facing my friend. "Finn, this is Zachary Paleki. Zachary, Finn Nolan."

"I'm so glad to finally meet you," Finn exclaimed with a wide smile as they shook hands. "Please tell me you're planning to move in."

Zachary looked surprised at that and mumbled, "You actually want me to?"

"Absolutely. Chance has been worried about you and we were both hoping you'd take him up on his offer," Finn said.

"Are you sure? You don't have to say yes. I can figure something else out."

"We both want you here, Zachary," Finn told him. "Our door's always open for family."

"But I'm not family," my friend said softly.

"Of course you are," Finn said. "I recommend the yellow bedroom, by the way. The red and orange rooms turned out pretty day-glow and I think it'd be really hard to relax in there."

"I'll take that under advisement," Zachary said as the little grin returned.

Someone tapped my shoulder. I spun around and exclaimed, "Oh my God, Nico!" I hadn't seen my friend since August, and I grabbed him in a hug. Greetings were exchanged all around, and then I asked him, "How've you been?"

"Alright, I guess. Congratulations on the new place, it's terrific."

"Thanks. So how was Italy? I heard you stayed an extra couple weeks."

"Italy was…complicated," he said, knitting his brows slightly.

I took a good look at him. Nico was usually fastidiously groomed, but he sported a five o'clock shadow, his button-down shirt was wrinkled, he looked tired and was past due for a haircut. There was something in his eyes, an almost haunted look, and I just had to ask. "Jessie said you met a guy in Italy. Would that be the complication?"

His frown deepened and he said, "Oh yeah, and I really don't want to talk about it."

"Fair enough."

Finn pulled my phone out of his pocket and glanced at the screen. We'd been sharing it because he'd given Elijah his phone and hadn't had a chance to get a new one yet. He told me, "Jessie's about to pull up out front. He says Nana had him make some modifications to the limo and wants us to come out and take a look."

We went out the front door with a couple dozen of our party guests, and we heard the limo before we saw it. Jessie was blasting Elton John's Crocodile Rock from a set of exterior speakers. Two little rainbow flags waved proudly from either side of the hood, and the top of the car had been painted in a big rainbow, end to end. Also, a wide pink stripe had been added to each side of the limo. While they were probably just meant to be accents, the fact that they were rounded off where they met the front bumper kind of made them resemble two colossal dongs.

Nana poked her head out of the sunroof and waved to us before ducking back down. A moment later, she and six of her little senior girlfriends piled out of the limo, along with my father, who was blushing vividly, and Cory Previn. My dad had taken my suggestion. When he met Cory to give him the camera, he'd spent a couple hours talking to him. That conversation had been enough to convince Tony to sign on as the boy's foster parent. It was still a fairly new arrangement, and I was looking forward to hearing how it was going.

"Jessie always makes me get out of the limo for this part," Nana yelled over the music. Her driver leaned out the window and smiled at the crowd, and Nana told him, "Show 'em the improvements you made, Jessie!"

The car dropped down low, and then the front end lifted at a forty-five degree angle. Jessie bounced the front of the limo up and down before raising it up again. Just as the song reached its conclusion, twin glitter cannons that had been built in above the headlights fired two big bursts of silver sparkles, which made the pink stripes even more brow-raising. The car then lowered slowly to its original position while everyone cheered.

I turned to my father and said, "Welcome back to San Francisco." I smiled as I stuck my hand out.

He grinned and went in for a slightly awkward hug instead. "I feel like I just landed in Oz."

"You might as well have."

We slapped each other's backs as we hugged each other and when we let go, Tony said, "This is Cory. He has something he wants to say to you."

The redhead colored beneath his freckles and looked at the ground as he said, "Sorry I stole and wrecked your car. Thanks for not pressing charges. Thank you for the camera, too, and the photos, and for returning my stuff to me. I know I didn't deserve any of that."

"You're welcome."

"Thanks for sending a limo to get us, too. That's the best thing I've ever seen in my entire life," he said with a crooked grin as he glanced up at me.

"You're welcome, although last time I saw it, the limo was solid white. I didn't realize Nana and Jessie had gotten creative."

Jessie bounded up to me and grabbed me in a hug as Finn, Colt and Elijah introduced themselves to Cory. "Congratulations on your new home, Chance," he said, "and on getting custody of the boys. I'm so glad everything's working out for you!"

"Thanks. And thank you for getting my dad at the airport."

"It was fun," he said, pushing his black chauffeur's cap to the back of his head. "Nana likes to think she's the city's goodwill ambassador, so she enjoyed greeting your guests."

"San Francisco really should appoint her to that job."

"Agreed. Oh hey, before I forget, I wanted to let you know that Sharona is back together and running like a dream.

You can come pick her up tomorrow. Just wait until you hear her engine purr!"

I reached in my back pocket and pulled out a folded envelope, which I handed to him. "About that. This is for you."

He pulled a slip of paper out of the envelope and his eyes went wide. "Oh my God Chance, you signed Sharona's title over to me! I can't possibly accept this!"

"The Civic needs to belong to you, Jessie."

"You don't want her anymore?"

I told him, "I don't really need a car, since Finn and I are always driving each other and the boys around in his SUV."

"Well, then I'll buy her from you. You're always working all those double shifts at the restaurant, so I know you could use the money."

"Money may be tight, but I'm not going to accept any from you, Jessie. I absolutely refuse, just like you refused to let me pay you for all that work you did. Now please, say yes and give Sharona a good home."

"But—"

"But nothing. You put hundreds of hours and your heart and soul into fixing it up, both before and after the crash. I know you love that car and it has to belong to you."

Jessie teared up as he crushed me to him in an embrace. "Thank you so much, Chance. I promise I'll take good care of her."

"I know you will."

Nana called for him and Jessie thanked me about a dozen more times, then hurried over to help her with something in the trunk of the limo. My dad was still beside me, and Tony smiled and said, "That was a really nice thing you just did."

"Well, it's no fire truck, but I'm glad it made him happy," I told him with a little grin.

"You knew about that?"

"Yeah. I googled you when I was in Gala and came across a couple articles in the local newspaper."

"I see."

Finn went to help Nana with whatever she was getting out of the trunk of her car and Colt, Elijah and Josh led Cory to the buffet. I went inside with my dad and asked him, "So, how's the whole foster dad thing working out?"

"I'm trying my damnedest to do right by that kid, which would be a lot easier if he'd just talk to me."

"Well, it's still a pretty new arrangement. Just give it time."

"You're right, and I'm always reminding myself to be patient. He's good with small-talk, he just won't open up about anything serious. That's probably true for most teenagers, and I can only hope he'll eventually trust me enough to confide in me."

"I can tell you really care about him. That's nice to see."

"I do. He's so bright, and funny, and incredibly talented. It's sad that no one ever bothered to look past his acting out."

"I'm glad it's going well for you two."

"It is. I've actually started the paperwork to adopt him. More than anything, Cory needs to know he has someone in his corner, someone who's there for the long haul. He's been in thirteen different foster homes since he became orphaned three years ago. Once the adoption is final and I can relocate with him, I want to move us out of Gala. He'll always be written off as a delinquent in the eyes of everyone in that town, just like I'll always be a thought of as a drunk, no matter how long I'm sober. I think he and I both need to start fresh somewhere else."

"Wow, that's huge. How does Cory feel about being adopted?"

Tony said, "He's so used to rejection that he refuses to get his hopes up. I don't think he'll believe it's real until I put the adoption certificate in his hands."

"Poor kid. Where are you thinking about moving, Gillette?"

"No, I'm thinking about San Francisco, or maybe a smaller town right outside it, since this city might prove to be pretty overwhelming. I want to be close enough so that you and I can keep building on what we started. Cory and I are going to look around a bit while we're here this weekend, just to get a feel for the different communities. Of course, I won't be allowed to move him out of state until the adoption goes through, but we can still get the ball rolling." I grinned and he asked me, "Does that smile mean you approve of this idea?"

"Definitely," I said. "It'd be great to have you closer." That made Tony grin, too. "What're you going to do about the bar, though?"

"One of my regulars is interested in buying it, so this is a good time to let it go. That place has been my security blanket for far too long and I need to move on to bigger and better things."

Finn walked up to us just then with a bemused expression on his face. He was carrying a large terra cotta pot, which held a thin, upright, three-foot-tall cactus, flanked by two small, round cacti. "Hi honey. Where'd you get the cocktus?" I asked, my grin widening.

"It's a housewarming gift from Nana. The soil spilled all over her trunk when the limo was getting ready to ejaculate, but she got it sorted."

"I hope you thanked her," I said.

"Oh, I did. Want to come with me to find it a place of honor?"

"Love to." I turned to Tony and said, "Come on in, I'll introduce you around."

After we got my dad situated, Finn and I went upstairs and put the cocktus on the second floor landing, out of toddler range. I happened to glance downstairs, and had to pause for a moment and take it all in. Our home was so full of life and happiness and people who loved us, and it made me feel incredibly good.

Finn brushed off his hands and drew me into his arms, then looked down at the party and said, "Great turn-out."

I nodded. "It's amazing to look around and see almost every single person I love, all in one place. About the only people missing are my friends Gianni and Zan, but they have the great excuse of sailing around the world, so I won't hold their absence against them."

"I wish they could have been here, but you'll just have to tell them about this later." I thought he meant the party, until he called down to our guests, "Could I have everyone's attention, please?" As our friends and family turned to look at us and someone turned the music down low, Finn said, "I have something I need to ask my boyfriend."

I stopped breathing when he went down on one knee and took both my hands in his. "I'll never find the words to tell you how much I love you," he said as I looked into his beautiful blue eyes. "So instead, I want to spend the rest of my life showing you. Will you marry me, Chance?"

"Holy shit," I whispered as my breath caught and my heart leapt. I had to be dreaming. I just had to.

From downstairs, Colt yelled, "What are you waiting for? Say yes already!"

"Yes!" I exclaimed. "Oh my God, yes, of course!"

As our family and friends cheered and applauded, Finn leapt up, took my face in his hands and kissed me passionately. Then he rested his forehead against mine and said, "You just made me the happiest man alive."

"I love you so much, Finn," I told him, hugging him tightly.

We went downstairs hand-in-hand, to a deluge of congratulations. Colt got to me first and grabbed me in a huge embrace. Tears of happiness shone in his eyes and Elijah's, who hugged us both quickly when my brother let go of me.

Nana pushed her way through the crowd, smiling ear to ear, and pulled us both down into a hug before saying, "This is great news, and the timing is perfect! I just got ordained by one of them, you know, online thingamajigs. I can legally perform weddings now, and yours can be my first!"

"Really?" I asked.

She nodded and fished around in her giant black purse. "I got the certificate in the mail three days ago," she told us. "Hang on, let me show you." She started handing things from the handbag to Colt, including a big box of condoms, a rainbow colored lollypop shaped like a penis, and a silver flask. When she handed my brother a .44 magnum, Finn quickly plucked it from his grasp and checked and emptied the chamber before handing it back to him and pocketing the bullets. Finally, she pulled out a laminated half-sheet of paper and said, "See? All official and everything." It actually did look legit.

Finn and I glanced at each other, and I said, "Sure. Why not?"

"Wonderful! Let's do it tonight!" she exclaimed, clapping her hands.

I said, "Tonight? Shouldn't we do some planning first? And don't we need a marriage license or something?"

"What's to plan?" Colt said. "You love Finn, he loves you, and everyone's already here, including your dad. Let's do this thing!"

"You can always follow this up with a civil ceremony at City Hall to make sure it's all legal and stuff," Elijah suggested.

I looked at Finn again and he smiled and said, "I'm game if you are. I can't wait to be married to you."

Laughter bubbled from me, just from the sheer joy of it all, and I told him, "Like Colt said, let's do this thing!"

Nana let out a whoop and grabbed her phone from her purse. "All I need is one hour. You boys go celebrate with your guests until then." She hit speed dial, and when the call connected she put it on speaker and yelled into it, "Mr. Mario, we got us an impromptu wedding! Chance and Finn are tying the knot tonight and we need to bring the magic for these boys, stat! You know what to do, right?"

Her hairdresser's heavily accented voice came through the speaker, yelling over a Katy Perry song in the background. "I got you covered! I'm calling the family as soon as we hang up, you text me the address."

"I'm counting on you, Mr. Mario!" She ended the call, fired off a text by holding the phone right in front of her face and typing with one finger, and then turned to us and said, "We got any champagne around here?"

"A couple bottles, I think," Finn said, putting his arm around my waist.

"That won't do." She started poking out another text message. "I'll have the family pick up a couple cases on the way over. You can't have a wedding without champagne!"

"The family?" Colt asked. "Are you calling in the mafia to throw my brother a wedding?"

"Yes and no," she told him as she hit send. "I called in the gay homosexual mafia, not the Dombrusos. My hairdresser and his friends are the men for the job, just you wait and see!" She recruited Colt and Elijah to help her, and they rushed off to get things ready.

Finn took my hand and led me out the back door. We went to the edge of our property beside the bay and he turned to me and asked, "Are you really okay with all of this, Chance? That snowballed in record time. I don't know if my proposal even had time to sink in yet, and now apparently we're going to be married in about an hour!"

As I put my arms around him, I said, "There's no reason in the world to wait. I'm absolutely sure of this and of us, Finn. It's impossible to picture my future without you right there by my side. In fact, if you hadn't asked me, I was going to ask you."

I put my hand on the back of his neck and pulled him down for a kiss, which went on for a long time. When we finally broke apart, he let out a joyful whoop, grabbed me around the waist and swung me around as he yelled, "We're getting married!" I threw my head back and laughed, and when he stopped spinning I wrapped my legs around his waist and kissed him again.

*****

The gay mafia arrived forty-nine minutes later, according to my brother, who'd been timing them. Apparently Mr. Mario had been participating in a drag show when Nana called him, because he rushed in dressed like a rather statuesque Lady Gaga in a (fortunately simulated) meat dress, followed by at least twenty more drag queens in full regalia. They brought cases of champagne, a big, pink bakery box, armloads of flowers, and DJ equipment. The latter included a light machine containing dozens of prisms, which bathed the room in rainbows once it was plugged in.

Our guests arranged themselves into two sections with a path down the middle, and we sent Colt, Elijah, Zachary, Jessie, Shea and Christian to stand in front of our new mural and be our groomsmen. Tall, metal pails brimming with multicolored flowers punctuated the room, and Finn turned on the garlands of white lights overhead. Between that and the rainbows cast by the light machine, the warehouse looked magical.

Skye grabbed my camera and started snapping pictures for us, and Nana climbed onto a case of champagne, flanked by the groomsmen. She'd borrowed a huge, white, bouffant wig with an off-center hat shaped like a pirate ship from one of the drag queens. I wasn't sure if she'd done that to make herself three feet taller, or possibly to give herself a regal air.

I pulled my father out of the audience and asked, "Will you please walk us down the aisle?" He seemed a bit choked up as he nodded and linked arms with Finn and me.

Nana yelled, "Hit it, ladies!" A dozen drag queens preceded us up the aisle, strutting their stuff like they were on a runway and throwing colorful flower petals into the air, while the rest of their equally colorful party formed a chorus to our left and started singing an *a Capella* version of I Say a Little Prayer for You.

Tony muttered, "I'm definitely not in Kansas anymore." Then it was our turn. Everyone turned to look at us as we walked down the aisle. When we reached Nana, Tony shook

Finn's hand and said, "You got a fine young man here. You treat him right, you hear?" Finn assured him he would. Then Tony grabbed me in a hug and whispered in my ear, "I love you, son."

"I love you too, Dad," I told him. He was dabbing his eyes with the back of his index finger as he took his place at the front of the crowd beside Cory. To his left stood Nico, who'd borrowed Colt's laptop and had gotten hold of Gianni and Zan. They were both on the screen, Skyping via web cam from some sunny tropical location, looking tan and incredibly happy. They smiled and gave us two big thumbs up, and I grinned and waved at the screen before turning to face my soon-to-be husband.

The entire audience had joined in on the song, serenading Finn and me as we laughed and joined hands. I felt like I was in a movie. When they finished the song, everyone applauded and whooped, and we turned to face Nana.

She began with, "Gentlemen, ladies, and gentlemen who are also ladies, thank you for being here. Neither of these boys knew today was gonna be their wedding day when they woke up this morning, but just take a look at all the love and joy on their faces and you'll see why they didn't want to wait to tie the knot. These two are meant to be together, and meant to be a family along with these two cute kiddos right here." Nana beamed at Colt and Elijah. Jessie handed her a pair of big, round glasses and his phone, and she said, "This is my first time officiating, but I've thrown plenty of weddings, so I know how this is supposed to go. Just in case though, I had Jessie pull up some nontraditional wedding vows on his phone so we don't skip something important."

Finn and I held each other in a loose embrace and smiled at each other as Nana skimmed the screen and said, "Let's see. Dearly beloved, yada yada yada…gathered here to witness the union, well that's pretty obvious! I guess we should probably do this part: does anyone object to this marriage? If you do, you're gonna have to answer to me!" She adjusted her glasses and squinted at the crowd menacingly, and I snuck a quick look at Zachary, who I really hoped wasn't uncomfortable with all of this. He gave me a smile, and I grinned in return.

"Okay, here's the meat of it," Nana said, turning her attention back to the screen. "Do you, Finn Nolan, take Chance Matthews to be your lesbian life partner?"

"Oh shit, sorry," Jessie said, stepping up quickly and taking the phone from her. He scrolled past a few screens, handed it back to her, and flashed a big smile and a thumbs up at Finn and me as he returned to his spot.

"Ah, okay, this makes more sense," Nana said, putting the screen right in front of her face. "Do you, Finn Nolan, take Chance Matthews to be your husband, in sickness and health, in good times and bad, as long as you both live?"

Finn smiled at me. "I most definitely do."

"Chance, same question," Nana said.

"I do, absolutely."

"I know you didn't have a chance to write any vows, but do you two want to say a few words?" she asked.

Finn nodded. "I'll go first." He took my face in his hands and looked in my eyes as he said, "I feel like I came to life the first time I held you in my arms, Chance. Before that moment I was only existing, never truly living. I was lonely and unhappy and pretty much suffocating in the closet, and then you came along and pulled me into the light. You taught me what it feels like to really, truly love and be loved, and I'm going to make sure you know, every day, that you're absolutely cherished. Thank you for showing me what it feels like to be a part of a loving family, and for the incredible gift of getting to spend my life with you. I love you beyond words."

I clutched his hands to my chest as I said softly, "Before I met you, I used to watch the world through a camera lens without really being a part of anything. My life is so different now, all because of you. Thank you for loving me, and for this home, and for making us a family. I never thought I'd have any of that, and I never dreamed I'd find a man like you. I'm so incredibly grateful for you and the love and devotion you show me, every minute of every day. I adore you, Finn, and I'm so excited about the life we're going to build together."

Nana sniffed loudly and pulled off her glasses. Jessie swapped out the phone with a tissue, and she said as she wiped her eyes, "You're both such good boys, and I'm honored to pronounce you married. Now kiss your husband already!"

Finn and I gathered each other in an embrace and he smiled at me before kissing me. The kiss was so sweet and tender, full of love and promise. I forgot about everything but him as I returned the kiss, running my fingers into his short hair as he tipped me back and held me securely in his arms. When he finally pulled back a couple inches and looked at me, his eyes sparkling with happiness, I whispered, "God, I love you."

He swung me upright and hugged me, and after a moment I realized all of our family and friends were cheering and applauding. A bubble of laughter slipped from me, and he said in my ear, "I love you too and I'm so happy to be your husband."

We joined hands as we faced the audience. Then I reached for Colt's hand on my right, and Finn took Elijah's hand on his left, and our family walked back down the aisle together as the DJ, who was dressed like Marilyn Monroe with a full beard, played The Beatles' Here Comes the Sun. There were even more hugs and congratulations, and we posed for some photos as Skye continued to act as our photographer.

One hell of a party followed, with lots of champagne and laughter and dancing and a wedding cake that was randomly in the shape of a rainbow-colored princess castle. Bearded Marilyn, who turned out to be a bakery owner named Phil, explained that it was the best of what he had on hand that night, an order that had been cancelled after it was already made. I thanked him and assured him it was perfect, which it really was.

Finn and I danced until dawn, amid family and friends and cops and drag queens. It was the most wonderful wedding I could possibly imagine. Finally, as the sun rose, casting a golden glow through the warehouse, my husband and I curled up together on the couch.

I looked around at our family, several of whom had opted to crash in the warehouse instead of driving home. Colt and Elijah were asleep in an upholstered chair, cocooned in each other's arms, and Shea and Christian were asleep in the other chair with Christian curled in his husband's lap. Nana was stretched out and snoring on the couch across from us. She still wore that huge bouffant wig, which jutted from her head at a sharp angle, and her stockinged feet were on Jessie's lap as he slept on the other end of the couch. Tony, Cory and Zachary had gone upstairs at some point and claimed the red, orange and yellow bedrooms. One of them was also snoring, oddly in sync with Nana. Jamie and Dmitri slept facing each other on the area rug with Lily between them, their arms draped over her and over each other protectively.

There was so much love in this house, and my heart was so full. But none of it made me happier than my sweet, beautiful husband, who drew me into his arms. Finn kissed my forehead and I put my head on his chest. His heartbeat was steady beneath my cheek, his clean scent familiar and soothing. I knew without a doubt that I was right where I should be. We both were.

I smiled and whispered as I let my eyes slide shut, "I'm finally home."

The End

#####

Coming Soon

The Firsts and Forever series will continue with Nico's story in late 2015.

That book's timeline will overlap with the one in Coming Home as we travel to Italy with Nico, Nana, and Jessie. Badly burned by his last relationship, Nico Dombruso has learned to keep the world at arm's length and guard his broken heart at all costs. When he meets a gorgeous, mysterious stranger on vacation, he decides to make an exception and enjoy a summer fling. It's just sex, after all, so what's the harm?

He's shocked when he finds himself able to open up to this man, and for the first time in years, Nico starts to consider the possibility of trusting his tattered heart to someone again. But when a secret is revealed that shakes him to his core and threatens to tear his family apart, Nico retreats, so far and so fast that no one, not even the man who was starting to make him believe he could love again, might ever be able to reach him.

Thank you to my readers, who keep asking for more!

For information about Alexa Land and her books, please visit http://alexalandwrites.blogspot.com/

Find Alexa on Facebook And on Twitter @AlexaLandWrites

Books by Alexa Land Include:

Feral

The Tinder Chronicles

And the Firsts and Forever Series:

Way Off Plan

All In

In Pieces

Gathering Storm

Salvation

Skye Blue

Against the Wall

Belonging

Coming Home

Made in the USA
San Bernardino, CA
04 September 2015